LOVE AND MAYHEM

ON THE SILK ROAD

HONG KONG TO LONDON

A TRAVEL NOVEL

DONALD HOUSER

ISBN: 978-1-7339175-4-4 (Donald Houser)

2

No one saves us but ourselves. No one can and no one may. We ourselves must walk the path.

Buddha

DEDICATION

I dedicate this book to all travelers seeking to understand the world and the many facets of humankind.

ACKNOWLEDGEMENTS

Although this book is based on actual circumstances and issues, any resemblance to real people or places in this book is purely coincidental.

I want to thank my editors Ioanna Carlsen, John Voorhees, and Marianna Versteeg for all their help.

1- HINDU KUSH MOUNTAINS: MARCH 1, 1970

Hank opened his eyes as the morning light filtered through the burlap bag covering the tiny window, shooting tiny specks of light around the room. His forearm was throbbing, reverberating in his head with an increasing drumbeat. The searing pain forced him to clamp his tearing eyes shut as the waves of nausea climaxed. He spewed the contents of his putrid meal from both orifices, feeling as if his insides had been turned out. He didn't know which was worse: the smell of the vomit, the smell of his shit soaked jeans, or the rotting offal smell of his swollen arm. He couldn't remember how long he had lain on the concrete in this bare room— many weeks or more. What did they want from him?

He tried to slow his breath and damp down the pervasive pain. He couldn't take much more of this. He could attack these men. Get it over with. He didn't want to die, but he didn't want to endure this agony anymore. Death would be a welcome end to this madness. He would die anyway if his arm continued to fester. He heard the guards talking in the other room in their Afghan language. He hoped they would leave him alone today and not take him out in the cold for his drenching. It had been several days since his last drenching. No... he'd prefer the drenching. The smell was too overwhelming. Let them come. He would welcome the fresh air. His eyes were smarting from the acrid smell. Hopefully they'd even clean the room.

When he heard the door open, he twisted away and tensed. The guard yelled what was probably an expletive as he entered, pulling the tail end of his turban across his face, before kicking Hank. Hank gulped for air as the guard yelled the word that Hank had come to understand was a command to get up. Hank attempted to get to his knees, but couldn't lift his head. He collapsed as the guard delivered another stiff kick to Hank's stomach. A second guard entered, yelling, and spit on Hank, then both pulled him to his feet. They dragged him outside in the freezing, morning air, untied his hands, pushed him against the wall, and laughed as he was doused with water from a bucket. Hank shivered in the cold as several more buckets of icy water were splashed over him causing him to slump down in agony.

They pulled him up and retied his hands before dragging him back inside. His putrid room had been cursively cleaned, but the stench was still overpowering. They threw him down, sending waves of excruciating pain from his arm pinned beneath him. He rolled to his side, but the pain continued like endless ocean waves hitting the shore. His soaked, icy cold clothes caused him to shiver relentlessly as he curled into a ball to warm himself. His stupid bluster had brought him to this horrendous situation. He wasn't as tough as he had imagined. What had he been thinking? Why couldn't he have been more sensible, more restrained?

James and Sally had probably gone to the authorities, but he doubted that the authorities could do much. His friends would never find him. Why had these men taken him from the hash sellers and moved him to this remote house in the mountains? How were they associated with the hash sellers? Were they going to keep him barely alive until the infection spread throughout his body and he died an agonizing death? Torture him passively just because of an insult? What other explanation could there be?

Useless questions and conjecture. He closed his eyes and hoped for sleep— escape the soul-splintering pain, engulfing putrid smell, and bone shaking shivers. But sleep had fled. He held his bound arms up slowly, ignoring the pain, and studied his swollen arm wrapped in the dirty blood stained cloth. In the splintered light, the redness seemed to be spreading. Was his arm going gangrene? It all made no sense. Why go to all this trouble? They could have killed him long ago. They must be keeping him alive for a reason. Were they tying to exact a ransom for him? His friends had little money. How could they pay a hefty ransom?

2- HONG KONG: OCTOBER 20, 1969

James arrived in Hong Kong after a week or so of sightseeing in Japan. He was on his way to visit his uncle in India after being discharged from the Army after his stint in the war in Vietnam. He was a young twenty-four and was elated to be traveling and in such a famous city. He had enjoyed his time in Japan, staying longer than he had planned, and was looking forward to learning about Hong Kong and seeing the sights. The skyline was dotted with high rise skyscrapers and hotels as the taxi from the airport took him to the modest hotel he had reserved at the airport tourist information. After checking in and depositing his bags, he decided to venture outside. As he stepped out onto the street, he stopped to view the mostly Chinese pedestrians hurrying up and down the busy street. A completely different ambience from Japan— less relaxed and almost frantic.

A black man approaching stopped to the side of him. "You look lost," the man said in his American accent.

James turned and smiled. "I'm not really lost. I'm just taking it all in. I just arrived this morning from Tokyo."

The man extended his hand. "I'm Ron. I work on the QE 2. We docked yesterday." He was a head shorter than James and was many years his senior—

perhaps in his early forties. He had a thick mustache and short cropped curly, wiry hair. Even with his prominent broad nose, he was quite handsome with a warm smile. "I've been here many times. I could help you orient yourself. Tell you about the most famous attractions. I take it you're an American like myself."

"Yes," James replied.

"It's nearly lunch time. If you're not otherwise engaged, I would be happy to offer you lunch with the crew aboard the QE 2. I can show you around the ship after. It is the finest ocean liner in the world."

"I'd like that." He had never been aboard a luxury liner let alone one of the world's most famous. He suspected the lunch would be quite delicious.

He walked with Ron to the harbor and went aboard the massive Queen Elizabeth 2. They had a delectable meal of orange chicken, spicy green beans, and jasmine rice accompanied by an excellent white wine with the other crew members still on the ship while Ron explained the main attractions in Hong Kong he thought James shouldn't miss. After lunch, Ron took him on a tour of the ship's ornate high end suites. In one of the grander suites as James stared in wonder at the mahogany paneling, gilt mirrors, and immense round bed, Ron suggested they could try out the bed. James surprised by the comment stared at Ron momentarily, then declined rather abruptly when he realized what Ron was asking. Feeling awkward, he thought of fleeing, but didn't want to insult Ron. He moved away from Ron. "Well, maybe I should be on my way."

"No need," Ron said and smiled. "I'm sorry if I offended you. You're a handsome young man, and I felt an affinity for you as soon as I saw you in front of your hotel. I understand your reluctance for my offer. I won't accost you again, I promise. We can still be friends. How long are you staying in Hong Kong?"

James felt a surge of relief. He wouldn't need to flee. "A least a couple of days," James replied, glad the situation hadn't escalated.

"There's a great night club in town that you would like. There should be plenty of young ladies there tonight. I was planning on going. It's just a few blocks from your hotel. If you walk south on your street you'll see it, Club Majestic. You should come if you don't have other plans. It's a fun place. I'll buy you a drink."

"Maybe I will." James thanked Ron for the lunch and tour and left the ship.

***

In the evening after dinner near his hotel, James went to the night club, hoping he might meet other travelers. He hadn't met any Western travelers in Japan, having spent most of his time with a young Japanese student, who had latched on to James, offering to show him around and hoping to practice his English. The student's English was almost indecipherable, but he was a jolly person and was keen to show off his country.

When he entered Club Majestic's large interior, the place was extremely crowded. Two beautiful Chinese bartenders in their matching dark-blue, embroidered, high collar dresses mixed and served the drinks with showmanship alacrity, their pony tails swinging back and forth as they moved. The accomplished band was playing a rock and roll cover of the Rolling Stones' *Honky Tonk Women,* which reverberated across the high ceiling. James liked the festive atmosphere as he surveyed the surroundings before selecting a stool at the bar to watch the performing bartenders. He ordered a Heineken beer and leaned back to listen to the band. He was soon joined by Ron, who he hadn't noticed when he came in.

"Hey, James, glad you could come." Ron selected a vacant stool and pulled it next to James. "This place is hopping." He ordered a single malt scotch and clinked James's glass. "Cheers."

James, surprised by Ron's appearance, remembering his rebuff of Ron's advances toward him, nodded. "Cheers," he said. He hoped his apprehension at seeing Ron again wasn't visible in his face.

Ron smiled and held up his hand. "Don't worry as I said before I won't try any more moves on you. I enjoy talking with you. You are a polite and thoughtful young man. Often a rarity on my travels."

James, relieved by Ron's declaration, was pleased with the prospect of talking with him. Ron was gregarious and quite the joker.

James halted his conversation with Ron when a tall, attractive, young woman drifted to the bar and slipped next to him. She was followed by a taller muscular blond man in a bush hat.

"Hello," she called to the gyrating bartenders. "Give us a couple of Fosters, please." She turned to James and, stepping closer, smiled, her emerald green eyes shining like beacons. "Hello, mate. Where're you from?"

"United States," James said, mesmerized by her smile and fascinating face. He felt as if his body was tingling with an intense emotion and closed his eyes briefly to savor the feeling she caused. He liked her effervescent spirit, stunning beauty, and was intrigued by her accent.

"Long way from home, Yank." She grabbed her beers and thrust one at the tall blond man. "Me and Hank are Aussies. On our way to India. What's your story?"

"I'm going to India too." James held out his hand. "James Handel."

She grasped it and pulled James toward her nearly pulling him off the stool. Her subtle perfume reminded him of spring flowers— lavender, and lilacs. "Good on you, mate. We came here on a freighter. Damn stinking ship." She took a long swallow of beer. "How'd you get here?"

"I flew from Japan," James said.

"Cool… that's the way to travel. We're going to Bangkok first, before India." She turned to Hank. "We should fly to Bangkok. I'm not ready for another damn freighter." She twisted back to James. It was obvious she was a little inebriated. "How long have you been in Hong Kong?"

"Arrived today," James said.

"Say hello to Hank." She pulled Hank forward, and he and James shook hands.

"Pleased to meet ya, mate," Hank said. James was somewhat cowed by the height and breadth of the muscular man.

"Hank is like a brother to me," she said, releasing Hank and taking a swig of beer. "You wanna dance. Hank is a terrible dancer and kind of a stick in the mud."

"Love to." James waited, eyebrows raised, hoping she would reveal her name.

Instead, she grabbed James by the arm and pulled him to the dance floor. "I'm Sally." She proceeded to bounce and gyrate her shapely body to the rock music, a cover of the Rolling Stones' *Paint It Black*. Her emerald eyes were set in an oval face with high cheek bones, a small delicate nose with tiny freckles, and dimpled chin.

She was wearing tight jeans and a cerise silk blouse. Her flaming red hair, parted in the middle, swished against him as she spun and dipped. When the song finished, she hugged James, sending waves of yearning throughout his body.

"That's more like it," she said before releasing him and sauntering back to the bar. She chugged her remaining beer. When James returned to his stool, Ron was staring at them with rapt attention.

"Who's your mate?" she asked.

James thrust his arm toward Ron. "Sally, this my friend, Ron."

Sally maneuvered around James and seized Ron's hand. "Pleased to meet you, mate." She grabbed Hank and pulled him toward Ron. "This is my traveling friend, Hank."

Ron stood and shook hands with Hank, studying him cautiously. Hank towered over Ron.

Hank smiled self-consciously and pushed his hat up. "Pleased to meet ya."

Just as James was taking a swallow of beer, Sally pulled on his arm again as the band began playing a cover of the Temptations' *I Can't Get Next To You.* "Come on, this is another good one."

James wiped the spilt beer from his chin and allowed her to lead him to the dance floor. She clasped him around the waist, nearly toppling over backwards before gaining her balance. "Wooo, sorry. Too many beers." She started moving around the dance floor, spinning and slipping between people. James followed spellbound by her movements. She stopped on the other side of the dance floor in front of the all Chinese band in their baby-blue suits and waited for James to catch up, then grasped and spun him around. She let go and placed her hands either side of her head. "Oh, I'm feeling a little dizzy. Better sit this one out."

Back at the bar, James offered Sally his stool. "How gallant," she said and dumped herself on the stool. She leaned forward over the bar and raised her hand. "Hey up, lady," she called to the bartender. "Bring us another round."

Sally discussed the band and her joy about being on dry land. Ron told her about his purser position and the tour he had given James.

"Wow, the Q.E. 2. Hey, mate, can Hank and I get a tour too." She sidled up to Ron and placed her arm on his shoulder.

Ron looked away briefly. "Sure. I'd be glad to show you around the ship."

"That would be so cool." She gazed back at James, placing her hand on his chest. "Will you join us?"

"Thanks, but I was planning to ride the tram up to Victoria Peak and do some shopping tomorrow. I'm not staying in Hong Kong very long. The tour of the Queen Elizabeth 2 was interesting. You'll like it."

"Okay mate, but you've got to promise to come back here tomorrow night," Sally said.

"Sure. I'd be happy to meet you here tomorrow night." James liked her no nonsense manner and was flattered that she had initiated additional contact. Her beauty was so striking. He had never met a red-headed woman with brilliant green eyes, let alone an Australian.

"We rode the tram up the Peak today," Sally said, staring unabashedly at James. "The view was fantastic. You could see all the way to Kowloon."

After the band's break, Sally dragged James back on the dance floor. She had found her second wind. Hank and Ron were in ardent conversation. Ron leaning close to Hank, who was now sitting on James's stool.

James was captivated by Sally's shapely body as she moved back and forth, periodically focusing her enigmatic smile on him. He leaned closer. "Have you and Hank known each other long?"

"Yeah, we grew up together." She grabbed his arm and pulled him nearer. "He's like a second brother. He's not my boyfriend. We're just traveling together." She spun away and then slipped closer. "My brother was going to come too, but his girlfriend is pregnant, and they're getting married. He wanted me to stay to help with the wedding, but I didn't want to waste the rest of the year and not see India. I've been planning this trip for a while."

They continued dancing most of the night except for periodic returns to the bar to slake their thirst. When the band stopped for the night, James and Sally strolled arm and arm back to the bar. They both had worked up quite a sweat. He liked the way the few stands of hair clung to her cheek, framing her beautiful face.

"They're closing," Hank said. "Reckon, we should head out."

"This is a great club we should all come back tomorrow night," Sally exclaimed.

"Yeah," James said, "this place is great.

"See you and Sally tomorrow, say twelve noon," Ron said as he stood and faced Hank. "Just come up the gang plank and ask for Ron."

James decided he better act if he wanted to spend more of the evening with Sally. He rested his hand on her shoulder to get her attention and ignored the glare from Hank. "Would you like to come back to my hotel for a night cap?"

"Mate, I'd love too, but I'm exhausted. I desperately need to recharge my batteries. I loved talking and dancing with you. Thank you for a great evening. I'll see you here tomorrow night. I'd love to dance more with you and get to know you better."

***

James rolled out of his lumpy bed in the early morning. His recurring nightmare had upset him—the haunting Vietnam memory wouldn't let go of him. He splashed his face with water and stared in the mirror. He thought about the previous evening to dispel the gloom of the nightmare. Sally was a breath of fresh air, and he was excited about seeing her again. Should he go with them for lunch aboard Q.E. 2? No, he needed to see the attractions in Hong Kong and travel onward. He had already spent more time in Japan than he had planned. His uncle, Martin, would be wondering where he was.

He wished he had gotten a better hotel. This one appeared okay from the outside, but was a little rundown. Sally wouldn't be impressed. Last night after walking back from the club, feeling somewhat dejected that Sally declined his invitation, an older Chinese woman had joined him in the elevator and offered her services. He wasn't interested in prostitutes, but wished the lady well. He still carried the guilt from his exploitation of the young women in Nam to drown out the sorrow he felt for being a part of a criminal war.

He ate a hearty breakfast of eggs, sausage, English bacon, and endless slices of toast at the hotel, which made up for his uncomfortable bed. He walked to Victoria Park and rode the slow moving tram up the peak. Sally was right, the view from the peak was spectacular. In the afternoon, he wandered around and visited several camera shops. He wanted to buy a camera and some lenses. He had inspected cameras when he was in Japan, but the Zen student he met there had said they would be cheaper in Hong Kong. Hong Kong was famous for knock offs, so he would need to make sure the cameras and lenses were genuine.

For lunch, he had fresh fish with ginger and bamboo shoots in a small cafe. He had mastered the chop sticks in Nam on his leave trips to Saigon and declined the proffered fork. As he envisioned Sally's angelic face and enticing shape, he contemplated the prospect of another evening with her and hoped he could persuade her to come back to his hotel. He hadn't met many Australians. Her boldness and fiery personality had captured his entire being like a soothing breeze of cool air on a hot night and allowed him to briefly forget the burden that haunted his sleep and waking life.

3- HONG KONG: OCTOBER 20, 1969

When they sailed into the Hong Kong harbor, Sally's excitement caused her whole body to tingle as she and Hank stood on deck with their luggage. After visiting the tourist bureau and getting an inexpensive hotel, they rode the tram up Victoria Peak where they lingered, enjoying the view of the island. She made a few sketches while Hank took photographs, insisting that she be in most. She gave into his assertions although she would have preferred to continue silently sketching. Still Hank had agreed to accompany her, and she wanted him to enjoy their journey.

After a satisfying dinner, Sally insisted that they go to a nightclub she had heard about. Upon their arrival at Club Majestic, she raced into the packed nightclub, sifting through the crowd, pulling Hank with her. Hank had wanted to go back to their hotel, but she wanted to have some fun and meet other travelers after eight days on the ratty freighter with nobody to talk to but Hank.

She liked the song *I Heard It through the Grapevine* the band was playing and shimmied to the beat. The dance floor was full of Chinese and a few Westerners moving to the music. Her memory of the freighter slipped to the back of her mind. She grabbed Hank's arm. "Come on, let's dance."

Hank pulled his arm back. "Nah, you know I don't dance."

"Christ, Hank. We're in Hong Kong. Don't be such an ass."

"Leave me be. I need a drink." Hank walked to the bar while Sally toured the room checking for other travelers and possible dance partners.

She wasn't going to let Hank spoil her fun. She was dying to dance, get her body moving to counteract the sedateness of the freighter voyage. After investigating the long bar that ran the entire length of the club and tables to the side of the dance floor, she was drawn like a magnet to a young man on a stool at the bar next to an older black man. The young man was incredibly handsome with his sculptured face, strong thin nose, dimpled chin, intense eyes, and engaging smile, but there was something more about him than just his enticing looks. What was it? His smile... his demeanor... his sumptuous eyes. Whatever it was, he took her breath away. Luckily, he didn't appear to be with any woman. She desperately needed to talk to this man. She rushed back to Hank at the bar and gulped her beer. "Hey, I spotted an interesting bloke down the bar." She yanked Hank away from the bar and pointed out the young man in the short blond hair, mustache, and hazel eyes that seemed to sparkle as he talked to the black man, who gazed at the young man with veneration.

"Looks like a soldier on R and R," Hank said.

She studied the young man more. Even though he had short hair, she had a feeling that he wasn't in the military, but could have been. She had met Aussie and American Rest and Recuperation men in Australia. R and R men had a certain air about them that was hard to explain. They were relieved to be out of Vietnam, but had a reluctance and fear of return. She sensed the man at the bar lacked this fear of return, but still had an air of melancholy.

"Come on," she said, "let's go over and say hello." She tried to pull Hank with her.

"Hey, we've got drinks at the bar," Hank said, pulling his arm away.

She had to meet this man, and she needed Hank with her to steady her. "Leave your drink," Sally said and grabbed Hank's arm again. "They're almost finished. We'll order more."

As she neared the man, she felt an overwhelming desire to claim this handsome man, wondering how this stranger could excite her so.

She danced most of the night with James and was captivated by his gentle manner. Completely different than most Australian men. He was a great dancer and seemed to like her company. Plus he was going to India as well on his round the world plane ticket. If she could meet him in Bangkok and India, she could hopefully convince him to travel with her and Hank. Give her some relief from Hank's boorish nature.

After the band called it a night, she and James sauntered back to the bar arm and arm. She felt a glow of satisfaction and almost overwhelming desire to be in James's arms and feel his taut body, but knew she was too exhausted to properly present herself to this handsome man after all the nearly sleepless nights on the freighter.

When James invited her back to his hotel, she was delighted that she had aroused his interest. For a brief second, she thought about changing her mind and going with him to experience his arms around her, probe his mind, and savor his muscular body. Hank was obviously jealous and hurt that she had ignored him most of the night. Upsetting Hank unduly could be a problem. An upset Hank would make her journey more difficult than it needed to be. She wanted to assuage his bruised ego so that tomorrow night there'd be no incident when hopefully James would again invite her back to his hotel, and she would be rested enough to partake fully in their mutual delights.

"Mate, I'd love too, but I'm exhausted. I desperately need to recharge my batteries. I loved talking and dancing with you. Thank you for a great evening. I'll see you here tomorrow night. I'd love to dance more with you and get to know you better."

"I'll look forward to it."

She felt her excitement rise like a soaring airplane. Hong Kong was turning out great. She would make sure to be in her best form tomorrow night.

***

Sally entered the Club Majestic with happy anticipation of spending time with James. The night club was again packed and the same band in matching yellow suits was playing their energetic music. There were two electric guitars, a bass guitar, two drummers and a horn section. The female singer, although Chinese, sounded American. The dance floor was full, shimmering reflections from the mirrored ball bouncing off the shaking dancers. She spied James talking to Ron and an older Chinese gentleman in a tailored, blue, linen suit. She rushed across the club. As James turned with an expression of surprised joy, she hugged him tightly, relieved that he was still present. "Sorry we're late," she said with a frown. "Hank took me on a wild goose chase."

"Why?"

"Never mind that. I'm dying for a drink." She looked around James at Ron. "Thanks for the great tour of the QE2 and satisfying lunch, Ron. It was a real treat."

Ron placed a hand on the Chinese man's back. "This is my good friend, Chu Lee. He owns several shops in town and has a great house up on Victoria Peak."

Chu Lee offered his hand to Sally and bowed. "Nice to meet you. Allow me to get you all a drink."

Sally suspected that Chu Lee was a homosexual like Ron, but couldn't be sure. Not that it mattered to her in the least.

The same pretty Chinese bartenders were wearing matching red embroidered silk dresses, their silky black hair hanging lose. Chu Lee signaled the bartenders just as Hank joined the group and was introduced to Chu Lee. James talked about his planned travels and his wish to buy a camera and lenses while Hank drifted away after he was handed his beer by Chu Lee.

Sally was glad that Hank had left. He could be easily provoked and associating with two gay men might be more than Hank could take. After their tour of the QE2, Hank had become upset that Sally hadn't told him about Ron being a homosexual. She had responded by telling him to lighten up. His dislike of homosexuals was absurd. She had warned him that he better not cause any scene with Ron when they returned to the club in the evening, or there'd be hell to pay.

Chu Lee placed his hand on James's arm. "I own a very fine camera shop." He gave James a card from his shop and his personal card after writing something on the back in Chinese. "Show my card at the shop, and you will get a significant discount."

"Thank you," James said. "That's very kind."

"It is my pleasure," Chu Lee said as he stared unflinching at James.

The look Chu Lee gave James solidified Sally's suspicion. Seemed James attracted interest from all sides.

"Why don't you tell James and Sally the history of Hong Kong," Ron said.

"Ah yes," Chu Lee said with a slight smile, "a most interesting history. Prior to the arrival of the British, Hong Kong was a fishing village and haven for pirates." Chu Lee surveyed his listeners, seemingly gaging their interest before continuing. "Once the Europeans discovered the wealth of China, they were eager to exploit it. They used the port of Hong Kong to purchase goods. Initial trade for Chinese tea, silk and porcelain was conducted by the exchange of mostly gold before Britain introduced the sale of opium from India. The exchange of opium for goods was quite lucrative for Britain, but caused a serious drug problem for the Chinese. When the Emperor banned the sale of opium, Britain attacked. After a brief war, the Emperor surrendered and ceded Hong Kong to the British in 1842. Opium continued to cause problems for the Chinese, and the Emperor tried again to ban opium, causing the second Opium War, which Britain won again with their superior weapons. The Emperor ceded more territory around Hong Kong to the British as part of the surrender. Hong Kong commerce increased as Britain took advantage of the riches of China, and everyone prospered."

Chu Lee took a drink and smiled before his expression turned dour. "Then in 1937, Imperial Japan invaded China, beginning the world war in Asia. The Japanese were brutal. They quickly conquered the main cities, but a small contingent of Chinese forces were able to keep fighting in the interior, reaching a stalemate with the Japanese.

The Japanese forces invaded Hong Kong and forced the British to surrender Hong Kong in 1941."

Chu Lee paused. "Anyone need another drink?" When there were no takers, he continued. "After Japan's defeat by the Allied Forces, Britain regained control of Hong Kong. The civil war between the Nationalists and Communists in China, which had begun before the Japanese invasion, became a full scale conflict after the war. When the communist won, hundreds of thousands of mainland Chinese fled to Hong Kong." He nodded to James and took a drink of his cocktail. "Now, we are an economic power."

"Do you like that the British control the colony?" James asked.

"Oh, yes." Chu Lee laughed. "I'm deeply anti-communist. I like my freedoms."

After another round of drinks, Chu Lee invited them all back to his house. Sally was glad when James declined. They said good night to Chu Lee and Ron.

Hank rejoined James and Sally. "Where'd you're poof friends go?" he asked James.

James smiled at Hank wryly in silence a few seconds before answering. "They had other plans. They're both interesting people. I'm sorry you didn't like them."

Sally pushed Hank. "Jesus, Hank don't be such a Neanderthal. They were nice. Hey, the tour and lunch aboard the QE2 was fabulous." She shook her head and grasped James's hand. "Let's dance."

***

When the band finished for the evening, Sally strolled back to the bar, dragging James with her. "I'm going with James back to his place for a night cap," she said and clasped Hank around the waist before kissing his cheek.

Hank scowled at James. "We gotta get up early tomorrow, Babe, to catch the freighter."

"I know," she replied. "I won't be too late."

"You're leaving tomorrow?" James said his face stretched in disbelief.

"Yeah, we got a tip from Ron on a freighter sailing for Thailand tomorrow," she said with a frown and placed her hand on James's shoulder. "We had a peek. The cabins are somewhat nice, a big step up from the one we arrived on." She was pleased that James seemed disappointed that she was leaving in the morning, but also felt bad about leaving him for what she hoped would only be a temporary stint.

***

"Not a bad room," Sally said as she toured around James's hotel room. She peaked into the bathroom. "Nice tub. Better than our hotel." After sitting down on the bed, she patted the space next to her. "Come on, sit down. Have you anything to drink?"

"I've a bottle of cognac."

"Break it out then."

He retrieved the cognac and two glasses, which he filled halfway. "Here you go."

She gripped the glass and took a sip. "Good stuff." She swirled the cognac and savored the aroma before drinking the rest. She pulled James to her, planted a warm moist kiss, and parted his lips with her tongue.

When she pulled away, James opened his eyes wide, and smiled before he downed the rest of his cognac. She watched him for a few seconds, thinking his apparent embarrassment delightful, and then pulled him to her and kissed him again. He was a good kisser and she savored the warmth she felt. She wondered if she was being too aggressive. It had been a long time since she had had sex with someone. The anticipation she felt was nearly unbearable. When he leaned back to gaze into her face, she marveled how the light caught his eyes and her excitement expanded like an inflating balloon.

She smiled demurely and placed her hand on his thigh. "Well mate, that was nice."

They continued kissing, each probing with their tongues, and he eased her back on the bed, running his hand over her leg and kissing her neck. She caressed his back and moved her hand down to his rear. A stab of excitement like a jolt of electricity careened around her body as she arched her back. Continuing to kiss her, he ran his hand up her blouse to her bra and petite breasts. She moaned and thrust her hips against him before wiggling out of his grasp and standing.

He scanned her face with a worried expression. His concern was endearing. She desperately wanted sex with this enticing man and couldn't help herself. Her efforts to keep Hank at bay had made sex a common thought. When she began unbuttoning her scarlet silk blouse, his face expanded in a smile. She threw her blouse on a chair and unclasped her bra, freeing her breasts. The look on his face was priceless.

She unbuttoned her jeans, her anticipation skyrocketing. "Don't just lie there, mate," she said. "Get with the program. Lose those clothes."

James rose and quickly disrobed. She sat back on the bed and slipped her jeans off. She lay back on the bed, her flaming hair spread out on the pillow glistening in the soft light of the bedside lamp. When James laid down next to her, she pulled him to her and kissed him deeply before pushing his head to her breasts. He suckled her breasts and ran his tongue around her nipples and kissed his way down to her panties. He slipped them off, exposing her red triangle of pubic hair. He placed his tongue on her moist labia surrounded by the forest of hair. Their coupling was long and frantic. After multiple climaxes, he fell back and sighed. She closed her eyes, bathing in the fire engulfing her body.

After what seemed like hours as they lay clasped in each other's arms, she parted his arms and reluctantly got up. "I better get back before Hank comes looking for me. He can get jealous. We've got an early start tomorrow." She desperately wanted to stay with this handsome man, who had made her feel wonderful with a satisfaction she couldn't put to words. She hoped her leaving before morning would not compromise her allure. She desperately wanted to meet him in Bangkok where she hoped she could unite him to her and get him to travel with her and Hank. She desperately needed to be with this man. She started to mention meeting in Bangkok, but stopped herself, thinking it would be more binding if it came from him.

"Couldn't you stay a little longer and catch a later ship?" he asked breathlessly. "We're just getting to know one another."

"Unfortunately, Hank already gave them a deposit. I would have enjoyed staying here longer and getting to know you better." Could she stay? What would Hank do? Was she being stupid? Was she risking never seeing this man again? She stood naked unmoving, holding her breath, waiting for his response. As the seconds ticked forward, she worried that he wasn't going to mention Bangkok.

"What time do you sail tomorrow?" he asked. "We could meet in Bangkok."

She closed her eyes and breathed in deeply. Her gambit had worked. "That would be lovely."

4- KABUL: JANUARY 28, 1970

As they descended toward the Kabul valley, Sally called to the back of the van, "There it is. Have a look. The mountains are majestic."

"The famed Hindu Kush," Harry added as he stuck his head forward into the front seat. Hank, Bridget and Monica moved forward as well to look out the windshield at the inviting valley.

The golden light of the setting sun on the brown mud buildings of the valley spread a welcoming cloak across the city as they descended. James honked his horn while the rest cheered, glad to be out of Pakistan. Harry directed them through the narrow streets of the old town to the hotel section where he had stayed when he came through eastward.

They selected a hotel on a street filled with shops selling all manner of goods and assorted restaurants and hotels. The street was called Chicken Street because of the large number of chickens, alive or dead, for sale. They rented two rooms, a smaller unheated room for James and Sally and a larger room for the other four with a central wood stove, laid down their packs, and ventured out to buy the famous aromatic brown hash that was readily available. Men in turbans and long Afghan shirts roamed the streets, shuffling along in their baggy pants and sturdy sandals. Afghan women in colorful head scarfs and tribal skirts walked among the crowd as well as women in business suits with bare heads. Western tourists were mixed in the mélange— mostly young people, but a few older men. Harry led them to a shop where they purchased blocks of hashish.

After returning to their big hotel room, its blazing wood stove radiating out welcome warmth kept stoked by the house boy, they lit their chillums and enjoyed the soothing hashish. Well stoned, they all left for a restaurant that several Americans at the hotel had recommended. They hurried along hunched over against the cold night in their meager coats.

When they parted the quilted blanket inside the door of the café, they were hit by the comforting warmth of the central wood stove. Harry ordered for them. They talked about their journey through Pakistan and the welcoming, friendly atmosphere and exotic nature of Kabul. Everyone was in high spirits. When the food arrived, they gobbled the lamb kebabs accompanied by the leavened sheets of Afghan bread and the steaming rice with assorted vegetables, finishing with the sweet rice pudding.

"Finally some good meat," Hank said rubbing his stomach. "I'm tired of this endless tea. I could sure use a beer."

"Me too, mate," Sally said.

"It's available," Harry said. "I know a shop where we can buy, but it's expensive."

"Let's stop on our way back to the hotel," Hank said with a big smile. "I'll treat."

Hank purchased several beers for each of the group and they hurried back to the hotel. As soon as they entered the hotel room, they gathered around the hot stove rubbing their hands, soaking up the radiating warmth. Once warmed, one by one, they retreated to the beds and popped their beers. Hank, after gulping most of his beer, stoked up his chillum and exhaled a cloud of the pungent smoke before passing the chillum around the room. The round of chillums continued.

Later in the evening, James and Sally excused themselves and returned to their unheated room. James was glad to be alone with Sally despite the cold room. They disrobed quickly and hunkered down in their bed until their bodies warmed the bed up before they began their sexual escapades, enjoying their heightened senses from the euphoric hashish.

After their romp, James expelled a long breath. "Well, we made it. I'm gonna love Afghanistan."

***

For several days they roamed the city. The ladies bought embroidered sheepskin coats to stave off the cold of the nights. Hank and James bought embroidered sheepskin vests and several Afghan shirts. They were often joined in the large room in their bouts of hashish smoking by two American men, Bud and Sam, who were staying at the hotel and obviously had their eyes on the Swedish ladies. Bud informed them that it was easy to ship hash back to the States from the post office if you slipped the postal clerk a good bribe. They had shipped several pounds to a friend in California with no problem.

"You should send some hash back to Freddy," Sally said to Hank.

"Yeah, that would be cool," Hank said. "What could I pack it in?"

"How about inside the lining of one of those fur lambskin hats that are so popular," Sally said.

They discussed other options and where to get the best hash.

"We're going up north past Charikar tomorrow to get a couple of kilos," Bud said. "You can buy the hash there for nearly half what it costs here."

"Can I go with you guys?" Hank asked.

"We're going to Bamyan in a couple of days," Sally said. "Why not wait 'til then."

"Nah," Hank said. "Half the price sounds too inviting. Will we be back the same day?"

"Oh yeah. It's about forty miles," Bud said. "The road is terrible. But if you just take it slow, it's doable."

"You can see the guys making the hash," Sam said. "It's really amazing. Handmade, man."

"Can I come?" Monica asked.

The two Americans perked up. "Sure," Bud said. "We've got plenty of room in the van."

James watched the two Americans as they eyed Monica. Oh yeah, they want Monica to go. They'd love to lure her away from Hank. She was almost as beautiful as Bridget and obviously enjoyed flirting with them while Bridget seemed to ignore them, happy to be with Harry.

5- MANILA: OCTOBER 24, 1969

"This was a big mistake," Sally said as she and Hank were sitting on their separate beds in the freighter cabin with its faux wood paneling and worn carpet. The ship had stopped and was off loading and loading goods. "You said four days. You didn't tell me we were going to Manila first. We won't get to Bangkok for another four days."

"What's your hurry?" Hank said. "A flight would have cost five times as much. This is a nice cabin. Quit your complaining." Hank crossed the room and sat down close to her. He put his arm around her. "Don't be mad at me. Come on let's make the best of it." He tried to kiss her.

She shoved him away "No. I'm not in the mood."

"We had a good time last night."

"You mean you had a good time."

"What do you mean?"

"Forget it. I'm going up on deck to get some air. It's hotter than hell in here." Succumbing to Hank out of boredom and to bolster her control over him had been a big mistake. What had she been thinking? She had resisted him all the way to Hong Kong. Did her night with James stir her passion too much?

The harbor was teeming with ships off-loading and loading a myriad of cargoes— coconuts, bananas, mangoes, bales of jute, motorcycles, scooters, cars, appliances. The air was hot and humid. Her sweat engulfed her. Would James wait for her? He had said he needed to get to India before his uncle in Madras left, but didn't say when that was. Hank had probably purposely agreed to a longer sailing time, so she would miss hooking up with James. Sometimes Hank made her so mad she could spit. Damn, her plans were disappearing before her eyes. She had really liked James. If James was gone when they reached Bangkok, she'd be stuck with Hank.

***

"We're coming into port," Sally said while shaking Hank from his slumber. "Let's go up on deck."

Hank rolled over. "What time is it?"

"Just get your butt in gear," she shouted. "I'll meet you topside." She left the cabin excited that they were finally arriving.

They had sailed from Manila four days ago in the early evening. Sally had to repulse Hank repeatedly. Why did she allow the intimacy after they left Hong Kong?

The teeming port was huge and tall skyscrapers flooded the skyline. Something was wrong. Hank arrived at her side, his hair a mess, rubbing his long neck. "Jesus, it's already hot."

"This doesn't look like the pictures of Bangkok."

"Why should it," Hank said, putting his arm around her waist. "It's Singapore."

"What!" She pushed him away. "You sack of shit, you knew all along. You planned this."

"Hey, it was such a good deal. We couldn't pass it up."

"But you didn't think to consult me?" She slammed her fist on his chest. "You're an asshole. We'll probably miss meeting James. Get the hell out of my sight." Tears flooded down her face as she walked away down the deck. Five days and probably at least another three to Bangkok. "He'll be gone for sure," she said to herself.

***

The first day after Singapore she ignored Hank and avoided his company as much as possible. She spent a lot of time on deck sketching and ate her meals quickly. At night in the cabin when Hank made more advances, she dismissed them with angry and acerbic comments. After two days, she realized that taking her anger out on Hank was not productive. She might never see James again, and she would have to continue to travel with Hank. She softened her repulses, but refused any intimacy.

The third night as she was dropping off to sleep she felt Hank lay down beside her. She rolled over and pushed him away. "Come on Hank. This is getting old. What do you think you're doing?"

35

"I'm trying to make up." He grasped her and pulled her to him.

She kneed him hard in the balls. He doubled over, and she jumped out of bed. "Cut the bloody shit, asshole. Just because I relented once doesn't mean were going to make a habit of it."

"Jesus, you don't have to get nasty. That fucking hurt."

***

"We made it," Hank said as they watched the approaching skyline of Bangkok. "Just think of all the money we saved."

"I'd be surprised if James is still here," Sally said, squinting in the bright sunlight. "He was nice." She was enraged that her enticement of James in Bangkok might not be possible, but realized taking her anger out on Hank was useless. Hopefully James had left his uncle's address in Madras at American Express.

"I'm nice. Who paid our way here?"

"Yes and thank you." She placed her hand on his chest. "When I say no, it means no from now on."

The last three days had been one long ordeal that Sally didn't want to ever repeat. Although she was still fuming at Hank, she needed to soften her attitude and get him to agree to fly from Bangkok to Madras if she had any hope of seeing James again. Still nobody was going to force sex on her. Hank was big and strong as an ox, but she could take care of herself.

"Okay. I'm sorry. You know I'm crazy about you. It won't happen again."

"All right, mate. No worries. I can't wait to get off this ship. I'm so sick of ships." She gave Hank a hug to keep him on her good side. "Let's go get our bags. First thing we're taking a taxi to American Express."

After docking they hurried down the gang plank. She felt like she was still at sea and the ground was swaying. Hank hailed a taxi and gave the driver the address to American Express. At the office, Sally went to the mail desk and retrieved two messages. The first was James's hotel address and telephone number dated seven days ago. The second message three days ago repeated his hotel address and announced he would have to leave the next day for Calcutta and then on to Madras. He had expressed his dismay at missing her and listed his uncle's address in Madras where he thought he'd be for at least a week or two. She was relieved that James had left his uncle's address and thought about catching the next plane for Madras. Hank had messed things up something terrible.

"What's he say?" Hank asked as he came up behind her. "I changed some traveler's check so we're flush. Let's check out the tourist desk and get a nice hotel. No rat traps. Okay." He placed his arm around her and gave her a kiss on the cheek.

"Great," she replied as cheery as she could manage. She wanted to strangle him.

***

The hotel was pleasant although a little pricey, so she agreed to pay half. She had insisted on two beds and a private bathroom. She didn't want any sneak attacks while she was sleeping. She knew she'd probably have to relent and let Hank have his way at least once to keep the noose tight and get him to agree to buy plane tickets to Madras. She wanted to see the important temples and other sites in Bangkok, but didn't want to miss James again. If she spent two days visiting the important attractions and then flew to Madras, she was hopeful James would still be there.

"Let's take a little nap, have lunch, and then go exploring," she said as she sauntered up to Hank on her tip toes and gave him a kiss on the cheek.

"Okay by me," he said, smiling brightly. "I'll set my alarm for an hour."

***

"What a sight," Sally said as the water taxi approached the Grand Palace. They disembarked and spent the afternoon wandering around, marveling at the beautiful palaces and temples. Hank took many pictures and seemed in good spirits. She made a few quick sketches.

When they had seen most of the buildings, sculptures and gardens, they went back to the hotel. Hank slumped down on his bed as the ceiling fan whirled. The room was somewhat cooler than outside, but still hot. Sally rested on her bed and filled out her sketches with more detail, using the post cards she had purchased as reference. After completing her sketches, she reluctantly decided to make her move and insure Hank would agree to plane tickets. She was still mad at him, but she believed plane tickets were essential if she had any chance of seeing James again.

Hank had grown up with her and her brother. They had spent many a summer diving the Great Barrier Reef. She loved the colorful fish, fans, and corral. It really was another world under the water. She had painted water color pictures of the fish and spectacular corral that she exhibited at a local Brisbane gallery. She wanted to be an artist, but, at the bidding of her parents, instead chose education as her major. She liked working with children, but her real passion was art.

After college, she had taken a job in Brisbane teaching young children. She often included art in her lesson plan. She and her brother had talked about traveling to India together. She had saved her money and investigated the most economical way to travel. She had dated a few men in town, but most were boring or too full of themselves. When summer came and school ended, she was excited to start their journey to India. She had been to Bali two years ago with her brother and was intrigued by Hinduism and Buddhism. She was devastated when her brother informed her he could not go to India. His girlfriend was pregnant, and he needed to make wedding plans. She wasn't going to travel to India by herself. Her brother Freddy suggested she go with Hank instead. She initially didn't like the idea, but, rather than scrap the trip, she asked Hank if he wanted to go with her. He had agreed on the spot.

She and Hank had gone to college in Brisbane and had dated briefly. They had grown up together, and dating him had been rather dull. She had a brief romance with a handsome bloke in college, but, when he went out with another women behind her back, she dumped him. The other men she dated never caught her fancy. Hank left college after two years and worked on and off at cattle stations or construction jobs. She knew Hank was infatuated with her, but she wasn't romantically interested in him. Hank was kind and somewhat considerate for a rough and ready Aussie, but he could get on your nerves. He wasn't interested in art and could care less about religions and culture. Still he was protective, and she had no other choice.

She swallowed hard and moved to Hank's bed. After sitting down, she leaned over, planting a moist kiss on Hank's lips. He opened his eyes. She ran her hand down his chest and stomach. His eyes got wider. She continued her hand to his groin and squeezed his growing member. She stood up and began quickly disrobing. Hank rose and wiggled out of his clothes. Their sex was quick and loud. Her moans of pleasure were somewhat faked, but they did the trick. Hank was beside himself.

"I'll go take a shower," she said, rising out of his arms. "You relax. Later we can go to dinner and even later you might get lucky again, mate."

His smile couldn't have gotten any bigger.

"We need to fly to Madras after we've seen the important attractions here. Two days and then we fly. Okay?"

"It'll cost...but okay. Yeah, I'm sick of freighters too."

James stayed in Hong Kong after his night with Sally, marking time, so when Sally arrived in Bangkok, they could explore together. He kept recalling their night of passion with a smile.

He and Ron visited the Che Kung Temple, built to worship General Che, military leader of the Song Dynasty, who many believed saved the Song Dynasty and was famous for his power to suppress plagues. Ancestral worship was strong in China. Temples were built for the Emperor and important dignitaries like General Che, so people could worship them publicly. Family ancestors were worshiped at a shrine in most homes.

On his visit to Japan, he had met the curious Japanese student, Nobo, at a Shinto Shrine in Tokyo and learned that ancestral worship was strong in Japan too. Shinto prayed to kami— animals, birds, trees, mountains, oceans, wind, and ancestors. James thought it was a type of animism. They had gone to Edo Castle, stronghold of the shoguns, and to Kyoto where they visited the imposing Shogun Nijo Castle and the Emperor's Palace with its curved pitched roofs and wooden floors.

They had also traveled to nearby Nara to the Todai-Ji Temple, the largest wooden building in the world. James was in awe of the massive building with its thick wooden beams and towering fifteen meter bronze statue of Lord Buddha, which in 751 had taken almost all the bronze in Japan and nearly bankrupted the country.

Zen Buddhism in Japan favored rigorous meditation practice— called zazen— to gain insight in the Buddha nature over study and knowledge of doctrines and religious texts. It seemed like a simpler Buddhism compared to Indian or Chinese Buddhism.

***

On the second day in Hong Kong after Sally's departure, James purchased his camera and lens at Chu Lee's store at a big discount and spent the day filming the boat people in Kowloon— thousands of families living on the water in sampans— Hong Kong's workers.

He went to the club in the evening, hoping to find Ron and Chu Lee to thank Lee and possibly get an invitation to his house on Victoria Peak. He imagined that the house would be palatial. The last two days he had felt a little doleful and his nightmares had invaded his sleep relentlessly. Sally had miraculously pushed his nightmares briefly to the background. He missed her exciting company. Would he ever be free of his haunting memories? How would he ever be able to accept and forgive himself for what he had done in the war?

He surveyed the club occupants, but didn't see Ron, so he selected a stool at the bar and ordered a beer. After he had taken a drink and was watching the band, he saw out of the corner of his eye a tall buxom mixed-race Chinese lady, who he had noticed earlier standing with a group of attractive well-dressed ladies, striding toward him. She stopped in front of him and narrowed her eyes with just a hint of a smile. She was wearing a tight fitting silver, expensive, sequined dress that set off her ample cleavage.

"You here all by yourself?" the lady asked as she leaned toward James, giving him a glimpse of her assets.

"Yes," James replied. He was intrigued by her shapely body and attractive face even though she appeared quite a bit older than him.

In her heels she was slightly taller than he was. "You want to dance?" she said and held out her hand. She had a husky voice and slight accent that James couldn't place. "My name's My Lin."

"Yeah, I'd love to. I'm James" He wondered why she had chosen him. She seemed way out of his league. There were older, affluent gentlemen present that seemed more suitable, but he was pleased with the prospect of dancing, hopefully remind him of his time with Sally and get his blood circulating to hasten a good night's sleep.

She grasped his hand and guided him to the dance floor. She moved provocatively and kept her eyes on him the entire dance. When the song finished, she seized his hand and escorted him back to the bar.

"Two Doctor Funks, Hing," My Lin said to the bartender, dressed tonight in a violet dress. My Lin handed the bubbling drink in the tall glass to James. "You'll like this— very refreshing."

James had never heard of a Doctor Funk—sounded ominous. The drink went straight to his head. My Lin kept him standing and squeezed her body up to his. He felt a little embarrassed by her actions.

After he finished his Doctor Funk, My Lin grabbed his hand. "Let's have another dance." She didn't wait for an answer, but dragged him out to the dance floor. She was very strong. The band was playing *Shake It Up Baby*.

My Lin did just that.

When the song finished, she held James's hand and waited. As the next song, *When A Man Loves A Woman*, began, she grasped him and pulled him to her. She roamed her hand across and down his back, pulling his hips into hers.

He thought My Lin was attractive, but he wasn't enthusiastic about her advances. After the sumptuous night with Sally, he wasn't interested in a liaison. After two more Doctor Funks and many dances, he was on the verge of drunkenness and wasn't sure what he wanted.

When My Lin went to the bathroom, Ron, whom he hadn't even noticed, came up to him. "James what do you think you're doing?"

"Hey, Ron. Sorry I didn't see you earlier and say hello. How's it going?" He felt light headed and had trouble focusing.

"Do you know who that lady is?"

"My Lin."

"I know you think you're gonna get lucky with this curvaceous lady," Ron said. "But she's not what you think." He laid his hand on James's shoulder. "She's a man."

"No way," James said and placed his hand on the bar to steady himself.

"Go across the street and look at the entertainment bill. She's the headliner."

James stumbled off his stool and slinked across the street. Surely Ron was mistaken. There on the bill My Lin was pictured in her sequined dress, flanked by a group of females or should he say males. World famous female impersonators.

He stumbled back to the nightclub, rushing past My Lin, who stood at the bar watching him with a beckoning smile. "Thanks Ron, I would have never known. That could have been embarrassing. I'm taking off." He placed his hand on Ron's shoulder. "You take care and thanks. I'm off for Bangkok tomorrow."

Ron slipped off his stool and gave James a hug. "Be careful, my friend."

James ignored My Lin's outstretched hand as he hurried past and headed for the door, glad he had been saved from an awkward embarrassment.

***

As James walked down the stairs from the airplane, he was hit by the intense heat and humidity of

Bangkok as the mirage heat waves flowed off the asphalt. Hong Kong had been warm, but nothing like this. Inside the terminal, he called a hotel he found at tourist information—a mid-priced hotel with private bathroom to impress Sally, who he expected to arrive tomorrow.

He hailed a taxi and entered the crowded city. The traffic was thick with small three wheel taxis, known as tuk-tuks that were everywhere. He liked the clean and tidy lobby of the hotel and was happy with his large room and pleasant bathroom with a tub. Sally would be pleased. He left his bags at the hotel and hurried to the American Express office to leave his address and telephone number.

He had bought an English paper at the airport and read it on the plane— the first news since he left the States. Viet Nam was still headlining the news, but nothing about a massacre. He had heard rumors of a massacre committed by Americans of an entire village when he was in Nam— women and children. He suspected the rumors were true, but doubted if it would ever come out. Some of the stories that soldiers, transferred to his artillery base, told of their fighting experiences in the jungle had turned his stomach with their brutality.

In Vietnam he had been a supply clerk at a forward Army artillery battery near Pleiku. He hated his time in Vietnam and felt guilty for the immense destruction that the Americans unloaded on the Vietnamese. His own actions haunted him day and night. He knew he needed to forgive himself and move on, but nothing seemed to help after his return to the States. He was so thankful when he was invited to visit his uncle in Madras, India. He would see other parts of the world, keep his mind engaged, and hopefully away from his haunting memories.

He waited for Sally's call for two days, keeping close to his hotel except for meals and strolls around the area. He checked back to his hotel repeatedly for any messages. It had been four days since Sally left Hong Kong. She should have been here by now. Why hadn't he gotten the name of the freighter? Stupid. He couldn't stay in Bangkok much longer. Martin would be leaving Madras soon, and James needed to get there so he could spend time with his uncle.

He worked on yoga poses, but his attempts at meditation were futile. His haunting memories of Nam would not let him be, nor the worries of never seeing Sally again. On the third day, he left a message at his hotel for Sally and went exploring.

The streets were full of people— monks galore in orange robes, street vendors, three wheel taxis, Americans on R and R, and Thai men and women in traditional and European dress. He took a water taxi, a long narrow wooden boat, to the What Pho Temple where the famous golden reclining Buddha was housed. Bangkok was known as the Venice of the East because of all its canals. The canal he went down was crowded with boats loaded with produce and goods. The boat drivers stopped at the various stilt houses on the sides of the canal to hawk their wares.

The buildings in the What Pho Temple compound were spectacular with their unique colorful architecture and carved spires. The gold plated reclining Buddha, the largest in the world, had been constructed in 1832 and was 46 meters long and 15 meters high. He hadn't seen anything like it.

He had studied Buddhism and Hinduism after his return from Vietnam. He was intrigued by other religions and wanted to learn more about them, another reason he had embarked on this journey besides his wish to get out of the States. Although he thought the teaching of Christ to be worthwhile, the dogma of the Christian religion annoyed him. He couldn't accept original sin and the Old Testament tenet of an eye for an eye. In Vietnam he had been enchanted by the Buddhist monks and their belief in non-violence, a stark contrast to the demeaning violence of war.

When he arrived back at his hotel, there was still no word from Sally. Out of boredom, he decided to explore some of the night spots. The clubs he visited were filled with a host of young Thai ladies in provocative dress and young Americans, soldiers on R and R. Bangkok was the most favored R and R location. He had taken his R and R in Hawaii. The war had not only destroyed the culture of Vietnam, but also the neighboring countries. Hundreds of poor women were selling their bodies to American soldiers.

He stopped in the third club where the Rolling Stones' *Sympathy For The Devil* was playing. Were the Americans the devil? He decided to stay in the lively club and ordered a beer. After watching for a time, he thought it would be fun to dance. He asked several ladies, who all declined. Disappointed, he went back to the bar to watch the twirling bodies. He wondered if there was some protocol required to get the ladies to dance.

A short Thai woman edged up to him at the bar. She was wearing a tight, forest green, mid-thigh dress with a Chinese collar that presented her shapely body well. "I dance with you," she said. "Those other ladies stupid. They no like your mustache. They think you might be ghost. Me, pay no attention to superstitions." She took his arm and coaxed him to the dance floor. The Beatles song, *She Loves You Ya Y*a, was playing.

The dance energized him, and he felt more relaxed as they returned to the bar. It felt good to get his heart pumping.

"You buy me drink?" she asked. He ordered her a rum and coke and himself another beer. She squashed against him. "You Army guy?"

"No. Just a tourist."

"Me, show you around Bangkok then. You like?" She put her arm around his waist and laid her head against his chest. Her gardenia perfume was luscious, and he breathed in the enticing fragrance. "Me good tour guide. No cost much. You pay me what you like." She was beautiful— eyes like liquid pools of black and long shining hair hanging down almost to back of her knees. She appeared young in her heavy eye makeup, but, studying her face, he could see the lines crinkling around the corners of her eyes. Not that young.

"Well, I don't know." He grabbed his chin. If Sally showed up, she wouldn't like it if he was with a beautiful woman tour guide. Then again what if Sally never showed. It would be nice to have a tour guide and someone to share the sights with. "I'll think about it."

"Okay, you think. Come dance."

They danced many dances and drank innumerable cocktails and beer. James became inebriated and wanted to lie down.

"I'm going to go back to my hotel," he said and patted her shoulder. "Thanks for the dances and your lovely company."

"Me, come too."

"No, that's okay."

"No, no. Me, get you taxi. You no pay tourist price." She grabbed his hand. "Me, no spend night. You trust. Me, good Buddhist. No cheat. Meet you in morning for tour. You see how good tour guide, me." She dragged him to the door.

He reluctantly went along. What could it hurt?

She gave a handful of bills to the doorman and dragged him outside to a row of three wheel tuk-tuks. She argued in Thai with the first taxi, then moved to the second in the row. They apparently agreed on a price, and she ushered him inside, squeezed in next to him, and kissed him on the cheek. "Me, save you much money. You see. My name, Farung."

***

"You have breakfast?" Farung asked as she stood in the lobby of his hotel at their appointed meeting time.

"Yes, I had breakfast early. Didn't sleep too well." Sally had floated in and out of his dreams all night, and his reoccurring nightmare had awakened him early.

"So sorry you no sleep good." She sidled up and took his hand. "We go." She had a tuk-tuk waiting outside.

The tuk-tuk took them to the river where they caught a river taxi to the old city, Rattanakosin. The immense Grand Palace was spectacular from the river. They went inside the walled compound and strolled around the many colorful temples and palaces. The multicolored Thai style pagoda spires and swooping roof ends were dazzling.

"The king lives here," Farung said. "Way beautiful. You like."

"It's great."

They spent most of the morning there. James took many pictures with his new camera. When they had seen everything, they left in a water taxi back up the busy canal.

After leaving the river, she took him to a rather dilapidated building and ushered him inside. "This good food. Me, order for you. You like prawns?"

"Yes."

She ordered several dishes and two Singlas, Thai beers. The delicious dishes were hot and spicy and the shrimp was gigantic. The cost of the sumptuous meal was next to nothing.

"We go hotel. You take nap? Yes."

In the lobby James obtained his key. "Farung, this was a lovely day. Thanks for showing me the Grand Palace and taking me to that great restaurant."

"Me, come too?"

"That's not necessary," he said.

"No cost you. Me good. Make you happy."

"I don't doubt that. Really it's okay."

"Yes, okay." She took his hand and led him to the elevator. He did not resist.

In the room she turned down the bed and began unbuttoning his shirt. "What's going on, Farung?"

"You no worry. Me clean. Just had test." Why he allowed her to disrobe him, he had no idea. "You ready to go. Me, like." She grasped his penis and started to kneel.

He pulled her up. "Really, this is not necessary."

"You no like Farung?" She rose on her tip toes and kissed him. "Me good lover."

"I'm sure you are, Farung."

"Good." She began undressing smiling demurely. She had perfectly formed little breasts with puffy dark nipples and a mass of black pubic hair.

She pulled him to the bed and lay down spreading her legs while she continued to pull him with her. Her hair fanned out on the bed like a cloak. "You no worry. Me, no make babies."

James shook himself from his acquiescent stupor, and stepped back from the bed. "Farung, I'm sorry you are a beautiful woman, but I can't do this."

"You no like make love?"

"Not now." James avoided peering at Farung's naked body. He had succumbed to the women in Nam, but he didn't want to continue to exploit poor women trying to make a living in this manner. The war had driven women to this degrading behavior. He had enough regrets about the war and didn't want to add to them in Bangkok.

"You want take shower together? I wash. Make you happy." She rose and inched up to him pressing her body against his.

He felt his desire rise, but gently pushed her away. "No...I'm not in the mood." His growing penis belied his comment, but she accepted his statement.

"Maybe later, then," she said cheerfully and began dressing. "You take nap. Me, come back tonight. We go eat. You like?"

Well she would know a good place to eat and he liked her company. "Yes. What time?"

"Eight."

***

After dinner at a small upscale restaurant—spicy fish with vegetables and jasmine rice— down the street from his hotel— they walked along the street looking in the shop windows.

"You buy me dress?" Farung asked, squeezing against him.

"Sure." He started for the shop door.

"No here. Too expensive. We go market tomorrow." She pulled him away from the shop. "Market better. You see." She hugged him around the waist and caressed his butt. "We go back hotel. Make love."

"No, Farung, not tonight."

"You missing wife?"

"Yes." He hoped his lie would keep her at bay.

"Me, understand."

They walked back to his hotel and he arranged to meet her in the morning to go shopping. At least he owed her the dress for showing him around.

He needed to get to Madras and spend time with Martin. He had saved quite a bit of money from his engineering job in Chicago before he was drafted, plus the money he was paid in the Army. He believed he could travel for some time on his savings. Martin had paid for his around the world plane ticket. He called the airline and made his reservation to Calcutta.

7- KABUL: JANUARY 31, 1970

As James, Sally, Bridget and Harry were passing around a chillum in the afternoon awaiting Hank's return, Monica burst into the room with a stretched, crimson face, her dusty cheeks stained by tears, her blue eyes puffy, rimmed in red. "They've got Hank!"

Sally jumped up and rushed toward Monica. "What do you mean?" she shouted.

"Hank insulted one of the Afghans," Monica said, her words trembling forth. "They just took him and made the rest of us leave at gun point. It was horrible. I was so scared." She dropped her head into her hands.

"Who's got him?" Sally growled, grabbing Monica by the shoulders. "What the hell's going on?" Gritting her teeth in anger, she stared wild-eyed at Monica. "We can't leave him there."

"There was nothing I could do," Monica said as she burst into tears. "They kept us at gunpoint until we left. Bud and Sam insisted on coming back for reinforcements."

Bridget went to her cousin and laid her hand on her shoulder. "Where's Bud and Sam?"

"There out in the street in their van," Monica said, "waiting for us to go back up to see if we can find Hank."

"Should we go to the police?" Sally asked, turning to James her face squished in anger.

"I don't think that's a good idea yet," Harry said. "Let's go back and see what we can find out first."

"I agree," James said.

They all piled into James's van and followed Bud and Sam back north. When they arrived at the house where the men had grabbed Hank, one man in a white turban was present sitting on the floor, cowering as the group squeezed into the small room.

James moved closer to the man, who reared back as if expecting an assault. "We are looking for the tall blond man, who was here earlier to buy hashish. Do you know where he is?"

The Afghan relaxed somewhat as he studied the faces behind James, then lifted his head toward James. "Me, not know… tall man and gunmen gone," the Afghan said forcefully before lowering his voice. "Go Bamyan. Ask for Mahmood."

"Did Mahmood take the tall man?" James asked.

"Don't know." The man hunched his shoulders. "Go Bamyan."

James watched the man in silence a few seconds, then thanked him, and ushered the others outside.

Harry laid a hand on James's shoulder. "Let's first check at the rest of the houses here for Hank," Harry said. "I wouldn't trust that guy. Makes no sense to take Hank to Bamyan."

"Yeah, could be the man said Bamyan because it's a well-known tourist destination," James said. "He just wants to get rid of us."

James and Harry went door to door among the few other houses of the village and asked about a tall Australian while the rest stayed with the van.

"Nobody knows anything," James said as he returned to the others. "I don't know what to do." He glanced at Sally.

Sally stared back at him in disbelief. "Jesus, James, where could he be? What are we going to do now? Damn, Hank can be so stupid."

"We can either return to Kabul and go to the Australian embassy and police or continue on toward Bamyan," Harry said. "I doubt the embassy or the police would be of any help. Maybe the guy was telling the truth. Nobody but him seems to have seen Hank. It's worth a try."

"Where's Bud and Sam?" James asked.

"Those fuckers left as soon as you and Harry went off," Sally said, narrowing her eyes. "Jesus, Monica, what did Hank do?"

"I told you all I know," Monica said and began crying

Bridget put her arm around Monica and hugged her. "It's not your fault."

James glanced at the small village and grabbed his neck. What to do? Harry was right they might as well check out Bamyan for this Mahmood. "Okay, let's go to Bamyan."

They drove off on the pot holed dirt road up into the mountains. When it was dark, they stopped and slept in the van alongside the road near a village. The night was bitterly cold and they had to start the car periodically to keep warm. They heard wolves howling in the night and slept fitfully.

59

8- CALCUTTA: OCTOBER 30, 1969

After exiting the plane to the overpowering heat, James went slowly through passport control and customs. The officials didn't seemed concerned about the long lines and took their time. Outside the airport, he was accosted by beggars of all sorts, and he had to push and shove to get a taxi. The taxi driver was dressed in a shabby khaki shirt and trousers and did not know the whereabouts of the hotel his uncle Martin had recommended.

The driver left him in the hot car and after some time returned, tilting his head from side to side. "Acha, I know the way now, kind sir. Very fine hotel. You will like very much, isn't it. Taxi will cost only eighty rupees." James was too hot and bothered to bargain.

As James left the airport the dwindling light gave a golden hue to the throngs of people, many with huge bundles on their heads, cows, taxis, bull carts, rickshaws, mopeds, and bicycles crowding the streets. The cacophony of horns was incessant and seemed a waste of time, since the drivers continuously honked their horns no matter what the circumstances. The sidewalks were crammed with a multitude of people, who appeared to be living on the streets— whole families sleeping, cooking on the cement. James was amazed at the number of homeless people. The smell of diesel fumes, burned oil, and smoke filled the air. After many miles, the multitude of people diminished as they entered the area of the upscale hotels.

James was surprised by the opulence of his hotel. He had thought Martin recommended a modest hotel based on the price. The front entrance was flanked by columns with an ornate carved door. A doorman in red Nehru jacket with gold embroidery, wearing a red turban opened the door and bowed. Inside men in turbans dressed in white Nehru jackets and trousers greeted him, grabbed his bag, and escorted him to the registration desk. The heavy-set woman behind the desk, dressed in a lime green sari with gold edging and sequins, smiled and asked his name. She signed him in, asking him where he had come from, and welcomed him, thanking him for choosing this fine hotel. She gave him a map of Calcutta circling the hotel location.

"Dinner will be in an hour," she said. She pointed to a courtyard with a gurgling fountain. "If you like, after you have freshened up, you can take a drink. It has cooled down a little. Today was very hot. It will give you a chance to meet our many European guests. I'm Missus Govinda, the owner. If there is anything you need, please just ask."

After perusing his small room containing a welcoming bed with mahogany carved headboard, a small mahogany dresser, and a small bathroom with a tiled shower, he washed his hands and face, then went downstairs into the courtyard. A man with a neatly trimmed beard and dark hair raised his arm and beckoned James. James settled at the table and was introduced to the two men, a German, named Willy, and an Englishman, named Captain Jeff. Willy explained that he was just visiting on his way to Germany after working in Australia for several years, but Jeff had lived in Calcutta five years.

James took the opportunity after some discussion of his past and planned travels to ask Jeff about all the people he saw living on the street.

Jeff pursed his lips as he regarded James before raising his hand to signal the waiter. "Calcutta is a poor city with many homeless and innumerable slums," he said. "A lot of the homeless have come from East Pakistan where there is considerable unrest. Of course you're familiar with the Indian caste system. Well, the Untouchables and Muslims are on the low end of the economic ladder. They are given only the most menial tasks if they can find work at all. Many end up homeless."

"I thought the caste system was abolished," James said.

"Yes the caste system was abolished in the Indian Constitution after independence," Jeff said. "Discrimination by caste is against the law. However, my good man, changing a system that has been in place for thousands of years is nearly impossible." Jeff finished his beer and grabbed the gin and tonic as soon as it arrived.

"When was the caste system introduced?" James asked

Jeff drank a copious amount of his drink before answering. "The Vedas, early Hindu religious texts, mentioned caste as early as 1500 BC. The Bhagavad Gita, one of their important religious stories from 200 BC emphasizes the importance of caste and defines the rights and duties of the four castes—Brahmins, priests, scholars, and teachers, Kshatriyas, rulers, warriors, and administrators, Vaishyas, farmers and merchants, and Shudras, laborers. Those outside the four castes are considered Untouchables, Dalit. They are literally to be shunned and a touch by them is considered a terrible affront and requires ritual purification."

James had read about the Untouchables in his Indian guide book but didn't realize the name derived from the affront of their touch.

Jeff stirred his drink as he watched James's reaction to his statement. "The only way Untouchables can rise is by leading a holy Hindu life and hope they will be reincarnated into a higher caste. There has been some progress through the courts to improve the lot of the Untouchables. Untouchables are even forbidden from most temples. There is almost no intermarriage among the castes. Nearly all marriages are arranged by parents. Women are treated as property. Caste can even determine what kind of job one can obtain. The government passes laws to try to integrate the Untouchables into society to little avail. If you stay in India very long you will see that the caste system is still pervasive."

James was surprised by Jeff's pessimism. He wondered, if the man disliked India so much, why he lived here. There were plenty of other countries where one could live cheaply. "I also saw long bearded men in orange and yellow robes walking among the homeless. One of them was carrying a trident. Are they the sadhus?"

"Probably. Most sadhus are charlatans if you ask me. Just a better way to beg and live off other people."

"Surely some of them are genuine seekers of enlightenment."

"Perhaps," Jeff said. "But what is this enlightenment? Bunch of crap if you ask me."

"You don't put any stock in yoga, meditation, and attainment of enlightenment?"

"Well I've read of some of the feats yogis can perform when meditating. I would imagine there is a benefit. But enlightenment and freedom from rebirth... I can't swallow that."

"You don't believe in reincarnation?"

"It's possible, I suppose. I don't worry about it. If there's no heaven nor rebirth, so what. If I die and that's it, that's fine with me. A lot of religion, it seems to me, is to keep people docile and willing to accept their wretched lot." He ordered another gin and tonic. "In India if people started questioning their lot and demonstrating for better lives, there would be a serious problem. There are way too many people in India and the population is increasing at an alarming rate. People keep having children so they will be supported in their old age. Female children are considered a burden because they will require a dowry. Thus the need for more male children. The government has those signs saying one or two children will do. You've probably seen them. Pathetic. There's already too many people in this country. It's overwhelmed."

James accompanied the men into the dining room when the gong sounded. They were joined by some Indian business men in collarless Indian style suits, wives in saris, and several more Westerners. After dinner of a delicious chicken curry, James accompanied Willy and Jeff to a bar on the outskirts of the city passing through enumerable slums before arriving at the bar in a stately house with Moghul style turrets. After more discussion of the state of the Indian morass as they consumed prodigious amounts of alcohol, Willy took advantage of one the many young women on offer. When he returned, the group went back to the hotel.

***

"Welcome to Madras," Martin, James's uncle, said as he gave James a hug inside the plane terminal. Martin was tall and lanky with gray hair at his temples. His gray eyes were wide and glinting in the sunlight streaming in the large windows.

After retiring in Calcutta, James had not been able to get the level of poverty he encountered in India and Jeff's pessimistic comments out of his

65

mind. He slept fitfully and woke in the middle of the night from his recurring nightmare. His lack of proper sleep and his stifling journey to the airport and subsequent flight to Madras had left him exhausted.

James released his hug, noticing the dampness of Martin's shirt. "Man, is it hot here," James said. "Calcutta was hot, but this heat is stifling."

"Yes, it's going to get even hotter. Let's get going. My apartment will be cool, and I've got iced drinks waiting. Grab your bag. My car is waiting outside."

The baggage claim was pandemonium as the multitude of Indian families retrieved their gigantic bags with the help of the ubiquitous porters. James couldn't even get close to his bag for quite a while as the sweat dripped from his brow. Outside Martin's driver was waiting along with an army of beggars. The driver took James's bag and opened the back door of the small tan car and shooed away the beggars that swarmed around the driver to grab ahold of James with their cries of 'baksheesh'. James was relieved when the door shut. Martin entered from the other side of the car, squishing in, pushing the beggars away gently.

"Wow, the beggars sure are intrepid in India," James said as they pulled away, entering the streaming, honking traffic trying to exit the Airport.

"Yes, there are many indigent people in India," Martin replied. "The government is trying to deal with the problem but is having little success."

Outside the airport the traffic was bumper to bumper with an array of vehicles and other means of conveyance of all types. Cows wandered along the streets and shoulders as mopeds darted around the cars, carts drawn by bullocks, rickshaws clanking their bells, and many bicycles. Men dressed in dhotis and women in saris thronged the sides of the streets, but he did not see whole families living on the streets like Calcutta. The ride to Martin's compound took over an hour at the creeping pace.

"Cracky, it's hotter than hell here," Hank said as they left the Madras airport terminal.

An Indian dressed in a kaki shirt and trousers grabbed Hank's backpack "Sahib, I help. No problem. I find excellent taxi for Sahib." The little man tilted his head from side to side.

Sally laughed. "Go ahead let him have the pack. This heat is killing me. Let's get the hell out of here."

They had trouble following the little man as beggars surrounded them. Hank bolted ahead, knocking beggars out of the way. The man ushered them into the backseat of a car away from the taxi stand. "My cousin. He's an excellent driver. He will take you wherever you wish. Very reliable." He deposited the bags in the trunk and slipped up to the car window with his hand out.

Hank handed the man a dollar bill. The man's face lit up. "Thank you very much, kind sir."

Sally handed the address of James's uncle to the driver. The driver studied the address. "Very far, Memsaab," he said.

"We need to get a hotel first," Hank announced.

"No... I want to make sure James is even here," Sally said adamantly, stretching her face. "We can find a hotel after. Hopefully there will be one near where James is staying... if he's still here."

Hank rubbed his face and scowled. "Okay."

"Is Memsaab ready to go?" the driver asked.

"Wait a minute," Hank said. "How much."

"Ah, Sahib not too much. One hundred rupees."

"That's outrageous...no way," Hank said, leaning forward.

Sally thought Hank had no idea that one hundred rupees was about eight dollars. Still bargaining was expected.

"Fifty," Sally said.

"Memsaab, it is long way. Eighty."

"Sixty," Sally said.

"Oh, Memsaab, this is not a fair price."

"Seventy," she said.

The driver tilted his head from side to side. "Yes Memsaab. You drive a hard bargain. My name is Madur. I'm am pleased to drive you to this address. Please relax. It is very hot today, isn't it?" He started the taxi.

***

The taxi driver attempted to enter the open compound gate, but the gate attendant stopped him. The driver and the gate attendant loudly exchanged words in a language Sally could not understand.

"What's the problem?" Sally asked.

"No problem, Memsaab. We shall wait here for gentleman, your friend, to verify our presence."

After a few minutes, the gatekeeper waved the car inside. The courtyard was wide with a few parked cars on the gravel. Two story buildings, apparently apartments, formed the other three sides of the courtyard.

Sally saw James and another man coming down the stairs and burst out of the car. She ran to James and gave him a big hug. "I was so afraid you wouldn't be here," she said, kissing him on the cheek.

"I'm glad you found me. I waited in Bangkok as long as I could."

"I'm sorry. Hank booked us on a freighter that went to Manila and Singapore before it sailed to Bangkok. I didn't know. I'll tell you all about it later. I feel so relieved that you're here."

"This is my uncle, Martin. He has an apartment here. Why don't you and Hank come up for a cool drink."

"Well, we need to get a hotel," Sally said. "We came here straight from the airport. I had to know if you were still here. It took forever to get here. I've never seen so many people. Hong Kong and Bangkok were crowded but nothing remotely like here. The streets are so congested it's a wonder that anyone bothers to drive."

"I'll help you get a hotel," Martin said. "I'll have my driver take you later. Just deposit your bags with the gatekeeper. He will store them and keep them safe. My apartment is nice and cool. After that long drive in this heat, you'll need a cold drink."

"That sounds wonderful." She waved at Hank. "Hank, come on. Give the bags to the gatekeeper, and we'll go up for a cool drink."

"How are we going to get a hotel?" Hank said, exiting the car. "We're out in the suburbs. We'll never get another taxi."

Martin walked over to Hank and introduced himself. He directed the gatekeeper to get the bags and took Hank by the arm.

"Wait a minute, I haven't paid yet."

Martin pulled Hank along. "The gatekeeper will take care of it. Please let's get out of this heat."

"You sure," Hank said.

"Yes, it's okay."

***

The apartment was luxurious and cool. Hand carved mahogany furniture was spread around the living room as the fan overhead whirled. Beautiful Persian carpets on the cool terracotta tile floor and original paintings of the Indian countryside and fabulous buildings adorned the colorful apartment. They all were sitting around the coffee table, sipping their gin and tonics.

"This is lovely. What a cool apartment," Sally said holding the glass against her cheek as she sank back into the sand colored soft leather sofa. "I love your artwork."

"It's all done by local artists. I'm glad you like it."

"Yeah, mate, this is great," Hank said. "Thanks for the drink. I really needed it. Is it always this hot here?"

"It's always hot in Madras, but the rains should be here soon. They're late this year. The buildup to the monsoons is always one of the hottest times here. The monsoons will cool it off a little."

"How long have you been here?" Sally asked.

"I'm going on four years. I'll be leaving in a week. My tour of duty at the consulate is up. I was worried that James wasn't going to make it here before I left."

James leaned forward, pursing his lips. "I was late leaving the States and fascinated with Japan. I shouldn't have stayed so long in Hong Kong and Bangkok either." He glanced at Sally. "I made it though."

"That you did," Martin said. "There's a hotel near here that visitors to the consulate usually stay at. I can make arrangements for you, Sally, if you like. I need to go to the consulate this afternoon. Why not stay as my guests for lunch and when I return my driver can take you to the hotel."

"Oh, that sounds expensive," Hank said sitting erect. "We're on a budget."

"Of course. I should have explained the hotel will be on me. I have an account there. How many days will you be staying?"

Hank's face went blank.

"We're not sure," Sally said. "How long are you staying, James?" She focused her green eyes on James, her smile bright. This was better than she imagined. Her instinct about James was spot on.

"Two weeks," James said. "Martin will be here another week and has arranged for me to stay in his apartment another week after he's gone before the movers come in to pack everything up."

"Oh, we couldn't accept your hospitality for that long," Sally said and trained her eyes on Martin. "A couple of nights if that's possible, and then Hank and I can get a more economical place."

"Nonsense. Two weeks is no problem. I'll make the arrangements. If you want to leave earlier you can. I get reimbursed for my expense account. It really would be my pleasure."

Hank appeared dumbfounded, staring at Martin.

Sally sat up and smiled brightly. "How lovely. I don't know how to thank you."

"Any friends of James are friends of mine. James told me what a wonderful time you had together in Hong Kong. I love Hong Kong. I go there for most of my suits, electronic equipment, and other sundries. They make great suits here too. I've purchased a few Nehru jackets here that I wear occasionally to stir up the uptight Americans." He paused and finished his drink. "I will enjoy your company this last week here. It's nice to be around young travelers. The consulate people and guests can get rather staid after a while. James has always been my favorite nephew. I was so worried he would be hurt in Vietnam." He got up. "We've time for another drink before we go down to lunch. Gin and tonics all around?"

"Sure," Sally said. "Thank you."

"You wouldn't have beer by any chance," Hank asked.

"I should have guessed, Hank, and offered you a beer," Martin said. "I know you Aussies like your beer. I've no Fosters. Will King Fisher do?"

"Yeah," Hank said and pushed his hat back.

"Anyone else for beer?" Martin said.

"Beer sounds good," James said.

"Sounds good to me too," Sally added.

Martin left the room for the kitchen.

"You didn't tell me you were in Vietnam," Sally said.

"It's not something I like to talk about. I was against the war, but was drafted. I didn't want to go, but didn't want to go to jail for refusing."

"I understand. I can't believe Australia got involved," she said before rising and settling next to James.

Martin distributed the beers and settled next to Hank. "Cheers." He clinked bottles with Hank. "Were you in the military in Australia?" he asked Hank.

"Nah," Hank replied. "I was lucky that my lottery number wasn't called."

***

"What a room," Sally said plopping down on the bed. "This hotel is fantastic."

Hank sat down next to her. "We didn't need two rooms."

"Relax and enjoy it," Sally said. "The American government is paying. I will enjoy having my own room and bathroom."

Would she ever. She could relax completely and not have to worry about Hank coming after her. She could entice James without interference.

"Go to your room or whatever. I want to take a nice long bath. Martin is picking us up for dinner in two hours."

"We could take a bath together," Hank said, raising his eyebrows.

"No way. You need to find your own female friend, Big Guy." She gave him a soft punch on the arm. "I want to relax in that luxurious tub all by myself." She pushed him. "Go on, get. I'll meet you in the lobby in two hours."

Hank reluctantly left. Sally went into the bathroom where the golden marble tile reflected the afternoon sun spilling through the translucent gothic arched window. She ran the warm water in the large ceramic green bath, whistling to herself. She was so elated. The horrible rides on the freighters slipped from her mind, and she focused on her memory of James's face and taut body as she slipped into the warm water. India was going to be great.

***

The sitar and tabla player, sitting on a dais, were deep in song at the spacious restaurant. The hostess, a dark young Indian woman in a purple sari with delicate facial features greeted them with a Namaste and bow. She told Martin she was glad to see him again and led them to a table near the dais. Martin ordered for everyone. When the food came out, Sally thought the parade of dishes would never end.

"Here in Southern Indian most of the people are vegetarians," Martin said. "The people in Madras are decedents of the Dravidians, the supposed original inhabitants of India before the Aryan invasion. Dravidians are darker skinned and more finely featured than the northern Indians, who have more Mughal features, larger noses and paler skin. Some think the inhabitants of the Indus Valley civilization were Dravidians." He paused and studied the dishes. "This one contains chicken and is red hot and this one has lamb. All the others are vegetarian. Help yourselves."

Sally loaded up her plate with a variety of the dishes, then dug into her food. "Ohhh, this is delicious. So many wonderful flavors. The Indian food back home is nothing like this."

"I'm glad you like it," Martin said. "How do you like the music?"

"I love it," Sally said. The rhythmic sounds of the sitar, harmonium, and tabla drums were flowing together in a wonderful melody that made her feel as if she was floating.

"The music is another reason I like to come here. The tabla player is excellent. I can't believe how nimble his fingers are. Indian music is based on a twelve note scale in contrast to the eight note scale of Western music."

"It sounds so ethereal," Sally said.

"It does indeed," Martin replied.

Her mouth was tingling from the hot spices, but she was loving this. She had never tasted so many different and unusual flavors. She and Hank would never have been able to purchase a meal like this. "So, Martin, what work do you do for the consulate?"

"I'm a liaison officer. I mostly meet with the local and visiting dignitaries and business men, listening to their needs and wants, promoting American goods and services. I try to get things expedited for them if I can. The bureaucracy of India is staggering and requires concerted efforts. Good contacts are essential."

"That sounds exciting," Sally said. She wondered if he had CIA connections.

"I'm sure it sounds more exciting than it is," Martin replied. "I like India, but I am looking forward to being back in the States."

"Are you married?" Sally asked. She thought Martin would be a fine catch for an older woman.

"I was, but I'm divorced. My ex-wife didn't like all the traveling and living in foreign countries. It can get old, but as far as jobs go, it's great for me. My regret is we never had children."

"Well, you're not that old, you could meet someone and still have children," Sally said.

"Yes, one never knows. I regard James as my god child. I'm so glad he could come visit. Even if he was a little tardy." He slapped James gently on the back.

***

"I'll stop awhile here," James said to his uncle as they pulled up to the hotel, "and have a night cap with Sally and Hank."

"Okay, I'll continue on," Martin said. "Just have the desk call for a taxi and have them put it on my tab." He yawned. "Excuse me, I'm rather tired. I've had a few late nights at the consulate getting everything in order for my departure. But I'm free tomorrow. Would you all like an excursion to Mahabalipuram? It's a fascinating place. My driver can take us. How about we leave around nine tomorrow morning. It's not that far."

"I'd love that," Sally said.

"That'd be great, Uncle Martin."

"Thanks for the dinner," Hank said somewhat nonchalantly. He exited the car and sought Sally's arm, but Sally pulled away. When James got out, she grabbed his arm. Hank frowned but didn't say anything.

The three went into the lively bar and ordered drinks. There were quite a few men and women, who were talking animatedly, in business suits and modest dresses. There were a few women in saris.

Hank ordered beer and Sally and James asked for cognac.

"What's this Mahakam or whatever you call it?" Hank said before taking a large swallow of beer. "I'm not comfortable taking all this charity from your uncle."

"I wouldn't call it charity," James said. "My uncle is generous, but he'll probably write off most of this on his expense account." James glanced at Sally and raised his eye brows.

"I'm perfectly fine with your uncle's generosity," Sally said. "I think he is a suave gentleman, and I like his company. Mahabalipuram sounds fascinating, Hank. It's supposed to have important sculptures and temples."

Hank ignored Sally and said that he needed to change money, and he wanted to get a map of Madras so he could figure out where they were. He liked to get oriented properly. James suggested he ask at the front desk to change money and request a map. James would bring a good map in the morning in case the hotel did not have one. They had a second drink.

"James, you want to see my room?" Sally asked. "This is really a fine hotel."

Hank glanced at James then glared at Sally.

"Sure," James replied. "Let's go."

***

"This really is a nice room," James said as he toured Sally's room. The room was compact but had a spacious feeling. The white walls had several watercolor painting of Indian agriculture scenes and the furniture, a double bed, chair and small desk was made from carved, dark mahogany. The bed had a print bedspread with elephants dispersed amongst the tendril design.

"It's so great to not have to share with Hank," she said.

"If I'm not mistaken, Hank is jealous of me. You told me he was just a traveling companion, but he seems to believe he's more than that."

"He's definitely sweet on me and is becoming somewhat possessive and a bore." Sally slipped up to James and gave him a warm kiss and laid her head against his chest. "I like you James. I wish we were traveling together. Hank deliberately booked an extended journey to Bangkok on that damn freighter without telling me. When we sailed into Singapore, I knew he had tricked me. I was so pissed at him when I found out." She pushed James toward the bed her anticipation increasing like intensifying sunlight at dawn. "I had to throw a fit to get him to agree to get plane tickets to here. I was so afraid we would miss you again." She tumbled down with him onto the bed. "Did you enjoy Bangkok?"

"Bangkok was great. I loved all the canals and colorful temples." He settled back on the bed. "It seems a difficult arrangement between you and Hank."

"You can say that again. I didn't think I could travel in this part of the world on my own. He's definitely getting on my nerves."

"I'm thinking once I leave Madras, I'll take the train to Bombay. It would be great if you could come with me. I suppose Hank could come too. If he's your brother's best friend, I guess you need to stick with him."

"Yeah." She was elated that James had invited them to travel with him. Things were working out great despite Hank's attempt to sabotage her. She climbed on top of James, and began kissing his neck. "Let's not talk about Hank." She rose and started disrobing.

10- MAHABLIPURAM: NOVEMBER 4, 1969

The carved granite, stepped pyramid glowed golden in the sunlight with its intricate carvings. There was a welcome breeze off the ocean, which mitigated the searing heat a little.

The ride from Madras to Mahabalipuram had started with the usual crowded streets and slow pace, but, once they got out of the city, the journey proceeded smoothly. The roadside was thronged with people— men pushing carts, women with brass containers balanced on their heads, water buffalos being washed in the river, cows roaming between the huts, fields of rice paddies shinning in the sun as women in saris attended the paddies.

"This temple is to the glory of Shiva," Martin said as they walked along the path to the temple.

"What do you think of the Hindu religion?" Sally asked.

Martin watched Sally, her green eyes holding his gaze like magnets. "I find it fascinating. Hinduism has a long history and is considered the oldest organized religion."

Inside the temple the large central sculpture drew Sally closer. "My god it's a giant penis."

"Yes, it's the symbol for Shiva," Martin said, laughing while he smiled at James. "The lingam sits in the yoni, the feminine symbol for Shakti. The lingam and yoni together represents the merging of the male and female. The creation of life. The lingam and yoni symbolism is very old."

James had read about the yoni and lingam. He was impressed that Hindus did not shun sexuality. The importance of the female in the cycle of life was revered even though most women in India were treated like chattels. James felt privileged to be able to see this impressive dual granite, carved, stepped pinnacle temple. The intricate carvings of the stepped layers were elaborate. They walked through the temple to the porch at the back on the Bay of Bengal. Sally nudged up to James and placed her arm around his waist.

James noticed Hank's face of derision. He saw Martin squint, and knew Martin noticed the derision also.

"Shall we carry on to the next temple?" Martin said.

***

"This is the Pancha Rathas," Martin explained as they strolled down the path. "A Hindu shrine of five chariot temples carved from a single rock."

The heat had increased and was nearly overpowering. Everyone was sweating profusely.

"Wow, carved from a single rock," Sally said as she took James's hand.

Hank drew abreast of the two, leaving Martin alone. "Man... that took a lot of work."

Sally placed her other hand on Hank's back. "Unbelievable. Just hammer and chisel." She gave James's hand a squeeze and prodded his hip with hers. He felt a wave of desire spike like a muscle spasm.

Outside the first of the Rathas, they stopped and marveled at the intricacy of the shrine. "These shrines are older than the shore temple," Martin said. "Carved about the mid-5th century. They are modeled on wooden chariots."

James asked Hank to take a picture of Sally, Martin, and him. "Try to get all the shrines and elephant sculpture in the picture."

Hank accepted the camera from James with a frown. The three assumed a pose with Sally in the middle. Hank snapped a few pictures.

"Here, Hank, you get in the picture," James said as he approached Hank and retrieved his camera. He took several pictures, then switched to Hank's camera, which seemed to please Hank.

After coming to the end of the shrines, Martin clapped Hank on the back and suggested going for lunch.

Hank dropped his shoulder and shifted away as if Martin's hand stung him. "Yeah, I could sure go for a steak."

Martin laughed. "Well, I don't think you could find a steak here." He started for the car. "There's a restaurant in Madras that serves a good steak. We could go there tonight. The best restaurant here is traditional. The cow is sacred to the Hindus. They do have some delicious sea food as well as the gamut of vegetarian dishes." He glanced at Sally and James, who were smiling at each other. "The beer's cold."

"Amen to that," Sally said and moved to the side of Hank. "We're ready for that, hey mate." She jostled his arm.

***

"This is the last shrine we'll visit," Martin said as they walked toward the massive rock sculpture. "I need to get back and visit the consulate before it closes."

"Good," Hank said. "I'm tired of this heat. It's like a bloody oven."

They had finished a delicious lunch of vegetable and sea food curries. Hank had four beers and was slurring his words a little.

Martin nodded. "It's certainly hot." He gave Hank a smile. "This is carved from two single boulders and is considered one of the finest examples of relief Indian rock sculpture."

"It's so intricate," Sally said.

"It's titled the Decent of the Ganges and Arjuna's Penance," Martin said. "Arjuna is a hero in the Mahabharata, the longest poem ever written." He turned to look at the group. "The Mahabharata was written around the fourth century BC and some think it defined the meaning of a just war."

James doubted if there was such a thing as a just war. Some people thought the Second World War was a just war. He had his doubts. He knew for certain that the Vietnam War was unjust, a manufactured lie. He had contributed to the lie and had blood on his hands that he would never be able to wash off.

Martin moved closer to the stone relief. "The Ganges River is considered sacred and supernatural." He waited until they all joined him and pointed to a crevice in the sculpture. "Notice the natural fissure and the carvings inside representing the cosmic event of the Ganges descending to earth at the command of Shiva."

***

James entered the hotel and called Sally and Hank from the lobby. After returning from Mahabalipuram, he had taken a short nap at his uncle's. The evening had cooled somewhat, but by any standard was still very hot. He was eager for another evening with Sally.

Sally came down dressed in a reddish orange sari with a gold band and tiny gold crosses she had purchased at a shop in the hotel.

James stared, his eyes wide. "You look fabulous." Her firm midriff stirred his passion.

"Thanks," she said and spun around. "They helped me figure out how to put this on in the shop. It took me a while to get it right."

"That color sets off your hair. What a great idea."

"You look handsome yourself, James. Where'd you get the Indian jacket?"

"It's my uncle's."

Hank finally appeared in his jeans and short sleeve tan cotton shirt. "What's going on? You two've gone native."

"Yeah, isn't it great, Hank," Sally said, her enthusiasm apparent.

"Let's go then," Hank said. "I'm sure yearning after that steak Martin promised me." He nodded at James. "Aren't you hot in that jacket?"

"Of course."

The ride to the restaurant was short. The décor of the restaurant was Mughal with carved intricate wood panels and a bubbling fountain.

"This restaurant is owned by Muslims, a rarity here in the South. Hence the large number of meat dishes. There's a lot more Muslims in the North of India. Are you all planning to visit any other locations in India after Madras?"

"For sure," Sally said. "James and I have been talking, and we're going to take the train together to Bombay when we leave here."

"Excellent idea," Martin said. "Here's to a fascinating and safe trip." He raised his glass and clinked with the Sally and James before trying to clink with Hank.

"What?" Hank said. "Who cooked this up?" He glared at James his brow crunched.

Oh-oh, Sally obviously hadn't mentioned their plan to Hank. "You're of course invited, Hank," James said.

"Nobody asked me." Hank focused his scowl on Sally.

"We talked about going to Bombay, Hank," Sally said her eyes wide. "It will be fun if we all go together."

"I wanted to go to Goa," Hank said.

"And so we will," Sally replied.

"Goa is nice," Martin added. "I went there last year for a week and relaxed on the beach. It was a former Portuguese colony. Quite different than the rest of India."

When the food came the conversation ceased as Hank dug into his steak. "Not bad, Martin. Not as tender as I like it, but a welcome change from those curries."

***

"We weren't trying to keep the trip to Bombay secret," Sally said as she clinked her beer glass with Hank and James in the hotel bar. "We talked about it last night and I forgot to mention it to you." She rubbed Hank's arm. "You're cool with it aren't you?"

Hank nodded. "Yeah, sure traveling together to Bombay will be cool as long as we go to Goa after." He took a big swig of beer. "It just caught me by surprise at the restaurant."

Martin had dropped them all off at the hotel where they ordered drinks in the bar. He had suggested that they explore Madras the rest of the week, and this weekend they could all travel to Bangalore for the annual festival of lights.

"The festival of lights sounds cool," Sally said. "Your uncle is so nice. I'm so glad I was able to meet up with you here."

"Yeah the Diwali as they call the festival of lights is supposed to be spectacular in Bangalore."

"I've read about the numerous religious festivals in India," Sally said. "I'm so glad I'll be able to see one of the most famous."

"I'm glad I will be able to see it too," James added, then raised his glass. "Here's to a great trip to Bangalore."

Hank scowled, but raised his glass. "Yeah, I hope it won't be boring. I've never been one for religious festivals."

James wondered if Hank really disliked religious festivals or was just being difficult to somehow denigrate James. All religions had festivals to highlight the aspects of the religion and induce participants to honor the religion. Most indigenous societies large and small had some kind of religion. Was religion, as Captain Jeff believed, a means to control the masses? The clash of religions throughout history had caused great suffering in the world. Still he was intrigued by the religions of the world and was glad he was learning so much about the Hindu religion.

They continued discussing their trip to Mahabalipuram and their journey to Bombay. When Hank went to the restroom Sally said, "I think you better not stay tonight." She kissed him. "Hank is acting weird. If you excuse yourself and say you have to get back, it might help cool him down."

James exasperated with Hank and Sally's intrigue asked, "Are you sleeping with Hank?"

"No," she replied curling her lips and keeping her face neutral. "He's come on to me big time, but I've repulsed him. I feel obligated to include him since he's a family friend and agreed to come on the trip." She grasped James hand. "I wouldn't be here if he hadn't agreed to come along."

"Okay." James wondered if she was really telling the truth or was playing Hank and him against each other.

Hank returned and plopped down in his seat and signaled the waiter for more drinks.

James downed his beer and turned to Sally. "Mahabalipuram and dinner was fun. It's great we were able to see it together. I'm rather tired, and I need to get back to talk to my uncle about the trip this weekend." James stood. "I'll call tomorrow about going to town."

***

"You're back early," Martin said as James entered the apartment. "Is everything all right? Did everyone enjoy the evening?" He closed his book and set it on the coffee table. "Hank seemed to like his steak."

"Everyone thought the meal was great," James said. "I'm just a little tired and want to have an early night. The trip to Mahabalipuram was fantastic. Thanks so much. You've been so generous."

"Think nothing of it. I'm so glad you were able to come. I've made the same offer of a plane ticket to my other relatives, but you're the only one that has taken me up on it. I think traveling is such a great education. I believe Saint Augustine said that traveling was like a book and not to travel is to stay on page one. I'm paraphrasing of course."

"I agree. I've learned so much already, and I'm looking forward to my continued travels."

"I hope you don't think me impertinent, but I couldn't help but notice that Hank seems jealous of you. Were Hank and Sally past lovers?"

"I don't know. Sally says he's just a friend, but I think they might have been more."

"I got the same feeling. She's a lively, lovely, young woman. I'm glad you've found such a great traveling companion." Martin glanced around the room before continuing. "You'll need be careful on your trip around India. She'll attract a lot of attention. It may be good that Hank goes with you, even though he appears to be a pain in the ass. Someone would think twice about confronting the two of you."

"You're probably right there."

Martin shifted in his seat and stretched his neck. "Would you like a nightcap? This brandy is quite good." He held up his glass and took a sip.

James declined.

Martin set the brandy glass on the table. "I heard you call out in your sleep a few nights ago. Was it a war memory?"

"Yes, I often have a reoccurring nightmare. It used to happen almost every night. But its frequency has started to wane."

"If you feel like talking about it. I'm here for you."

"Not tonight anyway. Getting out of the States and coming here has been a dream come true. And as you've noticed, meeting Sally has been wonderful."

"I know you didn't want to accept the draft. Your letter to me talking about going to Canada was heartbreaking." Martin took another drink of brandy. "I'm glad you decided to stay. I hope you don't hold my encouragement to go into the Army against me."

"No, I don't. My dad and almost everyone else agreed with you." He thought about what his life would have been like if he had gone to Canada. He wouldn't be burdened with the horrendous experience of war and his own part in the staggering deaths of Vietnamese. Useless thoughts. He did go. He did take part in the killing. He had to live with that forever.

"You record is unblemished. You'll find this invaluable in the future, when you start building your career." Martin leaned forward and placed his hands on his knees. "I didn't agree with the mammoth escalation of the war. Sending hundreds of thousands of American troops was a mistake. I think LBJ got drawn in and felt he had no choice. I do think the US needs to counter communism though. Perhaps in less violent ways than war."

"I think the war is terribly wrong and we should get out as soon as possible," James said with more force than intended. "The North Vietnamese will win in the end." He hesitated and let his anger slip downward. "We should have never contravened the 1954 Geneva Accords and stopped the election. Ho Chi Minh would have won the election, united the country, and the horrible suffering the Vietnamese have endured for all these years could have been avoided. Communism is an economic system not an ideology."

"I can't say I agree. I suppose I worry about the Soviet Union and China's influence, and their desire to expand their type of communism."

"Let's agree to disagree," James said and slumped back into the soft couch. He didn't want to upset Martin and realized that Martin's government position colored his views "What do you think of the Indian Government?"

"It is a democracy of sorts. Corruption is rife and the majority of people suffer terrible poverty. There is a following for the communist party here. The Soviet Union and China are trying to have a significant influence. Something we are trying to counter."

"Are you connected somehow to the CIA?"

"No, but the CIA has a presence in the consulate, and I have to interact with them." Martin paused and stared staidly at James. "I'm telling you this in the strictest confidence."

"Of course." He wondered if Martin was being truthful. If he was connected to the CIA he would never admit it.

11- BANGALORE: NOVEMBR 8, 1969

"They call Bangalore the Garden City," Martin said as they exited the car at the luxurious hotel.

They had arrived in Bangalore in the late afternoon after a winding seven hour ride with a brief stop on the way for a light lunch. The climb up to Bangalore replaced the heat of the low lands with a slightly cooler temperature. The cooler temperatures had improved everyone's mood.

The hotel was across from the golf course and the grounds were spectacular. They went to their individual rooms through the cool interior of the ornate hotel. Sally was in awe of the décor and smiled to herself. Things had unfolded so wonderfully. Her room was superb— magnificent mahogany furniture, full size bed, dramatic bathroom, and a window view of the exquisite garden.

After unpacking in her room, she strolled down into the garden, trying to imagine what it would have been like in the past. She stood spellbound in front of the huge banyan tree with its descending prop trunks to form additional roots, allowing the tree to expand outward. She envisioned men in uniform and women in period dress with their umbrellas strolling around the grounds. She herself could have been an aristocrat with a handsome officer on her arm. She laughed to herself and spun around, marveling at how good she felt.

She called James from the lobby and asked him to meet her in the garden for afternoon tea. How civilized she thought as she hung up. She chose a table in the pavilion of white lattice wood, surrounded by sumptuous flowering beds and bushes. Rich purple bougainvillea climbed up the posts in stark contrast to the white lattice. She ordered a gin and tonic and closed her eyes as the bitter tasting ice cold liquid flowed down her throat. She took out her sketch book and began sketching the garden. She felt so relaxed. When James arrived at the table, she felt a stirring of passion for this man, who had made her introduction to India such a wonderful unfolding experience.

"I thought you said afternoon tea," he said.

"Yes well, it may be cooler here than Madras, but it's still too hot for tea." She stroked his damp hair. She would have liked to have showered with him. "Your uncle is so great. Just think I would never have experienced this wonderful trip if we hadn't met in Hong Kong." She leaned to the side of the table and gave James a kiss on the cheek and took his hand, pulling it to her chest before placing it back on the table.

James lifted the sketch book from the table and began thumbing through the sketches. "These are beautiful. You are quite an accomplished artist." He held open the sketch book toward Sally. "I like these drawing of the temples in Bangkok. They were incredibly beautiful. You've captured them so well."

"I'm glad you like them." She sipped her drink to dispel her blushing. "I had wanted to become an artist, but instead got a teaching degree at my parent's insistence."

"Well you can still be an artist."

She nodded and raised her eyebrows in assent, leaned back with a small smile, and studied the colorful flowers. "This garden is so serene."

She was happy to be alone with James and felt a kinship deep into her being. Her situation seemed too good to be true— almost like a dream. She understood Hank's displeasure with the fancy hotels and James's uncle. This grand hotel was another vestige of British colonialism like her country. Yet, she was enjoying the ambience and delighted that she was able to experience the past grandeur of colonial India.

"So tell me about how the British took over India," she said. "We studied it in school, but I've forgotten most of it."

"I don't really know much about British history in India. I read a little about it in my guide book." James pursed his lips. "We'll have to ask Martin."

"Of course he will know." She placed her hand on James's shoulder. "Go ahead order your drink." She thought Martin was an arm of American colonialism that wanted to exploit India, but he was thoughtful and seemed genuinely interested in helping people.

James signaled the waiter and ordered a gin and tonic and, pakoras, deep fried battered vegetables. "Where's Hank?"

"In his room, I reckon. I almost wish he had stayed in Madras." She checked herself. Sure Hank could be a pain in the butt, but she owed him for agreeing to accompany her. She felt safe with him, and, although his advances toward her were annoying, he had a good heart and would do anything to protect her. She was happy that James was open to including Hank despite Hank's obvious animosity toward James. She knew her sexual manipulation had fueled Hank's anger. She felt guilty and wished she had found another way to convince Hank to fly to Madras. Water under the bridge. She was here and would relish her time with James and his uncle.

***

As night was approaching they caught a taxi to the Vidhana Soudha, the legislative building, a large expansive structure built in 1956 with its grand cupola, side cupolas, and multistory, arched balconied wings covered in thousands of lights.

"The procession should begin soon," Martin announced. "Let's get a good place to watch." He moved ahead into the crowd, and the rest followed.

When the music sounded the procession began led by the Maharaja on an elephant covered in lights followed by camels and dancers ahead of the band of musicians.

James snapped pictures seemingly mesmerized by the spectacle. Sally had never seen anything like the unfolding procession. She was in another world of unbelievable ancient splendor that lifted her back into another century.

Hank moved behind Sally and slipped his arms around her dispelling her reverie. She allowed the intimacy briefly before removing his arms and moving to grab James's arm.

After most of the procession had passed Martin said, "Let's walk to the Palace." He began moving out of the crowd. "I've seen the Diwali procession several times, but I never cease to be amazed and transported."

Sally took both James's and Hank's arm and pulled them along behind Martin. The walk was short to the massive, towered palace covered in lights, sparkling against the dark sky. She'd seen palatial houses in Australia, but they paled against the opulence of the palace before her.

"The Palace was built by a rich Englishman, in eighteen sixty-two before it was purchased by British officials for the young maharaja. He, of course, has made many renovations."

After walking around the periphery of the imposing Indian version of an English castle, they returned to the hotel for a quick nightcap before retiring.

***

Sally knocked on James hotel room with ballooning anticipation. As soon as he opened the door, she pushed him inside and whipped the door closed. "Oh James, what a night. The festival procession was unworldly. I loved it. The pageantry was beyond words." She hugged him tightly. "Your uncle was so kind to bring us here. He definitely likes you. I'm quite fond of you, myself." She kissed him pushing her tongue deep into his mouth. "I can hardly believe I'm here. The grandeur is overwhelming." She grasped him around the waist. "I'm so happy." She pushed him backwards across the wide room, laughing, and landed on top of him as they lurched to the bed. She rolled off him to the middle of the bed. "Come on," she said holding out her arms. James crawled to her. She grasped him and pulled her hips to his. "Oh James what a wonderful day."

He kissed her beckoning lips and neck before pulling her tan cotton trousers and pink panties off. As he kissed his way up her thigh, she sat up and removed her green linen blouse. James tongued her perky breasts, slipping her back as he worked his lips and tongue down to that fiery patch of hair.

She moaned and pressed his head down. "Ahhhh, that feels so good." She pulled him up and guided his erection home. Their carnal pleasures continued until late in the evening.

***

At breakfast, Sally felt enlivened after her night with James despite the athleticism of their antics. She was tingling with enjoyment. After they all had ordered, she asked, "Martin, can you tell us how Britain came to power in India?"

"That would be a long discussion," Martin replied. "Summarizing, the British East Trading Company, a private company chartered in 1600 to trade with India began an increasingly lucrative trade in India. To protect their commerce, the Company established fortified compounds and private armies with former British officers and Indian soldiers willing to join the Company for the generous pay. The Company also elicited the help of the local rulers and rewarded them by collecting taxes for them and providing protection. The Mughal Empire that had controlled most of India had been split into local factions, and the Company was able to increase its influence and control to such an extent that by 1760 the Company had influence over most of India. In 1858 the British government took control of the Company and began the colonial administration of India."

"Well said, mate," Sally said, captivated with Martin. She couldn't understand why he didn't have dozens of women after him. She wondered what India would be like if the British had not taken control. Would it be a group of separate states ruled by Maharajas or would some other colonial power have usurped control?

"Knowing Indian history is part of my job," Martin said. "Come on, let's enjoy this great breakfast."

"Thank you so much Martin for bringing us here," Sally said. "The festival of lights was so beautiful and unworldly."

She was impressed by Martin's smooth manner and wondered again if his liaison work was a front for spying. She understood from James that Martin wasn't a big supporter of the Vietnam War, but she knew he had encouraged James to accept the draft. If James hadn't gone to Vietnam, she probably wouldn't have ever met him. It was obvious that he had had a terrible time in Vietnam that was still affecting him. She was so glad her brother and Hank hadn't been drafted into the stupid war.

"You are quite welcome," Martin said. "I've enjoyed our time together immensely." He dug in to the remainder of his breakfast as did everyone else.

"Martin, how did the British view the caste system?" James asked.

"They liked the system and used it to control the population. At the time, England was quite a class society as well. So the caste system fit right in with the idea of how to administer India. There is very little interaction between castes and intermarriage almost never takes place."

"Do you think the relationship between the castes will improve in time," Sally asked.

"There has been some progress, but, when you consider that the caste system was abolished in nineteen forty-seven, it does not seem like much."

When everyone was nearly finished eating, Martin said, "I thought that we might, if you all agree, head out this morning to Mysore before driving back to Madras. The Mysore Palace is one of the largest palaces in India. The Mysore Maharaja was one of the last hold outs against the British. It's an amazing palace that I'm sure you would enjoy seeing."

"Oh yes," Sally said. "I read about the palace. How far is it to Mysore?"

"It's about a hundred miles, three and a half hours. From there we can drive back to Madras, a long drive or spend the night and leave early in the morning. I would suggest we spend the night and leave early in the morning, I need to be back in Madras on Monday night to take care of any lose ends in the morning. It's a nine to ten hour drive back."

"I don't know," Hank said. "I'm tired of riding in the car in this weather."

"Come on Hank," Sally said pushing him on the shoulder. "Where's your spirit of adventure, mate? It's not nearly as hot as Madras."

"Okay, Mysore it is," Hank said with a smirk.

***

"There it is," Martin said as the main gate of the Palace came into view.

"What a gate," James said as he stared up at the huge serrated arch of the elaborate gate. They stopped and James took a series of photographs.

"We'll have to drive around to the South Gate to enter the grounds," Martin said as he gestured for all to get back in the car.

Sally was spellbound by the three story grey granite palace with its pink marble domes as they pulled into the parking lot. "I've never seen anything like it."

"Spectacular," James said after exiting the car. He began snapping photographs. He asked the group to gather in front of the imposing palace for a group shot.

Inside the palace, they walked past the doll room to the massive gallery with its series of blue fluted pillars supporting vaulted domes intricately painted with calligraphy in the Muslim style. The marble floor shined brightly in the sunlight filling the large gothic windows. They strolled through the gallery to the room used by the Maharaja for private audiences. Inside was a shrine to Ganesh, the elephant headed son of Shiva riding a mouse.

"Ganesh is the lord of success and destroyer of evils and obstacles," Martin said. "He is a very popular deity in the Hindu religion."

"He's cute," Sally said.

They continued to the octagonal marriage hall with its stained glass ceiling of peacocks and the towering columns and peacock mosaic floor. They stood gazing up at the high ceiling before they continued on to the rest of the palace and out into the gardens where the cries of the peacocks reminded Sally of humans crying in distress.

***

"Would you like to visit the Chamundeshwari Temple," Martin asked after they finished their luncheon repast of chicken and vegetable curries at the hotel. "It's just outside town. It's a unique temple, seven stories high. It's the divine seat of

Shakti, the active feminine spirit of Shiva. She is considered the Devine Mother. The temple sits on a three thousand foot hill. It has a huge Nandi Bull statue as well. Nandi serves as the mount for Shiva."

After the visit to the Mysore Palace they had driven to the nearby hotel another colonial grand hotel with sumptuous gardens and lavish rooms.

"I'll stay at the hotel," Hank said. "The immense Palace was plenty for me. I'll hold up in the bar. It may not be as hot a Madras here, but it's plenty hot."

"I'm game," Sally said. "The temple sounds interesting." She initially felt she should prod Hank to come, but then decided she would let him be. Things were going well. No reason to rock the boat.

***

"You should have gone," Sally said as they approached Hank in the bar. "The temple was gorgeous. Another fantastic experience." She plopped down in the chair next to Hank. "Don't just sit there. Get me a beer, mate. I'm gasping."

Hank stared back at her with a deadpan expression. "Hey, barkeep. A round of beers." His eyes were drooping as he scowled at James and Martin.

Sally hoped Hank wasn't going to become belligerent. Maybe not encouraging him to come along, which allowed his continued drinking, had been a mistake. When Hank was intoxicated, he was easily provoked.

The man behind the bar wiggled his head. "Coming right away, sir."

Hank just stared back at Sally without speaking for a moment. "At least it's cool in here."

"Yes, that it is," Sally said smiling widely as she reached for her beer. She clinked everyone's glass. "Nothing like a cold beer after an excursion in this heat."

***

After dinner, they dispersed to their rooms. Sally told James she would come to his room after freshening up. In her bathroom after slipping off her dress, she regarded herself in the mirror. She knew her green eyes and red hair were considered striking, but she didn't consider herself beautiful. She disliked her pale skin and freckles. She was a little too skinny. She had chosen James in Hong Kong. He hadn't chosen her. He seemed to like her appearance, and they got on well. Did he like her personality— really like her as a person— or was it just sexual. Time would tell. She'd have to be patient. Something she was not known for. James's guilt from the war was a glaring weight that seemed to hold him back. She hoped she could help him overcome his grief.

Hank had been rather rude at dinner. His jealousy of James became more apparent with each drink. She would have a talk with him before going to James's room. She slipped on her jeans and pulled her green shirt over her head and brushed her hair.

As she left her room she thought about giving Hank a pass, she didn't need any agro, but decided she needed to set him straight about James and get him to stop his rude behavior. The last thing she wanted was Hank's behavior causing James to flee away from them.

Sally knocked on Hank's door. "Open up," she said. She could hear Hank stumbling to the door.

Hank answered the door in his underwear obviously completely soused. "What are you doing here?" he said, slurring his words. "I'd a thought you'd be with your precious James. I know you're fucking him."

"Easy, mate." She gently placed her hand on his chest, slowly pushed him further inside and shut the door. "You want the whole hotel to hear?"

"I don't give a fuck," Hank said. "I've about had it with you and your darling James and his rich uncle."

"Easy there, mate." She sat down on the bed. "I'm sorry if you're not enjoying our excursion. We came to India to see the sights and discover the culture. You should try to make the best of it. I would have never gotten here without your help, but our intimacy is over. I should have never succumbed to your advances. I'm sorry, but your rudeness to James and his uncle needs to stop."

Hank staggered to the chair opposite the bed. "These fancy hotels and meals aren't us," he said.

"I know... but it's been exciting to see the amazing temples and palaces. We probably wouldn't have come here on our own. We would have never been able to stay in these grand hotels." She saw that her statement was having little effect on Hank and raised her voice. "You're always going on about money. Just think of all the money we've saved." She stopped and just stared at him a few seconds. "James's uncle is nice. Yes, he's probably a colonialist and may not have the best interests of the Indians in mind. You think the Australian diplomats are any different." She blew out her breath to calm herself. "We're still friends, aren't we?"

"Fuck if I know?" Hank sniffed and took a swig from his beer.

"Come on, Hank. Please... can't you be more accommodating. What if you take off for Goa when we get back to Madras? James and I could meet you there after Bombay."

"So you're ditching me," Hank stood up and swayed as he approached the bed.

"Hey up, Hank," Sally said and stood, pushing her hand out. "What's going on?"

Hank stopped, clenched his fists, and grit his teeth before returning to his seat. "I feel like beating some sense into you."

"Hank if you ever lay a hand on me, I'll leave. I don't care if you are my brother's best friend." She knew Hank could be aggressive, but she had never seen him act this way toward her. It was scary.

"Don't worry. I swore to your brother I'd protect you. I'm not leaving."

"Okay, Hank, relax. That's fine." She took a deep breath. "I'm hoping to stay at the apartment with James after his uncle leaves until we all leave for Bombay. That is if it's okay with James." She thought James would welcome having her stay, since they could be alone without Hank. "Could you handle that?"

"What the fuck." Hank stretched his face before scowling. "You're leaving me on my own. Fuck that."

She raised her voice. "I'm not leaving you on your own." She realized her anger wasn't helping. "Please take it easy. We will still travel together, all three of us. I like James and want to spend more time with him, get to know him better."

She stared unflinchingly at him. She would relish not having to deal with Hank's jealousy. Things were going great with James, but their relationship was new and could easily vanish. How much of Hank's brutish nature would James be willing to tolerate?

"Why can't I stay there too?" He had trouble keeping his eyes open.

"There's only going to be one bed. Martin's room is already being packed up and as soon as he leaves they'll pack up his bed. Besides, you'll be more comfortable here at the hotel. I want to be alone with James and learn more about him. I really like him." She suspected that most of her talk was probably futile. Hank was too drunk to talk rationally. Still she had made herself clear enough. She rose. "Go to bed,

Hank." She gave him a kiss on the cheek. "See you in the morning."

She walked down the hall to James's room. She had been up front with Hank. At least she hoped she wouldn't have to repel anymore of his advances. She smiled to herself as she gently knocked on James's door.

"Hey up, Hank," Sally said as she and James approached Hank in the hotel bar after accompanying Martin to the airport for his return to the States. She placed a hand on his shoulder. "I see you're well on your way."

Hank frowned and picked up his beer. "Shit, it's past noon. What's the problem?"

"No problem, mate," Sally said. "Sorry we were gone so long. Martin's flight was delayed." She moved next to Hank and rubbed his back. "I'm going up to get my stuff. James has invited me to stay at the apartment the rest of the week."

Hank's face went blank before frowning, gritting his teeth. "Yeah, I knew that was coming." He stood and stared at Sally. He felt like thrashing both of them, but knew that wouldn't help him with Sally. He'd have to tolerate this haughty American for now until Sally got tired of him.

"We already talked about this," Sally said, stepping back. She placed her hand on Hank's shoulder. "The hotel is paid for. Enjoy it." She stretched and glanced with a frown at James before concentrating on Hank. "Next Monday we'll come and get you and we can catch a train to Bombay."

Hank sneered and narrowed his eyes. "You're leaving me here the rest of the week on my own?"

The fuckers were trying to ditch him. He wasn't going to let this happen.

"No, silly. I'll go pack up and we can all go to James's and then into town." She hit his arm gently. "We're not abandoning you. I'll just be sleeping at the apartment. We'll still do things together." She grasped his beer and took a swallow. "I'll be back down in a jiffy. You and James have a drink. It's hotter than hell out there."

Hank forced a smile and plopped back down on his stool. "What're you having?" he asked James, keeping his anger in check. There wasn't much he could do anyway. In reality James wasn't so bad. Maybe he should try and accept the guy. He seemed to really like Sally, and Sally undoubtedly was enchanted by this American. At least his rich uncle was gone. Now he and James were somewhat on equal footing.

James took a seat next to Hank and spread his hands on the bar. "I'll have the same as you."

"Barkeep, another two Fosters."

The bartender wiggled his head and placed two cans of Fosters on the bar and a glass for James. James poured his beer and chinked his glass to Hank's. "Cheers," he said.

"Cheers, mate," Hank responded and took a big swallow.

***

They took a taxi to the center of Madras, a bustling crush of people and shops after a quick stop at the apartment where Sally stored her backpack. Hank was always amazed at the huge loads of merchandise the emaciated men were able to pull and push along in their carts as the cars, trucks, mopeds and bicycles darted around them. Their loads would be hard for him to maneuver, and he was twice the size of most of them.

"I want to get more saris," Sally said as they started down the bustling sidewalk accompanied by a group of children and adult beggars whose call for baksheesh was incessant. "The one I got at the hotel was expensive but nice. I'd like to get another." She grabbed Hank's arm. "What are you gonna buy?"

"Shit, I don't need anything," Hank said pulling his arm in so that Sally was next to him. He couldn't help himself. He knew he needed to accept the situation, but still felt he had a chance with Sally if they could get rid of James.

"You gotta get some souvenirs. How about a sari for your girlfriend." She retrieved her arm and separated from Hank

"First though, we need to find the hash store," James said.

"Good idea," Hank said, perking up. So James wasn't as straight as Hank envisioned. Probably hadn't mentioned it before because he didn't want to offend his uncle. Maybe traveling with him for a while wouldn't be so bad.

Sally stopped. "I keep seeing these red stains on the sidewalk. What's that about?"

"It's spit from chewing betel nut," James said. "I noticed it when I first arrived here. Betel nut has a mild narcotic effect. They say it's like chewing tobacco, but much stronger. It's very popular. I tried it. It tastes horrible. I had to spit it all out."

"Sounds horrible," Sally said and avoided stepping on the stains.

"I wouldn't mind giving it a try," Hank said. He had chewed tobacco briefly when he worked at cattle stations.

James led them to a kiosk that was selling the betel nut concoction. "Here you go."

Hank purchased the nut wrapped in betel leaves accompanied by a wedge of lime and stuffed it his mouth. He started chewing as they continued down the street. Soon the insipid, disgusting taste of the concoction was too overwhelming. With a screwed up face, he hurried ahead to the alley and spit out the concoction. He wiped his lips. "Damn, that tasted horrible." He started to feel a numbing affect from the concoction.

"At least you gave it a try," Sally said, laughing. "Let's get the hash and have a drink. I can tell you're in bad need of a drink." She gave Hank a shove.

Was he ever in need of a drink? He spit a few times, but knew Sally detested spitting and suppressed his urge. He felt an increasing buzz from the betel nut. Maybe he'd try it again when alone. His attempt to show up James had failed.

They located the government hashish shop and bought several charas of hashish and a pipe. Hashish was legal in India and was used in religious ceremonies. They had a quick smoke of the hash in a small park, then proceeded to a restaurant where Hank had a beer, and James and Sally had a mango lassie.

Hank felt so much better with the buzz from the hash and the soothing beer. They went in many of the other shops, perusing the many items for sale and made their few purchases. Sally purchased an emerald green sari that Hank thought matched her eyes. When she came out of the dressing room, Hank watched her twirl in front of the mirror with aching desire. She was so beautiful, and her delight at the new sari was infectious. Hank purchased a blue sari for his latest girlfriend in Brisbane, Vivian, more to please Sally then himself. He liked Vivian, but his heart belonged to Sally.

After the sari shop, James steered them into a carpet shop. Hank wasn't much interested in rugs but was impressed by the variety. James purchased several carpets that he was going to ship back to States with his uncle's apartment furnishings. Hank was surprised at how inexpensive the rugs were compared to what they would have cost in Australia. He would have liked to buy a rug, but knew shipping it back or carrying it with him would be a hassle.

"Did you see that beggar with the huge legs," Sally asked as they left the rug shop. "What the hell is it?"

"Elephantiasis," James said. "Apparently there's quite a bit in India."

"Jesus. How do they get it?"

"Apparently a mosquito carries a round worm that infects the body. It multiplies causing the lymph nodes to swell, stopping the flow of fluid, and the extremities swell. It's treatable if caught early."

"How horrible," Sally said.

Hank thought the gamut of ailments amongst the beggars was sad. The medical care in India had to be a mess. The poor and destitute seemed to suffer needlessly around the world, including Australia, but it wasn't in the same league as India.

As they made their way back to the taxi stand, the rains started and they became soaked. Soon the streets were muddy thoroughfares as the rain came down in an unrelenting torrent. Back at Martin's apartment, they ran laughing up the stairs as the rain pelted down. They were drenched to the bone when they hurried into the apartment.

After beers and a round of the charas pipe, Hank said, "Reckon, I'll go back to the hotel and take a shower." Sally and James had changed into dry clothes and James had lent Hank some shorts and a shirt that Hank was barely able to get into. He could tell that the tight clothes were giving Sally a chuckle, but was glad she didn't mention it. "Are we going out to eat tonight or are you guys staying in?"

"Of course we're all going to dinner together," Sally said. "I'd like to go back to the restaurant that Martin took us to with all the amazing dishes and music."

"You mean the steak place," Hank said, purposely to get a rouse from Sally.

"No, mate, the other one. Nice try."

Sally frowning lowered her eye lids in such a way to convey to Hank that he had to be kidding, a look he knew well. The look gave him a chuckle. Well, she and James could screw their brains out for all he cared. He did care, but there was nothing he could do. He told himself he should try and make the best of it. Maybe he could meet somebody back at the hotel. Unfortunately, most of the apparently single women there were much older than him. He had nothing against older women. He could try talking to one. Better than drinking alone.

"We can go to the steak place tomorrow night," Sally said.

"I'll hold you to it, mate."

The gothic immense Bombay train station was wall to wall people as the train pulled in. The week in Madras had been fun and exhilarating. James's nights alone with Sally had been so satisfying. His nightmares continued, but whenever he awoke still feeling the agony of the dream, Sally was there to comfort him.

The crazy Vietnam War continued on endlessly. He thought about the My Lai massacre he had read about in the paper. The massacre exposed that Americans were capable of ugly savagery up close and personal. Sure napalm, Agent Orange, aerial bombing, and artillery bombardments were savage. Their remoteness made it seem less vicious than eye to eye death. He wondered if the US would ever give up and allow Vietnam to have their country back. Didn't seem like it was possible. He felt sorry for the other soldiers that would have to endure the horrors of the insidious war, and the unfortunate Vietnamese who had to endure the death and destruction the US dispensed indiscriminately.

It was obvious to James that Hank hadn't liked staying at the hotel by himself, but he masked his anger with plenty of beers and hash and made only a few complaints. Sally had insisted that they join him for breakfast each day and include him in their day's activities, visiting the town or hanging out at the apartment. It even seemed as if Hank was warming a little to James.

It took some weaving and concerted effort for the three to thread their way out of the station. Porters were carrying numerous large Indian sleeping bags, suitcases, and all manner of bundles wrapped in cloth on their heads, going every which way. Outside there were innumerable people streaming by as they took in the panorama of the immense colonial train station.

"It's called Victoria Terminus," James said. "It was built in 1887 to commemorate the Golden Jubilee of Queen Victoria."

They were soon surrounded by a circle of beggars. One lady carrying a small emaciated baby latched onto Sally's arm repeating 'baksheesh... baby' over and over. James removed the lady's hand and gave her a few rupees, which increased the enthusiasm of the other beggars. A tiny man in his kaki shirt and trousers, which appeared two sizes too big, had grabbed James's bag and yelled at the beggars in Hindi. He pushed several away and led the three to a taxi as the beggars trailed clamoring for baksheesh.

James was relieved to be inside the taxi as the beggars surrounded the vehicle. The beggars in Bombay were much more aggressive than Madras. Dealing with all the impoverished people was depressing. The extent of the poverty seemed worse than Madras. What extreme contrasts this country held. Sure there was poverty in Hong Kong and Bangkok— the thousands of people living on boats in Kowloon and the beggars— but they didn't approach the degradation of the poor in India. Many seemed like they needed to be in a hospital. What a contrast to the delight he had experienced visiting the splendor of the temples, palaces, and ornate hotels.

He had gotten a reluctant rest from their athletic sex on the train ride in the sleeper compartment. Hank was slightly courteous toward him, but he suspected Hank could erupt easily. He didn't want to offend Hank. He was still trying to figure out the best way to act around Hank and Sally. Some of the comments Hank spouted incensed him, but he kept his disgust to himself. Thankfully the night train to Bombay had been void of any undue confrontation.

***

James and Hank went down together to the restaurant next door to the hotel at James's suggestion after they checked in while Sally freshened up. James thought he needed to try and ingratiate himself more with Hank to blunt Hank's jealousy.

Sally joined them at the restaurant. "You didn't order me a beer?" she said with a faux frown.

"Shit, how were we to know when her ladyship would be down," Hank said. He had already consumed several beers.

"Easy, mate, with the ladyship crap. I've not been gone that long." She caught the waiter's attention and ordered a beer. When she looked back at the two she had a questioning smile. "So what have you boys been talking about?"

"I was telling Hank," James said, "about Ajanta and Ellora. I thought it would be cool to go there after checking out Bombay before we go to Goa. It's not that far away."

"Fuck that," Hank said. "I wanna go to Goa and relax on the beach and get some more hash. I'm almost out." He glared at James and Sally, eyes wide, brow stretched. "I want to have some fun."

"Wow, mates, I just got here," Sally said and placed her hand atop Hank's. "Let me have a beer and catch up with you. Let's enjoy Bombay. We're not in any hurry. We can get more hash here." She removed her hand from Hank's when the beer arrived. "Here's to a great time." She clinked her beer with Hank and James. "I read that the Gateway to the West is near here. Once we've finished our beers, why don't we walk down?"

"Walk?" Hank said. "How far is it? I'm tired. I didn't sleep well on the train."

"Take a nap then. James and I will go."

Hank glowered at Sally. "Fuck, you're not getting rid of me that easy."

James marveled at how easily Hank's anger rose. It didn't take much.

Sally took a long swallow of beer. "Come on Hank. Cool it."

Hank pushed his hat back and grasped his forehead. "Sorry."

"Right on, mate." She clinked her beer again to the other two and laughed. "We're in Bombay. How cool is that." She swallowed the last of her beer. "Let's get going before it rains again."

***

The imposing yellow basalt arched structure stood on the quay shining in the hot sun. They strolled into the eighty-five foot arch, through the domed interior, and out to the quay and the Arabian Sea. The clouds were building rapidly, but they could see the islands in the bay.

James consulted the plaque on the gateway. "The gateway was built to commemorate the visit of King George V and Queen Mary in 1911," he said. "It was finished in 1915."

"Another monument to British imperialism," Hank said.

"Yeah, for sure," James replied. He agreed with Hank that Britain's conquest of India had been wrong. The era of colonialism by European powers was distasteful and a blot on history that many developing countries were trying to recover from. France had tried to re-establish their colonial rule of Vietnam after the Second World War by attacking the Viet Minh, who, led by Ho Chi Minh, had defeated the Japanese. The Viet Minh wanted no part of continued French colonialism. They defeated the French in 1954. The US took over from the French and tried to accomplish what the French had failed to do, supposedly to stop the spread of communism, but in reality was an effort to establish another type of colonialism.

Sally took James's hand and pulled him to Hank, then grasped Hank's hand. "I feel great. I can't believe I'm standing in such a historic place." She swung both their arms back and forth and kissed each on the cheek. "Let's get a taxi to the markets."

"How about a rickshaw," Hank said. "We've not been in one yet."

"I hate how those poor guys have to run. The three of us will be too much for them."

"Shit, I've seen them pulling many really fat Indians." Hank grabbed Sally around the waist. "You weigh little." He hoisted her off the ground.

She accepted the hoisting with good humor. "Okay, mate."

James was glad that Hank had perked up. He marveled at how well Sally dealt with Hank. She knew him well, and her gentle maneuvering was something to behold. He wouldn't have been able to tolerate Hank's advances so calmly if he had been her.

"Let's take two rickshaws. Me and James in one and you, big guy, in another. Distribute the weight for these poor runners."

"Fine, let's go." Hank walked down the quay and talked to two rickshaw drivers.

"You should go with Hank," James whispered. "Cheer him up some more."

"Okay." She was obviously pleased with James suggestion. She hurried to Hank. "I'll go with you. Pick the fastest, mate."

She and Hank got in the rickshaw and off they went. James proffered the next rickshaw. He wondered if Hank would ever stop his boorish behavior. How wonderful things would be if they didn't have to deal with Hank. Well that didn't seem like it was in the cards. Oh well, he would swallow his pride and go along with the machinations necessary to keep the three of them cordial toward each other. Sally wasn't going to ditch Hank.

The runners moved into the choked street, ringing their bells and shouting at the congested traffic. The runners wove their rickshaws through the bumper to bumper traffic, dodging the cars, three wheelers, bullock carts, cows, motorcycles, bicycles and pedestrians, who seemed to think nothing of veering into the street when the sidewalks were too crowded. James wondered if there were many accidents. He hadn't seen many. The way the traffic meshed together was quite amazing.

The Crawford Market wasn't that far, but the journey seemed protracted through the choked streets. They stood outside admiring the imposing Victorian structure and were soon surrounded by beggars.

"It's huge," Sally said. "Come on, let's go inside."

They wove their way through the beggars and temporary stalls outside, many on the back of carts or motorcycles. They stopped to watch a man blowing his melodious flute as a cobra swayed from the basket, something Sally always wanted to stop and see. They had seen a few in Madras. The cobra was such a majestic snake with its unique hood. He wondered how these men trained their cobras.

Inside the market the narrow aisles were full of people— ladies in colorful saris were common along with men in all manner of dress. The stalls offered the gamut of food and spices. The multitude of smells was inviting.

Sally ducked into a spice stall. A portly lady in a purple sari approached Sally. "Namaste." The lady bowed. "Yes, madam, what are you wanting today?"

"Just looking."

"Please madam. Take a look. Here we have turmeric, cayenne pepper, cardamom seeds, fennel, coriander...." The Indian lady jiggled her head from side to side. "Yes madam, I have also mixed spices. Here is masala, curry powder.... Where are you coming from?" Upon Sally's answer, the lady jiggled her head. "Very fine country."

They continued through the market impressed by all the different vegetables and fruit, many unfamiliar to James. When they reached the pet area with its assortment of animals in cages, Sally hurried through to the outside.

"The Mumba Devi Temple is ahead," James said. "Shouldn't be too far."

They continued north down the narrow alley crowed with pedestrians, past shops selling a dazzling array of goods. Wherever Sally went she attracted stares. The towering presence of Hank was enough to keep most at bay, but many maneuvered closer, which made negotiating their way up the alleyway more difficult. James could tell the immense crowd was annoying Hank.

When Sally saw the Mumba Devi Temple, she grabbed James's and Hank's hands. "Let's go inside."

Inside the statue of Mumba, an incarnation of Devi, the Mother Earth Goddess, patron goddess of the original inhabitants of salt sellers and fishermen of Bombay, was dressed in a robe with a silver crown, nose stud and golden necklace. The statue was draped with garlands of chrysanthemums. The interior was crowded, but not as much as the street outside and it was much cooler. The air was suffused with the smell of enchanting incense. James breathed in as Sally pulled him through the crowd.

"It's a relief to be inside," Sally said moving closer to the statue still holding James's hand. "I like the nose stud." She turned her head sideways and stretched her neck. "How do you think I'd look with one?"

"Great."

Hank hung back, rolled his neck, and watched the crowd moving around him like a rock in a stream. James wondered if Hank actually disliked temples and learning about the Hindu religion or was being difficult because James was with Sally. Maybe a little of both.

They went back outside and pushed their way through the crowd, past the inviting fabric shops. "Wow, I should've bought my sari here," Sally said sidling up to James.

"Let's stop and see what another sari will cost," James said. "I bet they're much cheaper here." Sally had the svelte body that looked fabulous in a sari, and he wanted to treat her to show her how much he was enjoying being with her.

"Oh yes, James, what a good idea."

"Fuck," Hank said, "not more shopping. How you going to carry all your shit?" He pointed across the street. "I'm going over to that restaurant stall for a beer."

"Easy mate," Sally said pushing Hank in the stomach. "Let me worry about carrying my stuff. Go ahead get a table and your beer. We won't be long."

***

"Won't be long," Hank said in a falsetto voice as Sally approached his table. "You were in there nearly an hour."

"I ordered two more saris," Sally said rising on her toes before plopping down in her seat next to Hank. "What a selection of fabrics. They said they'd be ready in two hours. Can you believe that?"

"Sounds like bullshit to me," Hank said.

Sally stuck out her tongue. "Mate, don't be so critical." She leaned forward and grasped Hank's beer, downing the remainder. "Ahhh, that's better."

She raised her arm and signaled the waiter in his white, slightly soiled shirt and trousers. "Beers all around."

The waiter smiled broadly, shaking his head from side to side. "Acha, madam. Coming right up."

Sally leaned to her left and gave James a kiss. "Thanks James. You're so kind."

They drank their beers while Sally described the myriad of fabrics she saw and the two saris James bought her. James nodded and smiled as Sally held forth. He liked how her excitement ebbed and flowed. She was a joy to be with. He could tell, although Hank was sitting stoically, that Hank was enjoying Sally's oration.

"I'm getting hungry," Hank said. "Shall we eat here?"

"Nah mate, this place is all right for drinks, but it's kind of grungy for food," Sally said. "Let's carry on and find a better restaurant."

They left the area of fabric shops, walked past the stalls of plumbers sitting on their stall floors surrounded by their myriad of pipe fitting and fixtures, and continued past the gold shops with their shinning necklaces and baubles.

"That's a nice mirror," Sally said as she headed for a furniture shop displaying in the window a gold leaf mirror with semiprecious stone inlays. Inside there were peacock rattan chairs of amazing craftsmanship and other sumptuous furnishings. "Oh, I would love to have things like this in my apartment." She sat down in one of the peacock chairs, threw her head back closing her eyes, and smiled with contentment. "It's really comfortable."

The shopkeeper slipped up behind James. "Ah, Madam, you look like a queen. He moved past James and the towering Hank. "Excuse me, gentleman." Turning back to Sally he said, "Madam, only one thousand rupees for such a fine chair. We can ship anywhere in the world, isn't it." He jiggled his head with a big smile.

"Interesting." Sally nodded to the merchant and rose to move around the shop, marveling at the many wonderful furnishings. Hank plopped down in one of the chairs and soon was dozing off. James followed Sally and the proprietor around amused by Sally's excitement and captivated by the assorted display of beautiful things.

Sally, having snaked through most of the shop, started for the door. "Hank, come on, we're leaving," she called.

"Madam, please come back. I have best deals in Bombay."

"Thank you," Sally said. "Maybe we will." She moved out into the crowed alleyway, her long stride carrying her into the crowd, which melted away as she moved, closing quickly behind her like the wake of a ship. James and Hank had to shove their way through to keep up with her. She spied an attractive restaurant ahead and strode toward it just as the rain deluge started.

14- HINDU KUSH MOUNTAINS: MARCH 10, 1970

Hank alternated between bone shaking shivers and feverish flashes, unable to sleep. He was so tired. The putrid food, which in the early evening was placed near his body, lay untouched. He knew he needed to eat, but he didn't have the energy to scoot to the steel plate and eat like a dog. Besides he would probably end up puking or shitting the food out before getting much if any nutrients. He was tired of laying in his watery shit for days. He was tired of the stink. He was tired of his throbbing arm. The swelling had reached his shoulder and the pain was unbearable. Whatever was happening, he had had enough. Could he will himself to die— stop this nightmare?

He pictured Sally in his mind. He had always been in love with her. She had been the light that pushed the debilitating loss of his parents to the background. Her parents had taken him in and attempted to soothe his pain and help him grieve, but it was Sally that drew him out of his shell. Her brother, Freddy, helped, but without that joyous little girl with her amazing green eyes and silky red hair, he would have been lost.

He remembered the wonderful days diving the barrier reef with her and Freddy. He marveled at the myriad of colors of the corral and fish. Often though, his eyes were on the beautiful teenager, who darted from place to place on the reef pointing out amazing sights: anemones, moray eels, sea horses, and tiny fishes hidden in the corral. Her excitement was contagious. When he had to surface having exhausted his air, she would still have plenty of air but would surface too. They went everywhere together, the three of them. Such happy times. When Sally and he dated in college, he knew she considered him as a brother and romance with him was not going to happen.

When she asked him to come on the trip to India with her, he jumped at the chance. They hadn't seen each other for a while. He had left college and gone to work in the outback on cattle stations. She had finished college and gotten a position teaching kids at the local school. He had been so hopeful that he could seduce her on the trip and get her to see how he would protect her and honor her. He had been so stupid. When they met James in Hong Kong, he had hated him for taking Sally away from him. On the freighter to Bangkok and in Bangkok, his hope had risen only to be smashed in India. James and his hotsy-totsy uncle made him sick. When he met Bridget, he thought he could make Sally jealous, but grew to be infatuated with the long-legged Swede. Little did he know Bridget's real motive for coming on to him. He had been so gullible. His anger and stupidity had landed him here in hell. He just wished to die.

He hadn't realized he had fallen asleep until he felt the kick to his side. He opened his eyes. The guard kicked the plate of putrid food across the room and ordered Hank up. Hank raised his head, but couldn't get his body to move. He closed his eyes as more kicks were administered. He heard a loud noise and gunshots in the other room followed by shouting and more gunfire.

The next thing he knew someone was kneeling close to him and cutting his bound hands. Another man came in and helped the first man lift Hank up and carry him outside. They carried him quite a distance and placed him in the back seat of a vehicle. They had not kicked him, rebound his hands, or shouted at him. He gazed down at his swollen arm that stunk to high heaven wrapped in the dirty cloth. Looked like it needed to be amputated or he'd probably die. Were they taking him to do just that? Why else take him away? After they started off, bouncing on the rutted road, his arm recorded each bounce with rocketing pain. He closed his eyes and pushed his rising nausea to the background. He didn't want to puke and upset the men. Who were they? What did they want with him?

15- ELLORA: NOVEMBER 19, 1969

James was pleased that Sally had convinced Hank to come to Ellora and Ajanta from Bombay instead of heading for Goa. He had been afraid if Hank had refused that Sally wouldn't have agreed to come.

The train ride to Aurangabad was the usual packed train. Arriving in the afternoon, they got a taxi to a guest house in town and walked across the street to a restaurant. After dinner they retired to their room and played cards. In the cool morning, they caught a taxi to the Ellora temples and caves to begin their visit.

When James came upon the immense Kailasa Temple he was astonished by the sculpture before him. The Kailasa Temple, designed to represent Mount Kailash, the home of Lord Shiva, was a free standing gigantic four story sculpture carved down out of the rock. The enormous size was daunting. The second story displayed life size sculptures of elephants and other animals. As he gazed at the astonishing temple, he raised his face to the warming sun, glad for the cooler weather the rain had brought.

Even Hank stood dumbfounded by the size and intricacy of the temple. The horse shoe shape of the area had been excavated out open to the sky. The three intricately carved structures of the courtyard were surrounded by carved three story galleries. The thirty foot high bull, Nandi, held up by elephants was the leading carved sculpture followed by the gargantuan main temple. Inside the main temple was an immense lingam.

"Wow, this puts the other temples to shame," Hank said. "When was it built?"

"It was started in the late seven hundreds and supposedly took one hundred years to complete." James was happy that Hank had finally taken an interest. He had been worried that Hank's acquiescence to coming here would turn into a malevolent attitude. "It's the largest ancient temple in the world. It is estimated that two hundred thousand tons of rock were cut out."

The rest of the morning they strolled around the many caves and temples: twelve Buddhist caves carved from 200 BC to 600 AD, seventeen Hindu temples from 500 AD to 900 and 5 Jain temples from 800 to 1000 AD.

Nothing, however, was nearly as stunning as the huge Kailasa Temple. There must have been thousands of workers hacking away with hammer and chisel. The amount of rock they removed was staggering. The guide book claimed it was bigger than the Greek Parthenon.

They hurried through the latter caves. James sensed that Hank was losing interest and was in bad need of refreshment. They got a taxi back to town and had an early dinner in the small restaurant across the street from the guest house. After dinner the three retired to their shared room and played cards as they discussed the amazing sculptures they had seen.

***

"This is enchanting," Sally said as she stood in front of the Ajanta cave painting depicting a scene from the life of Buddha. "I've never seen paintings like these. There is some kind of perspective here that defies understanding."

They had taken a taxi to Ajanta right after an early breakfast. There was no rain in the night and the day was already heating up.

James moved to the side of the painting and pointed to the center. "The painting spreads out from a central figure in all directions giving a false sense of perspective." He turned to Hank who stood behind. "What do you think, Hank?"

"They're cool, but awfully faded."

"Well given their age they are remarkably well preserved," James said. "This style of painting is found nowhere else in the world."

"Oh James, I'm so glad you convinced us to come here," she grabbed him around the waist. "The painting has a subtle beauty. It is quite a masterpiece. When was it painted?"

"200 BC."

"Incredible." She nudged her hip to his. "They must be the most accomplished paintings for this age anywhere in the world."

Her nudge reminded him that he had missed their intimacy last night, sleeping in the same room as Hank.

They wandered around half the caves marveling at the many paintings and stone sculptures. When Hank expressed his hunger, they left the cave platforms and walked down to the grassy area near the stream. They ate their box lunches the restaurant had prepared while sitting on the grass. The sound of the beautiful and colorful song birds accompanied their lunch as the birds flitted from tree to tree. All the caves, high above the trees, were visible in the U-shaped cliff.

James read from his guide book after their light lunch. "The caves were abandoned around 500 AD and were covered by the jungle until they were discovered by the British military in 1819."

"Discovered bullshit," Hank said. "I bet the locals knew about them. The British are arrogant assholes."

"You're right there, Hank," James said. "I'm sure the locals knew about them. Well, shall we go visit the rest of the caves?"

Sally jumped up, and James joined her.

Hank remained lounging on the grass. "What's your hurry? I need to digest my food."

"Come on Hank," Sally said taking his hand and trying to pull him up.

"You guys go ahead," Hank said and lay back. "I'll catch you up."

James and Sally hiked back up to the platforms that allowed them to go from cave to cave. The paintings and sculptures continued to depict the life of Buddha from birth to enlightenment and previous incarnations of Buddha.

They continued through all the caves and started back when they encountered Hank strolling along, talking to a tall blond woman. He looked so relaxed and engaged.

"Hey up, mates." Hank called. "I'd like to introduce you to Bridget." Hank gestured toward the attractive young woman and introduced James and Sally. "Bridget is from Sweden. She's at the same guest house in Aurangabad."

"Hello," Bridget said. She was thin with legs that seemed as long as Hank's and beautiful high cheek bones, small thin nose, dazzling long golden hair, and intense deep blue eyes. "Isn't this an amazing place? I'd read about the paintings here, but seeing them in person is awe inspiring. I love how they created depth without perspective. Have you seen all the caves?" Her voice was as smooth as a jazz singer, and she pronounced her English with a sing song lilt.

"Yeah, we've been through them all," Sally said. "The paintings are beautiful." She moved closer to Bridget. "What a truly remarkable experience." She placed her hand on Bridget's shoulder. "Carry on. We'll go down and wait for you two to finish." Her smile encompassed her entire face. "Are you here by yourself?"

"Yes, I traveled to India with some friends, but they didn't want to come here. They're at Anjuna Beach in Goa."

"Take your time, and, if you like, we can share a taxi back," Sally said.

"Oh yeah-yeah," Bridget said. "That would be great."

When Hank and Bridget moved on, Sally dug her elbow into James side. "You can close your mouth now."

"What are you talking about?"

"I saw how you looked at her," she said, pushing him forward. "She's a beauty. Hopefully she and Hank can hit it off."

"That would be great. Take some pressure off you."

"You think," she said and grabbed his hand and started swinging it back and forth. "I knew this was going to be a great day."

***

"How long are you staying in India?" Sally asked Bridget as they were sitting at the restaurant across from their guest house.

"I don't have a set schedule," Bridget said. "I took a semester off so I don't have to be back in Sweden until next fall. Of course, I wouldn't want to stay in India until then. All the poverty is depressing."

"That's great," Hank said staring at Bridget with eyes wide. He had taken off his hat and combed his longish blond hair. The two could have been brother and sister.

"Did you already see Ellora," Sally asked Bridget.

"Oh yes. That big temple, Kailasa, was incredible. I can't imagine the people and time required to carve out such a gigantic temple. Even after seeing it, I still find it unbelievable."

It was obvious that Hank was mesmerized by Bridget's beauty. Her eyes lit up when she talked and any pause was accompanied by a broad smile. She was nearly as mesmerizing as Sally. How could Hank resist.

"Bridget, where are you planning to go next?" James asked.

"Goa, to meet back up with my friends."

"That's where we're going," Hank said. "That's right isn't it? We agreed, right?"

"Yes Hank," Sally said. "We can all take the train together." She focused her eyes on Bridget. "You up for that Bridget?"

"Of course," Bridget said, stretching upright. "I would love your company. I was disappointed when my friends wouldn't come here and a little afraid to travel on my own. I haven't had too many problems. I got a few bruises on my butt in Bombay, walking on my own."

I know what you mean," Sally replied and placed her hand on top of Bridget's.

James remembered the men that moved toward Sally in Bombay with a glint in their eye before hesitating when they noticed James or Hank. Bridget would enjoy the safety of the group.

16- AURANGABAD: NOVEMBER 19, 1969

Bridget had been at Anjuna Beach a week and wanted to see other parts of India, but her friends had been so traumatized with their few days in Delhi with the constant accosting by beggars and men in the crowds that they were reluctant to travel anywhere else. She had read about the famous temples, sculptures, and paintings at Ellora and Ajanta and tried multiple times to entice her friends to accompany her on a short visit there to no success.

She had enjoyed her time at Anjuna Beach where the locals were more courteous and there were almost no beggars. It was certainly relaxing after the shock of arriving in Delhi with its pervasive poverty and misogyny where they had all been touched repeatedly on their few excursions to check their mail at American Express and to eat.

Bridget was determined to see Ellora and Ajanta despite having to go on her own. It wasn't that far away— a quick ride to Bombay a change of trains and a short ride to Aurangabad— so she had reluctantly left her girlfriends. After arriving in Bombay, she ventured out of the train station, hoping to see some of the city before her train to Aurangabad. She didn't get very far in the crowd amongst the outside vendors as a melee of beggars accosted her and numerous men slipped close to touch her. She retreated back into the station to await her late morning train. As she was sitting in the first class waiting room, she hoped that Ellora and Ajanta wouldn't be crowded, and she wouldn't have to fend off any Indian men.

One of the main reasons she had come to India was to see the art and artifacts. She was getting her Masters in Art History and was fascinated by what little she had learned about the art of India. She never expected her girlfriends to be so afraid. The sun, beach, and hash were enjoyable, but she could have gone to Spain if that was all she sought. She wished she could find other suitable Europeans or Americans to travel with so she could see more of India in some semblance of safety. In Anjuna Beach, the Westerners she had met were mostly aimless scruffy young men, who didn't really appeal to her. Men sought her out repeatedly, obviously attracted to her looks. She knew she was a striking young woman. She still held out hope that she could eventually meet a suitable male traveling companion that would want to see more of India with her.

When she arrived in Aurangabad, there were only a few beggars outside the train station, and she had no trouble getting a taxi to the small village guest house, where she procured a room, and stowed her luggage before taking another taxi to Ellora. She ambled along through the many caves marveling at the temples and sculptures. The place was interesting and she felt blessed to be able to see the artifacts. She had not been accosted at the site and her fear of being alone waned, but the looks and stares of the visiting Indian men kept her on alert. There were almost no Westerners visiting the site.

When she came upon the gigantic Kailasa Temple, she stopped and gazed up at the unbelievable sight with awe. She spent hours walking around, taking pictures of the gargantuan sculpture. She was reluctant to leave, but the site was closing. After arriving back at the guest house, she had a quick dinner at the restaurant across the street and went to bed happy she had forced herself to come to Ellora and had seen the amazing Kailasa Temple.

She was late in rising in the morning, still overwhelmed and exhilarated by what she had seen at Ellora. She had a quick breakfast and took a taxi to the caves at Ajanta. She had seen pictures in books of the some of the cave paintings and was anxious to experience them. She hurried up to the wooden platform that linked the caves. The day was already hot and she removed her shirt down to her tee shirt and folded the shirt into her handbag. The painting in the caves were stupendous, and she felt blessed to be able to see them up close.

Because of the looks and stares she was receiving, she put her shirt back on despite the heat, worrying that the outline of her breasts was too provocative for the Indians. As she was leaving a cave, she saw a tall blond European-looking man wearing a wide brimmed hat ahead. She caught up to him and walked alongside. When he noticed her, he turned toward her.

"Hi," he said.

"Hello there," she replied, flashing her smile and stepping closer. He was handsome and appeared alone. "The paintings in these caves are amazing," she said.

"Yes they are," he replied, staring at her in astonishment, his eyes wide.

She thought she recognized his accent. "Are you from Australia?"

"Yeah, mate. Where are you from?"

"Sweden. My name's Bridget." She held out her hand. She hadn't met anyone from Australia, but had heard the accent on TV. She liked the look of him and wanted to find out more about him.

"I'm Hank," he replied and grasped her hand. His huge calloused hand engulfed hers as he gave her hand an enthusiastic shake. "Are you here by yourself?"

"I came to India with two girlfriends of mine, but they didn't want come along to Ajanta. Are you traveling with anyone?"

"Yeah, my friend from Australia and an American we met in Hong Kong."

"Sounds exciting. Do you mind if I accompany you while you visit the caves. The Indian men sometimes can be a little pushy."

"Yeah, I know what you mean. Sure, let's visit the caves together."

Things were looking up. This tall Australian might be a suitable traveling companion, and he's with other Westerners. Traveling in a group would be even better.

They preceded through the caves, taking in the amazing paintings. She made sure to give him plenty of smiles, removed her shirt again to expose more of her sculptured body, and stood close to him as they discussed the paintings. She was sure her allure was provoking plenty of interest from this tall Australian. As they were nearing the end of the caves, they came upon his friends. The woman with her sumptuous red hair and green eyes was incredibly beautiful, and she had her arm hooked into a very handsome young man with blond hair and a mustache. She was intrigued by the couple and especially the man that caused her heart to jump. His endearing smile and hazel eyes penetrated her being, and she felt an immediate attraction.

When the lady named Sally learned that Bridget was staying at the same guest house as them, she suggested they all share a taxi back. Bridget happily agreed.

***

In the evening she joined the three at their invitation for dinner. When Sally learned Bridget was going back to Goa to stay with her friends again, Sally asked if they could come along with her, since they were planning to go to Goa too. Bridget couldn't believe her luck. Maybe after staying awhile in Anjuna Beach, she could convince them to allow her to join them on additional travels to other parts of

India. She had missed the attractions in Delhi except what she saw on their taxi rides to American Express and restaurants. She had considered going to some of the sites on her own, but felt, since they were newly arrived in India, she needed to stay together with her friends.

The beach scene in Anjuna Beach had been pleasant enough, but was not the primary reason she had organized the trip to India with her friends, who seemed content to just stay at the beach community.

Her travel alone to Ellora and Ajanta, had been fortuitous. Meeting people like Hank, James and Sally was what she had hoped for. They were obviously interested in art and culture and were planning on visiting more of India. Hank was handsome, big, and strong, and she sensed traveling with him would provide the safety she sought. She felt a strange affinity with James that she couldn't put her finger on. He was more handsome then Hank and had a gentle and intellectual quality about him that was enticing. She was so happy all three were going to accompany her to Anjuna Beach. Such an excellent opportunity to get to know them better.

That evening she invited Hank to her room. They cuddled and kissed, but she repelled his more assertive advances. She wanted to postpone any sex until she knew him better. She hadn't liked his aggressiveness. She knew she would eventually need to sleep with him if she wanted to travel to other areas with him, but oddly enough wasn't looking forward to the prospect. She liked sex and was not prudish about sharing her sexuality, but the underlying brutish nature of Hank was somewhat off-putting.

***

"I'm so glad we traveled together," Bridget said as the train rolled into the small Thivim station.

Hank grabbed Bridget's large shoulder bag, his backpack, and started for the exit. He was the first off the train, pushing through the crowd, pulling Bridget with him. Sally and James followed. A small group of other travelers had disembarked and were also seeking taxis. Hank bulled through the small crowd and easily grabbed a taxi. Bridget didn't relish being pulled along but accepted it. There was no doubt Hank was a force to be reckoned with. She would need to tone down his impulsive nature. She'd sleep with him tonight in hopes of being able to assert more influence over him. The journey to Anjuna Beach in the sunny moist heat was relatively short. Bridget directed the taxi to their rented bungalow.

"This is it," Bridget said when the taxi stopped outside a yellow bungalow with a wide porch and pitched, green roof. "Come on inside. There's enough room for everyone, for tonight. I'm sure the girls will know of a place to rent nearby."

"Sounds great," Sally said and followed Bridget inside.

Bridget's friends were not home. "Why don't we leave our stuff here and change to our bathing suits," Bridget said. "I bet they're at the beach."

"Great, mate," Sally replied.

148

They found Bridget's friends lounging on the beige sand of the long beach. Many of the women sunbathers were topless like Bridget's friends.

"Hey, ladies," Bridget called as she moved toward her two friends. Hank was right behind her. "I've met some people. We traveled down from Ajanta together."

The two women sat up, their tan full breasts gleaming with suntan oil, and shaded their eyes. "Oh yeah," they said in unison. "Good."

"This is Hank, Sally, and James," Bridget said. "And these are my friends Monica and Lisa."

Sally, James and Hank exchanged handshakes with the ladies. Sally marveled at how attractive the women were. She thought they were brazen by lounging topless when it was obvious the passing men were mesmerized by the sight of the ladies bare chests.

Bridget laid her beach blanket down and pulled Hank down with her. Hank removed his tee shirt exposing his lily white chest and back. Bridget began applying sunscreen on herself with Hank's help and rubbed the sunscreen on Hank's back.

Sally and James moved to the other side of Monica and Lisa. She was pleased by Bridget's attention to Hank. Things were going so well. "You ladies know of a good bungalow or hotel room nearby we could rent?" Sally asked.

"The house two doors down is becoming vacant tomorrow," Lisa said. Her dark hair was in a ponytail and her blue eyes were spaced wide apart from her narrow nose. Her prominent square chin dominated her face. "It's the same landlord as ours." Her smile was a little lopsided, and she had a small scar under her nose.

"Oh, that's lucky," Sally said. "How can we meet with the landlord?"

"We were just talking about getting some lunch," Monica said, her golden hair shining in the sun. She too had penetrating blue eyes and bore a remarkable resemblance to Bridget. "We could relax for a while and then go to the restaurant shack." She pointed to a restaurant set back from the beach. "After lunch we can go to our landlord's house."

"That would be great," Sally said. "Monica, are you and Bridget related? You look so much alike." She removed her wrap to expose her muscular legs with their tiny freckles, but kept her tee shirt on. She had applied sunscreen on her pallid skin before leaving the bungalow. She was quite susceptible to sunburn.

"We're cousins. We're often asked if we're sisters."

"I can see why," Sally replied. She pulled off her tee shirt, but left her bikini top on before lying back on the blanket.

After about an hour in the hot sun, Hank stretched. "I'm getting thirsty."

"Me too," Sally added.

"Let's go to lunch then," Bridget said.

After a delicious lunch of fish curry in coconut sauce with ice cold beers, they traipsed back to the bungalow through the grove of palm trees. Sally was feeling great. Meeting Bridget had been fantastic. She couldn't have contemplated a more propitious event.

***

"I read that a lot of the Goans are Christian," Sally said as they were sitting around the Swedish ladies front room, drinking King Fisher beers as a cool breeze from the ocean suffused the room stirred by the ceiling fan. "I wonder if that's why they seem so different from the rest of the Indians."

"Well most Goans are Hindu, but, as you say, there are a lot of Catholics here," Bridget replied. "I find religions, culture, and the art associated with them fascinating. I liked the Aborigine art when we studied it." She stared at Sally momentarily. "Did you ever visit Aborigine settlements?"

"Yeah, my brother Freddy was very interested in Aborigines," Sally said. "His fiancé is part Aborigine. Unfortunately the government has treated the Aborigines terribly and there is a lot of poverty and alcoholism. But their religion and culture is captivating. It's probably the oldest surviving culture in the world."

Sally swallowed a gulp of beer and leaned forward. "Before the Europeans arrived they were dispersed throughout the country. They didn't build stone monuments, farm animals, or cultivate crops. They never had a formal written language. They recorded their culture in rock art, which I've seen at Kakadu— beautiful paintings of fish, turtles, lightening man, rainbow serpent. The paintings were full of mysticism. Some rock art is said to be fifty thousand years old."

"I thought the Ajanta paintings were old," Bridget said. "I can't get my head around fifty thousand years."

Sally looked toward Bridget, feeling a strong affinity for the beautiful Swede. "Each tribe had their own deities," Sally continued. "There are the creation beings who brought forth the people, landscape, and environment. The ancestral beings taught the people how to make tools, hunt, and gather food. The totemic beings are the original animal or plant beings. Aborigines believe that dreams are memories of things that happened during the creation period and give great significance to their dreams. They follow song lines as a ritual enactment of the Dreamtime during creation."

"Yeah-yeah, you know a lot about the Aborigines," Bridget said. "What a concept— Dreamtime. I think their rock art and contemporary art is beautiful. I've seen pictures of the Kakadu paintings," Bridget placed her hand on Hank's shoulder. "Have you seen the rock paintings?"

"No I'd didn't go on that trip," Hank said, dropping his head. He quickly perked up and placed his hand on Bridget's thigh. "I've worked with Aborigines, though, at cattle stations. They're interesting people."

Sally and James had met with the ladies' landlord after lunch and had procured the two bedroom bungalow two houses down for a week with the option to stay longer. Sally hoped Bridget and Hank would build on their relationship, that she and Bridget would become good friends, and they all could go traveling together after a relaxing stay in this laid back beach village.

Monica produced a fat doobie, lit it with a big smile, sucked in a big hit, and passed it on. Bridget took a long toke and expelled the fragrant smoke of hash and tobacco with a satisfied smile.

Sally found it hard to refrain from starring at Monica and Bridget. She noticed that James was often watching the two also. Both were so much more attractive than herself. Hank had been incredibly lucky to have found Bridget. Hopefully, they would get along well. She accepted the doobie from Bridget and took a long drag before passing it to Hank.

"This is fine hash," Hank said after his hit while he slumped back against the couch. "I need to buy some of this."

"No problem," Lisa said. "We'll introduce you to our local dealer. He'll be at the beach restaurant at sunset. Saves going into town. You can buy some then."

"You sure it's okay for us to stay here tonight?" James asked.

"It will be fine," Lisa said. "One of you can sleep on the couch and we can put the cushions on the floor for the other two."

"Yeah, it will be great," Sally replied. She had wanted to be alone with James, but she could wait another night. She hoped Hank would sleep with Bridget and she and James could put all the cushions on the floor and sleep together. Hank had spent time in Bridget's room at the Aurangabad guest house, but had come back to their room to sleep late at night. She had wanted to ask Hank if he had had sex with Bridget, but thought it might upset him. There was no doubt in her mind that Hank was totally smitten. Bridget seemed to like Hank's company, but often was secretly glancing at James. Well James was very handsome and had been a magnet for her. She hoped Bridget's interest in James was just friendly curiosity.

Hank and the three Swedes went back to the beach. Sally and James stayed at the Bungalow agreeing to meet them at the beach restaurant just before sunset. Sally needed be careful with the sun.

"Okay, mate. Get over here." Sally held open her arms. James rose and slipped into her arms. It felt so good to be alone with James.

***

There was a large group of hippies on the beach drumming as the sun sank low in the sky. Hank had his arm around Bridget and was obviously several drinks ahead as Sally and James joined the group at the restaurant. Hank and Bridget were the perfect couple, both well over six feet tall, both with stunning blond hair.

"This is too perfect," Sally said before taking a large drink of beer. She knew she was going to have a great time here. Sun, sand, hash, and loving. What could be better? The Goan people seemed so tolerant. No wonder all the hippies had congregated here.

After the sun sank into the ocean to the shouts, wild calls, and crescendo drumming, they ordered dinner— fried vegetable appetizers, more fish curries, and many beers. The fish was fresh and delicious in the piquant coconut curry sauce. A group of musicians— two guitars, a flute and a drummer— gathered out in front of the restaurant on the wooden patio and started playing Dylan's *Like A Rolling Stone*.

Sally pulled James up and they began dancing. Lisa and Monica joined them, and after some coaxing, Bridget got Hank up.

"Wow, Bridget got Hank to dance," Sally whispered. "She really has conquered the Big Lug." She smiled to herself, grasped James around the waist, and tipped him from side to side. "Don't get too tired, mate. You've got a lot more work to do tonight." She laughed as she spun him around and watched the big smile grow on his face.

After many more beers and dancing, the group trudged through the coconut palms to their bungalow by the light of the waxing moon. Back at the bungalow they smoked several more hash doobies. Late in the night, Monica and Lisa excused themselves.

"Come on, Hank," Bridget said, standing and pulling on Hank's arm.

Hank with a surprised expression rose quickly and followed Bridget into her bedroom. When the bedroom door closed, Sally smiled and reached for James.

***

The group settled into the beach scene. Sally and James moved into the bungalow two doors down. Hank had initially joined them, but spent many nights with Bridget— yet not always. When Sally asked him what was up when he slept at their bungalow, Hank just shrugged and said Bridget wanted to be alone.

One week became almost two. Sally spent time on the beach in the shade adding to her sketches and making new ones. She regulated her swimming and often wore a tee shirt in the water to insure she didn't get sun burned. They were able to buy some snorkel equipment from some Italians, who were leaving. She enjoyed their snorkel excursions watching the bright colorful fish in the bay. She was able to foster a light tan and felt so relaxed, but she could tell that James was getting restless.

When he called out in his sleep, she wanted to wake him, hold him, and kiss him to banish his nightmares, but thought they were therapeutic. He needed to work through his Vietnam experiences. All she could do was support him. She tried to get him to talk about his experiences more, but he usually changed the subject after a brief discussion. She sensed something awful happened that he was not telling her. She hoped with time he would confide in her.

"You know this is great here in Goa— sun, surf, hash and you," James said. "It's wonderful... but I feel we should be moving on to check out some of the other great wonders of India. I'd like to eventually work my way north and go to Nepal."

"Yeah, I know what you mean. This place is idyllic, and being with you here has been wonderful." She rubbed his chest and stared at his face as his smile made her heart thump. "But as you say there's a lot more of India to see. I would love to come with you to Nepal."

"What do you think Hank wants to do? Would he want to come with us or stay here with Bridget?"

"Let's ask him. I bet Bridget would like to come. She liked seeing Ajanta and Ellora, and she loves art." Sally rotated away. "She seems enamored of you."

"What? Come on, she's with Hank."

"I know, but Hank's not much of a scholar and he's a typical Aussie male— full of himself."

"Sally and I are thinking of taking off and traveling north eventually making our way to Nepal," James said as they were smoking in the Swedish ladies bungalow.

Sally blew out a cloud of smoke and studied the group. "Anyone else interested in traveling north with us?"

"When would you leave?" Bridget asked.

"Couple of days," James said.

"So soon," Hank said. "It's so great here."

"Hey, you can stay," Sally said. "We can meet up later."

Hank frowned at Sally. He had promised Sally's brother he would protect her. He wanted to stay. He was having such a great time, lounging about with the beautiful Bridget. The hashish was good and the Goans were great people. There were hardly any hassles here. He wasn't up for dealing with the beggars and crowding that further travel would entail.

"I'd like to go," Bridget said. "I'd love to see more of India."

"Great," James said.

"I'll stay here," Lisa said. "Traveling in India seems so difficult. All the poverty, crowds, and beggars...."

Monica placed her hand on Lisa's shoulder and smiled. "I'll stay with you, Lisa."

If Bridget was going, Hank felt he would have to go too. He needed to continue fostering his relationship with Bridget. They were getting along well, but he sensed a kind of reluctance toward him sometimes. He had put it down to her moody and bookish nature. He also needed to honor his pledge to protect Sally. He didn't think James alone would be able to protect both women very well. The two of them together would garner lots of interest. He liked Bridget's friends, Monica and Lisa, and would miss them. He was just getting to know them. Monica was almost as beautiful as Bridget and had a killer body. He was having fun for a change.

"So Hank what do you think?" Sally said. "You're coming aren't you?'

Shit, he had no real choice. "Yeah, I reckon," Hank replied. "Could we stay a little longer? A week would be good."

"No...no," Bridget said. "I'm excited about traveling more in India." She leaned her golden body against Hank.

"Okay three days then," Hank said and grasped Bridget to him. He savored her acceptance of his grasp. Maybe she'd be more into him on the trip.

"Yeah-yeah," Bridget said pulling away from Hank. "This is going to be great. Where to first?"

"I read about the palaces in Udaipur," James said. "Sounded like a good place to break the journey to Delhi."

""Yes, I've heard of the palaces there," Bridget said. "Wonderful idea, James."

More palaces and temples.... Hank felt James could be a pain in the ass sometimes with his tour directing and wish to see all the temples and tourist sites. He was more for kicking back and taking things slow and easy. Oh well, nothing else to be done. He was committed, and Bridget was over the moon with the prospect of more traveling.

"Oooo, I'd like to stay there," Bridget said as she pointed at the dazzling island palace, reflecting the bright sun off its white exterior. She separated from the group and walked to the edge of the lake. "The palace across the lake on the bank is even bigger."

After the four had arrived in Udaipur in the early morning on the overnight train from Bombay, they had gotten a taxi to a modest hotel near the western shore of Lake Picholo. They had shared a sleeper compartment from Bombay after their morning second class train ride from Goa. Everyone was in high spirits as they stowed their packs and bags at the hotel and walked down to the lake for a view of the famous palaces.

James was relieved that he didn't have to confront Hank's jealousy. He thought Hank and Bridget seemed to be meshing well. Being with Sally in Goa had been sublime. His recurring dream still often haunted him in the night and left him morose on waking, but he was able to push the nightmare to the back of his memory.

"We could get a taxi around the lake to the City Palace and then a boat to the Jagmandir Island Palace," James suggested, dragging Sally to the lake edge to stand next to Bridget. "Both have recently become hotels, but we can still visit."

"I'm hungry and I know Hank needs a beer," Bridget said before giving Hank a shove.

Hank grabbed her from behind and kissed her long neck. "You think you know me?"

"No, Big Guy," Bridget said. "But I'm certainly ready for a beer myself and lunch. All the Indians on the train eating their snacks stirred my appetite."

***

They leisurely walked from the restaurant in town that they had taken a taxi to, ignoring the few beggars following them. They stopped at the gate to the Mewar City Palace and gazed up.

"Shall we," James exclaimed. They strolled inside. "The series of palaces were begun in 1559. They were expanded for three hundred years, sprawling across the face of the lake."

"What an immense conglomeration," Sally said

"There are eleven palaces in the complex," James added.

"Eleven," Bridget said, "My god, these Mewar princes must have really liked their palaces."

They wandered through the palaces, following the twisting corridors that seemed never ending. They stopped in the Dunbar Hall where official business of the Mewars was conducted with its grand ornate ceiling. They moved through the palaces to the outside and walked to the towering, carved stone temple on the hill. The walls of the temple were decorated with images of Vishnu, Krishna, and cavorting nymphs.

"This temple is for Lord Jagannath, an incarnation of Vishnu." James announced.

"The carvings are so intricate," Bridget said.

"Jagannath... another incarnation." Sally shook her head. "These incarnations of Vishnu and Shiva seem endless."

Bridget laughed and moved to Sally, taking her arm. "Endless...yeah-yeah. You are so right."

James was glad that Bridget and Sally were getting along well. Even Hank seemed to be enjoying himself. Undoubtedly, Bridget was keeping him in a good mood. They proceeded to the Mor Chowk square where three large peacock statues covered with a mosaic of colored glass sparkled in the sun. They continued their tour and eventually strolled out the back wall of the complex to the quay at the lake edge.

Sally grabbed James. "This is one massive series of palaces. It's bigger than the Mysore palace, but lacks the continuity or beauty of Mysore."

"They're both massive, and you're right this complex is bigger than Mysore, but the Mysore Palace is larger than any of the individual palaces here. I agree Mysore was more beautiful and stunning."

Sally separated from James and pointed at the wall of the complex, shading her eyes from the sun. "It's like the Mewars couldn't stop building."

"Yeah-yeah, an obvious obsession," Bridget said. "They were all beautiful. I'm sorry I didn't see the Mysore palace. I'm so glad you suggested coming here, James." Bridget nudged James in the side before grabbing Hank's hand. "So Hank what did you like best?" She pulled Hank to her and walked down the quay leaning against him.

"It was all interesting, but I liked the peacocks best," Hank said.

"Me too," Bridget said, her face stretched in surprise.

James was relieved that Hank was getting the hang of it with Bridget. He had been worried that Hank's brutish nature would come out on the trip and turn Bridget off.

The massive palaces and monuments attested to the lavish life style the royalty of India enjoyed. The amazing structures were impressive, much like those produced by European royalty. Exploitation of the masses seemed to be universal.

"Let's go back to the hotel and relax," Sally said. "Wandering around these endless palaces was enough for me for the day. We can go the island palace tomorrow before we catch the train to New Delhi. It's getting hotter by the minute and I'm palaced out."

***

The morning ride to the island palace was short and cooling. They strolled up the jetty through the entrance pavilion with its carved elephants on each side of the entrance steps. The towers at the corners of the main palace rose with octagonal cupolas. In the center was a three-domed building, its marble interior walls inlaid with precious stones.

"I want to get a drink here," Sally said. "I don't care how much it'll cost."

"Of course," James said, grabbing her around the waist. "Let's splurge and enjoy the ambience."

"Yeah-yeah," Bridget said and reached for Hank's hand.

They walked through the garden courtyard to a small bar with its panorama view of the lake. Sally signaled the waiter in his red turban, white suit, and red sash. "Four King Fishers, please."

They clinked their glasses together. "Skol," Bridget said. "I'm having such a great time. I love seeing these magnificent palaces. They are incredible works of art." She took a long swallow. "Here's to my new friends. Thanks so much for including me."

***

"The Maharanas of the Mewar kingdom sure knew how to live," Sally said as they waded into the crowd waiting for the train. "I wonder how their subjects faired. Probably not so great."

They had packed up after an enjoyable lunch near their guest house and took a taxi to the train station. They paid for first class tickets so they could rest after their sightseeing. They chose a place at the back of the crowd that was spread out across the concrete platform awaiting the train.

"I'm sure glad we sprang for the first class," Sally said. "We can relax. It always seems more people are waiting for the train then the train can accommodate, yet they all get on somehow."

When the train rolled in, the mass of people rose and moved to the train. The third class carriages seemed to be already full. People with their bundles were sitting on the roof or hanging out the windows. Nevertheless, the sea of people slowly disappeared into the train cars or onto the roof.

They waited for most of the crowd to disperse before walking up the platform to the first class carriages. Many of the Indian men, streaming from the first class waiting room, were wearing Western or Indian suits while most of the women wore colorful saris and were decked with gold jewelry.

Their reserved seats were two together in one row and two together in the next row. They were the last to board and ignored the stares and frowns of the seated occupants.

James settled back into the plush seats. He felt a welcome nap coming. Ever since Hank and Bridget had joined up, his time with Sally had been wonderful.

20- DELHI: DECEMBER 7, 1969

The New Delhi train station was immense and filled with people. They had trouble getting off the train as the porters swarmed in to grab the baggage of the wealthy. The porters tried to seize their bags and back packs. Hank and James were able to fend them off.

"I need to go to American Express and check my mail," Bridget said as they were finally able to exit the train to the multitude of people moving every which way on the platform. "My Dad was going to send me some money."

"Let's get a hotel first," Sally said. "We need to relax and cool out. We can go in the morning. She had attempted to catch a nap on the train, but wasn't able to. Even with Hank and James towering over most of the scurrying people, she felt the occasional hand touch her bottom. She wondered what it would have been like traveling on her own. The thought was too frightening. Bridget had been remarkably courageous going to Ellora and Ajanta on her own. The multitude surrounding her made her feel dirty. She needed a shower and a lie down.

"I stayed at a nice place when we first got here," Bridget said. "It was clean, inexpensive, and had private bathrooms."

"Let's check it out," James replied.

They pushed their way out of the station with Hank leading the charge— Bridget and Sally following with James bringing up the rear. The crowd thickened outside the station with the beggars making a dash toward them. The refrain 'Baksheesh, Sahib Baksheesh, Memsaab Baksheesh' filled the air.

One emaciated young lady with only a few teeth dressed in rags, who would have been rather attractive had she been eating regularly, latched on to Bridget. Hank pushed himself between them and handed the lady several rupees, which, as expected, emboldened other beggars to crush forward. Hank, swinging his shoulders to dispel the people trying to get his attention, strode forward, grabbed a taxi door, and pushed Bridget and Sally inside. James scurried in after.

Hank, apparently tired of all the hands thrusting toward him and grabbing his shirt, pushed himself toward the crowd like a rugby player. "Get the hell back," he yelled before spinning and jumping into the cab.

"Jesus, Hank," Sally said. "Take it easy."

"These little shits get on my nerves," Hank said and scowled at Sally, then turned forward again.

Sally raised her eyebrows and jiggled her head like the Indians while pursing her lips and sticking out her tongue. Bridget laughed, and Hank swung back to glare at the three.

"No worries, Hank" Sally said and placed her hand on Hank's shoulder. "Thanks for leading the charge to the taxi. You were great."

Hank's anger slipped away as he stared at Sally and then Bridget. "Sorry."

"I'm sure glad you're here, Hank," Bridget said and placed her hand on his shoulder and squeezed.

Hank smiled, rubbed her hand, and twisted back to the front. Bridget and Sally exchanged a knowing glance.

***

James and Sally's hotel room was small but cozy with a tiny bathroom. As soon as Sally dropped her pack, she moved to James and gave him a hug and kiss. "Want to shower together?"

"I don't know," James said. "Do you have any enticements?"

"Mate, you won't believe the enticements I've got." She pushed him down on the bed and giggling ran into the bathroom, pulling her shirt off as she went.

"Okay, I want to see these enticements," he said and quickly stripped off his clothes, before dashing into the bathroom, whooping.

"Christ there's no hot water," she said and sprang out of the shower.

James grabbed a towel and wrapped it around her, kissing her neck. "We need to work up some heat then before we shower in cold water."

***

As they lay resting on the bed in the morning, they heard a knock. "Hank and I will meet you in the lobby if you want to go with us to American Express," Bridget said.

"Okay. We'll be down in a few." Sally tried to rise against James locked hands.

"Wait a minute," James said. "What about the rest of the enticements."

"Don't worry... there's plenty more," Sally said pulling away. "You haven't even begun to realize the store of enticements I have for you." She rose and hurried to bathroom. "I need to rinse off. Come on, get in here and rinse off."

Downstairs Bridget was sitting in the wicker peacock chair in the lobby, watching the multitude stream by outside.

Sally's face was flushed, her wet hair shining and her tiny freckled nose was pink. James was smiling broadly his wet blond hair sticking out at odd angles.

"Oh, you two look blissful," Bridget said. "The mysteries of India seem to agree with you." She stood up. "Hank's got a cab waiting."

The taxi, honking endlessly, wound its way through the clogged streets dodging the multitude of conveyances and streaming pedestrians. The American Express office was crowded with Europeans and Americans. They got in line at the mail desk.

"This is gonna take a while," Hank said "Think I'll go find a beer down the street. Meet you guys there."

"What about your mail?" Bridget said.

"I doubt I've got any," Hank said as he walked away.

"He won't have any mail?" Bridget asked Sally.

"Probably not," Sally replied. "His parents are dead. My brother would write to me for both of us."

"Oh, he didn't tell me about his parents," Bridget said.

"Yeah, he was ten," Sally said. "They died in an auto accident. Afterwards my parents took him in."

Sally backed up against James and grabbed his arm and pulled it around her. She knew that Hank had never really gotten over the death of his parents. Who would at that age? She was fond of Hank, even though he often got on her nerves. She was delighted that Hank had found Bridget. She hoped that they all would continue to travel together. If Bridget left Hank, the pressure would be back on her for sure. Stop fretting.

After getting their mail the three, shooing away the beggars trying to latch onto them, joined Hank in the tiny restaurant. Hank saw them entering and summoned the waiter requesting three more beers. "Was there mail from your brother?" he asked.

"Yeah, mate," Sally said. "He sent me some money too. They've postponed the wedding."

"What's up?" Hank asked.

"Nothing really. They just want us to be there."

"That's cool. I was sad that we were going to miss it."

"Yeah, he needs his best man." She was glad that this had made Hank happy.

"Here's to Freddy and his lovely bride," Hank said, raising his glass.

Sally clinked her glass followed by Bridget and James. "Cheers, mates." She nearly downed the beer in one go. "I needed that." She gave James a shove "Where to next?"

"Well, the Red Fort is supposed to be spectacular and the Jain temple is nearby." He took a large swallow of beer. "Tomorrow or the next day we could take a train to Agra and the Taj Mahal."

"Yes I want to see the Red Fort," Bridget said. "Let's go to Agra early in the morning so it won't be so crowded. I've heard it can get packed with people. Going the day after tomorrow might be best. We've got to go to the National Museum tomorrow. I'm dying to see the Taj Mahal, but the museum has a fantastic art collection."

"Yeah, I don't want to rush around," Hank said. "Our hotel is a good one. I need a day to cool out."

"My sentiment indeed," Bridget said, and grasped Hank's hand.

***

"Wow, it really is red," Bridget said as they walked toward the imposing fort. "It almost matches your hair, Sally."

"Right on," Sally replied.

Hank grabbed Bridget's hand and began pushing his way through the crowd.

"Here we go," Sally said. "The bull is off." She could tell by Bridget's frown that Hank's dragging her about was not to her liking. Was Hank's impulsiveness turning Bridget off?

They walked through the Chawari Bazaar ignoring the beggars and entered the massive red sandstone Lahori Gate— three stories high, crowned by a series of white domes above arches with towering pillars on either side. The gate was flanked by the high walls of the fort with its crenellated battlements.

James pulled out his guide book. "The fort was constructed in 1648 by the fifth Mughal Emperor. It was the zenith of the Mughal Empire. He built it when he shifted his capital from Agra to Delhi."

"Interesting," Bridget said and rubbed James's back.

"Lead on maestro," Sally said, pushing James forward. They walked through the Chatta Chowk passageway with its domed, covered roof and side arcades selling all manner of souvenirs. They continued on through the outer court to the Diwani-i-Aam section with its towering columns and serrated arches.

"This is beautiful," Bridget said. "Get together, and I'll take a picture."

They took turns taking pictures "That raised marble balcony in the back is where the emperor gave audiences," James said.

They continued to the inner courtyard. A series of the imperial apartment pavilions on a raised platform overlooked the river.

"The British defeated the Emperor's forces in 1857 in the Indian uprising and ended the emperor's rule," James said.

"The damn British," Hank said.

Sally laughed and gave Hank a shove. "They sure exploited this country. When was India granted independence?"

"1947," James said. "Indian troops fought for the British in the Second World War."

"As did Australia," Hank said.

"My country, officially neutral, collaborated with the Nazis," Bridget added. "War is terrible. Sally tells me you were in Vietnam, James."

"Something I'm not proud of. I was drafted. I was at an artillery base so I didn't see much intense action."

"Let's go to the Jain temple," Sally said to change the subject. She could tell that James was turning morose with the talk of Vietnam. The call out in his sleep of 'no...no, I had no choice' had scared her at first, but she was getting used to it. She wished he was more forthcoming about Vietnam and his future plans.

"I don't know anything about the Jains," Bridget said. "I'm excited to see the temple."

They walked arm in arm through the crowded streets to the imposing Jain temple with its red, sandstone towering pyramid like towers.

James stopped and pointed at the shrine. "The main shrine contains a statue of Lord Mahavira, who was born in 599 BC. He was born a prince, but renounced worldly pleasures and went in search of enlightenment. He is considered the founder of Jainism."

"That sounds a lot like the story of Buddha," Bridget said.

"Jains seek enlightenment the same as Hindus and Buddhist. They follow non-violence and are strict vegetarians. Bounty is to be shared."

"Who came first Buddha or Mahavira?" Sally asked. Jainism seemed to her a more strict religion than Hinduism or Buddhism.

"I think Mahavira came first," James said. "Although they were contemporaries."

Sally wondered if Mahavira and Buddha were actually real people or myths. She wondered the same thing about Christ. She was quite the sceptic. So many different schools of thought on almost everything— religions, economics, political organizations and you name it. What a jumble?

They walked through the temples with their elaborately painted scalloped domed ceilings and arches and finely sculptured Jain saints.

"The paintings are so intricate and the statues are dazzling with all the gold leaf," Bridget said. "Their attention to detail is so precise."

They lingered in the temple studying the elaborate painted interiors before strolling out to the bird hospital where the temple complex received injured birds of all kinds and nursed them back to health to be released back into the wild.

"Oh James, this was great," Bridget said. "I like the Jains."

"Where to next?" Sally asked. She was irritated by Bridget's fawning over James. It didn't bode well. Of course Bridget was right, the Jains were very interesting.

Hank didn't seem to like the attention Bridget displayed toward James either. He grasped Bridget around the waist. "I'm thirsty as hell and getting hungry."

Bridget leaned back into Hank and rested her head on his shoulder. Sally was relieved that Bridget was still showing Hank affection. Still Bridget seemed to be beginning a play for James. She hoped she was mistaken, and it was just Bridget's way of being friendly.

"Lunch it is then," James said. "Let's walk down the road and see if we spy a good restaurant."

"Just down the road is Jama Masjid, India's largest mosque," James said as they were paying the bill at the small restaurant. "We should have a look. We don't have to go inside."

After several blocks the immense mosque came into view. The three onion shaped domes with their alternating red sandstone and white marble stripes shone brightly in the sunlight. The two towering minarets at each end of the front façade of arches were massive and rose over a hundred feet.

"This courtyard can hold twenty five thousand worshippers," James said. "If you want to go inside we'll have to rent robes and the ladies will have to wear scarves as well."

"Fuck that," Hank said.

"Doesn't sound appealing to me," Sally added. "It's getting even hotter. I'm dripping. Let's carry on."

"I would go inside with you, James," Bridget said, stepping toward James. "If you really want to."

Bridget had resolved that traveling paired with James would be much more enjoyable than Hank. Hank's aggression and brutish nature was getting her down. He was actually a bit of a boor, who had little interest in culture or art. He was a disappointing sex partner as well. James has a keen interest in art and liked learning new things. Would it be possible to switch partners? Didn't seem like an odds on possibility. Sally wouldn't go for it. It was obvious that James was infatuated with Sally. Sally was an interesting and captivating young lady. Not as educated in art as herself, but seemed to be an accomplished artist. Bridget's attempt to produce art had been mediocre. She didn't seem to have the impetus or patience.

Despite the poor odds of success, Bridget fantasized about how she could attract James away from Sally. Men were often easy lured into her web with the expectation of sex. She hadn't encountered any man in the past who she couldn't entice if she really put her mind to it. Perhaps taking James away from Sally was not the best move. She wanted to continue traveling across India and seeing the many attractions. Pursuit of James could blow up in her face and ruin her excursion. Was it worth the risk? Maybe... being near James made her so excited. The thought of being together with him was extremely inviting.

Sally slipped up and placed her arm around James, shuffling Bridget to the side. "It's too hot for robes and scarves."

Bridget was surprised by Sally's quick intervention. Maybe Sally sensed Bridget's infatuation. She suspected Sally was very intuitive. Maybe a little competition would make the traveling more exciting. She never winced at competition.

"I agree," James said and leaned into Sally before walking away with her. "We could go to the Lakshmi Narayan Temple, which is just down the street, or get a taxi to the National Museum. Or bail and go back to the hotel.”

“Hotel sounds good to me,” Hank said. “All these temples are interesting, but a lot to take in all at once.”

“Well, why not go to the Lakshmi Narayan Temple since we’re so close,” Bridget said. She wasn’t ready to fend off Hank or submit to his hurried idea of sex. “We don’t have to stay long.” She knew James with his keen interest in culture and art would want to go.

“There’s a big park associated with the temple,” James said. “We could relax there if need be.” He moved closer to Sally and bumped his hip against hers. “The museum would probably be too much for today. What do you think, Sally?”

Bridget watched James hip bump with jealousy. He was so attentive to Sally. She would relish experiencing the same attentiveness.

“I’m of two minds,” Sally said. “I’d like to relax. The hotel sounds inviting, but I suppose the temple would be the best. Then tomorrow we can go the museum and quit the sightseeing early so we’re well rested for the trip to Agra.”

“Okay— does that work for everyone?”

“Oh yes,” Bridget said, slinking up to Hank. “Come on Hank.” She took his arm. She’d keep Sally guessing what her intentions were toward James for now.

***

"This looks fairly new," Bridget said as they walked into the temple grounds."

"It was built in 1938 by a wealthy industrialist," James said. "It's dedicated to the Hindu goddess of wealth and prosperity, Lakshmi, and the god Narayan, the Preserver. Mahatma Gandhi inaugurated the temple and it is open to all castes."

"I like the carvings," Bridget said as she moved closer to James and placed her hand on his shoulder before staring up at the brilliant white marble carvings. "I can't wait to go inside. Why did you say it was open to all castes? Are there temples that are restricted to certain castes?"

"Most temples are forbidden to the Untouchables," James said.

"Really, how crude," Bridget replied.

"You're right there, mate." Sally added and led the group inside.

The temple interior displayed the boldly painted statues of Narayan and Lakshmi in their ornate gilt pavilions. "Lakshmi is the female counterpart of Vishnu and Narayan is an incarnation of Vishnu," James said. "He and Krishna are the often considered the same."

"The Hindus sure have a slew of these gods and goddesses," Hank said. "Christianity is so much simpler."

"You're right there, mate," Sally said and slapped Hank lightly on the back before moving in between Bridget and James. "Let's go back to the hotel and get some drinks at the restaurant next door. I could do with a smoke and a nap before dinner."

"Yeah, a smoke and a beer would be great," Hank said, and moved to take Bridget's hand.

Bridget sensed that James was flattered by her attentions toward him and knew he found her beautiful and sensuous. He had often gazed at her perfect golden body as she sun bathed in Goa. Maybe she needed to be a little more aggressive to make sure James understood her interest in him. Get him thinking about a possible liaison with her

***

"Oh James, I wonder if I could borrow your guide book for the night" Bridget asked as the four were sitting in the restaurant discussing the day's visits and what each liked the best out of the places they'd seen. They all had consumed a number of beers. Even she was slurring her words slightly. "It's a lot better than mine." She had decided that getting him alone so she could make a move on him was the best way to launch her enticement. Since he had consumed three beers, he might be more easily manipulated.

"Sure, no problem," James said.

Bridget lowered her eye lids slightly. "Can we get it now?" She rose. "I'd liked to start reading before dinner." She placed her hand on James's back.

"Sure," James replied and stood. Turning to Sally, he tapped his hand on her shoulder. "I'll be right back."

Sally stared at James squinting slightly. Bridget saw Sally's obvious jealousy, but paid it little mind. James hadn't seemed to notice, which was good. She damped down her rollicking anticipation so as not to appear too obvious.

"I think I'll read and take a nap," Bridget said, placing her hand on Hank's back.

Bridget walked with James up to his room, followed him inside, and closed the door behind her. James retrieved his guide book from the side table close to the bed and handed it to her.

"Thanks James," she said, then sat down on the bed, and started thumbing through the book. James, obviously surprised she hadn't left with the book, sat down on the bed also. She laid the book on the bed and pulled James to her. "Oh James I wish I was with you and not Hank." She kissed him. "I've always been drawn to you." She tried to kiss him again, but he pulled away.

"I'm sorry Bridget," he said and stood. "You are an intriguing and beautiful woman. If I wasn't with Sally, I would be happy to get to know you better."

"We have so much in common," she said and grabbed his hand to pull him back. "You're interested in art and culture like me. We would be good together."

"It wouldn't be fair to Hank or Sally."

"I don't care about them. Let them go off on their own. Hank is more interested in her than me anyway."

"They grew up together," James replied. "They're like brother and sister. Hank still seems infatuated with you to me. He doesn't want to go off with Sally." James went to the door and opened it, waiting for her to exit.

Unfortunately, her first attempt to woo James hadn't gone as well as she would have liked, but she had initiated her intentions and considered her actions a good first strike. She stood and walked away with a smile on her face.

***

Bridget wondered what her next actions to bring James closer to her should be. She needed to be cautious how she proceeded. James's rejection didn't deter her. She had considered that he was a man of conscience and might not fall for her first strike. His comment about her being intriguing and beautiful had gratified her. She understood his infatuation with Sally. What man wouldn't be? She found Sally quite alluring and wouldn't have minded a sexual relationship with Sally herself. She had had female lovers in Sweden. She had even had a liaison with Lisa in Goa to relieve herself after getting tired of her periodic masturbation. She relished sex and was longing for an exciting sexual union.

She and James really did have a lot in common. More so than Sally and him. She wondered if she was being stupid, but in reality she couldn't help herself. James was like a promising elixir to her. She wanted him so badly. She often grew tired of the men she was involved with. She liked the thrill of new sexual encounters. Considering the way James treated Sally, she knew he would be a caring lover. If she planned her maneuvers carefully, she believed she could at least entice him into a sexual dalliance. Maybe she could even take him completely away from Sally. She fully understood that Sally looked on Hank like a brother and wouldn't wish to leave James to go off with Hank. This was definitely an impediment to a partner switch, but the brotherly bond Sally held for Hank might mitigate the sting of losing James for Sally. If Bridget could pull James away from Sally, Sally would have no choice but to travel with Hank. That had been their plan when they left Australia.

***

They started their excursion through the National Museum early in the morning after a quick breakfast near their hotel and a taxi ride. Bridget, excited to be in the museum, waded ahead of everyone to the display cases. "The Harppan civilization began around 3,000 BC in the Indus Valley," Bridget announced to Hank as she read the plaque on the case of bronze articles. When the rest arrived to her side, she moved to the side of James. "Sweden was still in the stone age." She grabbed James's arm. "This is so cool." She reached for Hank. "This is great, isn't it?"

"Yeah," Hank said. "It's pretty cool."

As they moved through the museum, Bridget often took James's arm and engaged him in conversation, displaying her interest and appreciation of the art. Sally kept breaking them apart. It was obvious Sally was getting perturbed with her, but Bridget didn't relent. She had decided there was no going back— the game was on.

"Bronze tools, terra cotta figurines… absolutely amazing," Bridget said. She hurried ahead to the glass display case of the Nal pottery. "The craftsmanship of these pots are superb. Made on a pottery wheel. The red, black, and yellow colors are still vibrant."

Sally had taken James's arm and slowed their walk. Bridget knew Sally was trying to keep James away from her. When they came up to Bridget, Sally stared staidly at Bridget, then narrowed her eyes in an obvious fake smile. Bridget suspected Sally was signaling her that she understood what Bridget was attempting and was determined to get her to stop.

"The oldest polychrome pottery known," James said after consulting the plaque on the Nal pottery display case.

"Where was the Indus Valley?" Sally asked as she moved her hand across James's back. She was just as interested in art and culture as the Swede even if she didn't express it every time she turned around.

"It's in Pakistan. The Indus River flows from Tibet through Pakistan to the sea," James said. "The Indus Valley civilization included most of Pakistan, Eastern Afghanistan, and Northwestern India—contemporary with the Chinese Yellow Valley, Mesopotamia in the Middle East, and Ancient Egypt."

They continued on to the Mauyan Empire collection with its red and tan sandstone sculptures with refined features and fine bronze castings.

James opened his guide book. "The great Mauyan Emperor, Ashoka, controlled nearly all of India, Pakistan, and Eastern Afghanistan," he said. "He converted to Buddhism after a bitter war with the Kalinga Empire, which was along the eastern coast of India, in which over one hundred thousand soldiers died in 260 BC. Greatly saddened by all the death and destruction, he devoted his rule to the spread of Buddhism."

"Was his reign peaceful after his conversion?" Sally asked.

"Yes," James said. "He adopted nonviolence, and the arts flourished. Thousands of stupas and monasteries were built during his reign."

Sally made a note to find out more about Ashoka. He sounded interesting— a peaceful reign amidst all this history of war.

They continued through the museum to the Kushana collection. Kushana was an empire covering northern India and Afghanistan from the first to the third century AD. It's finely featured spotted red sandstone sculptures of voluptuous women were exquisite. Then they continued on to the ancient Gandaharan youthful Buddhist sculptures, and finally to the Gupta Art Collection where Indian art flourished in stylized depictions in the 3rd and 4th century.

Sally liked that the ancient Indians were upfront about sex in their art. The union of the male and female was to be celebrated as opposed to Christians, who believed Eve's seduction of Adam caused humanity's downfall. How absurd. Women were the life givers as the Hindu religion trumpeted. The voluptuous sculptures had caught the eyes of James and Hank. Neither she nor Bridget had anything near the stylized bodies of the sculptures with their round buxom breasts and fleshy bottoms. Did men prefer the voluptuous bodies? Why then did models have tall lanky bodies like Bridget?

Bridget slipped to James's side when Sally stopped to view a painting. "I never realized the extent of India art."

Sally sprang forward and took James's hand. Easy there Bridget. "Certainly a rich artistic history," she said as she maneuvered James away from Bridget. "I want to get a book with pictures of the major artifacts. I'd love to do a painting incorporating some of the more beautiful pieces." Bridget with her art history degree may be the better scholar, but she was the creative one.

"Let's go see the miniatures," Bridget said placing her arm around James's back and pulling him forward away from Sally.

Sally witnessed the exchange with a neutral face, but she was stewing inside. They needed to get out of the museum and back to the hotel. The Swede was unrelenting.

***

Sally stretched out in the first class train carriage to Agra and rested her head on James's shoulder. She planned to be on him today like glue. James was still more attentive to her, but the wily Swede was hard to ignore. The rhythmic swish of the train lolled her, and she closed her eyes, glad to be able to relax. After her brief nap, feeling renewed, she got up to use the rest room. When she came back, Bridget was ensconced in the seat next to James. Bridget had the guide book out and was talking about the Taj Mahal. Sally stopped and stared at the two momentarily, then took the empty seat next to Hank, her anger rising like a spouting geyser.

Sally leaned in toward Hank. "Is something going on with you and Bridget," Sally asked in a whispered voice.

Hank, who was slumped down in his seat, straightened, pushed his hat back, raised his eye brows, and pushed his lips out. "What do you mean," he said. "We're okay."

"Are you having sex?"

"Jesus, Sally," Hank replied, his face stretched.

"Come on," Sally said. "I've noticed that she hasn't been paying you the same attention she was in Goa and Udaipur."

"Well, I'm not sure, but I think she might be on the rag."

"What do you mean... not sure?" Sally said, lowering her head and voice even further. "You're in the same room." She nudged his arm with her elbow. "So you haven't had sex since Udaipur?"

Hank pushed his lips to the side and shook his head.

She knew it. Damn. "You need to be more romantic, mate." She nudged him again with her elbow, "You've got to woo her. You can't just take her for granted. Pay her compliments. Take more of an interest in the things she likes. More hugs and kisses... foreplay."

"Okay," he whispered angrily with a frown and turned his head away.

"I'm serious, you Big Lug." She shook her head, hoping her talk wasn't a waste of time. She grasped the seat in front and pushed her head over the seat. "So what are you guys talking about?"

James twisted around. "Just the places to see in Agra," he said. He seemed to be enjoying Bridget's interest with his big smile.

"Good, you can tell me all about it when we get there," Sally said and rose to stand next to Bridget. Get up you Swedish siren.

Bridget ignored Sally momentarily before she smiled at her, rose, and moved back to her seat. Sally raised her eye brows at Hank and nudged her head toward Bridget. Hank nodded with a scowl.

Hank was about as romantic as an old dish cloth. How could Hank not know if Bridget was menstruating? Talk about clueless. If Hank and Bridget weren't having sex, then no wonder Bridget was pursuing James.

***

The Taj Mahal gleamed like a precious jewel in the morning sun. The group were spellbound by the spectacular building as they stood gazing down the walkway and long rectangular pool that led to the mausoleum.

"What a view," Bridget said.

"Yeah mate, this is one beautiful building," Sally added before taking James's hand and pulling him forward, leaving Hank and Bridget behind. "Let's get closer. You can take pictures later." She needed to give Hank some space to rekindle his relationship with Bridget. What better place than the most beautiful building in the world.

"Okay, Sally, let's slow down," James said. "We're not in a hurry. We've got all day."

"You're right there," Sally said and slowed her pace before glancing back at Hank and Bridget, who were walking slowly hand in hand. Her little talk with the big lug looked like it was working. She smiled to herself. "So give me the history, Maestro."

"The Taj Mahal was built by Emperor Shah Jahan after the death of his third wife, who died in childbirth in 1631. The complex was completed in 1653."

"The white marble seems to glow and what beautiful inlay," Sally said. "It really is the most beautiful building."

"The Shah was madly in love with this wife and was heartbroken by her death. After he had the mausoleum built, he was over thrown by his son and was imprisoned in the Agra Fort where he supposedly gazed out at the Taj until his death."

"Nice son."

As they both stood contemplating the intricate scroll work and inlay of semiprecious stone, Bridget and Hank came up behind them. "I'm speechless," Bridget said. "It's perfect."

"Yes, absolute perfection," Sally replied. "Let's go inside."

Inside the interior walls were covered with the same style colorful inlay work. The false tombs surrounded by a perforated marble screen were set in the center of the dome that rose up over one hundred feet. The interior was dim, the only light coming from sunlight through the door and perforated scroll work at the entrance.

"I can't believe my friends are going to miss seeing this fantastic building," Bridget said.

"I'm not big on temples and monuments," Hank said, "but even I wouldn't have missed this."

"Good on you," Sally said. "Let's go back to the hotel we passed with the rooftop restaurant and have lunch. I bet the restaurant has a nice view of the Taj as well."

The afternoon sun was hot as they maneuvered through the crowded alley to the Benares guest house. The clouds drifted slowly overhead. The ride from Delhi had been the usual packed train. Hank had held the sea of Indians back in Delhi at the train door as the ladies and James ducked under his arm and dashed for seats as people came through the windows of the train. Their exit at the Benares station had been the familiar crush.

A young boy greeted them in the small lobby of their guest house and took them to their rooms, a ladies pack on each arm, chatting away, asking where they were from, how long they were staying, how they are liking India, and telling them Benares is the most holy city in India.

After they separated into their rooms, Bridget stowed her suitcase and left Hank in the room. He wasn't looking well and complained of a stomach ache. She went to Sally and James's room and knocked. "It's Bridget, can I come in."

James after a delay opened the door. "What's up?"

As soon as Bridget entered, she could tell she had interrupted them. The bed was ruffled and Sally's hair was in disarray. "I wanted to see your room and see if you had a great view like ours." Undeterred, she walked toward the balcony, and

James followed while Sally remained at the balcony door, her face contorted.

"The sun rise on the river will be spectacular," James said and glanced back at Sally, who was watching them intently.

Bridget's wish to get James alone out on the balcony and induce a kiss was not going to happen. "Yeah-yeah, sunrise should be wonderful," Bridget replied. "You picked a great hotel, James." She walked back into the room and smiled at Sally, who had changed her frown to a pseudo smile. "Hank was going to take a quick shower, and then we were going to go up to the rooftop restaurant for lunch that is if he's all right. He was complaining of a stomach ache. I hope those meat filled chapattis he ate on the train aren't going to cause him problems. You guys going to join us?"

"Of course," Sally said and moved to Bridget. "Why don't you go back and surprise Hank in the shower." She placed her hand on Bridget's back and ushered her toward the door. "We'll be up in about thirty minutes."

Bridget stood outside the door for a few seconds listening, but could not hear their conversation clearly through the door. Bridget knew Sally was irritated with the attention Bridget was showing James, but she had no intention of stopping her pursuit. She had successfully repulsed Hank since Udaipur, claiming she was menstruating, which had some truth for a while. She couldn't maintain the ruse for long.

She had tolerated sex with Hank in the beginning and was content with the arrangement as long as it allowed her to travel with the group, but her increasing infatuation with James had soured any affection she felt for Hank. Even though she felt a little sorry for Hank, she wasn't going to stop her pursuit of James. Whenever, she gazed into his eyes it was like getting lost in the amber and multicolor hues of his hazel eyes, traveling along a sumptuous tunnel of desire. She was sure the interest she was showing James was working to increase his interest in her. She felt his acquiesce and surrender to her was just a matter of time.

When she returned to their room, the stench from Hank's trip to the bathroom hit her as soon as she opened the door. She could hear Hank in the bathroom moaning. His eating of street food and resulting diarrhea had presented her with a convenient opportunity. She could be with James and Sally without having to pay attention to Hank and consequently devote more attention to James. She was surprised at how horrible Hank looked when he came out of the bathroom, his face white and drawn. She felt a hint of regret that she was trying to ditch him. In many ways, the big guy had made her trip to India so much better. Nevertheless, her desire to be with James consumed her like a raging fire.

"Jesus, I've got the shits something terrible," Hank said. He grabbed his stomach. "What's their room like?"

"Same as ours. We're going to go up to the rooftop restaurant for lunch. Were you thinking of coming?"

"I... oh no." He grit his teeth and rushed back into the bathroom, not even bothering to close the door. The sound of his evacuation was loud and the smell was awful.

"I'll leave you to it then," Bridget called. "I probably won't be back until later."

"Okay," he weakly called and moaned as another evacuation hit him.

She was glad to exit the room— the overpowering smell made her gag. She went up to the restaurant, breathed in the outdoor air, selecting a table with a nice view of the river, and ordered a beer. With Hank out of commission, she had free reign to try and get James alone. Sally would undoubtedly try to prevent this. She ran through various scenarios in her mind that would allow her to be alone with James. If successful, she would waste no time in seducing him.

***

After lunch on the scenic rooftop café of various curries and cold beers, where Bridget focused on James like a cat ready to pounce on its prey, the three made a quick visit to Hank. As soon as they entered the room, they all dropped their heads and pulled their hands to their nose.

"Hank, we're going to walk to the Dashashwameth Ghat," Bridget called. "You think you're able to come with.

"Fuck, no way."

"Okay, I'll be back later." Bridget turned to Sally and James, squinting from the smell, and pushed them out the door. "Looks like a bad bout," Bridget said hooking arms with Sally and James. "Too bad. He saw all the others on the train eating those horrid stuffed chapattis and couldn't help himself."

"Yeah, he can be very impulsive, often to his own detriment," Sally added.

They went outside and wove their way down the alley crowded with people, cows, goats, garbage, and plethora of feces, shooing away the flies, breathing through their mouths to avoid the stink, ignoring the pervasive beggars until they reached the Dashashwameth Ghat, one of the largest Ghats on the river. James wanted to see the famous Ghat in the daylight in order to make sure they could find it for the evening fire ceremony.

The Ghat steps were crowded as the many bathers walked down the wide steps to submerse themselves in the sacred river, hoping to remove their bad karma. A small, shikhara style, tan temple rose up from the back of the Ghat plaza where many devotees made their prayers before going to the river. Hawkers at the souvenir tables engulfing the sides of the plaza called out to them.

A number of sadhus in their orange and saffron costumes were bathing in the murky water amongst the women in colorful saris and men in their white dhotis, all making their prayers, submersing in the water, disappearing briefly from view. Bridget was stunned by the number of bathers and felt a brief desire to bath in the river.

"Are you going to bathe in the Ganges, James?" Bridget asked, interrupting his reflections with a hand to his shoulder.

"Not today anyway," he replied.

"Me neither," Bridget said. She was glad it wasn't so hot this time of year, or she might have been tempted. She thought the idea of ritual bathing in a sacred river as a purification a meaningful ritual. In Christianity baptism with water was used as an ablution. The Greeks considered bathing an essential purification.

"You'll not get me in that polluted river," Sally said. "All the sewage and crap on the streets and alleys just flows into the river. Plus all the ash from the dead bodies. I don't think it would be very therapeutic. We could end up like Hank."

"He's pretty bad," Bridget said. "I warned him about eating those chapattis filled with god knows what."

"Big mistake," Sally said. "Poor guy."

"I feel bad leaving him on his own," Bridget said. She hoped her face did not belie her statement.

They stayed for a while on the steps, watching the bathers and fending off the hawkers, who were trying to sell them boat rides or trinkets and the army of beggars, many with shocking ailments that continued to amaze Bridget. Medical care in India seemed to be a luxury only the well to do could access.

"What do you guys think about a boat ride?" Bridget asked. "It would be a good way to see all the Ghats and orient ourselves."

"Yeah, we could get him to drop us off near our hotel after, so we don't have to crush through all the people, cows, and beggars in the alleys to get back," Sally said.

"Okay, I'll see what kind of deal I can make." James walked down among the boatmen and, after lively bargaining, waved. "Come on."

The ride down the river was relaxing as they passed the many Ghats with the colorful steps, temples, hotels rising behind, and numerous bathers. All seemed a little dilapidated. The colorful saris of the women bathers contrasted with the muddy, brown water. They passed several Ghats where funeral pyres were burning the dead.

James consulted his guide book. "To be cremated on the banks of the Ganges in Benares is considered the ultimate Hindu funeral and supposedly liberates you from rebirth." He glanced at the blazing fires momentarily. "The ashes are allowed to smolder for three days before they are emptied into the sacred river. It takes a lot of wood to properly incinerate a body. Sandalwood is considered the ultimate wood for cremation, but it's incredibly expensive. Most just get a few shavings to add to the pyre."

"When I die I want to be cremated," Bridget said. "I think burial is a waste of land. I think the Hindu way of cremation is rather antiquated, but I understand the tradition."

The boatman took them all the way down to the Harishehandra Ghat, one of the last cremation Ghats, and then back up past the Dashashwameth Ghat to the Manikarnika Ghat, considered the most sacred cremation Ghat.

"They sure burn a lot of bodies here," Bridget said as she exited the boat. She could feel the heat of all the fires.

"It's the most auspicious and most expensive Ghat for cremation," James said. "The people who handle the bodies are called doms and are considered outcasts."

"What a job," Sally said. "Considering the importance they give to death, you'd think the doms would be revered. Not a job I would like."

"No," Bridget replied. "The boat ride was interesting and sad at the same time. I felt strange being around all the dead people." She paused and watched the cremation fires. She found Hinduism fascinating but thought the cremation enterprises in Benares excessive and quite polluting. She exhaled deeply and sucked in a breath with a shudder. "I better go back and see how Hank's doing."

"He's probably still on the toilet," Sally said.

"Now, now," James replied. "Let's not be mean."

"How do you get mean from that?" Sally said. "I'm just stating fact." She bumped her hip against James. "Just kidding."

***

They all visited Hank when they got back to the hotel. Hank was lying in bed shivering despite the heat.

"You don't look good," Sally said, sitting down on the bed and feeling his forehead. "You've got quite a fever."

"Should we take him to the hospital?" Bridget said.

"No way," Sally said. "You don't want to go to the hospital in India."

Sally explained that they had talked to a young man, who had gone to a hospital with the runs, ended up with hepatitis, and almost died. Proper sterilization and hygiene in Indian hospitals was almost nonexistent according to the young man. James's uncle had also told them to avoid the Indian hospitals if possible.

"Sally's right," James added. "I've got some aspirin. That should bring down his fever. I'll go get some soft drinks. He's lost a lot of fluid."

After James left, Bridget turned to Sally. "Maybe if I went and got some Pepto Bismo or something like it, it would help."

"Couldn't hurt."

***

Bridget found a chemist and was able to buy Pepto Bismo. When she returned Sally was gone, and James was sitting on the other bed encouraging Hank to drink the soft drink he had brought. She sat down on Hank's bed and got him to take a spoonful of the pink liquid. Hank expounded on how horrible it tasted, causing her and James to chuckle. She gave James a knowing wink. "I hope this helps some. Where's Sally?"

"She went to take a shower."

As Bridget discussed the boat trip, the cremation Ghats, and her feeling that burning so many bodies and dumping them in the river was terribly polluting, she hoped her raging desire was apparent in her face as she focused on James. He seemed to be watching her intently. She could feel her desire building like a thunderstorm.

When Hank slowly slipped into sleep, she put her finger to her lips and rose, taking James's hand and lifting him up. The confused expression on his face was charming as she pulled him into the bathroom, continuing to admonish him to silence with her finger to her lips. She closed the door silently, pulled James to her, and kissed him deeply. When he did not resist, she began unbuttoning his shirt. He placed a hand on her arm but didn't use enough force to stop her. She continued to kiss him and opened her shirt, squashing herself against him rubbing her bare breasts against his chest. His eyes expanded with obvious desire.

She removed her trousers and underwear and knelt down to remove his trousers. She sensed his reluctance despite his obvious arousal. She needed to act fast. She squatted down, pulling him with her, and laid back on the cool tiles grasping his erect penis and inserting it into herself. Their coupling was quick and, she clasped him too her with vigor as he climaxed. The guilt of what he had done was visible in his face, and he rose grabbing his head. She got up and pulled him to her, but he put his hands on her chest and shook his head.

When he turned on the shower and moved into the spray, she joined him and attempted to engage him in a standing copulation. He repulsed her, swiftly finished his shower, and left the bathroom. She heard him exit the room as she continued her shower, feeling ecstatic about their interlude, despite the quickness and his obvious guilt. Finally she had succeeded. The sex was hectic but a valuable strike. Even though she knew James was feeling guilty about the sex, she had broken through his resistance. She would bide her time, continue to engage James in conversation, and stay close to him until the next opportunity presented itself. She believed his memory of her body and her continued pressure would eventually bring James totally to her. Then she and James could go off together, leaving Sally to Hank.

24- HINDU KUSH MOUNTAINS: FEBRUARY 1, 1970

In the morning at first light, James rose shivering, roused the rest, and drove off for Bamyan. The road became even worse with immense pot holes and boulders. Often Harry had to get out and direct the navigation around large rocks and other obstacles when they were near the precipitous drop offs down the mountain. The villages were small, and they saw very few people out and about. They drove down into Bamyan in the afternoon. The fertile valley with its shimmering lake, was back dropped by the brown cliffs north of the city where the towering carved Buddhas stood in their alcoves absorbing the bright sun.

They asked in a few shops of the small town for Mahmood, but to their dismay were dismissed abruptly.

"Looks like we were sent here on a wild goose chase," James said. "We can go back to the village where they were selling the hash and talk again to the man that sent us here. He might know more than he let on."

"No," Sally exclaimed. She didn't exactly know why she was adamant they should continue searching in Bamyan. "Please, let's try some other places."

Her vehemence seem to surprise James. Sally felt it was necessary at least to talk to this Mahmood character. He must be somewhere in Bamyan.

Finally, after several more dead ends, one of the shopkeepers, an old man, who squinted at them and spoke broken English, wanted to know why they sought Mahmood. After explaining they had been told to seek Mahmood to find their Australian friend, they were directed to a compound on the outskirts of the city.

Sally felt vindicated that they had finally been directed to Mahmood. She spurred the group onward, praying that it wouldn't be another dead end.

The walled compound had large, solid-metal gates painted blue with a small door in one of the gates. After knocking repeatedly, the door opened and a boy appeared. James attempted English, but the boy just stared back at him. He switched to sign language by pointing to his eye repeatedly and saying Mahmood. The boy nodded and shut the door. After several minutes, the boy reappeared and beckoned them into the large compound. There was a sizable mud brick home at the back of the compound and several out buildings. A few goats roamed around the open courtyard and a group of blue turbaned men, sitting against one of the walls, drinking tea, their rifles propped against the wall, stared with stark expressions as the group crossed the yard.

The boy ushered the group into the house and led them through a long hallway into a large room with a multitude of deep red Turkmen carpets spread on the floor, multi-colored applique wall hangings, and a decoratively-painted, beamed ceiling. The boy indicated with extended hand that they should sit. A heavy-set man in a dark blue turban and matching embroidered robe with a neatly trimmed beard and piercing dark eyes was sitting on a raised platform at the back of the room behind a small table, watching them intently.

Sally was beside herself, but remained quiet, not wishing to offend this undoubtedly important Afghan on his raised platform as if on a stage, who she assumed was Mahmood. She desperately hoped that this man could help them find Hank.

The man said in surprising good English, "Salam, welcome to my home. What may I do for you?"

"Our friend, Hank, was taken prisoner in a village north of Charikar," James said. "We were told he had insulted a man over some dealings for hashish. We looked in the village for our friend, but could not find him. The man at the house where he was taken told us our friend had been removed to Bamyan. He suggested we go to Bamyan and ask for Mahmood."

Mahmood had listened carefully nodding often. "I am Mahmood, and I know nothing of this. I doubt that your friend was brought to Bamyan." He sipped his tea. "There is little that goes on in Bamyan that I do not know about." His serious expression changed to a smile. "I am happy that you have come to my beautiful village. It is a very famous village, and you are most welcome. Is your friend, Hank, an American like yourself?"

"No, Hank is Australian," James said and placed his hand on Sally's shoulder. "Sally, who grew up with Hank, is Australian." He indicated Harry. "Harry is from England." He extend his arm toward Bridget. "Bridget is Swedish." Then indicated Monica. "Monica is Swedish also, and I am James."

"I am pleased to meet all of you," Mahmood said. "It is most pleasant to meet young people together from so many different countries. I am sorry to hear of your friend's abduction." He reared back and took a drink of tea. "Miss Sally, is this Mister Hank your brother?"

Sally surprised to be addressed directly looked to James, who nodded. "No, his mother and father died when he was young, and my family took him in. He is like a brother to me."

"I see. Miss Sally, I must say your red hair and green eyes are most unusual. You are a beautiful young lady as are all you young ladies. I am pleased that you have graced my humble abode. I have traveled extensively and have never met another women with such rich red hair and green eyes. I feel blessed to meet you all." He paused and stared at Sally before straightening in his seat. "I will make enquiries about the whereabouts of your friend. I am well known, and many men owe me allegiance." He leaned forward, placing his hands on the small table, and studied the group in silence that seemed interminable.

Sally wanted to break the silence, but held her tongue. She slipped her hand into James's. She didn't know how to take Mahmood's compliments. They had actually scared her a little. Mahmood finally motioned toward the boy, who bent down to hear Mahmood's whispered instructions, then hurried from the room.

"Please be my guests for this evening," Mahmood said. "I will send my men out to make enquiries about the whereabouts of your friend. God willing, I hope to have some news tomorrow morning for you."

The boy returned, and whispered to Mahmood. Mahmood nodded. "Mohammed," he said, indicating the boy, will show you to your quarters." Mahmood spoke to Mohammed in his native tongue and smiled as Mohammed led them out. "Relax and do not worry. I will get to the bottom of this. We will talk again in the morning."

They were shown to a room through a series of corridors where they were to sleep and eat. The room was small and several rugs were placed on the floor, but there were no beds. A small wood stove in the corner kept the room somewhat tolerable. In the evening, they were served a goat stew with bread and rice and offered handmade hash.

Sally was beside herself and ate little. "What could have happened?" she said and burst into tears. She had hoped Hank would be here. He could be anywhere if even still alive. She didn't trust this smooth Mahmood, but what could she do. How had things gotten so screwed up? "Jesus, James, what are we going to do?"

James put his arm around Sally. "We will have to wait until morning and see what Mahmood has learned." He rubbed her back. "He seems to be the head man in the area. He was quite taken with you. Hopefully he will have some news of Hank in the morning."

"What if Mahmood says he doesn't know anything?" Sally said before standing and walking around the room. "Those damn Americans never showed. We don't even know the full story of what really happened."

"There's nothing Bud and Sam could add," Monica said. She rose and approached Sally. "I'm scared too for Hank."

"Hopefully, Mahmood will find out something," Bridget said. "Why would anyone want to keep Hank?"

"Who the hell knows," Sally shouted, brushing past Monica and dropping down next to James.

"Sally, we're all worried," Bridget said. "There's nothing else to do but wait."

Sally stared at Bridget. Easy for you to say you betraying hag. They could kill poor Hank. He may be a pain in the ass sometimes, but she loved him like a brother.

They bedded down for the night on the rugs and no one slept much. The room became increasingly colder as the night progressed, the small wood stove having gone out. The heavy sheep skin blankets they were given were warm, but Sally shivered nevertheless. James held Sally all night. In the morning, Mohammed relit and stoked up the wood stove, which mitigated the bitter cold of the room somewhat.

Sally wanted to see Mahmood as soon as possible, but her questions to Mohammed were answered with shakes of his head. Later they were served a breakfast of meat and vegetable stuffed pastries. Finally Mohammed reappeared, ushered them to the graciously warm grand room, and indicated for them to sit. The raised platform was empty much to Sally's dismay. She grabbed James arm to damp down her impatience.

After a few minutes, Mahmood entered from a door in the back wall of the platform. He nodded and took a seat on the cushions behind the small table and smiled. "Good morning, I hope you slept well and enjoyed your breakfast."

"Thank you for your hospitality," James said.

"I imagine you are anxious to hear what I have learned about your friend." Mahmood raised his hand. Mohammed rushed to the small table and poured Mahmood a glass of tea and then came down and poured a glass of tea for each of the group. When everyone had tea, Mahmood placed his hands on his table and leaned forward. "Your friend, Mister Hank, is still alive." He paused and took a drink of tea. "But as I suspected, he is not in Bamyan. He is being held somewhere in the mountains by the hash-sellers. I will endeavor to find out his exact location, and what the hash-sellers want. I suspect they are holding him for ransom to make up for the insult one of them received." He leaned back. "I would suggest returning to Kabul. I will contact you when I have more information. What is the name of your hotel?"

"Shaheed," James replied.

"Yes, I know it well," Mahmood said, nodding. "I cannot promise anything, but I will do my best on your behalf." Mahmood clapped his hands and Mohammed poured them more tea. "The standing Buddhas of Bamyan are fantastic sculptures to behold. You must visit these important sculptures. Bamyan was once a Buddhist pilgrimage location, and learned men from around the world came to visit. It was an important stop on the Silk Road to China. Please enjoy this beautiful valley before returning to Kabul." He extended his arm toward them, and Mohammed went to stand beside them. "Mohammed will show you out. Please be assured that I will contact you at your hotel in Kabul when I have more information. This may take some time." He placed his hand on his heart. "Go with God."

***

The days waiting for word in Kabul seemed endless. The foreboding amongst the group could be cut with a knife as they lost themselves in the hashish smoke. Sally became more morose with each passing day. James's frantic call outs in his fitful sleep didn't help her mood. She knew his war nightmares were back with a vengeance.

"I can't take much more of this waiting," Sally said as they were sitting around the stove in the larger hotel room. "We need to do something. We should go back and talk to this Mahmood again. It's been over a week. He must know more than he let on. How else would he know that Hank was alive?"

"I'm not sure that would be such a good idea," James said. "Men like Mahmood put a lot of stock in their word. He might take our return as an affront. Losing face is anathema to them."

"Exactly right," Harry said. "I'd recommend giving it at least a few more days."

"Well, we could go back to the village where it all happened," Bridget said.

"I'm not sure that's a good idea either," James said. "It would probably get back to Mahmood."

"What the hell was this insult, Monica?" Sally asked. "What could be so bad that they would take Hank?"

"I don't know," Monica said. "They were discussing price and quality of the hash in the first room. Hank wanted to see the different types, so he and two men left the room. Then one of the men came back with a rifle and shouted out and began waving the gun at us."

"They must have said something?"

"The man with the gun kept shouting a word in the native language, and the other man, who told us to go see Mahmood, said 'bad insult... you must go'. He seemed scared too."

"Jesus, how could it get so fucked up?" Sally said and collapsed. "Hank, you idiot, what did you do?"

James tried to comfort her as best he could. Sally ran through horrible scenarios in her head. What if they killed him? How could she ever face her brother and family? How long could they wait for Mahmood to find Hank? She felt she should be doing something.

The group assuaged their fear and distress with continued rounds of the chillums. The young man, who kept the fire going in the big room and brought them tea, would often exclaim as he entered the room, waving his hand at the ubiquitous smoke, "Too much hashish. Not good."

To which Harry always replied, "Yes… hashish very good."

Sally partook of the hashish and welcomed the calming effect that kept her from nearly going insane with worry. Each morning Sally hoped there would be word from Mahmood. The end of the second week, Harry came to James's room early in the morning and said there was a man downstairs asking for him. They both went downstairs. Sally remained in bed.

When James returned to the room, he said, "Mahmood sent this note asking us to return to Bamyan" He held up the note. "It's in excellent English script."

Sally shot out of bed. "Let's go then."

***

"Thank you for returning," Mahmood announced. "I am sorry that you had to travel here again, but I thought you would appreciate what I have to tell you in person rather than in a note." He clapped his hands and tea was brought.

Sally was beside herself. She wanted to jump up and shout at Mahmood. James took her hand and squeezed gently. She knew she had to sit quietly while the men discussed the situation. All so civilized.

Mahmood waited until they each had a drink of tea then continued. "We have located your friend. Apparently, Hank insulted one of the men he was going to buy hashish from by grabbing this man with his left hand and calling him a cheat." He paused to observe the reaction of the group. "This is a grave insult. Touching someone with one's left hand is unforgivable. Luckily, I have interceded, and they have not unduly harmed him, but to save face they are requiring payment."

James looked at Sally then Harry. "Okay," he said. "What payment is required and how do we make the payment?"

"I would be pleased to be your intermediary. If you pay in dollars, the ransom would be five hundred dollars." He paused and drank his tea until his glass was half empty before setting the glass on the table in front of him. The young man immediately refilled his glass holding the glass and tea pot a large distance apart and moving the pot up and down. "This is a small sum compared to the insult given."

"Well, I think we can get that amount together," James said. "Will you accept traveler's checks?"

"I'm sorry to say that traveler's checks would not be acceptable to these men." He again began sipping his tea. "You can easily exchange the checks in Kabul at the money changers for a fee. Not a large fee. Probably around five percent. They will ask for ten percent, but you should be able to bargain for the five percent. I would avoid the banks."

"We'll go back to Kabul and get the money," James said. "Hopefully we can return tomorrow."

"I must warn you that the men, who are holding your friend, are not patient men." He sipped his tea, and his glass was filled as soon as he set it down. "If they were my men, there would be no ransom. Unfortunately, these men do not owe me allegiance, but do respect my position."

"Thank you for your help," James said. He finished his tea and stood. "We will return as soon as possible with the money."

Sally rose with James's help. She bowed to Mahmood and gave him a lingering stare. She had a litany of questions she wanted to ask, but knew she was expected to remain silent. How had Hank got himself in such a dire situation? Her journey that she had hoped would allow her to solidify her relationship with James now seemed doomed.

"Until we meet again," Mahmood said. "Please remember that we Afghans are proud men. Reputation is very important to us. What your friend did could have easily cost him his life." He paused and took another sip of tea. "Go with God."

***

"Can you believe the nerve of that guy," Sally said when they were alone back in their hotel room. "Five hundred bucks. I don't have that kind of money to spare. Hank knows that in this part of world touching someone with your left hand, the hand you wipe with, is an insult. How could he be so stupid?"

"Don't worry, I'll pay the ransom. I could have paid it on the spot if they would have accepted travelers' checks." He joined her on the bed, placed his hands on the back of her shoulders, and massaged her back and neck. "The ransom will put a dent in my traveling money, but there is nothing else to do." He smoothed her hair and kissed her cheek. "We'll change the checks in the morning and go back up tomorrow."

"What if they take the money and don't release Hank?"

"I don't think Mahmood would do that."

"You trust that son of a bitch?"

"In fact I do." He let out a rush of air between his pursed lips. "Reputation and a man's word are sacrosanct to a man like Mahmood."

"Yes, but someone else has Hank." She wiped her tears. "They could take the money, then later ask for more. They could bleed us dry. Mahmood may be in on it."

"Mahmood could have taken us all prisoners for that matter and taken all our money," James said

"We should go to the police."

"I wouldn't advise it."

Sally got up and rushed down the hall to the bathroom. She threw up repeatedly. After splashing water on her face, she glanced into the mirror and started crying.

When she came out of the bathroom, James was standing outside looking woeful. She was thankful that James wasn't falling apart like her. She wished she could be stronger, but the waiting was like a cancer eating away at her. "I need to lie down."

James escorted her back to the room, helped her disrobe, and eased her into bed. "I'll go see if I can get some broth from the restaurant for you." He felt her forehead. "You have a fever. Just relax and try to sleep."

"That damn Hank. He can be so stupid sometimes."

"I have a good feeling about this. Don't worry. We'll get out of this."

Yeah, right. He may have a good feeling, but she was scared to death. Yes, we'll probably get out of this, but will Hank.

Bridget, James, and Sally hired a boat to the Dashashwameth Ghat for the burning ceremony on the advice of the guest house receptionist, who told them that they would be able to see a lot better from a boat. When they arrived at the Ghat, there were already quite a few boats floating with tourists in front of the Ghat.

Hank had remained in his room during their dinner on the roof. Bridget had been friendly to Sally, telling her how Hank was doing and discussing the Hindu religion. Her friendliness and her bright smile added to Sally's suspicions that something happened between Bridget and James. Bridget was mooning over James even more than previously, and James was acting funny, almost embarrassed. It was strange that James took a shower in Hank's room because he didn't want to wake her from her nap. If he had come to the room to check on her, she hadn't heard him.

"Oh, here they come," Bridget said, sitting behind Sally and James, leaning over James's shoulder.

It was cooler on the river and the hotel was right— they could see well. The priests on their daises, facing the river, began their chanting, conch blowing, and fire lamp gyrations. At the end of the ceremony, many people sent the little candle lights in remembrance of loved ones floating down the river in a spectacular display.

"This is so cool," Bridget said. "What is the ceremony for?"

"It's a dedication to Lord Shiva, the River Ganga, the Sun, and Fire," James said.

Sally suspected that Bridget already knew the purpose of the ceremony. Bridget's fawning was driving her mad. She need to be on her guard and more attentive to James to counteract Bridget's actions.

The boatman when it was his turn took them back up the river to the brown stepped Lalita Ghat, the Ghat closest to their hotel with its Mughal like temples either side.

James helped Bridget from the boat. "Lalita was a consort of Shiva and is considered the embodiment of female power and beauty," he said. After he helped Sally disembark he placed his arm around her and pulled her to him. "Lalita reminds me of you except Lalita has four arms."

"I'll give you four arms," Sally said slamming her shoulder into his chest. "Power and beauty I'll accept." She grabbed him around the waist. "Come on let's all go see how Hank's doing,"

At Hank's room, Sally followed Bridget inside. "Hey, Hank. How's it going?" Sally said with as much jocularity as she could muster. She was still stewing over what Bridget and James might have been up to.

"I'm feeling a lot better," Hank replied. He was sitting up in bed reading Bridget's Ginsburg Indian poems. "I may even try to eat something in the morning."

"That's great," Sally said "Well then, we'll leave you and Bridget in peace." She was surprised to see Hank reading poems. Maybe Hank had taken her harangues to heart. "Give us a knock when you go up for breakfast." Sally ushered James out of the room.

"Goodnight," James called as Sally pushed him into the hallway.

***

Sally grabbed James in their room as he started for the bathroom and held him at arm's length, studying his face. "Don't be long in there, mate." She thought for sure she saw some consternation as he smiled weakly.

"I'll be right out," he said and continued into the bathroom.

Sally wondered if James's shower at Hank's room might have been a means to hide an encounter of some sort. She had been asleep long enough for anything to have happened. If so, what could she do about it? Even though her jealous anger was like a raging bull, shouting at James and accusing him of betrayal wouldn't solve the situation. James was still with her. She had tolerated Bridget's infatuation and even James interest, but a possible sexual engagement between them was outside the bounds of tolerance. She didn't want to overreact and drive

James away. Continuing on with only Hank would be abhorrent. Maybe she should forget about the damn shower and what it might have entailed, and instead use her guile to keep James tied to her— pull out all the stops and give James a night to remember.

***

"Let's walk to the Golden Temple," James suggested after breakfast at the guest house. "It's not far from here. It's dedicated to Vishwanath, Shiva as Lord of the Universe. It has gold plating on the tower and dome." His smile couldn't have been bigger. Sally knew he had enjoyed the escapades last night as much as she had.

Hank perked up. "Gold... I'll come too," he said. He had joined them for breakfast and had a small portion of rice. He was a little drawn, but seemed in good spirits. "I'm feeling a lot better."

Sally was impressed that Hank was continuing to show interest in their explorations. She hoped now that he was feeling better that he could rekindle Bridget's interest in him and stop Bridget's relentless pursuit of James.

"Vishwanath...that's a new name," Bridget said. "How do they keep them all straight?"

"Who knows... maybe the average Hindu doesn't. The various names represent different aspects of the deity." James started for the hotel lobby door "Brahman is the ultimate reality or God."

"I find it confusing too," Sally said, following James outside. "I thought Brahma was the Lord of the Universe."

James stood outside, waiting until the entire group had joined him. "Brahman and Brahma are different. As you said, Brahma is the Lord of the universe and the creator deity, who brought forth Vishnu and Shiva. Very few temples are dedicated to Brahma, and he is not often worshipped. Then there are avatars, which are the deities' incarnations on earth— 24 for Vishnu and 21 for Shiva. Some of the famous ones are Rama, Krishna, and Narayana for Vishnu. For Shiva there is Sharabh, Durvasa, and Hanuman."

"I thought Greek Mythology was hard to keep straight, but the Hindus have made an art out of the different names and incarnations," Bridget said, moving to the side of James. "Religion in Sweden has lost its appeal. It is amazing how Hinduism is so suffused in Indian society."

Bridget the scholar. Well Sally could expound also. "Seems to me that if you're cremated here in Benares and are automatically released and enlightened that most Hindus would want to bring their failing loved ones here," Sally said.

"If most could afford it, they probably would come here to die," James replied, grabbed Sally's hand, and started off down the alley.

"Wow, could you imagine all the people in India coming here to die," Hank said as he took Bridget's hand. "It's physically impossible. Seems that this release from rebirth from just being cremated here is a kind of bypass to the whole Hindu religion." He laughed. "This is one crazy country."

***

"So that's real gold," Hank said as they stood in front of the Golden Temple. "Damn, that's a hell of a lot of gold."

"When was the temple built?" Bridget asked.

"The present temple without the gold plating was first built in 1780," James said. "The gold plating was added in 1835. One ton of gold was used for the plating."

"Imagine the value of all that gold," Hank said.

"Yeah, no kidding," James replied. "Let's see… gold's about $40 an ounce." He stood a moment musing. "A ton would then be worth over a million dollars."

Hank whistled. "Man, that's a ton of money." He laughed. "Imagine what that would buy."

"Way to calculate in your head, mate," Sally said. "I would go for just a small square of that gold." She grabbed James's hand and pulled him through the crowd at the gate to proceed inside and up to the central sculpture. "Another big dick," she whispered to James and slipped her arm around his waist. James smiled at her and grabbed her arm pulling it tight around him. Sally closed her eyes and breathed in. Maybe she was mistaken about any impropriety between James and Bridget. He didn't seem to be paying Bridget any undue attention today. He had been a dynamo last night.

"This temple is considered one of the most holy of Hindu temples," James said. "Many great sages have visited."

"It's certainly impressive," Bridget said as she moved toward James.

"Yes, it was well worth a visit," Sally said as she grabbed James's arm and pulled him away from Bridget toward the exit. As she maneuvered her way through the arriving crowd, she noted the number of entering Western youths. Benares sure attracted them. Many living on the streets or in the numerous flea bag hotels looked destitute. Most were probably searching for something greater than themselves in the mystery of the Hindu religion— existing on their meager savings or relying on generosity of others. Some were obviously college types like themselves, possibly searching as well or just visiting in order to learn about different cultures. She had certainly learned an immense amount about Indian culture and wanted to continue the learning with James. She wasn't going to let Bridget interfere with the continuation.

26- KATHMANDU: DECEMBER 13, 1969

Sally hugged James as she stood outside the minibus that had taken them from the border to Kathmandu. "Thanks for bringing us here. I thought the journey from Benares would never end. But it was well worth it. The air in Kathmandu smells so clean and fresh after all the pollution in India."

They had left Benares for Gorakhpur, the last train station before the Nepalese border, early in the morning, hoping that the train might be less crowded. No such luck. They had gotten seats in a second class carriage thanks to Hank holding the crowd back.

"Yeah and it's not so hot," Hank announced. "Let's get some of that black Nepalese hash."

A boy, who overhead them, approached them. "Gentlemen and ladies, I can take you to a good shop for excellent hashish," he said.

"Lead on, mate," Hank said. "Good English."

The boy smiled and bowed, then led them to a busy street of shops selling arts and crafts. The street was thronged with young Westerners and Nepalese walking at a leisurely pace.

Hank was pleased by the lack of squashed crowds and innumerable beggars. He was going to like Kathmandu. He and James each bought several round black balls of hash, stone chillums, and tobacco. Just outside the shop men were smoking chillums. The fragrant hash filled the air as they strolled away.

The boy led them to a street where many Westerners were walking about. "Freak Street," the boy said. "Many fine hotels. Many hippies here."

"Take your pick ladies," Hank said.

"Let's see if we can find one with private bathrooms," Sally suggested.

After visiting several hotels, they chose a hotel that seemed more upscale and acquired two rooms.

***

As the four smoked a chillum in Hank's and Bridget's small room, each bed against the wall leaving only a small space to walk between the beds, they each professed their joy of being in Nepal. The room's bathroom had an in-the-floor toilet that you flushed with a bucket of water and an open shower that washed into the toilet. After savoring several chillums of the strong hashish, James and Sally retreated to their room.

Hank moved to Bridget's bed. "I'm gonna like Nepal." He placed his arm around Bridget and pulled her closer. "The air is much cleaner here. I can feel the altitude a little, but I'm feeling so much better than Benares. How about a little bed action."

"Oh, Hank," Bridget replied and placed her hand on his shoulder, "the packed train and those border vans have tired me out— not to mention the strong hash. I need a nap. You were wonderful holding back the crowd at the train so we could get seats. I'm happy you are back to your old self. You looked terrible in Benares. I felt for you. Let's just relax. We've got plenty of time to renew our intimacy later." She kissed him and ruffled his long hair.

"Sure. I'm a little tired myself." He move back to his bed and lied down. He was disappointed, but believed her statement. As he closed his eyes, he envisioned a future energetic session with Bridget and slowly began to relax.

***

In the late afternoon, Sally banged on Hank and Bridget's door. "Hey up, mates. I'm starvin'. Let's go eat."

Hank looked over at Bridget who was rising to a sitting position and rubbing her neck. God, she is so beautiful. He was dying to grab her and take her into his arms, but sensed it would be a bad move. He needed to be patient, something he often found difficult. He understood her standoffish behavior in Benares. His diarrhea was disgusting. He wasn't sure what the best approach was to get her back in his bed. Her fawning over James seemed to be increasing, but there wasn't much he could do about that. He'd be patient, pay her compliments, and show her how much he liked her. Sally was right. He had taken his pairing with Bridget for granted.

"Hold your horses. We're coming." He went to door and flung it open.

"Speaking of horses," Sally said. "I could eat a whole one by myself.

"I doubt that," Hank replied. "You're skinny frame couldn't even finish a hindquarter."

Bridget walked to the door, laughing. "I hope we don't have to eat any portion of horses. I'd die for a salad?"

"Fat chance of that," Sally said.

They went out into the street and sauntered along, looking in the window of the few restaurants until they spied a small restaurant where several other Western youths were eating.

"This looks inviting," Bridget said. They all agreed and went in. The restaurant's menu was limited to bowls of rice served with buff, chicken, or just vegetables, mostly potatoes and carrots, and an assortment of soups.

"What's this buff?" Hank asked. "Is it beef?"

"I think it's water buffalo," James said.

Hank frowned as he ordered the buff and rice. He didn't like the sound of buff but was tired of chicken or fish. The place had no beer and the lady that served them looked like she could have used a good meal. The situation did not raise his expectation. The rest ordered the chicken and rice.

As soon as the food arrived Hank looked at his bowl of chunks of meat a few potatoes and carrots on top of white rice. He was hungrier than hell so he dug in. "This buff meat is a little tough but tastes okay," he said, pleasantly surprised.

"I'd say the same about this chicken," Sally said. "Compared to the delicious food in India this is disappointing."

"Speak for yourself," Hank replied. "I like simple food." He had grown tired of the curries in India, but agreed with Sally the food in India had been much better. Not that he would admit it. He was glad to be in Nepal. There wasn't the hassle with crowds, and the few beggars were not nearly as aggressive or appeared to be as ill as the beggars in India. Kathmandu was going to be interesting and relaxing. The black hash was excellent. Better than the hash in India.

"Ahhh, rest, relaxation, and food—just what I needed," Sally said as she leaned back. "Where to next, James?"

"We can walk up to Durbar Square," James said. "It's full of temples and is across from the royal palace."

"More temples," Hank said. "Christ, don't you ever get tired of temples?" Actually he wanted to see the temples, but enjoyed giving James a hard time.

"I'd love to go," Bridget said opening her eyes wide at James.

Sally gave Hank a dig in the side with her elbow. "Come on. Don't be difficult."

Hank was amused that he had even gotten a rise out of Sally. Now that he was with Bridget, Sally was much nicer to him. He was even warming to James. He didn't like all the attention Bridget paid James, but understood his appeal. James studied his guide book and was well informed about the many attractions. He could understand why women were drawn to him. Sally was crazy about him. Maybe if he emulated James a little more he could get back into Bridget's good graces.

"It's only a couple of blocks," James said.

"Yeah, Hank, get with program," Sally said.

"Okay, mate, I'm down with the program." Hank rubbed his chin, frowning at Sally. "Actually, I would like to see the square. I'm really liking Kathmandu. Lead on." He took Bridget's arm

"The pagoda style temples are in the indigenous Newa style," James said as they stood in front of the three story, wooden temple atop a nine-stepped, rock mason platform. "This temple is dedicated to Shiva. Let's walk up. We'll be able to get a good view of the city."

"This is a great view," Bridget said. She pointed up at the carved roof struts. "The carvings are pornographic. Take a look."

Hank studied the roof struts and felt a stirring. "Yeah, they are definitely cool." He looked down for Bridget, but she had placed her hands on James's shoulders and was following him inside. Hank strode inside after them.

"Ah, another lingam," Bridget said as she moved closer to sculpture.

Inside the temple, people were crushed together, annoying Hank, reminding him of the crowds in India. He left the temple and stood outside in the warm sun. He was tired of crowds and had seen enough lingams to last a lifetime. He inhaled the sweet air. The view of the Dunbar square from on high was quite impressive. He liked that the

Nepalese had used wood for their temples. He had always liked working with wood and thought when he returned to Australia, he'd try his hand at some carving. When Bridget came outside, he wrapped his arms around her, and she laid her head on his shoulder. He felt energized and hopeful.

"When was this temple built," Sally asked.

"1690 by the mother of Bhaktapur's king," James said.

"Where's Bhaktapur?" Bridget asked, removing Hank's arms and moving next to James.

"It's about twelve miles east of Katmandu," James replied. "We can take a tiger taxi there tomorrow or the next day. Supposedly you can see Mount Everest from there."

Sally squeezed between Bridget and James. "I want to see Mount Everest." She steered James back down the steps. "This is a lively plaza. I could go for some snacks. They smell good." She pulled James toward the food seller. "What are they?" she asked the man.

"Momo, very good," the man said.

"Momo? Okay, yes." Sally held out her hand and flapped her fingers. The man handed her several momos on a sheet of paper." She handed the man a few Nepalese rupee notes. She took a bite of one. "It's like a Chinese dumpling with some kind of meat. Tastes good." She held the other momo out for James.

"No thanks," James said.

"You want one, Hank?" she asked.

"Sure," Hank replied and took the momo and stuffed it in his mouth.

"This small white temple in the shikhara style is a temple to Kama Deva, the Hindu deity of love and desire," James said, caressing Sally's back and moving closer.

"Speaking of Kama Deva," Sally said enthusiastically. "I could go for going back to the hotel."

"I'm up for that," Hank said and moved to Bridget's side to take her hand.

"Let's go to the Kathamandap temple first," James said and started walking toward the temple. "Kathmandu is named after the temple."

Bridget caught up to James and took his arm.

Sally slowed and walked abreast of Hank. She nudged his shoulder. "You need to pay more attention to Bridget."

He was tired of Sally trying to tell him what to do with Bridget. "What the fuck for?" he responded

"Yeah, mate, exactly. For the fuck, you idiot."

"I tried to get it on after you guys left the room, but she was not having it."

"You see those two ahead," Sally said. "She's got his arm and is making a play for him."

"So?" Hank replied. "That's your problem. You need to take care of that."

"I am taking care," Sally said, "but I need your help too. You need to bed that wench. Romance... you fool. Pay her some interest." She shoved Hank forward. "Go get her. Hold her hand. Snuggle up to her. Give her kisses. Do I have to spell it out for you?"

Hank snarled. "Okay." He sped ahead and grabbed Bridget's arm. He knew Sally was right. He had allowed Bridget's interest in James to get out of hand. He was upset with Bridget for shunning his advances and had out of anger ignored her somewhat. He would stick close to Bridget and renew their passion. Ignoring Bridget hadn't worked at all.

"This temple was supposedly built from a single tree," James said as they stood outside the beautifully carved three story pagoda temple.

"You're joking, mate," Sally said. "No way was this built from a single tree."

"That's the legend," James said.

"Must have been a gigantic tree," Hank said. "Hey, there's another guy selling some of those momos." Hank started for the seller. "Let's get a few more."

"Not for me," Bridget said.

Hank walked up to the momo seller and held out his hand with a few rupees. "Okay, I'll take a couple."

***

"I'm so glad we came to Nepal," Bridget said as they were all sitting around James and Sally's room smoking chillums. "Those wooden pagodas were beautiful." The room was almost identical to Hank's and Bridget's. "What do you think about going to that yogurt and tea house that the American told us about?"

"Good idea," Sally said. "They've got western music, you can smoke there, and they have an assortment of goodies. I've got the munchies."

Hank blew out a cloud of smoke. "You think they've got beer?"

"Probably for a price, mate," Sally said.

The tea house was down the street from their hotel. The small place was filled with hashish smoke. The sound of Blind Faith's *Can't Find My Way Home,* radiated from large speakers. All the tables were taken.

Sally strode forward and went to a table where she spotted a red haired young man with a trimmed beard sitting by himself. "Hey up, mate, you mind if we join you,"

"No," the man replied. "Help yourself."

Sally waved to the others. Hank put his arm in Bridget's and followed James to the table.

"Where do you hail from?" Sally asked as she ran her fingers through her hair and widened her eyes. "I'm Sally from Brisbane." She extended her hand.

"Harry from Somerset," the man replied, shaking her hand and staring at her.

As the others joined them, Sally said, "Hank is from Brisbane too, James is from the States, and Bridget is from Sweden." They all shook hands. "What's good here?"

"Lassies are good," Harry said as he appraised the group. "Yellow curd is good too."

"They got any beer?" Hank asked.

"They don't keep it here, but you can send out for one," Harry said. "They're comparatively very expensive. Come from India. Of course most things do except for local food and craft."

"Mango lassie for me, please" Sally said to the small boy, who came up to the table and asked them what they would like in perfect English.

Bridget and James ordered the lassie also. Hank wanted a beer. Nothing went better with hash than beer. He pulled out his chillum and loaded it up before taking a long drag and offering the chillum to Harry. Harry accepted and, cupping his hands, took a drag and passed it on.

When the drinks came, Sally greedily drank half her lassie. "Man, this is good. Harry, thanks for the tip, mate." She swayed to the music as *Well All Right* blasted from the speakers.

Hank took a few gulps of beer when it arrived and settled back with a grin. They continued passing the chillum back and forth. When he had finished half of his beer, he started sweating, had stabbing stomach pains, and bent forward with a groan.

"What's up, mate," Sally said and placed her had on Hank's shoulder. "You look terrible."

"I don't know," Hank replied and removed his hat. "My stomach aches something awful." He doubled over again. "Uh, man, that hurts."

"Now that you mention it," Sally said. "My belly's getting uncomfortable also."

James lit his chillum and passed it to Sally who took a small toke and handed it to Harry. "I hope it wasn't those momos you and Hank ate," James said as he watched Sally screw up her face as she took a deep breath.

"Oh no, mate," Sally said and leaned forward over the table. "Jesus, I better go back to the hotel." She blew out air between her lips and groaned.

"Me too," Hank said.

"You want me to come with you?" James asked.

"No stay," Sally said as both she and Hank pushed themselves up. "I think we better hurry."

"Uh oh," Bridget said. "Hank was just getting over his last bout."

"Your friends ate some street food?" Harry asked.

"Yeah," James said. "Some of those momos."

"Big mistake," Harry said. "About half the population of Nepal at any one time suffers from intestinal problems. It's rife here. Nobody seems to wash their hands" He raised his bushy, red-haired head and pushed his glasses up on his nose. "When'd you guys get here?"

"Today," Bridget said. She moved to the seat to next to James. "Is the food here okay?" She took James arm.

"Yes, it's fine," Harry said and stroked his red beard. "I've been here a week. Usually come here every day. Never had a problem."

Bridget and James finished their lassies and then shared Hank's beer after obtaining glasses. They smoked chillums and enjoyed the familiar music.

"They've got a great sound system here," Bridget said. "And the latest albums."

"That's why I'm here," Harry said. "I come most days and hang out. I would like to go trekking, but I don't want to go by myself. Are any of you interested in trekking?"

"Can women go trekking?" Bridget asked.

"I suppose," Harry said. "It would probably be hard without a pretty big group. I don't think a couple going on their own would be advisable. Nepal seems rather lawless to me."

***

Sally was lying on the bed, clutching her stomach, when James and Bridget entered.

"You okay?" James asked.

"No," Sally said. "I've just shit my guts out." She glared at the two. "Fuck...." She rose, doubled over, and rushed into the bathroom.

The sounds of evacuation and groans drifted from the bathroom.

Bridget hunched her brow and curled her lips. "That sounds bad."

"See if you can help Sally," James said. "I'll go check on Hank."

When James came back, he placed his hand on Sally's forehead. "You're burning up."

"No shit, Sherlock," Sally said. "I need something to drink. I'm dying of thirst."

"Hank's as bad as you if not worse," James said. "I'll go get some soft drinks. See if I can find some mineral water or tonic." He hurriedly left.

When he entered Hank's room with the drinks he had purchased for him, the stench caused his eyes to water. It was even worse smelling than in Benares. Bridget was sitting on the bed with the

Pepto Bismo bottle and a dejected frown. "It didn't help," Bridget said. "What should we do?"

"Here Hank," James said as he handed him the lemon soft drink. "Drink as much as you can."

***

"Come in," James said to the soft knock.

"He's finally asleep," Bridget whispered, noticing that Sally was also asleep.

"Good, let's go out," James whispered and followed Bridget into the hall. "I'm hungry."

"Me too," Bridget said. "We need to be careful what we eat."

"Let's go to the restaurant Harry recommended with the traditional Nepalese food—dahl, bhat, and tarkari."

"What's that?"

"Lentil soup, rice, and curried vegetables."

They walked past the Durbar Square to the Thamel shopping district. They strolled through the crowded alleys where shops sold a multitude of different items until they found the restaurant.

They chose the traditional offering. The dahl was spicy, the rice brown, and the tarkari, steaming curried potatoes with eggplant and onions. The meal was quite filling.

"This is tasty, but I liked the other restaurant better," Bridget said. "Shall we go back and check on the invalids?"

"Yes, we better," James said.

As they were walking back Bridget took James's arm. "I don't want to sleep in the same room as Hank. It stinks something awful." She stopped James and kissed him. "We could get another room." She squeezed against him. "This is our opportunity. Please, James." James allowed the intimacy. He thought back to the quick episode in Benares. He knew he was being stupid, but her soft lips had aroused his passion, and he wasn't looking forward to sleeping in his stench filled room either.

***

Bridget stretched her arms out and arched her sleek body. "I've been imagining us together like this." She rolled toward James and placed her hand on his stomach. "I feel so released."

James had been apprehensive about getting the extra room, but Bridget's enthusiasm had won out.

"This was great," James replied, but knew it wasn't great. He had again succumbed to Bridget's charm and placed himself in an impossible position. He was so weak. He had enjoyed their sex. Bridget's long legs had clasped him tight as she arched in climax. He had to admit it felt great. He knew it had to stop. He could hardly blame Nam for his acquiesce to Bridget. She could manipulate him so easily. He needed to end their exploits. He had betrayed Sally again and the consequences if Sally found out could be devastating. She had suspected something in Benares, but hadn't reproached him. If she found about the room, she would know for sure that he had betrayed her.

He could feel Bridget's golden pubic hair against his thigh as she draped her leg over him. He ignored his reignited arousal. "We better go back and sleep in their rooms," he said. "We need to keep this room secret."

"Why James?" Bridget said. "Let's come clean and tell them. I don't mind sharing you with Sally."

"Wait a minute," James said. "Sally would never go for that and neither would Hank. Sally would be livid, and Hank could get violent."

"I don't want to have sex with Hank anymore," she said. "He doesn't really like you. He's a bore. He's very aggressive and not much for cuddling. You're tender and considerate about my feelings." She snuggled against him and grasped his penis. "We could have a threesome with Sally. Ahhh...that's got you stimulated."

"That's probably impossible," James said, pushing her hand away.

"Let me work on Sally. I could seduce her. I think she's incredibly beautiful. Her red hair and green eyes— she excites me."

"Are you telling me you're bisexual?"

"A little," she said pushing her lips out. "I've had sex with women. My friend and I even had a threesome with her boyfriend once. I'm crazy about you James."

Things were getting out of hand. He was letting his dick do the thinking. How would he ever get out of this mess? Could they foster a threesome relationship? Jesus, what was he thinking? He was being completely stupid. This had to end. He suspected that Hank and Sally had been lovers on their journey together, but believed Sally had been true to him since they left Madras. Sally had captured his heart. She was fun to be with and made him laugh. Why was he so weak?

"I'm going back to my room," James said. He stood and dressed.

"I'm sleeping here," Bridget replied. "I can't take the smell in Hank's."

"Okay, see you in the morning."

"You can come back down in the morning for quickie before breakfast." She jumped up and hugged James from behind. "I'm going to tell Hank I got another room for myself."

***

Sally was asleep when James snuck into the room. He undressed and slipped into the other bed. The room stank, and he couldn't get to sleep. Once Sally learned that Bridget had her own room, she would suspect his betrayal. His sleep was fitful. His recurring nightmare had woken him. When he fell back asleep, he dreamed of falling down a dark sink hole as Sally and Hank laughed.

"What time did you get in," Sally said shaking James.

James rolled over and rubbed his eyes. "I don't know. Didn't pay attention to the time. I was too tired after all the chillums we smoked at the tea house." He averted his gaze, hoping she couldn't read his embarrassment. "How are you feeling?"

"A little better. But after I take a drink of tonic water, I have to go again. It's like I can't stomach anything." She focused intently on him as her smile disappeared. "So you and Bridget stayed up smoking chillums?"

"Yeah, we closed the tea house. This Nepalese hash is heavy duty." He rubbed her back. "You need to keep drinking fluids. You've lost a lot of salts too. After breakfast I'll go to the chemist and see if they have any salts we can add to the soda."

"James I'm so sorry. I ruined Kathmandu for you. I was so stupid to eat the street food. I should've known after Hank's bout in India."

"No reason to beat yourself up. We'll conquer this."

"Will you help me take a shower? I feel so weak."

"Sure."

"Let me sit for a while. Go check on Hank and Bridget and see how Hank's doing."

"I'll wait and help you shower. Maybe then you'll feel strong enough, and we can both go." He needed to ingratiate himself as much as possible with Sally to dispel any thoughts she might have of his betrayal with Bridget.

James helped Sally disrobe, and, after disrobing himself, stepped with Sally into the shower. He soaped her up and washed her hair. He dried her off and helped her back to sit on her bed. "You want to get dressed."

"I don't have the strength. Leave me be and go check on Hank."

"Okay." James went down the hall and knocked on Hank's door.

"Come in," Hank called weakly.

"How you feeling, mate?" James asked.

"Like I've been run over by a truck. I've shit so much I've got a damn pile."

"Ewe, sorry."

"Where's Bridget?"

"Don't know. I thought she'd be here." He hoped his lie was convincing. He'd let Bridget make her own excuses.

"How's Sally?"

"About the same as you. I helped her take a shower, and she's resting. She's very weak."

"Will you help me take a shower?"

"Sure. You ready."

"Yep." Hank rose and toppled back down. 'Woo, I'm a little dizzy."

After helping Hank out of his underwear, James pulled Hank up and put Hank's arm around his head. "Nice and easy." Jesus he stinks. He weighs a ton.

The bathroom was a mess and the floor level toilet was covered in shit. James turned on the shower and pushed Hank inside. While Hank leaned against the wall and let the water run over him, James cleaned up the toilet, then disrobed and helped Hank wash.

When Hank was finished showering, he helped him dry off and escorted Hank back to his bed.

"You think Bridget went on her own to breakfast?" Hank asked.

"I doubt it. She could have gone for an early walk. She really liked Durbar Square." James went to the other bed. He racked his brain on what he could say to keep Hank from focusing on Bridget's absence. "Maybe after a rest you and Sally can take a short walk. The exercise might do you some good. I was planning on all of us going to Bhaktapur today. Probably not a good idea for you and Sally to come. What do you think?"

"No way could I handle a taxi ride," Hank said. "I need to be close to a toilet. I don't even know about a short walk."

Suddenly Bridget swished into the room with a big smile and glowing cheeks, her sapphire blue eyes clear and bright. "Hey Hank, how are you feeling?"

"Better," Hank replied weakly. "James helped me shower. Where have you been?"

"Don't get mad... but I couldn't sleep in here, so I got another room," Bridget said.

"What?" Hank sat up. "You didn't need to do that."

"I thought it would be better, and you wouldn't be concerned about waking me when you went to the loo."

"Well, I reckon it wasn't very pleasant in here with all the trips to the loo."

She dodged the bullet there. Hank is still smitten. Who wouldn't be? She's so beautiful, and I'm so unbelievably weak. Damn, I've been so stupid.

James stood. "I'll go back and check on Sally." He moved to Hank and placed a hand on Hank's shoulder, purposely avoiding the scintillating stare from Bridget. "Catch you later."

28- BHAKTAPUR: DECEMBER 14, 1969

"The road is terrible," Bridget said as they bounced around in the taxi striped with black paint like a tiger, hence the name tiger taxi. "I'm glad we could go to Bhaktapur on our own." She grabbed James's hand. "I like being with just you."

They had left Hank and Sally in their rooms resting. Neither Hank nor Sally had thought they were well enough to come along. James and suggested waiting a day or so, but Sally had encouraged James to go, professing that he shouldn't have to hang around because of her stupidity.

Bridget was feeling enlivened by her conquering of James and their sexual exploits late into the night in her room. She had shown James what a powerhouse she was in bed. He had slept soundly for a few hours after she had thoroughly worn him out. Hank and Sally's stupidity on eating street food in a country like Nepal had provided her with such a wonderful opportunity. She couldn't have imagined things working out any better. She believed she had James finally in her orbit and was determined to consolidate her conquest.

She snuggled up against him, placing her head on his shoulder and rubbed his chest. "Oh James, last night was so fulfilling. I feel complete. You were wonderful. We were meant for each other." When she looked up into his face, his half smile and silence gave her pause. He didn't appear genuinely happy. Was he still feeling guilty about his betrayal of Sally? This didn't bode well.

They disembarked at the town square in Bhaktapur that also was called Durbar Square, which translated to Royal Square, where many Newa style pagoda temples stood opposite the fifty-five intricacy carved wooden windows of the palace. There were only a few Western tourists mixed in the small number of Nepalese walking around the square.

"I like it here," Bridget said slipping her arm around his back. "It's so peaceful." She grabbed James's hand and drew him across the square. She needed to engage him intellectually, dispel his guilt. Show him she was the ideal partner. She stopped in front of the tall temple. "This pagoda is more dramatic than the ones in Kathmandu."

"It's the tallest Newa temple in Nepal. It's called the Nyatapola, which means five stories. We can't go inside, but we can walk up the steps. "

They ascended up the five brick tiers past the warrior, elephant, griffin, tiger, and lion goddess stone sculptures on either side of the steps to the temple with its beautiful carved struts, windows, and doors.

Bridget shaded her eyes and looked off in the distance. "Is that mountain range, Everest?"

"Yes it's that peak that's a little taller than the rest." He pointed at Mount Everest.

"Wow the tallest mountain in the world. I'm so glad we came here and caught a glimpse of Mount Everest. I love all these beautiful temples." She wrapped her arms around him from behind and held him tight. "I'm getting hungry."

***

"This is a quaint little restaurant," Bridget said. "You think the food here will be okay. We don't want to end up like Hank and Sally."

James had led her to a small restaurant just off the square where an attractive Nepalese woman had greeted them with a Namaste and pointed to a table near the window.

"I asked our Kathmandu hotel clerk about a good restaurant here," James replied. "He recommended this one. I think it will be okay. I'd suggest getting the traditional fare with no meat."

They ordered the dahl, bat, and tarkari. The Nepalese woman with delicate features, her eyes highlighted by kohl with lines extending out like wings from her dark eyes, dressed in a black velour type blouse with strings of silver necklaces and colorful full skirt, nodded with a big smile and left for the kitchen.

"Our waitress is a stunningly beautiful woman," Bridget said. "What do you think?"

"Yes, I agree. She's beautiful. Lovely smile."

"Well don't get too enamored."

"Don't worry. She's stunning, but she can't hold a candle to you."

"Thank you, James," she replied, taking his hand. She was buoyed by his comment, thinking he was definitely succumbing. "You're a great traveling companion. Wouldn't it be wonderful if just you and I could continue traveling together like this?"

"I don't think we can abandon Hank and Sally. It wouldn't be fair."

Uh-oh... he hasn't been completely conquered yet. She still needed to continue to work on him. Another night together would hopefully do the trick. She thought of different ways she could orchestrate something dramatic tonight, take him to the heights of ecstasy. For now she had him all to herself and would make the most of it.

After lunch, they walked to the front of the sprawling palace and studied the intricate carvings of the long row of windows. Bridget had her arm around his waist. "This is stupendous. When was it built?"

James opened his guide book. "It was completed in 1754."

"The never ending windows give it a welcoming appeal." She turned to look at the nearby shining golden gate. "Let's get closer to the gate. It's incredibly beautiful. Such intricacy. Truly striking."

"Supposedly after it was completed, the king had the artists' hands cut off so nothing so beautiful could be made again."

"That can't be true. That would be crazy."

"Yeah, sounds pretty crazy to me too. Must be some kind of myth."

They continued around the square hand in hand, looking at the dramatic temples and sculptures. "Well, I think we've pretty much seen all we can see," James said after they had completed several circuits. "Shall we get a taxi back?"

"Okay." Bridget pulled James to her and kissed him strongly. "When we get back, we could go to my room for an afternoon snuggle."

***

When they arrived back at their Katmandu hotel, Bridget pulled James up the stairs toward her room, hoping for some late afternoon sex she had been contemplating on the ride back. Outside her door, James declined entry and turned to go. She grabbed him tight. "Hey, we could have a quick tryst. It won't take long. Sally's not going anywhere. I've been thinking about us on the ride back, and I'm primed and ready."

"Bridget ... I... I would...." He looked down his face flushed red in embarrassment. "Not now... maybe later."

She reluctantly released him and watched him walk down the hall to the stairs. Damn, she hoped he wasn't going to end their assignations. She had grown excited on the return trip and really wanted to extend their intimacy to strengthen her grip on him. She would have to wait until the evening to try and complete her hold.

"You're back," Sally said sitting up in bed as James entered their room. "How was the trip?"

"It was great," James replied. "We saw Everest in the distance from the five story tallest pagoda. The palace with its 55 carved windows was striking. All the other temples were beautiful as well. It was a most beautiful square." He approached her bed and felt her forehead. "How are you feeling?" He dispelled Bridget's invitation for a tryst from his mind, hoping his face didn't project his embarrassment.

"A little better. The salts with the tonic water tastes horrible, but I think it's helping." She stared up at him without speaking. "Well, are you going to give me a kiss? I'm not contagious."

He gave her a hug and kiss. "You feel like trying to eat something?"

"No... no. I'll stick with the tonic water and salts for today. I'm definitely not out of the woods yet." She shifted in the bed and scooted down to lay back. "I feel so weak. I walked to Hank's room earlier and hardly made it back. I think I'm doing better than him."

"Good."

"What's this about Bridget getting her own room?"

He knew Sally would find out about Bridget's room and had worried about how he would answer her questions about the room. He was still at a loss on how he was he going to explain the situation without incriminating himself. "She said she couldn't get any sleep with Hank getting up and down all night. She couldn't stand the stench in the room."

"Did you sleep with her?"

James tried to keep his face without expression. *Jesus, she's on to me. What should he say? He was tired of lying. He suspected it was useless anyway. His sex with Bridget would eventually come out. More lying would make it worse. Why had he been such a fool? He'd have to take his punishment. He hoped Sally wouldn't drop him and would eventually forgive him. What else could he do? He didn't really want to go off with Bridget. Bridget was beautiful and a consummate lover, but there was a distance between them he couldn't put his finger on. He felt close to Sally and maybe really was in love with her. His stupidity and weakness was astounding.*

James readied himself for the onslaught his confession would induce. "I slept in her room last night."

"I figured as much," Sally said meekly, but James could tell she was stewing inside as her face hardened. "I woke up to go to the toilet late and your bed was empty." She pushed herself back up with a groan her face contorted. "Did you have sex?"

"You know I'm crazy about you, Sally." He rose and started pacing. He hung his head. "Yes, we had sex." He waited to see her reaction. Her stretched face of fury scared him. "I'm sorry. I don't want to destroy our relationship. I fucked up. What should I do? How can I make this up to you?"

"You fucked up is right," she shouted and grit her teeth. She narrowed her eyes. "Was this the first time?"

"What difference does it make?"

"Just answer the question, asshole."

"No, we had sex in Benares once."

"I knew it." She started crying her body shaking in spasms.

"I'm so sorry, Sally. It won't happen again. Please forgive me."

"Fuck you. You fucking bastard. Go ahead, go to your precious Bridget. I don't care."

"Sally... come on. We can work this out."

"Get the hell out of my sight." She tossed the half full bottle of tonic water at him.

"Okay... okay." He left the room. What was he going to do now?

30- KATHMANDU: DECEMBER 15, 1969

Sally woke early in the morning as the sky was beginning to brighten. She studied James, who was asleep on his bed with his back to her. She was feeling markedly better— not having to get up once in the night. She didn't know when James had come in. She wondered if he had snuck in after banging Bridget. He said it wouldn't happen again. Should she believe him? She didn't really want to drive him away— just punish him somehow— make him regret his betrayal and make sure it never happened again. Was she being childish? At least he was honest with her when confronted. She hadn't been with him.

She got up and went into the bathroom. She didn't appear so wan today. She could try eating something. She needed to make up with James. She had over reacted yesterday. She certainly didn't want to switch back to traveling with just Hank. She doubted that Bridget would rekindle her relationship with Hank, but stranger things had happened. Did Bridget want to conquer as many men as possible— something men were often fantasizing about? Even if Hank and Bridget didn't continue their sexual relationship, there was a possibility they could continue to travel together as friends. Was she being unrealistic? Perhaps, she could solve the quandary with some honesty.

She tiptoed to James's bed and rubbed his back. As he began to awaken, she kissed his cheek. "Wakey, wakey, mate."

He rolled over and smiled, his eyes opening slowly. He stared at her a few moments as if he was waiting for a barrage. "You seem much better today," he said hesitantly. "How're you feeling?"

"Better." She kissed him again and rubbed his chest. "I don't want to lose you James. I'm sorry I told you to fuck off."

"Hey, I'm the one who should be sorry." He reached his hand out and caressed her arm. "I blew it."

"You were honest with me," she said solemnly. "So I'm going to be honest with you. I did have sex with Hank on the trip from Hong Kong and in Bangkok." She breathed in deeply to gather her thoughts. "I wanted to get him to buy plane tickets to India and thought I needed to use sex to convince him." She bent closer and smoothed his hair. "I was so afraid of not finding you in Madras. It was stupid, and I've had to fight him off ever since." She stood up. "I know Bridget is utterly beautiful, and it's obvious she's hot for you. I don't want to share you with her, but I don't want to lose you."

"Do you hate her?" James asked and stood. As Sally backed up, he grabbed her. "You're more beautiful to me than Bridget." He kissed her. "It was stupid of me to succumb. I feel like an idiot. I can't believe how weak I was. I don't want to risk what we have together." He caressed her cheek. She leaned into his caress, lowering her eye lids and pushing her lips out. "Do you think we can get Hank and her to go off together?"

"I doubt she would go off alone with Hank," she said, screwing up her face. "No, I don't hate her." Well she actually did hate her, but hoped she could dispel her hatred with time. "I would love to punch her in the face though. I think Hank is still infatuated with her, but she seems to have had it with him." She had to admit Bridget had a much stronger allure than she had anticipated. "Maybe they'd be willing to continue traveling with us as just friends. Hank might be up for that, but I don't know about Bridget. It would allow her the continued safety of traveling in a group. I don't know if I could take her continued fawning over you though. I don't know what to do."

"Well, let's have a shower and then we can join them for breakfast. You and Hank can have some bananas and possibly a little rice and we'll lay our cards on the table. No more secrets. See what Hank and Bridget say."

"Okay, James. Sounds like a plan."

***

"So you think it's okay to have a little rice," Hank said as they were sitting at the tiny restaurant where other Westerns were eating. The walls were decorated with Buddhist flags of different colors. The elderly waitress shuffled around the patrons with a perpetual toothless smile.

"Yeah, but not too much," James replied. "How does your stomach feel after the banana?"

"Not too bad," Hank said.

"And you, Sally?" James asked.

"I feel great and I'm starving." She glanced at Bridget before reaching for James's hand. "Let's order."

Bridget stared at James with a furrowed brow. "What's going on? Something's up."

"Well Bridget," Sally said, "James told me about your sexual capers." Bridget twisted in her seat, glanced at James, then with a red face focused on Sally. "It's okay. I was mad at first, but realized that I'm crazy about James and don't want to lose him. Nor do I want to drive you away, Bridget. I like you and enjoy traveling with you." She paused and regarded each in turn. "Hank and I had sex on our way to India. So I'm as guilty as James. We're going to forgive each other and be completely honest from now on. Okay? No more sneaking around."

"James." Bridget reared back. "What does this mean?"

Sally placed her hand on Bridget's. Bridget withdrew her hand as if stung.

"Bridget I'm very fond of you," James said, "but I can't continue our sexual relations. It wouldn't be fair to Sally or Hank." He reached for Bridget's hand. "Don't be hurt or mad. We can still travel together and enjoy each other's company."

"You can, but not me," Bridget said, her contorted face flushed. "I'll leave today for India. Go back to Goa."

"Come on," Sally said. "Don't be rash. We can forgive each other and carry on as before."

"No way," Bridget said. "It's gone too far for that. I've enjoyed traveling with all of you. But, things have changed, and I can't go back or forget." She stretched her neck and blinked back her tears. "I would love for you to come with me, James."

Sally couldn't believe that Bridget was still trying to take James away from her. What a brazen hussy.

"I can't, Bridget," James responded. "I'm with Sally. You need to think this over. I made a terrible mistake. I'm sorry if I've hurt you. I want to remain friends." He watched Bridget's face as he took a drink of coffee. "Let's have breakfast and talk more later. Please... let's not allow my stupidity to ruin things."

"I'm not going to change my mind." Bridget looked from one to another, then threw up her hands. "Okay, let's have breakfast," she said with exasperation.

***

They all went with Bridget to the bus station. Bridget grabbed James and kissed him. "I'll miss you, James." She hugged Hank. "I'm sorry it didn't work out between us. I do like you. I didn't mean to hurt you." She turned to Sally. "Take good care of them." When Sally came toward her, she moved back, then set her hand on James's shoulder. "Thank you all for your friendship. If you're ever in Sweden, come visit." She pivoted and dashed into the minibus. Sitting at a window seat, she glanced out the window as tears slipped down her face.

Sally smiled at Bridget and grabbed James's arm. She felt relieved that Bridget was leaving, and she had James back completely in her fold. She was thankful that Bridget had taken the pressure of Hank off her and made the journey much easier for a time. She couldn't blame Bridget for dropping the big oaf, but couldn't forgive her for seducing James. Still... good luck to her.

"I would have gone with her," Hank said as the minibus pulled away. "It's not wise for her to travel alone."

"She can take care of herself," Sally said. "She wanted to be alone."

Hank glared at James. "You ruined it."

James hung his head. "I'm sorry."

"Hey, forget the blame game," Sally said. "Bridget is a beautiful and intelligent lady. We all loved her." She grabbed James and hugged him. Her hug sent waves of pleasure spinning around her body. "Maybe we'll see her again."

"Are we going back to Goa?" Hank said. "I really liked it there."

"We all did," Sally said, rubbing Hank's arm. "We'll see. Let's enjoy Kathmandu now that we're feeling better. No more street food." She pushed Hank. "To the monkey temple."

***

The three disembarked from the taxi at the bottom of the hill outside Kathmandu and began the climb up the many steps to the Swayambhunath Stupa. The azure sky was dotted with puffy clouds over the distant mountains and the sunshine was intense. They had seen the magical large eyes of the stupa spire in the distance on the drive. Sally was excited to see the temple. The absence of Bridget was a tonic to her spirit. As they ascended the stairs, the Nepalese devotees moving up the stairs stared at the strange Westerners with big smiles.

"This is one of the oldest Buddhist pilgrimage temples in Nepal," James said, placing his arm around Sally's back and helping her up the steep stairs. "It's been a place of worship since the fifth century."

"Why all the damn steps," Hank said, stopping to catch his breath.

James turned to Hank. "Three hundred sixty five for all the days in a year."

"Come on, I want to see the monkeys," Sally said.

"Let's take it nice and easy— you're both still not completely recovered," James said.

At the top of the steps, the round white stupa gleamed in the sun with the dazzling golden spire on top and the majestic eyes. A troop of monkeys scampered over the stupa. Sally stared up at the Stupa as she caught her breath.

"The two eyes on all four sides of the tower are symbolic of God's all-seeing presence," James said. "The elongated spiral between the eyes is the Nepali symbol for one, which represents the unity of all things."

"All seeing eyes of God would fit in any religion," Sally replied. "It's great up here. You can see all of Kathmandu. I love all the monkeys."

"What's that huge golden thing ahead?" Hank asked pointing to the double arrow like sculpture.

"It's the Vajra," James said. "The thunderbolt." He moved to the sculpture. "The lions on either side symbolize strength and purity and are often associated with Buddha. His teachings are called the roar of the lion." He put his arm around Sally. "The Vajra was initially a Hindu symbol. Buddhism evolved to incorporate a lot of the symbols in Hinduism."

"I like the prayer wheels," Sally said. "Can anyone spin them?"

"Sure, why not," James said.

"Let's go spin then," Sally said, grabbing James's hand and hauling him forward.

"The spinning of the prayer wheels is a recitation of the mantra 'Om Mani Padme Hum', which is recorded inside the prayer wheel on paper," James said as Sally pulled him into the group circling the stupa. "They were introduced for illiterate people so they could receive the benefits of the mantra."

"What's the benefit?" Sally asked.

"The sounds of the mantra are considered sacred vibrations," James replied. "They are to still the mind. The literal translation is sometimes said to be the jewel in the lotus. Although Buddhists maintain that the mantra is not translatable."

Sacred vibrations— she liked the sound of that. She had never been religious. Her parents would be considered Christian, but seldom went to church. The more she learned about Buddhism the more she liked it. Could she become a Buddhist? James seemed to gravitate more toward Buddhism than Hinduism, but was obviously interested in both. She imagined the horrors of war he experienced had a lot to do with his interest in Buddhism. Was the world really Maya, an illusion as Hindus and Buddhist seemed to believe? Sure seemed real to her. The aborigines believed dreams were more real than actual life, but still thought life was real— not an illusion.

Sally led James around the stupa until they reached the prayer wheels where she dropped his hand and spun the wheels like the many Nepalese, who smiled and nodded at her. She felt a sense of ease joining in the ritual.

After several circuits Hank stopped. "That's enough praying for me," he said.

"Yeah," Sally said. "It felt good." She snuggled up to James. "Shall we go back to town?"

He kissed the top of her head. "This way," he said. "There's a road in the back where we can catch a taxi."

"What!" Hank said. "Why'd we walk up the steps then?"

"To sense the ambience and enter into the ritual of the shrine."

"You're unbelievable," Hank said. "Where do you get this crap?"

"Don't be such a philistine," Sally said, grabbing Hank from behind and laughingly pushing him forward. She understood Hank's animosity. James had betrayed them both. She wanted to place the blame more on Bridget, but James was a willing participant despite what he said about Bridget enticing him. She was glad that Hank's anger and disappointment had not translated into violence.

"A what?" Hank shook Sally off and removed his hat to smooth his long blond hair. "You're as crazy as him."

***

"Hey Red," Harry called from his table in the tea and yogurt café.

Sally turned toward the call. "Hey up, Red, yourself." She swooped to the table as the Rolling Stones belted out *Street Fighting Man* on the stereo. "Is this your permanent spot?"

"Of course," Harry said. "Where have you guys been?"

"We went to the monkey temple," Sally said. James and Hank joined them. "It was so cool. I circled the stupa and spun the prayer wheels, so I'm in good shape, mate, with Lord Buddha." She reached out for the chillum Harry was holding. "Give us a toke." Sally accepted the chillum and cupped her hands to draw on the upright pipe. She expelled the smoke upward and cooed. "All right." She laughed and handed the chillum to Hank. "I'm good... prayers and smoke. I'm on the road." She really did feel good. The visit to the stupa had energized her.

"What road is that?" Hank asked before taking a long toke on the chillum and throwing his head back to expel the smoke.

"The Dharma road," she replied.

Hank threw his hand up and motioned to the young boy waiter.

The boy glided to the table. "Yes, lady and gentlemen what is it you are liking?"

Sally thought the boy waiter was cute and so courteous. She ordered a lassie for James and lemon sodas for her and Hank.

"Speaking of roads," James said. "How'd you get here, Harry?"

"I walked from my hotel," Harry said, squinting.

"No... I mean to Nepal," James said. "Did you fly or come overland."

"I came overland with some other English people from London to India. The Hippie trail. I left them in Delhi and came here to Kathmandu after Benares on my own."

"Overland... what countries did you come through?"

"Let's see," Harry said. He pushed his lips out and tilted his head back. "There was France, Germany, Switzerland, Italy, Greece, Turkey, Iran, Afghanistan, Pakistan, and India."

"What's this hippie trail?" James asked.

"That's what everybody is calling it now—Istanbul to India. It's becoming the in thing. You've seen all the European hippies in India and here."

"I'd love to do the overland route to London," Sally said. "Wouldn't that be cool, James?"

"For sure," James said. "How long did it take you?"

"The people I came with were always in a hurry to get to India," Harry said. "I would've preferred to take some time and enjoy the countries more. But these people were up early and on the go." He sipped his lassie. "It took about three weeks."

Sally reared back. "Three weeks. Jesus, how far is it?"

"It's about six thousand miles," Harry said.

"Well I reckon that's not so fast," Hank said. "I've driven from Melbourne to Darwin in less than a week and that's about twenty three hundred miles."

"I bet the roads in Australia are much better than the roads to get here," Harry said. "Plus, from Turkey onward, you shouldn't drive at night because the truck drivers will run you off the road."

"Crazy," Sally said.

"You give anymore thought to trekking," Harry asked. "I'd really like to go. The trek from Pokhara to the Dhaulagiri and Annapurna Mountains I thought might be the most interesting."

"How long would that take?" James asked.

"I'm not sure," Harry said and pushed his glasses up on his nose. "From what I've read maybe about two weeks."

"Would you take a bus to Pokhara?" James asked.

"No, you'd have to fly. There's no road."

"What... there's no road," Sally said. "How do the Nepalese get there?"

"Fly, walk, or horseback," Harry said. "I imagine most people don't go."

"You think it's safe to get a lassie, James?" Sally asked. "This hash has given me terrible munchies."

"Well, I don't know. You're doing well on the bananas, broth, and rice. Possibly a lassie would be okay. You're the best judge of that."

"I'm not risking it," Hank said. "My asshole is still painful."

Sally frowned and gave Hank a shove. "That's more information them we need, Hank." She leaned forward. "I think I'll give a lassie a try. I reckon I'm pretty much out of the woods." She laughed. "This trekking business sounds cool, but I'm not about to try it. Walking for weeks is not my idea of fun."

***

"You certainly got your energy back," James said as he lay back on the bed in their room, enjoying the afterglow of sex as he held Sally.

"That's right," Sally said, "and don't you forget it."

James stretched his arms and placed them behind his head. "I feel so much better now that Bridget is gone. I'm so sorry I fell under her spell."

"So you think she bewitched you. Good story, mate." She draped her arm across his chest. "That's water under the bridge. Let's not talk about it again." She got up and went into the bathroom.

Of course his dalliance with Bridget was not water under the bridge. His betrayal was lodged in her mind like a steel spike. She would forgive him, but the thought of them together infuriated her. She hoped her anger would wane. She needed to keep it under wraps. She splashed her face with water, studied her reflection, and pushed her hair off her flushed face.

When she came out of the bathroom, she said, "You seem intrigued by this trekking thing."

"It sounds fantastic. Imagine hiking between some of the highest mountains in the world. I need to find out more about it. Harry would be a good guy to go with. He's nearly as big as Hank and is in good shape."

"You're in good shape." She laid back down and nestled against him. "I love your body." She inched up and gave him a warm tongued kiss. "Your personality is pretty cool too. You know the overland trip from England to India Harry told us about sounded interesting. Hank and I had planned to return to Australia after India, but I've been thinking about all those countries we'd see. I've learned so much on our travels. The wealth of art I've been able to enjoy has been so rewarding. I'd love to continue on westward, learning about the other countries and of course spending more time with you. Plus, I've relatives in England I haven't seen since I was a kid. I've still got quite a bit of traveling money left. India and Nepal have been so inexpensive. My uncle Jeb lives in London. He came to visit us in Australia several times. He's richer than shit."

"What's richer than shit? Here shit is everywhere. You mean he's poor?"

Sally dug her elbow into his ribs. "I don't know where that expression came from. I agree it's rather lame. Jeb has his own company. He supposed to have a great house in Chelsea, London."

"I've been thinking about traveling overland too. Learning about the other countries with you would be wonderful as you've said. Much better than flying from country to country. I could trade in the rest of my plane ticket, I bet. Would you really be up for traveling to Europe by bus?"

"Yeah, with you."

"If I could find a vehicle to buy in India, we could drive to England. That would be even better. I could sell the vehicle in England and get some of the money back. What do you think?"

Sally brightened and grabbed James's arm. "That would be so awesome. Do you really think it would be possible?"

"I don't know if I could buy a car in India. A van would be ideal. Yeah, I like the idea. When we get back to Delhi, we can check if it's possible."

"I'm sure I could convince Hank to come along." Her remark about Hank coming had elicited a slight frown from James. She could understand why James wouldn't want Hank to come. She doubted Hank would be willing to let her travel with just James. He had promised her brother he would protect her. Hank wasn't one to go back on a promise to her brother. He'd like to see uncle Jeb as well.

James rubbed his head and forced a smile. "Yeah, Hank could come if he wanted to," James said somewhat reluctantly.

She understood James's reluctance. She was glad he put a pleasant face on his reply. He owed Hank plenty of deference for his liaison with Bridget.

"We could also advertise for other riders to share expenses. I bet there's other young people who would like to ride back rather than taking buses."

"Oh James that would be so cool, but what about trekking?"

"I'd love to do it. My only reservation is abandoning you. What would you do for two weeks?"

"I wouldn't want to stay here in Kathmandu with Hank."

"You could fly to Pokhara with us."

"Yeah, but still I'd just be hanging out." She laid back down and placed her head back on his chest. She thought about going back to Goa to wait. She was apprehensive how Bridget would treat them. But at least there'd be people they knew, and the beach scene would be relaxing. She and Hank could rent a small bungalow.

"You're right, I should give up the trekking idea."

"No James. I can tell you really want to do it, and as you say, Harry would be an ideal trekking mate." She placed her hand on his chest. "Hank and I could go back to Goa and wait for you. He's already missing Bridget. Not that I think he has much of a chance with her anymore, but who knows. Relaxing on the beach for weeks would be easy to tolerate while you go gallivanting."

"Would you really wait for me?"

"Of course," she said as she slipped her hand up his thigh and watched his eyes widen. "Let's sleep on it, and we can talk to Harry and Hank about it tomorrow."

31- BAMYAN: FEBRUARY 10, 1970

"I'm pleased to see you again," Mahmood said as the group was ushered into the big room. He clapped his hands for tea.

James approached Mahmood with an envelope, handed it to Mohammed and bowed before resuming his seat. Mohammed relayed the envelope to Mahmood.

Mahmood set the envelope on the table without checking its contents. "Thank you for your understanding," Mahmood said. "I will make the arrangements to have the money sent to the men holding your friend."

Mahmood drank his tea and scanned off into the distance before turning back to the group. "This may take a few days." He leaned back and took a deep breath. "They have gone into hiding, expecting that I might retaliate against them." He raised his hand. "I would not do that. But these men do not know me. They only know of me. Enjoy your tea and perhaps have another visit to our amazing statues. Many in other villages do not like them— thinking they are graven images, which as you may know is forbidden in the Muslim religion. Ignorant people can be so intolerant. Of course, we inhabitants of this beautiful valley treasure them as our heritage." He nodded to Mohammed. "I will send word when I have located your friend. Do not despair." He placed his hands together and raised his head upward.

"Your friend will be returned to you...God willing." He motioned to Mohammed, who hurried down the steps, moved to their side, and beckoned them toward the door. "Go with God."

***

"Jesus, it's been over a week," Sally said as she was sitting in the large room, soaking up the warmth of the wood stove as the group passed the chillum around. "Mahmood said a few days. I'm so worried." She grabbed her head. "Maybe we should go to the embassy."

Bridget looked over at Sally as she considered Sally's statement. She could tell that Sally was trying her best not to erupt into tears. Sally's suggestion of going to the embassy would most likely be useless and might anger Mahmood if he found out about it. Mahmood seemed to have great influence and undoubtedly had informers in the government. She did not trust Mahmood fully, but thought allowing him to pay the ransom to get Hank released was probably the best course.

The delay was worrisome, and she commiserated with Sally. Her romance with Hank had allowed her to know James, Sally, and Harry. She was thankful they had forgiven her for her dalliance with James and had included her in the journey back to Europe. For that she was supremely thankful. Hank's aggressive manner had driven her away from him and had caused his abduction. Had she been more patient with him and not so enamored of James could she have dampened his aggression and prevented his abduction?

She was glad that there was a ready supply of hash to dampen the morbid mood of the group. Of course it had been Hank's wish to obtain hash at a low price that led to the impasse they were in. Their journey back to Europe had turned grim. Without Hank's release the journey would be dreadful. If there were more delays and problems, she and Monica could journey on westward together taking public transport. She thought Harry would want to come too. He knew the route. James and Sally would probably stay for some time until finding Hank became futile. Could their relationship last if Hank was never found?

There was a soft knock on the door. When James opened the door, the houseboy handed him a note.

James read the note and turned toward the group. "We've been summoned." He frowned. "Maybe you ladies want to stay here. Harry and I can go."

"I'm going," Sally said as she jumped up, grabbing James's arm. "You think Mahmood has Hank?"

"I don't know," James replied, shaking his head. "Let's not jump to conclusions."

"I want to come too," Bridget announced. Besides wanting to go to find out about Hank, she felt she could help keep Sally from offending Mahmood.

"I want to come," Monica added.

"Okay we'll all go," James said. "Let's not get our hopes up." James paused and watched the group. "But there must be a development." He placed his arm around Sally.

***

"My friends, thank you for coming," Mahmood said as they were ushered into the big room. "I expect theses repeated trips are rather tedious for you. Please sit." He clapped his hands and tea was brought.

Bridget could tell that Sally wanted to speak out, but was glad that Sally constrained herself despite her obvious worry. She had placed herself on the other side of Sally in case she needed to reach out to her. Mahmood would not look favorably on an assertive woman, even though it was obvious that Mahmood was enthralled with Sally. She studied Monica's face, which displayed obvious worry, but nothing as severe as Sally's. She suspected Monica's pairing with Hank was a convenience for Monica as it had been for her. Poor Hank— he didn't instill deep devotion in any of the women he courted. Would this ordeal change him? Undoubtedly it would. It could either make him more aggressive or temper his rough nature. Mahmood always has to have the proper protocol and the tea. She wished Mahmood would drop the time consuming preliminaries and just tell them what's going on.

Mahmood sipped his tea and studied them before straightening and taking a deep breath. "I am sorry to tell you that there has been a difficult development. My rival, who some would call my enemy, has intervened and kidnapped your friend. He is trying to use the situation against me."

"What about the ransom we paid?" Sally blurted out.

Bridget cringed and placed her hand on Sally's back to distract her. Mahmood's expression conveyed his surprise at Sally's outburst, but he recovered his stoic face quickly. Mahmood's fascination with Sally was still holding sway.

James placed his hand on Sally's wrist and stared hard at her, furrowing his brow. Sally frowned back, but remained quiet. James was good at sensing the situation and adept at restraining Sally. Bridget was still infatuated with him even though she was content with her association with Harry. Harry was supportive, but did not come close to eliciting the desire that James aroused in her.

"What does this mean?" James asked.

Mahmood stared at the group in silence a moment before speaking. "The men asking for the ransom are also in custody of my rival." He glanced to the side and placed his hand on his cheek. "This has now become my problem. If more ransom is required, it will be my responsibility. I am now honor bound to resolve this situation." He stroked his beard. "My men are seeking information as to the whereabouts of your friend. It is a delicate situation. I must be very careful how I proceed to insure the safety of your friend."

"What should we do?" James asked as he squeezed Sally's hand.

Sally looked like she had been stabbed, her ashen face drawn in disbelief. Bridget hoped Sally would remain quiet. Another outburst would not be helpful.

"You can return to Kabul and wait, or you can continue your travels west," Mahmood replied. "You could see the other grand locations of my beloved country often called the crossroad to the East. We have a rich history. If you prefer to stay in Kabul that is acceptable. I thought further travel would help to occupy your minds. I know the situation is very vexing for you. Resolving the situation will take some time."

"We can't leave without Hank," James said and placed his arm around Sally as she slumped forward. "We will return to Kabul and wait."

Mahmood motioned to Mohammed behind him and handed him an envelope. Mohammed brought the envelope to James. "I am returning your money. Your friend's release and safety is my problem now. I assure you I will do everything within my power to find and release your friend. I shall, however, proceed with utmost caution. Haste would only endanger your friend. Hopefully my men will quickly discover the hiding place they have taken your friend. There are many hiding places in the hills and mountains, but I am sending my best men, who know the terrain like the back of their hands."

He sipped his tea. "My rival is being very foolish and will pay dearly for his actions. He is an evil, devious man, who would stop at nothing to embarrass me or attack me in some way other than going directly against my superior forces. He is a coward." He nodded to the boy. "Mohammed will show you out. Inside the envelope is an address to which you can write and indicate your location if you change your mind and want to travel west, so your friend can reach you when he is released. Of course I would ask that you not leave Afghanistan. Any letter with my name left at a post office, I assure you, will reach me very quickly. I have special dispensation at our post offices. I would strongly advise you not to go to the authorities. They have little sway in Afghanistan and would further endanger your friend. Upon your friend's release, I will insure that he has the means to safely reach you wherever you may be in Afghanistan." He threw his arm out. "Mohammed will show you out. Go with God."

Mohammed stood by their side. James, Harry, Monica and Bridget got up, but Sally remained sitting in a stupor. James pulled her up. "Would it help if we could raise more money?" James asked.

"No, money is not a problem," Mahmood said. "I am a wealthy man, and I will spare no expense in finding and freeing your friend. I have been gravely insulted, and, God willing, I will eventually triumph." He motioned for them to leave. "Please leave this in my hands. You have my word that is more valuable than all the money you could procure. Go with God."

279

The flight to Pokhara was in an old DC-10 airplane that had seen better days. There were no seats. Harry and James, the only Westerners, lounged on the floor with their packs along with the Nepalese. A group of women in colorful native dress with multiple heavy gold necklaces stared at them warily and talked in a clipped dialect.

The plane on landing sounded like it was ready to come apart, rattling and shaking as it hit the ground. The group of women clutched at their necklaces, eyes wide in terror. The group slowly relaxed as the plane came to a halt.

James and Harry were the first to walk down the stairs, greeted by the blue skies and snow covered mountains in the distance. James breathed in the clear air and smiled to himself. It was hard to believe he was even here and would soon be hiking in the Himalayas. Something he hadn't contemplated doing in his wildest dreams.

"There they are," Harry said pointing north at the mountains. "This is going to be so cool."

James laughed and nodded. "They look majestic, but very far away."

"Yeah, it's going to be a long trek for sure."

"I read about a Tibetan camp on the outskirts of town that would be a good place to stay the night and would be easy access to the trail north," James said excitedly. He was so glad he had met Harry in Kathmandu and was thankful that Sally had promoted him coming even after his betrayal with Bridget.

***

"Yuk, this tea tastes horrible," Harry said as they were sitting outside eating breakfast at the Tibetan camp, basking in the sun, a welcome relief to the cold night in the large tent of the hostel.

"It's got yak butter in it," James replied. "Rather salty but it's not that bad. It's hot and feels good in the stomach." He rubbed his belly. "This buckwheat porridge is pretty good."

"I need a proper cup of tea," Harry said. He called over the Tibetan waiter, whose smile in his soil stained face was wide and bright, and tried to make him understand that he wanted tea with no yak butter.

"Tea, yes, very good," the Tibetan replied repeatedly.

"Just give up and drink it," James said.

Harry frowned but grudgingly drank the tea. They ordered more buckwheat porridge, and James had another salty tea. After their breakfast, they set out on the trail for Nayapul. The incline was gradual and the walking was rather easy at first, but then the trail soon started climbing upward. They rested frequently to catch their breath but kept walking and a slow pace. They stopped at a trailside tea stand mid-morning near Sarangkot for a milky tea with sweet biscuits that they dipped in the tea and devoured.

"The map says were at 1590 meters," James said. "We've climbed 700 hundred meters."

"I can feel it. Man, am I out of shape." Harry closed his eyes as he sipped his tea. "I'm glad to have some semblance of real tea. That yak butter tea was horrible. I don't know how you drank two cups."

The snowcapped Dhaulagiri Mountain with its iconic shape and the three pinnacle Annapurna Mountains were visible in the distance. A walking train of six Nepalese men with large tins of cooking oil were at the tea stand as well. As Harry and James savored their tea, the group of Nepalese in their tattered shirts, shorts, and worn sandals hoisted the tins of cooking oil on the backs, slipped the rope and head band over their heads, and off they went.

"That's a job and a half," Harry said. "That would kill my neck carrying that weight like that."

"No kidding. We better get going if we are going to make Nayapul before dark."

"Hang about," Harry replied. "I need another tea. Our water tastes horrible with those iodine tablets. I'm tired already and this pack I brought is uncomfortable."

"What about this piece of shit pack I got in the Kathmandu bazar," James said. "Your English pack is way better. You want to swap."

Harry laughed. "No."

They had another tea and started off. The trail after Sarangkot was not as steep, but they were feeling the altitude and their legs were aching.

"So you were in the British Army," James said.

"Yeah, I grew up in a small village, Watchet, Somerset. Heart of cider country and fishing. Not many jobs. Got tired of working mindless jobs, so I enlisted in the Army." He adjusted his pack. "Big mistake. Talk about programmed idiots. After two years, I couldn't take much more of their crap. So I bought myself out."

"Bought yourself out?"

"Yeah, I had less than a year to go and paid to get out early."

"Wow, how cool is that. The US had nothing like that. I would have given every last cent I had to have gotten out of going to Vietnam."

"I understand completely. I haven't met one US vet that thought the war was justified."

"Believe me there are plenty that think the war was necessary to stop communism and were glad to participate. At least Britain didn't have the draft and didn't participate in the carnage."

"Harold Wilson saved us from that involvement. How that ever came about I don't know. Many rabid soldiers would have loved to have gone to Vietnam to fight."

They stopped at a house on the trail at Naudanda for a late afternoon lunch. The view of the Annapurna Mountains was spectacular as they relaxed outside under the house portal on woven mats. The sky and clouds seemed so close. They were served the traditional Nepalese lunch of dahl, bhat, and tarkari— lentil soup, brown rice, and curried potatoes— by the pretty lady, dressed in a pink high collar Nepalese shirt and wrap around black skirt.

When they finished the small meal, they paid the lady three rupees each and settled back against the wall, staring out at the mountains as they finished the last of their tea.

"I'm beat," Harry said. "It's already late. I wouldn't mind staying here for the night. We don't want to end up on the trail after dark."

"Yeah, you're probably right. I'm exhausted too." James signaled the lady, placed his hands together, laid his head on his hands, and pointed into the house. "Sleep here tonight?"

The lady smiled, nodded, and took them inside and pointed to an area and made the sign of sleeping.

"Thanks... Dhayabaad," James said. He and Harry removed their sleeping bags and rolled them out. James got out a book and began reading. Harry fell asleep.

Just before dark, a man entered the house. He stared momentarily at the two reclined on their sleeping bags, his eyes wide in surprise, before putting his hands together. "Namaste."

The woman, after brief conversation with the man, began cooking. They were served the same meal they had had for lunch. When they handed over the three rupees each after the family had finished eating, the man accepted the money with a big smile and exclaimed, "Namaste."

***

The next morning they were up early and moved outside to sit under the portal. A few song birds were singing and the view of the distant mountains in the morning sun was inspiring. James indicated to the lady that they wanted to eat. The lady didn't seem to understand. James got out six rupees and again made the gesture of eating. The lady nodded and fixed them the same breakfast as the evening meal. They lingered over their tea, sitting under the portal, reluctant to start hiking. The lady began thrashing rice.

"We better get going," Harry said. "I think we're overstaying our welcome."

They hoisted their packs, gestured Namaste to the lady, and started off. The trail climbed upward steadily. They plodded along with frequent pauses for a short rest, then stopped midday for the standard meal in a small village that didn't appear on the map.

"I feel better today," Harry said as he hoisted his pack. "We should make it to Nayapul with no problem."

They continued upward through the subtropical forest as the birds sang and glimpses of the mountains appeared through the trees. When they reached a peak in the trail, they plopped down to rest and soak up the view.

"The Annapurnas are spectacular," James said as he inhaled deeply in the thin air. "I think we're finally making good time. Course the Nepalese pack trains are passing us like we're standing still."

"Those little guys are amazing," Harry said. "Human pack trains. Unbelievable. It's like we entered a time machine, and we're in a past century."

"Yeah, it blows my mind that we're traveling through a timeless society at the foothills of the tallest mountains in the world."

"How much further you think?" Harry asked with exhausted breath.

"Let's see," James replied as he unfolded the map. "It's ten kilometers on the map."

"Well we better take off then," Harry said. "Ten kilometers on that map could be close to fifteen or twenty actual walking distance."

"Hopefully it won't be too difficult," James said. "It appears to be downhill from here most of the way to Nayapul, which is on the confluence of the Modi and Burundi Rivers." James stretched and rubbed his legs. "Ten kilometers...six miles." He rose and slipped his pack on. "Let's hit it."

Harry reluctantly rose and hoisted his pack. "Right then."

They continued on, slow and deliberate, down and up, but mostly down.

"So how did you meet Sally, Hank, and Bridget?" Harry asked. "Seemed like Hank and you didn't like each other that much."

"I met Sally and Hank in Hong Kong. We were supposed to meet up in Bangkok, but the freighter they took went to other ports and they didn't arrive until after I left. Apparently, Hank booked the extended sailing without Sally's knowledge in hopes of stopping Sally from seeing me again. He was extremely jealous and belligerent in Hong Kong. If Sally hadn't been such a beautiful and fun woman, I might have given up on her. I waited in Bangkok for her to arrive for five days, but had to move on because my uncle in Madras would soon be leaving India. He bought me my around the world plane ticket, so I felt obligated to spend some time with him before he left. When I left Bangkok, I doubted I'd ever see Sally again."

James paused as another Nepalese pack train approached and passed them. "I was severely disappointed that I had lost such an intriguing woman. She really made an impression on me. When they came to my uncle's in Madras, I was ecstatic. We stayed in Madras a couple of weeks. Sally moved into my uncle's apartment with me after my uncle left for the States, and Hank stayed at a hotel. Being alone with Sally without Hank was pure bliss. She captured my heart. After Madras, she and I along with Hank traveled together to Bombay and then to Ellora and Ajanta where Hank met Bridget. I was elated when Bridget hooked up with Hank. Man, did Bridget capture Hank. His jealously disappeared. He was still a bit of a butt-head, but travel was so much easier. We had a great time in Goa. When we left Goa and went to Udaipur and then Delhi, Bridget didn't seem to be that enamored of Hank anymore. Hank got sick in Benares and as you know in Kathmandu."

"So why did Bridget leave?"

"She had had it with Hank." He wasn't going to explain his betrayal with Bridget. He was ashamed of his weakness with Bridget and the schism that it caused. "How was your travel to India and Kathmandu?"

"I left the English couple in Delhi," Harry said. "Stayed in Delhi a few days. Of course went to Agra and then on to Benares. The Taj Mahal was incredibly beautiful. I thought Benares was interesting too, but the whole cremation business I found depressing. Plus all the hippie nuts there seeking enlightenment were irritating."

"I understand the motivation. Enlightenment sounds fascinating, and I think it is a worthy pursuit. But, I think it is a lifetime pursuit with no easy short cuts." Was he trying to pursue enlightenment? He didn't think he was really ready for such a pursuit. His Nam baggage or bad karma as the Hindus would call it was a block he needed to overcome. But how was one supposed to overcome such hideous actions?

"I agree. I'm interested in Buddhism and Hinduism, also. That's one of the reasons why I came out here. Also I wanted to see the Himalayas. I'm so glad you agreed to come trekking."

"If I hadn't met you, I probably wouldn't have come trekking. I didn't know anything about it until you mentioned it. It's an experience of a lifetime. Thank you."

"Do you believe in reincarnation?"

"I don't know. I have my doubts." He had doubts about most everything when it came down to it. He even doubted his infatuation with Sally. Were they meant to be together or was she a station on his journey? He was certainly missing her already. Did he feel true love for her?

"I have my doubts too. It's an interesting concept."

"The first law of thermodynamics that energy cannot be created or destroyed makes me think it could be possible. We are a type of energy. When we die our energy could live on in some other form or possibly in another person."

"Uh-oh, the engineer in you is coming out." Harry laughed. "I know nothing about thermodynamics, but it's an interesting way to think about reincarnation. It would be nice to believe that our spirit continued on after death."

33- ANJUNA BEACH: DECEMBER 21, 1969

"Hey up, mate," Sally said as she stepped into the house as soon as Bridget opened the door and hugged a surprised Bridget.

"Sally?" Bridget said, her face looking like she'd seen a ghost. "What are you doing here? And Hank?" She stared at the two as if they were an impossible mirage.

Sally and Hank had taken the bus and train from Nepal to Delhi, spent the night, caught the train to Bombay, spent the night, and then the train to Goa. They had not had many difficulties, but Sally had worried most of the journey how Bridget would take their arrival. Bridget was very upset when she left Kathmandu, and Sally feared Bridget would shun them.

Sally blew out a breath. She was relieved that Bridget hadn't closed the door in their face. She needed to insinuate herself as quickly as possible before Bridget's anger surfaced. "We came to stay a while if that's all right." She hesitated, hoping Bridget wouldn't tell them to leave. "We can rent another place if need be."

"Where's James?" Bridget asked as she went outside still seemingly unable to process their arrival.

"He went trekking in Nepal with Harry, the Englishmen you met at the tea place. They'll probably be a few weeks. Then they're both coming here." Sally debated if she should initiate additional physical contact— demonstrate she held no animosity toward Bridget despite Bridget's enticement of James.

"Why?" Bridget said with a screwed up face.

"So we can all meet up." Sally placed her hand lightly on Bridget's shoulder. "James, Hank, Harry, and I are going to travel overland to London. Either by buses or possibly buy a van and drive." She moved closer and put her arm around Bridget, who hunched her shoulders. "I'm so glad to see you again, Bridget."

"Drive back overland?" Bridget said. "All of you?"

"Yeah, if we can find a van to buy."

"I thought you and Hank were going back to Australia from India."

"We changed our mind. I have an uncle in London I haven't seen for years. The overland journey that Harry talked about sounded so cool and interesting. I didn't want to pass up the opportunity to continue traveling. The things I've seen and the wonderful artwork... it's been amazing."

"I'm dying of thirst," Hank said. "You got any beer."

Hank's comment seemed to shock Bridget out of her stupor, her face changing to a scowl. "No, we're out," she said. She softened her scowl and looked from Hank to Sally and then back to Hank. "We could go to the beach restaurant? Monica is at the beach." She placed her hands on her hips. "I was just going to go myself. Why don't you stash your stuff and get your suits on. You can have the spare bedroom. Lisa had to leave and get back home... family emergency. It's only Monica and me now."

Sally breathed out and felt the tension slip from her limbs. They had been accepted. She pulled Hank into the spare room and hurriedly donned her bathing suit. She thought about getting Hank to rub suntan cream on her back, but decided they needed to join Bridget as fast as possible, so Bridget wouldn't think more about their arrival and change her mind about them staying. "It's so nice to be back here." Sally beamed at Bridget and got a small smile in return. Things were still a little tense, but she felt if Hank didn't do something stupid she would be able to renew her friendship with Bridget.

After snaking through the coconut grove, the shining sea and beautiful sand beach came into view. Monica was laid out on a blanket, her bronze skin shining in the sun.

"Hey up, Monica," Sally called as they approached. "That's a beautiful tan you've got. Wish I could tan like that."

Monica shaded her eyes. "What the hell... Sally and Hank. Where'd you come from?"

"Nepal... we just got in," Sally said. "We're staying for a few weeks until James and our new friend Harry show up."

Monica glanced at Bridget, who was not smiling. "Oh... well, great."

"We're going for some beer and an early dinner," Bridget said. "You coming."

"Of course," Monica replied. She got up and gave Sally and Hank a hug. "Good to see you again." She rolled up her blanket, slipped on her tee shirt, and they walked over to the restaurant.

After a hot fish curry and innumerable beers, they waited for the sunset. The fiery globe sank in the turquoise ocean to sound of the drummers. They weaved their way back to the house through the coconut trees. Hank pulled out his Nepalese hash and chillum. They shared the chillum back and forth until late in the night. Bridget and Monica said good night and went to their rooms.

"Hey up, mate, you're not sleeping with me," Sally said as Hank followed her into the third bedroom. "It's the couch for you, Big Guy." She gave him a light shove and lowered her voice. "You need to try and get back in Bridget's good graces or try it on with Monica, but you need to take it slow. Try being subtle for a change." She patted him on the arm. "You can forget about trying your moves on me."

"Okay... okay," Hank said, shoving her back. "You don't have to get nasty."

"Yeah, I do. I don't want any more of that crap you tried in Delhi."

Hank frowned, grabbed his pack, and left the room.

He would've tried it on for sure Sally thought. He should stop being an asshole and try wooing Bridget again. Bet she's getting horny unless she's had some squeeze here. Course he could try Monica. She's almost as beautiful as Bridget, but a little heavier—much bigger breasts. She knew Hank liked them buxom. Monica was just his cup of tea. She personally thought Bridget was more enticing with her lanky model body. Either way, he needed to be on his good behavior. Something often lacking in Hank.

***

They settled into a beach rhythm and Hank's enticement of Bridget hit a stone wall. Sally stayed mostly in the shade, limiting her sun exposure to only a few hours. She made sketches of the beach scene and the many different Goans as she was sitting in the shade. She had to shoo off the many Western and Goan admirers she attracted.

Hank developed a golden brown tan again. He changed his pursuit to Monica and was surprisingly gallant and restrained. After several days, he was successful and spent the night with Monica. Bridget didn't seem to mind in the least. Sally thought things had worked out surprisingly well. Much better than she had envisioned.

They celebrated Christmas at the beach restaurant that had a decorated Christmas tree. They had purchased small little gifts for each other, and they had a jolly time. Hank and Monica became almost legless drunk late into the night. Bridget and Sally had to help them back to the bungalow.

Sally was surprised that Bridget wasn't still holding a grudge against her. Bridget sought her out, choosing to walk next to her to the beach, engaging her in conversation, and often placing her hand on Sally's shoulder. Bridget volunteered to rub sunscreen on Sally's back and grabbed the seat next to her during dinner at the beach restaurant. Sally was happy that they were getting on so well, but wondered why Bridget was being so nice to her. She still hadn't fully forgiven Bridget for seducing James.

***

"How much longer are you and Monica staying here?" Sally asked.

"We're not sure. I almost went back with Lisa, but Monica talked me into staying."

They were back at the house enjoying chillum after chillum. Several weeks had passed. Sally and Bridget were ensconced on the couch together. Hank and Monica had left to the bedroom.

Bridget picked up Sally's sketch book. "I love your sketches. The detail is so rich and such a diverse array. You are very talented." Bridget held up the sketch of herself sitting on the beach topless. "I wish I could draw like this."

"Thanks," Sally replied. She thought it was indicative that Bridget chose the sketch of herself for comment. She suspected the Swede thought highly of her beauty and wanted to reinforce her ego any chance she could. "I'd be at a loss without my sketch

295

book. I can't wait to turn the sketches into water colors and oil paintings when I'm settled."

"What a wonderful memento of your journey."

"Yeah, I guard this sketch book closely. I'd hate to lose it."

"That would be terrible."

Sally smiled at Bridget and placed her hand on Bridget's shoulder. "I've always liked you. I know I got rather nasty and unpleasant in Nepal. I couldn't help myself. I'm so crazy about James. I want to put what happened in Nepal behind us. I understand your attraction to James. He's an amazing guy. I hope we can remain friends."

She hoped Bridget swallowed her bullshit. She hadn't forgiven Bridget and doubted she ever would. She didn't really trust Bridget. If Bridget and Monica were invited to come with them overland, Bridget might try to rekindle a liaison with James. She wouldn't put it past her. Would she be able to take Bridget's overt attention to James? Not easily that was for sure even if it would be a good test of James's fidelity. Hank would be much easier to take if he was paired with Monica. Finding other suitable riders could be challenging. Many of the Western travelers were con artists. Some seemed barely sixteen. She didn't think Monica would come without Bridget. If Bridget came along, maybe she could hook up with Harry. Bridget seemed to like new conquests. Harry was handsome, tall, and had a pleasant demeanor. Seemed like the kind of bloke Bridget would go for. Everyone paired up would be ideal.

"Yeah-yeah, James is very handsome and interesting," Bridget said nervously. "I'm so glad we're friends again." She hugged Sally and pressed her chest against hers. "I think you're beautiful. I love your hair." She ran her fingers through Sally's long sanguine hair. "It's so soft and such a rich color." She pulled back slightly and stared with an enigmatic smile almost a smirk. "Have you ever been with another woman?"

"Wow... hang about, mate," Sally said and moved away a short gap. "No I haven't, and I don't think I want to try."

"Hey, no pressure," Bridget said. "I've been with women. I like men most, but being with another woman can be exciting too. The last sex I've had was with James and I'm getting way too horny. I almost thought about getting it on with Hank, but I'm glad I didn't. I'm happy he's with Monica now." She tossed her head back and laughed at Sally's stretched face. "Don't worry. I'm not going to jump you. If you change your mind, you might find it enjoyable." She kissed Sally on the cheek and rose. "Guess I'll go to bed. See you in the morning."

Sally didn't know what to think as she rubbed her cheek. So she's bisexual. Wonder if she and Monica get it on. They look so much alike it would be like screwing a mirror. Not for me. Although nothing tried, nothing gained. What? Easy mate. What the hell was she thinking? She hoped James would arrive soon. She was missing him and their athletic romps. Would his continued absence tempt her with Bridget? She leaned back and sighed. Go to bed.

James and Harry reached the river at Nayapul as the sky was darkening. They had descended about six hundred meters. The valley's green hills were terraced with rock walls for planting. The air was sweet as the river gurgled down the rocky valley. Birds swept from tree to tree, chirping their song.

They chose one of the few stone houses on the trail and greeted the man standing outside. He welcomed them with the Namaste greeting and motioned them inside with hand gestures, staring at them as if they were aliens from another planet. Two adolescent boys inside watched them with wide eyes and big smiles. They along with the woman of the house greeted them with Namaste gestures. The man indicated a space to the left of the central fire pit and put his hands together laying his head on his hands. James nodded, placed his pack down, and removed his sleeping bag. Harry followed suit. The woman began building up the fire and placed several pots on the fire. The kids were sitting in front of the sleeping bags giggling and shoving each other while they continued to stare.

"That seemed a lot more than six miles," Harry said. "I'm glad it was mostly downhill." He stared back at the kids. "These kids act like they've never seen Westerners before."

"Well, they probably haven't seen many," James said. "We've seen only Nepalese on the trail so far."

After the dahl, bhat, and tarkari diner served on metal plates while the whole family stared at them, they lolled back on their packs, and sipped their milky tea. The woman began mixing a brown powder in another pot with boiling water. The family ate the brown mush with the dahl and tarkari.

"What do think that brown mush is?" Harry said.

"I don't know," James answered. He set his tea down and held out his plate gesturing that he wanted to try the brown mush. The man waved James off. "Well I guess it's not allowed for us."

After the family finished their meal, the woman gathered the dishes and went outside followed by the giggling kids. When she returned she took her place next to her husband. The kids planted themselves at the foot of the sleeping bags. The man turned down the lantern and stirred the fire before laying his head on his hands and smiling.

"You going to undress while they just stare at us?" Harry said.

"What else can we do?" James said. "We're the entertainment."

James and Harry removed their jeans and shirt as the whole family laughed. As soon as they climbed into their sleeping bags, the family pulled out their sleeping pads and extinguished the lantern. James was glad to close his eyes and was soon asleep.

When James awoke to the sound of a crowing rooster, he was unsure of his whereabouts momentarily before he dismissed his nightmare. The woman was already up and working at a counter cutting potatoes. The kids were sitting at the foot of their sleeping bags, staring with big smiles as the morning light came in the open door. He smiled at the absurdity that they were such a source of amusement for these happy boys.

"Oh, my back is killing me," Harry said stretching his arms out of his bag. He glanced at the kids. "Well, I'm glad these kids get such a kick out of us."

"Happy to oblige." James crawled out of his bag and slipped on his jeans to the laughs of the kids and woman. He couldn't help but laugh himself. Harry began laughing too.

After they were dressed, the woman began cooking. The aroma of frying onions and potatoes infused the room and jump-started James's hunger. She motioned with two cups of tea for them to go outside and followed them out, indicating for them to sit under the portal on the women mats. The man was gone. The mist was clearing over the valley and the sun reflected off the mist still lingering over the roaring river. The sound of the river and the singing birds added a pleasant atmosphere to the morning air. They sipped their tea as the boys watched them intently. The woman called to the boys, who rushed inside. When the boys returned, they handed Harry and James plates of the dahl, bhat and tarkari.

"I could do with some eggs," Harry said. "I feel like I'm starved for fuel. I heard a rooster." He turned to the woman, who was standing in the doorway with a big smile, closed his thumb and finger together, and made chicken sounds. "Do you have eggs?" The woman shook her head as the kids guffawed.

"No eggs apparently," James said, laughing.

After they finished their food, James and Harry went inside, followed by the boys, to roll up their bags and ready their packs. The boys crowded around to make sure they didn't miss anything. Harry and James handed over another three rupees to the woman, who was very thankful. Outside the sky was nearly clear and the cold air was beginning to warm. They bowed and made the Namaste sign to the woman in the doorway and started off, the boys following along for a time, shoving each other and laughing before turning back.

Harry stopped and took a deep breath. "Those kids were a trip. I'm hungry already. I could have eaten three breakfasts. I'll be ready for lunch in an hour."

James laughed. "Yeah, we're burning calories like mad. Well, let's try for double portions for lunch. Onward and upward."

The trail was alongside the swift flowing Burundi River and air was cool and sweet. After several hours they stopped at a tea stand. The morning had warmed, and they removed their jackets and stuffed them in their packs. They leaned against their packs as they savored their tea and biscuits. After two teas, Harry nodded at James and they stood. Without a word they slipped on their packs and continued onward at a leisurely pace.

They stopped for lunch in Chandrakot at a trailside house for the standard meal. The tarkari was not that tasty, consisting mostly of undercooked potatoes and onions with a few spices, but the dahl was quite flavorful. The woman, who served them, chatted away in her native language as if she thought they could understand her or didn't care if they didn't. She served them outside as they lazed on the woven rattan mats. Harry after gobbling his meal tried to obtain additional portions, making motions of eating and holding out rupees, but the woman just laughed and continued to hold forth, happy to be talking.

"She doesn't want to give us anymore food," Harry said in exasperation.

"Either she doesn't understand or believes the portions served should be adequate," James replied. He tried his attempt to make the woman understand they wanted more food by rubbing his belly and pointing to his plate and pretending to eat invisible food. The woman laughed, then continued her discourse. "Well, we're not going to get any more food." He turned his empty cup upside down and made motions of drinking. The lady nodded, retrieved their cups, went inside, and returned with more tea. "At least we can get another milky tea."

They slowly savored their second cup of tea, reluctant to start off. James, closed his eyes and let the warmth of the sun sooth his aching body. He knew they needed to be moving on, but was enjoying the respite.

Finally, Harry said, "All right then. I suppose we should carry on."

"You're right. We've got a ways to go if we're going to make it to Ulleri before dark." They paid the lady, who stopped talking briefly to count the money, then continued on with her talk. When they donned their packs, she bowed repeating 'Namaste' incessantly and waved as they started off.

After they were out of earshot, Harry said, "That lady was nuts. She sure liked talking. I don't understand why she wouldn't give us more food."

"The mysteries of Nepal."

They reached the village of Thikedunga later in the afternoon and continued through the small village as a group of kids followed along laughing and asking 'how are you' repeatedly before veering off. After a short distance from the village, the trail became stone steps upward.

"My god," Harry said. "Those steps go up as far as you can see. I don't know if I'm ready for this."

"Yeah, they're almost straight up," James said and removed his pack. "We could stay the night in the village and do these stairs in the morning."

"Excellent idea."

They smoked a chillum and relaxed by the river soaking their aching feet in the water before walking back while birds sang and flew overhead. They choose a stone house in the village and were invited in. They were shown to a type of alcove where the woman indicated with hand signs the area they would sleep. They spread out their sleeping bags and laid down. James wrote in his journal and Harry read his book.

As the light was fading, the man of the house arrived. He greeted them with Namaste and spoke briefly to his wife before leaving. When he returned he had a live chicken by its legs. He thrust the chicken, flapping its wings, repeatedly at them and smiled, nodding continuously.

"He's trying to get us to buy the chicken for dinner," James said. "What do you think?"

"How many rupees?" Harry asked.

The man spoke, but in Nepalese.

Harry held up ten fingers. The man spread the fingers on his left hand four times. "Twenty... no," Harry said and held up ten fingers again. The man repeated the four hand spreads.

"That's a lot of meals," James said. "If you want, I'll go for it."

"No way," Harry said. "Besides that chicken has seen better days." He pushed his finger and thumb in a circle. "Eggs?" The man held the chicken up again. "No chicken... eggs."

The man left and came back with two eggs.

"Yes good," Harry said. "Rupees?"

"The man held up two fingers and then five fingers."

Harry nodded. "Yes...okay."

The man nodded and handed the eggs to the woman.

***

They rose very early at first light and without eating left for the steps. At the steps, they paused.

"This is going to be a killer," Harry said. "We should've had breakfast."

"The man didn't seem that friendly and was pretty blatant about us leaving," James said. "According to the trekking guide most Nepalese normally don't eat breakfast, but have a meal around eleven and their second in the evening after dark."

Harry glanced at James. "They've got much smaller bodies. Still we're at least well rested and those eggs were a welcome addition last night." He started the climb. "Alley-oop."

The steps seemed to go on forever. The burn in James's thighs was overwhelming. After nearly an hour he stopped and dropped down. "God, how many steps are there?" They were in an alpine forest surrounded by hills that gave an occasional glimpse of the majestic mountains.

"Whose idea was this," Harry said. "We could go back and forget it."

Approaching from below was a walking train of Nepalese with heavy goods on their back, supported by the head brace, their faces twisted in determination as they relentlessly stepped up the steep incline.

"If those little guys can do it, we can," Harry said. "Come on." Harry rose with a groan.

They continued on up and up, stone step after step. They negotiated over three thousand steps before they reached the summit.

Up ahead they spied the tea stand where the Nepalese pack train were sitting, drinking tea and resting. Before they reached the stand, the Nepalese men were up with their goods and off.

They reached the tea stand and collapsed with their packs still on their backs. After several minutes James rolled over and slipped his pack off with a groan. The two men in the tea stand stared at the two with wide-eyed blank faces.

"I can't move," Harry said. "Get me a tea and a packet of biscuits." He rolled out of his pack. "Jesus... that was one tough climb. Worse than all the physical shit I had to go through in the Army."

James fetched the teas and biscuits. The two Nepalese men started talking animatedly, periodically pointing at the two. Another Nepalese man approached from the North, ordered a tea, seated himself on a log, and stared at the two. He was dressed in a crisp white shirt and tan trousers, appearing much more affluent then most Nepalese. After several sips of his tea the man said, "Big climb."

"Yes, big-big climb," James said. "Do you speak English?"

The man twisted his hand. "A little English"

"Where is your village?" James asked.

"Ulleri, not far," The man said. "You come?"

James consulted his map. "Yes we go Ulleri, Banthanti, and sleep Ghorepani. We'll eat at Ulleri."

"Good," the man said. "I come with. Know good tea house for food. You relax. We go soon."

They had several teas dunking biscuit after biscuit in the sweet milky tea. The Nepalese man asked them where they were from. As he spoke, his English seemed to improve.

After more than ten minutes, James stood. "I'm starving. Let's go."

The three moved off at a leisurely pace up the gradual incline. They had ascended over 900 meters up the steps. At the village, the man led them to one of the larger houses on the trail. He motioned for them to stay and went inside. He soon reappeared. "Yes, come... come." Inside they were directed to a low table. "Sit. Good food here."

"Will you eat with us?" James asked, as he settled on the cushions around the table.

"No, but thank you." The man said and bowed. "Namaste." He smiled broadly. "Must go. Good trekking." He pivoted and left speaking to the woman as he left.

They were served the dahl, bhat, and tarkari. The tarkari had spring peas and a leafy green vegetables mixed in with the potatoes.

"Man, this is delicious," Harry said. "This sauce is great. This is the best tasting lentil soup we've had. And the portions are big."

"Just what we've been needing," James said in between the hurried bites of food. "The houses here seem studier then the houses lower down."

"Well I bet they get a lot more snow," Harry said. He scoured his plate with his fork and set it down with a whooshed exhale. "How much farther to Ghorepani?"

"On the map it's ten kilometers, but we have to climb up about eight hundred meters in elevation."

Harry stared at James and scrunched his forehead. "Not more steps?"

"I don't know." James hoped not. The steps had been difficult, but he felt a grace being on the trek. He was so happy that he had come and felt a growing kinship with Harry.

Bridget had been totally flabbergasted when Sally and Hank arrived. She thought she would never see them again and was surprised that Sally would ever contemplate staying with her. She doubted that Sally was genuinely happy to see her, but Sally put on a good act. Of course they were on their own, and had few choices of places to wait. Sally wouldn't have wanted to stay alone with Hank for two weeks. So coming here to stay with her and Monica made sense. Maybe Sally had thought Hank could get back together with Bridget.

Bridget had repelled Hank's advances when he and Sally first arrived and made it perfectly clear she wasn't interested in renewing any intimate relationship. Hank had pouted for a few days, but when Monica showed him some kindness, he switched his pursuit to Monica. Bridget was relieved but surprised that Monica would accept the brute. She had to admit her shunning of him and her pursuit of James in Kathmandu had seemed to mellow him somewhat. Monica was on her own. Her brief fling with a local man had been disastrous, so hooking up with Hank was understandable. He was handsome, strong, and kind.

Bridget wanted to be friends with Sally. She had wanted to take James away from Sally, but didn't dislike her. Actually she was drawn to Sally, thinking Sally was a beautiful, fun-loving woman. She paid

Sally a lot of attention, and they had a good time together. She found Sally alluring. She had attempted to seduce her briefly one night, but didn't push too hard as not to upset Sally unduly. She hoped with time Sally might fall into her web. She suspected her pursuit of James was partially because she wanted to compete with Sally and better the alluring red head. She liked enticing men away from other women. It was a game she enjoyed. She had almost lost Monica as a friend when she had taken one of Monica's boyfriends away from her in Sweden. Was she too competitive? She always wanted to be the best in everything.

Bridget didn't want Sally as an enemy. If she became enemies with Sally, James wouldn't want to have anything to do with her. She was convinced he had enjoyed their sex together unhindered in Kathmandu. Would she have an opportunity when James arrived to renew a possible liaison together with him and Sally? Was she crazy to even think about it? James was the only man, who had ever broken it off with her. She was always the one to break off affairs.

Sally lost her jolly nature after three weeks. Bridget stopped her subtle advances toward Sally, realizing Sally was too worried to accept any enticement. There was not much they could do but wait for James's and Harry's arrival. Maybe when James arrived, she could try wooing Sally again. If she could get Sally to agree, she suspected James would relish a threesome. She dreamed sometimes of the threesome and wondered if she was crazy to think a threesome was even possible.

***

After more than a month with no arrival of James and Harry, Bridget became extremely worried as well. She wondered if there was anything they could do to find out what had happened to James and Harry. Going to the authorities in India would be a waste of time. Maybe Hank and Sally should go back to Nepal to make enquiries. Bridget would like to go with them if they did, but she couldn't abandon Monica. Should they all go? How much longer should they wait? If James and Harry were lost in the mountains, would anything help? If they were injured in a hospital and conscious, James would surely would have sent a telegram to Sally care of the Thivim post office. Sally in her deep funk was hard to be around, but Bridget consoled her as best she could. If they didn't hear something soon, she was afraid Sally might fall ill. It took some coaxing to get Sally to even come to the beach with her anymore. Sally wasn't eating properly and had lost weight. She moped through the days often crying by herself in her room. Bridget profoundly hoped James and Harry would soon appear. Otherwise she decided they would have to travel to Nepal to find out what had happened.

36- GHOREPANI: DECEMBER 22, 1969

James and Harry reached Ghorepani late in the afternoon after walking through forested hills, passing several waterfalls. The trail didn't have any more long sections of steps just the occasional steps. The trail went up and down but mostly up. They had stopped midafternoon at a tea stand for a long rest, but mostly they had kept going.

They selected a large house in Ghorepani and were welcomed inside. They were given a separate room with no door for sleeping, which had an actual wooden floor. They unpacked and laid down on their sleeping bags.

Harry removed his boots and socks. "Ewe, do I stink."

"You're telling me."

"You're no rose either."

"There's a hill a few kilometers up the trail that's supposed to have a spectacular view of the mountains," James said. "If we get up early, we can watch the sunrise there."

"How early?"

"Six, I guess."

"Fuck, I'm beat." Harry rubbed his legs. "Those fucking steps killed me. My legs are numb."

"We can decide after dinner." James grabbed both knees and squeezed his legs toward his chest. "Poon hill is supposed to be spectacular."

"It's nice to have a semblance of privacy for a change," Harry said. "This is the biggest house we've seen. The village must be some kind of regional center. Did you see that building a couple of houses down? It might be a store of some kind."

"After a rest, let's check it out."

***

The sun broke over the snowcapped jagged Annapurna Mountains. The brilliance of the sun blinded them momentarily in the thin air. To the west, the snow on Dhaulagiri Mountain reflected the sun like a mirror.

"Oh, my god," Harry said. "Unbelievable. You were right. This was well worth getting up so early. Dhaulagiri has got to be the most beautiful mountain I've ever seen."

"The map says this hill top is 3200 meters." James was so happy to witness such a spectacular sunrise. All their effort had been well worth it. This was an experience he would never forget.

"I can feel the altitude." Harry stretched with a groan. "You know you called out in your sleep last night and the night before. What was it? Some kind of nightmare?"

"Yeah. I did things in Nam I'm not proud of. I often have a recurring nightmare that plagues me. Their frequency has diminished somewhat.

Traveling with Sally has helped." He pictured her beautiful face. Why did he ever jeopardize their relationship... stupid? He was glad that he had dreamed of Sally as well as the horrifying dream. For so long he had hoped that he would have other dreams. Sally had made it possible. "I'm missing her already."

"I can understand that," Harry said. "She seemed like a great energetic lass and really beautiful. I bet she's fun to be with. The other lady, Bridget, was nice too. She was incredibly beautiful—like a model. I liked her Swedish accent as well. Man, I could go for her. How come she left before Hank and Sally? I thought she was with Hank."

"She had a disagreement with Hank and wanted to return to Goa to reunite with her friends."

James pictured Bridget in his mind. He wished he had been stronger. He really did Hank a disservice... not to mention his betrayal of Sally. He would try to make it up to them when he got back to Goa. He hoped Hank had been able to renew his relationship with Bridget. It would make things easier if Bridget rode back overland with them. Another woman would make the journey more pleasant for Sally even if she still harbored ill feeling toward Bridget. One woman and three men might be difficult.

"Are Sally and Hank going to the same place as Bridget in Goa?"

"That was their plan." He wondered how the reunion went. He hoped Bridget didn't shun them.

She was very perturbed when she left. Well, if Bridget did shun them, there were plenty of other Westerners there they could befriend. "Do you have a girlfriend back in England?"

"Kind of. We've known each other since school. She was upset when I told her I was going to India and Nepal. After the Army, I needed to get away." He stared out at the Annapurnas. "I wasn't ready to settle down."

"Who were these people you traveled to India with?"

"I answered an advertisement asking for a rider to India to share expenses. The people were nice but too straight. They were coming to some kind of conference in Delhi. They were religious scholars. Man and wife."

"Were they interesting?"

"Sort of. Over educated idiots if you ask me. Still they were pleasant enough. I got the impression they looked down on me because I hadn't been to college. Both Oxford graduates."

They waited until the sun was well up above the mountains, then hoisted their packs, and started up the trail through the drifting clouds, climbing even higher before the trail started its downward drift. Down and up they went toward the valley.

They stopped at Chitre for their late breakfast. The tarkari had beans and greens with the potatoes. After savoring their tea, they paid their rupees and started off.

"I'm looking forward to the hot springs," Harry said. "That is if the map is correct."

"I hope so too. Soaking my aching body would be nice."

They reached Tatopani in the late afternoon. The village was even bigger than Ghorepani and there were several guest houses to choose from. They chose a guest house that actually had spacious rooms and even rope like beds, stowed their packs, and with their towels walked back to the hot spring pools. They stripped to their underwear and joined the two staring kids in the rocked off pool next to the rippling river.

"Christ, it's really hot," Harry said as he slipped into the steaming pool as the kids giggled.

They relaxed in the pools for over an hour, periodically dipping into the ice cold river. Whenever a villager walked past, they would stop and stare or exchange conversation with the kids that resulted in laughs and bows with Namastes. Finally satiated, James dried off, dressed, and they went back to the guest house.

"I feel renewed," James said as he laid down on his sleeping bag on the rickety bed.

"If I fall asleep wake me for dinner," Harry said. "That felt so good."

***

The following day they were slow to start their trek having enjoyed the luxury of a private room and several chillums. The trail wandered along the

317

cascading river most of the way. The air was fresh, suffused by the melodious birds trumpeting their progress. They had lunch at Dana a quiet little village next to the roaring Kali Gandi River.

After the trail ascended up, they were rewarded with the huge water fall at Rupse Chahara that caused them to stand in awe for many minutes before they continued further upward to Ghasa at 1960 meters where they spent the night.

Early up the next day to the sounds of birds welcoming the day, they had another hearty breakfast. They climbed upward through forests with lingering clouds. The wet mist felt good on their face. They were walking with ease now having acclimatized themselves to the regimen. They were even passing the Nepalese walking trains. Of course they were not carrying nearly the weight the Nepalese were. The beautiful mountains shining in the sun—the ever present back drop— made the hiking a joy.

They stopped for lunch in Larjung, a quiet little village along the river where the older Nepalese woman serving them had a plethora of colorful necklaces, a bright red patterned skirt, and an engaging laugh. They continued on following the river steadily climbing higher in altitude.

They reached Marpha a cliff lined village of stone houses on the river with its big Buddhist monastery at 2680 meters in the late afternoon and stopped for the night. The inhabitants had features similar to the Tibetans they had met. As the sun was sinking, they gathered outside their guest house and watched a group of Buddhist monks assemble in their orange robes on top of the monastery with huge long horns that they rested on the roof. Most of the village had gathered to watch. The monks played melodic, deep sonorous sounds on the horns until the play of colors of the sunset ended.

"I could feel my body vibrating with those sounds," Harry said. "Those horns are the biggest I've ever seen. What a fabulous experience."

"They've stored a lot of wood on their roofs. It must get really cold up here."

"Well it's not exactly warm now at sunset. I bet it will get pretty cold tonight."

James had to get up in the night and put on more clothes to keep warm. His sleeping bag that he bought in Kathmandu was rather paltry. Harry had a nice down bag, but even he complained of the cold.

The next day they savored a breakfast that included eggs with their tarkari. The portions were large and they lingered over several cups of the hot tea while the morning sun warmed the dining area through the open door and windows.

"What a day yesterday was," Harry said. "The sight of those monks playing their horns I'll never forget."

"It's been arduous, but so fulfilling."

"Shall we," Harry said reluctantly and hoisted his pack as he stood.

James nodded. "Hi ho, hi ho, up the trail we go."

Midafternoon they reached a narrow makeshift airfield and a small plane with a damaged nosecone. No one was around.

"Looks like they had a bad landing," Harry said. "Not much of an airfield. How far is it to Jomson?"

James retrieved his map. "I'd say eight or so kilometers."

They continued on and after a five kilometers, they saw two men sitting on rocks ahead. As they got closer to the men, they saw that the men were soldiers.

The two Nepalese soldiers rose when they saw the two approaching. Harry started to walk past them, but they stopped him and motioned for him to turn around.

"Jomson," Harry said and pointed past the soldiers.

"No Jomson," the soldier said. "Prohibited." He raised his rifle from against the rock and cradled it in his arms.

James held up his hands. "Okay, we go." He grabbed Harry's arm and pulled him back.

They started back the way they came. "What the hell," Harry said. "We hike all this way and we can't see Jomson." He shook his head. "That's a crock of shit." He was silent momentarily as they slowly shuffled back down the trail. "Fuck that. We could sneak around them and have a peak at the city."

James stopped, raised his brow, and studied Harry. "You think that's wise. I don't want to end up in a Nepalese jail."

"We better not go in, but I'd like at least to see it from a distance. If we're careful and make sure we're not seen, I bet we could get a peak."

James squished his lips to the side. "Okay. I'm game," he said.

They continued back on the trail until they rounded a corner and weren't visible. James turned to Harry. "All right, let's give it a try."

They climbed up the hill away from the trail into the pine trees and skirted their way around the soldiers. They descended back to the trail to get an unobscured view of Jomson in the small valley, making sure no one was watching.

"Not very big," Harry said. "I wonder why it's forbidden to go into the village."

"According to the map, it's an autonomous district separate from Nepal," James said. "Could be they don't want foreigners visiting. It's a picturesque village nestled nicely in the basin of the river surrounded by the peaks. It's only 2700 meters here. Too bad we can't go in."

"Yeah, it does look inviting. Oh well, we better go back before someone sees us."

They slipped back up the hill and wound their way through the forest until they were clear of the soldiers and descended back to the trail. They decided to have a chillum to celebrate their trek. They passed the chillum back and forth as they marveled at the mountains, breathing in the light air and savoring their accomplishment.

"Hey, what's that coming down the trail," Harry said as he squinted and pushed his glasses up.

A man was leading a white horse with a small man astride with glasses, an orange robe, and golden metal Brodie type hat. They stood dumbfounded as they watched the man on the horse approach. As he passed, he said, "Good morning." His smile radiant.

It took a few seconds before they could find their tongue. "Good morning," they said in unison.

They stood still as if frozen in time and watched as the man and horse disappeared down the trail.

"My god," Harry exclaimed. "Who was that?" He stared at James with a look of wonder. "I bet that was the Dali Lama." He shook his head as if he needed to wake himself. "It must have been. That helmet... was it gold or brass?"

"Heck if I know. Wow, the Dali Lama up here. Unbelievable."

37- ANJUNA BEACH: JANUARY 11, 1970

Sally suddenly vaulted up and began running when she saw James and Harry hobbling up the beach in the distance. She nearly knocked James down as she grabbed him to her. "You made it." She hugged him tight and then kissed him deeply before holding him at arm's length. "You've lost so much weight. What took you so long?" She continued speaking before James had a chance to say anything. "Jesus, I was getting worried. It's been more than a month. What the hell happened?" She moved to Harry and gave him a hug as James stood spell bound by Sally's excitement. "Oh Harry, I'm so glad you're here. My god, I was so worried."

Bridget, who had followed after Sally, gave James a quick hug and hugged Harry. "Welcome to Goa. We all were worried." She took Harry's arm. "Let's go see Monica so I can introduce you."

"Harry, you've lost weight too." Sally said before grabbing hold of James and pulling him toward Monica. "Damn mate, where in the hell have you been?"

Monica bare chested rose and gave James a hug. "James so glad to see you again."

Bridget placed her hand on Harry's shoulder. "Monica, this is Harry."

Monica hugged Harry. "Harry, great to meet you."

"Thanks. I'm so glad to be here," Harry replied, staring at Monica's shining full breasts.

Sally pulled James down to her blanket. "I'm so happy you're back." She cuddled against him. "I was going crazy with worry."

James stared at her in a daze before glancing around. "Where's Hank and Lisa?"

"Hank went into town for beer," Monica said. "He should be coming back soon. Lisa had to leave because of a family emergency."

"So, let's have it," Sally said, pushing against James's chest. "Why have you been gone so long?"

James collected himself and exhaled. "We got lost on the way back down from Jomson, the village we walked to way up in the Himalayas." He looked over at Harry sitting between Bridget and Monica, who appeared overwhelmed by their reception. "Instead of returning to Pokhara on the same trail, we thought that taking a different route back would be more interesting. There was another trek shown on the map that went around Tukuche and Dhaulagiri Peaks to the west. The first day was great. We took the new trail at Marpha. We made it to Yak Khara after a steady climb up to nearly 4000 meters and spent the night in the tiny village. There was snow and we celebrated Christmas with several chillums."

James stopped talking and took a deep breath as he raised his eyes skyward. "The next day we went through the Thapa and French Passes at 5,000 plus meters. We were way up there, the highest we had ever been and there was thick snow. It was hard going. When we came upon some water that was coming out of the rocks, we thought it couldn't be polluted. We hated the taste of the water with iodine tablets, so we filled our canteens with the clear water. Big mistake."

James again paused and glanced toward Harry as if he expected Harry to take over the story. Harry just smiled back still in awe of his reception. "I got sick that night and had terrible diarrhea— fever and chills. Harry came down with the crud the next day. We couldn't hike very far, but kept going on, believing we needed to get back to Pokhara in order to properly deal with our illness."

"Oh you poor dear," Sally said and caressed his cheek as a tear slid down her face. What would she have done if James had never come back?

"Go on," Bridget said. "What happened next?"

James, looking toward Bridget, continued. "The crud got worse. We lost our way. The names of the villages on the map didn't match the villages we came to. Why... I have no idea. Maybe because the trekking trail we were on was hardly ever used and the map names weren't accurate, or we were on the wrong trail. We never did figure out where exactly we were. Without Harry's help I might not have made it. One day, I was so sick I kept passing out on the trail."

"He's exaggerating about me saving him," Harry said. James became silent and with a gesture indicated for Harry to continue. "We were totally out of our depth. It's not easy walking with dysentery and the altitude was higher than we were used to. We were both scared. When we came to a village, we would try to figure out where we were by pronouncing the various villages on the map. All we got were blank stares." Harry paused and watched the ocean waves. "This is a great spot. Goa seems quite different from the rest of India."

Sally punched at Harry behind Monica's back. "Come on, let's have the rest of the story."

Harry returned Sally's gaze. "The only town the people seemed to recognize was Pokhara. They'd send us off on a trail out of the village in the morning that supposedly was the way to Pokhara. There are trails all over the place, so when we'd come to forks, where we didn't not know which way to go, there was usually no one to ask. We had to guess the way. The trail up was well traveled by the Nepalese walking caravans and others. People recognized the village names so it was fairly easy to get the right trail."

Harry leaned forward to get a glimpse of James. James just nodded and smiled back, happy to let Harry continue. "None of the trails we ended up on were well traveled and most of the villages were very small. The inhabitants seemed amazed to see us when we arrived. We never saw any Nepalese walking caravans either until we got closer to Pokhara where we encountered Tibetans, leading yak caravans, who passed us with looks of wonder. We mostly ate the liquid from the dahl and small portions of plain rice. We drank only purified iodine water, refusing any tea. We didn't risk walking too far in a day to make sure we were in a village in the afternoon, so we could get something to eat and sleep inside. It was extremely cold at night. My diarrhea let up a little before James's. I don't think I drank as much of the polluted water."

Harry appraised the group, who were all staring at him with rapt attention. "One night we didn't make it to a village before night fall. The trail was very narrow and the edge dropped off into a chasm, so we decided to sleep on the trail rather than risk the narrow trail at night. James had passed out a few times on the trail. We had flashlights, but we didn't want to waste our batteries. Getting replacements would be a problem. We put almost every piece of clothing we had on and got into out sleeping bags. The stars at that altitude were amazing. It felt like you could just reach out and touch them. It got too cold at the high altitude. We just couldn't take it, so with the aid of the flashlights we got up, and continued on just to stay somewhat warm. It was touch and go. I've never been so cold in my life. When we finally arrived in a village, we were so thankful. We relished the warm liquid from the dahl we were served and ate a few bites of rice. We rested against the house soaking up the sun for a time and then reluctantly continued on. It took much longer to reach Pokhara than the trek up to Jomson took. We may have taken a convoluted route back. When we finally were in sight of Pokhara we were so happy. We got a room in a somewhat upscale hotel and stayed a few days, eating modestly, but frequently to build up our strength before flying back to

Kathmandu. We stayed the night in Kathmandu and in the morning continued on to India."

Harry ended his tale with a stretch. "And here we are." He looked at James. "I'm starved. We didn't want to eat on the train."

"Let's go to the beach restaurant then," Sally said. "My god, mates, what a harrowing journey." She stood up and led the group to the restaurant.

As they were ordering their food, Hank arrived. He ambled up to the table and stood staring, dumbfounded. "James and Harry. My god...."

"Good to see you again," James said and stood to hug Hank. "You remember Harry."

Harry stood and shook hands with Hank. Hank still pumping Harry's hand looked from James to Harry and back to James. "We all were so worried. I was afraid something terrible had happened to you."

"We'll tell you about our trek later," James said pulling out a chair for Hank. For now sit down. We're starving. We haven't had anything to eat since breakfast in Bombay."

"Jesus, you look like your starving. You're both unbelievably skinny." He took a seat and placed his arm around Monica. "What a surprise. Wow, I need a beer."

***

After leaving the restaurant in the evening the group wove through the coconut grove toward the bungalow. Sally held James back from the rest of the group and gave him a passionate kiss. She explained that she had spoken to Hank about their plan to go back together overland to England, and Hank had agreed to come along. "As you probably noticed Hank has hooked up with Monica. He's going to be reluctant to leave Anjuna Beach. How long do think we should stay here?"

"At least a week or so. I need to build up my strength."

Back at the bungalow they continued drinking beer, smoking chillums, and staying up late into the warm night as Harry and James held forth on the rewarding and difficult trek. Sally expressed her excitement of traveling overland to England and her hope that they could find a van to buy and drive to Europe. Harry said he was happy that he could travel back with friends and knew the trip back would be more rewarding than his trip out. He was excited about the prospect of finding a van, but would be happy to take public transport if it came to that.

Hank expressed his enthusiasm about the overland trip as well and kept his chillum stoked as he kept asking questions about the trek. They stayed up late until James rose from the couch, said he was exhausted, and needed to sleep.

Sally rose and took his hand. "I'm exhausted myself from just listening to your amazing trekking adventures."

Bridget moved from the couch she was on to sit next to Harry on the other couch that Sally and James had vacated. "I bet you're tired as well," she said, placing her hand on Harry's shoulder. "I didn't know what to do when you guys were gone so long. I thought we'd have to go back to Nepal and contact the authorities for a search party."

"If we hadn't been able to continue trekking back, I don't know what would have happened," Harry said as he faced Bridget's focused smile. "I doubt any inquires with authorities in Kathmandu would have been much help."

Bridget ran her fingers through his curly red hair before standing. "I'm certainly glad you both made it back. Sounds like an extremely difficult trek. It was fortunate that you were able to help James."

"We helped each other," Harry replied. "No doubt, the return trek was difficult, but the trek, all in all, was a fantastic experience. I feel blessed that I was able to do it. James was an excellent trekking partner. I have enough wonderful memories of the trek and the amazing mountains to last a lifetime."

"Wow, you can tell me more about it tomorrow." Bridget patted the couch. "You'll probably be more comfortable if you put all the couch cushions on the floor. These couches are rather short." She stood and nodded to James and Sally, then strolled to her bedroom. "Good night."

Sally wasn't surprised that Bridget had wasted no time in making a play for Harry. She had to admit the Swede was a vision to behold and wasn't shy about making her intentions known.

"All right, to bed, my lovely." James said wrapping his arm around Sally's back. "Lead on." He placed his hand on Harry's shoulder. "Good night, Harry."

Harry stood and Sally slipped up to Harry and gave him a hug and kiss. "Sleep tight, Harry. I'm so glad you're both here. Good night."

***

They settled into the beach scene. James and Harry ate often at the beach restaurant and devoured snacks in the night relentlessly. They gained back their weight slowly. Sally initially took it easy on James with her pursuit of nightly activities, but as James gained in strength their escapades became gradually more strenuous.

One night after a vigorous romp as Sally lay in James's arms, she floated the idea of Monica and Bridget coming with them overland back to Europe. James had been back nearly a week and he had gained a good amount of his weight back.

James stared back in surprise. "I hadn't considered the idea of them coming. I thought they already had open ended plane tickets back to Sweden. I'm stunned that you'd want Bridget with us. Have you forgiven her? You think both of them would want to come?"

"They might. I'm taking you at your word about Bridget. I trust you. Since Hank and Monica are together now, it would be easier with Hank if Monica came also. Bridget has seduced Harry, and they seem to be getting on well. I doubt Monica would come without Bridget. Everyone paired up would be rather ideal.”

“As you say, everyone paired up would make the journey much easier. It would be crowded with six if we found a van to drive back, but I think it would be workable.”

“Shall we bridge the subject with them tomorrow then?”

“You sure you’d be good with Bridget coming with us?”

“Yes, we’ve been getting along well for the past month.”

“Okay, let’s see how they take the idea.”

***

In the morning as they were eating breakfast of peanut butter and toast with their tea, Sally got up and went behind Hank. She whispered in his ear, and gave him a nudge. She had already talked to him about the idea of Monica and Bridget coming overland with them. Hank had liked the idea.

Hank turned to Sally and nodded before focusing on Monica. “Monica, would you and Bridget be interested in coming with us back to Europe overland. I’d like you both to come. What do you think?”

Monica, caught unaware, stared back speechless for a few seconds before turning to Bridget. “I don’t know. What do you think Bridget?”

Bridget smiled back at Monica, then looked to Harry, who nodded. "Yeah-yeah I would love to go. We had talked about going back on public transportation when we first arrived, but decided it would be too arduous on our own. Lisa had been adamant against it. I would like to see the other countries, and traveling in a group would be exciting."

"Me too," Monica said enthusiastically and hugged Hank.

"It's settled then," Sally burst out. "Welcome aboard, mates."

***

"I was thinking of going back to Delhi soon to search for a suitable van," James said as they all were laying on the blankets at the beach a few days after Monica and Bridget had agreed to come with them. The sky was full of colors as the sun was setting on the aquamarine expanse of the sea. "Are you all sure you want to come overland and are willing to share expenses if we can find a suitable van?"

Bridget perked up. "Yeah-yeah, for sure. Monica and I are ready to go."

"Sally and I could go on ahead, and you guys could come in a few days if you want to hang out on the beach a little longer," James said.

"I wouldn't mind staying here a little longer," Hank said, "but I would like to participate in finding a van. What do you want to do, Monica?"

"Let's all go to Delhi together," Monica said. "It will be more fun, don't you think?"

"Shall we take the train in the morning then?" Bridget asked.

"Sounds like a plan," James said.

Sally jumped up. "Well let's go to the restaurant and celebrate our last day here." She rubbed her hands together, laughing. "This is going to be so cool. I can't wait to get started."

"I met some English tourists with a cool van, who were open to the idea of selling," Sally said as she rose from their bed in their Delhi hotel room.

They had taken the train to Delhi and had been there nearly a week. James had seen several Indian vehicles for sale, but their costs were prohibitive. There was a tax break if you were taking the vehicle out of India, but the cost still was very high and most of the vans weren't really suitable. The ubiquitous vehicle made in India was the small Ambassador sedan. Most vans were imported and scarce. The few tourists with vans, who they had met, were planning to drive back and didn't want to sell. He did look at a Volkswagen van a French couple wanted to sell, but the van was in terrible shape. He was getting worried that he wouldn't find a suitable vehicle.

James stared at Sally expecting her to continue. "Where?"

They had returned in the night to their room after enumerable beers and chillums in Hank's and Monica's room and gone right to sleep.

Sally remained silent, returning his stare with a smirk for a time before answering, "At that little grocery down the street." She laughed. "This kind of straight guy came on to me. He heard my accent and asked how I got here. Anyway, we got to talking, and he told me he had driven out in a van, but wasn't excited about driving back." She pulled her tee shirt on over her head.

"And?" James exclaimed. He knew Sally was purposely dragging out her explanation to tease him.

"I told him that we were wanting to buy a van to drive to England." She got up and went to the bathroom and came out with a carton of milk. She started heating water with her coil.

"Jesus, Sally get on with it. How can we see the van?"

"Hold your horses," she said, sitting back on the bed. "I'm in bad need of a cup of tea." She obviously enjoyed increasing his consternation. "I arranged to meet them at their hotel at two o'clock this afternoon."

"Great."

"See...what would you do without me?" She stood and regarded him from a short distance. "I did good, hey."

"Of course you did good, you little vixen." He grabbed for her, but she slipped out of his grasp. He enjoyed their comic antics, but he anxiously wanted to know more about the van.

"None of that until I've had my tea and one of these delicious samosas." She poured the boiling water into the two mugs with tea bags. "You've got a one track mind."

"Oh...I see. As if you don't."

"Mate, you're lucky I'm not some repressed hag."

"Hallelujah."

"Here, drink your tea and don't get any samosa crumbs on the bed. We don't need any distractions after breakfast."

"Oh, you think we're going to make love after breakfast," James said. "I was going to go to the American Express office and check my mail."

"Yeah... right." She removed her tee shirt. "As if you could resist. You still haven't caught up from all those weeks on the trail."

***

"Hi," Sally said as she approached the tall dark haired Englishman in the lobby of his expensive hotel. "This is my friend James who's interested in buying a van." She introduced the rest of the group, who had all insisted on coming.

"Pleased to meet you," the man said, shaking hands with all the group. "My name is Frank Cliffe." He moved closer to James. "Shall we get to it? I imagine you want to see the van."

They went out onto the street where the Austin, blue van was parked. The back of the van had been fitted with low cabinets on one side and seats around a table on the other side. The bench seat across back of the van behind the front seats extended to the cabinets, leaving a walking path between the table and the cabinets. The table top with its folding leg was removable and could be placed between the seats. The rearmost seat back folded down and a section of plywood attached to the bench seat could be fitted in the walking section area to form a sleeping platform across the entire back of the van. The vinyl covered foam cushions fit exactly together on the platform to make a soft bed. The seats also had removable wood tops for additional storage.

"Wow, you had this fitted out really well," Sally said. "What do you think, James?"

"I like it," James said. "What are you asking for it?"

"You're paying in US dollars, I assume?" Frank said. James nodded. "Well you know that to bring a vehicle into India you have to have a carnet to insure that you don't sell the car in India."

"What's a carnet?" Sally asked.

"It's a kind of insurance policy," Frank said. "If one did sell the car in India, the carnet policy would guarantee to pay the sizable import fee."

"So you mean there's some procedure required with the carnet before you can sell the van?" James asked.

"No. I shouldn't sell it to an Indian, who would keep the vehicle here, requiring the payment of the import fee. You'll need the carnet to get the van out of India, so it will have to be transferred to you along with a bill of sale. Since you will be taking the vehicle out of India, there will be no import fee. I had to pay quite a bit for the carnet. Consequently, I will need to include it in the sale price."

"Okay, what's the price?"

"Two thousand five hundred dollars complete."

"Wow mate, this is not a new van?" Sally said.

James thought the van was exactly what they needed. They could all sleep inside if need be—cramped for six, but still doable with five in the back and someone across the seats in the front.

"No it isn't. It's a 1966 model, but it is in good shape, has a sound engine, good tires, and is custom fitted," Frank said. "It comes with a carnet from the Royal Automobile Club." Frank closed the back door. "Check around and see what else you can find. I would suspect you'll find that this van is an excellent deal." He paused and studied the group. "Would you like to take it for a drive?"

"Yes, that would be great," James said.

James and Frank drove off leaving the rest to wait on the sidewalk. When they drove back, James, thinking the vehicle was just what they needed but didn't want to appear too enthusiastic in hopes of reducing the price, exited the van without comment.

"What do you think, James?" Sally asked.

"It drives well and the engine sounds pretty good," James replied. He approached Frank and offered his hand. "Thanks, we'll think about it and check some other places."

***

The group stopped at a small restaurant down the street from the van's location. Everyone ordered an ice coffee except Hank, who got a beer.

"That was a great van," Harry said. "It would be ideal, but it's rather expensive. I'd like to help you out with the purchase, but I'm short of funds. I'll pay my share of gas and things, and I could do a hundred towards the van for the trip. We could take public transport for a lot less."

"Monica and I could contribute a few hundred dollars each," Bridget said. "And of course share the expenses. The van would be great. It seemed in good shape."

"I never expected to go to Europe," Hank said. "Sally and I were going back to Australia after India. I'm looking forward to traveling farther, and I think the van would be so much better than public transport. We'll share expenses, but we can't help much with the purchase. We could manage a few hundred. That leaves you on hook for most of the cost. If it's not doable, then there's public transport. I'd be willing to go that route."

James was surprised by Hank's statement. He thought the only reason Hank had agreed to travel overland to England was because of his commitment to Sally. Maybe Hank's travels and his relationship with Monica had really changed him.

"Thank you all for your consideration," James said. "I have a money order coming any day now. With it, I will be able to make the purchase. I don't expect you guys to help with the purchase. I agree the asking price is rather high. Still, considering that I can sell the van when I get to England and the convenience and security of a van, I think the cost is acceptable. The van is really cool, but I want to check some other places. Just to be sure. I'll probably get a lot less back in England than I'll pay, but it should work out okay."

"That would be so cool," Sally said, bristling with excitement.

"Yeah James, that would be great," Bridget said.

"Let's get some beers and take them back to the hotel," Hank suggested. "And smoke on it. If we're leaving soon, I've got a lot hash to go through before we leave."

***

James searched for other vans for three days, but could not find anything as suitable as Frank's van. He did find a small Mercedes bus that would be roomy and luxurious, but the price was prohibitive. There was also a Volkswagen van that some Germans were willing to sell for less than the Austin van, but it wasn't fitted out well, and the smaller interior would be rather cramped.

James purchased Frank's van four days after his initial viewing. He was able to reduce the price down for the van to two thousand. The group was ecstatic. James took the van to a garage for an oil change and lubrication. They all cleaned the van and loaded it with food—canned goods, cereals, milk, eggs, peanut butter, cheese, bread, coffee, tea, soft drinks and condiments. There was a butane stove with the van with quite a few canisters and an assortment of cooking utensils. They celebrated the last days with another excursion to the Red Fort.

When James went to the American Airlines office to get a refund on his remaining ticket, he was told that they could not refund the remaining portion in India in dollars only rupees. Well, he couldn't use a plethora of rupees. They told him the nearest location he could obtain dollars for the refund of his ticket would be Frankfurt, Germany. Disappointed that he wouldn't have the extra traveling money, he thought he was still in good shape economically for the overland trip. Bridget and Monica had found out the same thing about their plane tickets, but didn't seem too worried. They would wait until they were back in Sweden to get their refund.

They set out from Delhi just after sunrise to beat the traffic. Even with the early start it took them a long time to get out of Delhi. The road west was full of traffic, mostly trucks going both directions. The pavement was in reasonable shape, and they made good time despite the traffic.

They arrived at Amritsar, the last town before the Pakistan border, in the evening. Hank remained in the back with Monica. Bridget and Harry were in the back also while Sally rode up front with James driving. They found a hotel in the old town and obtained one room for six people.

Hank was disappointed they had not gotten three separate room. He was enjoying his romance with Monica. She seemed always ready for his advances, and sex with her was very enjoyable. He was a little jealous of Harry being with Bridget, but understood it made traveling easier.

"If you want to see the Sikh's Golden Temple at its most spectacular time," Harry said as they were sitting around the table of their Amritsar hotel restaurant after their evening meal, "I would recommend getting up early and going before sunrise."

"Shit, we got up early today," Hank said. "I wouldn't mind sleeping in."

"The temple is fantastic at sunrise," Harry said. "It won't take long to see the place. We can come back here for breakfast."

"I'm up for the sunrise visit," Bridget said.

"Yeah-yeah," Monica said. "I want to see it at sunrise."

"Come on, Hank," Sally said. "You can sleep in the van after. Course if you really don't want to go, you can sleep in."

Hank scowled at the group. "I'll think about it." Even though he thought that visiting the temple at sunrise was a good idea, he wanted to maintain his image as the contrarian. Sometimes he thought maintaining his image was absurd, but for some reason beyond his comprehension he continued on with it.

In the morning Harry was the first up and woke the others. They all walked to the Golden Temple in the predawn light as the birds greeted the coming daybreak. The cool morning mist hung over the placid lake-like tank, known as the pool of nectar. The causeway over the pool to the temple was crowded with Sikhs.

The sun broke above the trees, reflecting brightly on the gold plating of the temple and the surface of the pool as they stood at the beginning of the causeway.

"That's a dazzling temple," Sally said, and hooked her arm with James. "How do the Sikh differ from the other Indian religions?"

"Sikhism was founded in the fifteenth century by Guru Nanak as a rejection of the caste system," James said. "Sikhs believe in one god and do not worship idols. They believe in reincarnation and enlightenment like Hindus. They have a strong military tradition and are known as ferocious fighters. They have controlled most of this region since 1799.”

Hank was glad he had gotten up with the rest of the group. The Sikhs were obvious quite rich and had carved out a strong position in Indian society. They were doing a lot better than the lower castes of the Hindus. He wanted to get the excursion to the temple over with quickly. They had seen the sunrise spectacle, touring the inside was going to be anticlimactic. He was anxious to get on with the journey. He’d had enough of India.

He took Monica’s hand and followed the others down the causeway. James was taking enumerable photographs. Hank took a few photos as well. He stared back at the gawking Sikh pilgrims. He and the rest of the group were the only Westerners that had come for the sunrise panorama.

“All people and religions are welcome at the temple,” Harry said.

“Good on them,” Sally replied and skipped ahead with James in tow.

They quickly toured the inside of temple, with its mural paintings and plaster scroll work depicting animals and flowers that resembled Persian carpets, then headed back to the hotel for breakfast.

***

As they approached the Indian Pakistan frontier James declared, “All right, here it comes, the Indian border.” He twisted to regard those in the back especially Hank. “We’re all clean... right.”

"Clean as a whistle," Hank replied. He had thought about hiding some hash in his toothpaste tube, but Harry's stories of Westerners languishing in Pakistani jails, and James's frequent harangues about making sure there was no hash particles anywhere had dissuaded him.

James drove up to the Indian border gate and handed over the passports. The policeman scrutinized the passports carefully, checking the passport picture against the person as each stuck their head when called into the front seat. The policeman had them open the back door to make sure there were no other passengers, stamped the passports and handed them back. When he studied the carnet, he asked, "Where is Frank Cliffe?"

"There is a bill of sale and affidavit of transfer of the carnet from Frank Cliffe to me," James said. "They're inside the carnet."

The policeman adopted a wry expression. "You must go back to the office to get approval for the sale of the vehicle and carnet transfer."

Sally grabbed her neck. Hank knew she hated border crossings and their often challenging situations. He wasn't fond of them either. He wondered if the people, who had these jobs, were assholes before they started or became assholes with the work. He suspected the former. He was glad he was in the van. Often when border guards saw his towering height, they got even more haughty and aggressive.

James turned the van around and drove back a hundred feet to the office and went inside. He was gone for nearly an hour.

Sally started fidgeting and complaining about the delay. Hank wondered what the problem was. They were taking the damn car out of India and had a bill of sale. So what if the name on the carnet is somebody else? Jesus, what if they made them return to Amritsar or even to Delhi. He wanted to get out of India and the plethora of beggars. He hoped Pakistan would be different, but from Harry's impression of the country it didn't sound very inviting.

When he saw James walking rapidly toward them, he was relieved, but then noticed his stark frown. Something must be up.

"Everything okay?" Sally asked as James got into the driver's seat. "Can we go?"

"No."

"What's the hold up?" Sally asked.

"Bureaucratic bullshit," James said, gritting his teeth and groaning. "The head honcho told me the car and carnet couldn't be transferred. I tried to reason with him, but it didn't seem to be going very well, so I gave him the card with the name and telephone number of the vice consul in Madras that Martin gave me in case I got in any trouble. The head guy told me to wait in the hallway. I got tired of waiting and thought I better update you guys on the situation."

"Can they stop us?" Bridget asked.

"Maybe."

"Fuck that," Sally said.

James had the carnet and sale documents in his hand. "Fuck it, is right," he said. "Let's go. They're so disorganized they might let us through. It's worth a try."

He drove to the gate. "They said it was all okay," James told the border policeman as he held up the carnet. The border policeman jiggled his head and raised the barrier. Off they went, continuing to glance back in case anyone was coming after them. When they were out of sight of the crossing, they began laughing and cheering.

Sally slapped James on the back. "Wow... that was ballsy, mate."

"Way to go, James," Hank added. He was glad they had gotten out of India. He had seen some amazing temples, and sculptures, but traveling around India had been difficult. He hoped they would get across Pakistan without any problems. He was anxious to get to Afghanistan. Afghani hash was famous the world over, and he was anxious to sample it at the source. He had initially been against traveling overland, but now looked forward to more adventures and eventually seeing uncle Jeb. He and Monica were getting on well, and he had almost forgotten about James and Bridget's betrayal. He doubted Sally had forgotten despite her friendliness toward Bridget.

40- BAMYAN: MARCH 10, 1970

Hank, prone on the backseat, bounced in agony while the two men in blue turbans drove along the rough road, clouds of dust trailing after them. Periodically the men would look back at him and say something to him. He didn't know what they were saying, but was glad they did not shout at him. Hank bore the pain of his arm quietly except for the occasion moan when there was a big jolt. He had no idea how long they had been traveling. He was glad the men had their windows open. The fresh air helped to lessen the horrible smell of himself. Eventually, he fell into a fitful sleep.

He was awoken from his sleep when they stopped in front of a large compound. The sun was bright against the mud walls. The two men left the car, and he closed his eyes again, glad to be stationary. His repose was interrupted when the rear door opened. The men carefully pulled him from the back seat and carried him through the door in the blue gates into a large compound courtyard. They placed him down on a stool and began gently removing his shirt. The manipulation of his arm to extricate it from his shirt sent shudders through his body. He leaned forward to vomit, but nothing but mucous came forth. The men removed his trousers and underwear that were stiff with dried feces. They carried him to a large galvanized tub, unwrapped the dirty rag around his wounded arm, and lowered him into the warm water. My god, it felt so good. They washed his body while a young boy stood by holding towels. It was such a relief to be rid of the smell of shit. What was going on? Why were these Afghans treating him so well?

They lifted him from the tub and carried back to the stool where the boy rubbed him gently down with the towels, avoiding his arm that had streaks of crimson radiating from the puckered, swollen wound. He was given a cotton Afghan shirt and trousers, then the two men helped him dress. Was he dreaming? This made no sense. They slipped sandals on his feet, lifted him up, and carried him into the house at the back of the courtyard to a large room. The room had beautiful carpets covering the entire floor where they positioned him against a pillow and left. Hank looked up at the large man sitting on a raised platform as if on a throne, starring at him.

"Mister Hank I believe," the man in his blue robe and turban said. "Salam and welcome. Do not fret. You are safe now and in due time, God willing, you will be reunited with your friends."

He couldn't believe his ears. Safe... reunited with his friends. He studied the man. The man's English was flawless, yet he undoubtedly was an Afghan.

"My men reported to me the horrible conditions under which you were kept," the man said. "I am Mahmood, and I humbly apologize for the terrible treatment you have endured in my country. I'm afraid you are gravely ill. My physician will treat you and hopefully save your arm, God willing. We will build up your strength. It is fortunate that we rescued you when we did. I don't know how you would have fared if you had been held captive longer. Your captors will pay dearly for their transgressions." Mahmood nodded to a man, who Hank noticed standing to the side of him dressed in a green robe and turban. The man kneeled next to Hank and gave him a pewter cup of foul smelling liquid.

"Please drink," Mahmood said. "I know it smells and tastes disgusting, but it will help your illness."

Hank studied the cup. Were they trying to poison him? He looked up at Mahmood.

"Mister Hank, I realize you have no reason to trust me. I have met with your friends, James, Harry, Bridget, Monica, and Sally, who were very worried about you. I understand you grew up with Sally, the red-haired young lady of surprising beauty with green eyes. You were kidnapped by my rival, who shall remain unnamed, from the hash sellers holding you for ransom because of an insult you gave. My rival is a most villainous man, who would stop at nothing to anger and attack me anyway he can. He thought by taking you from the hash sellers after I agreed to act as an intermediate to pay your ransom on behalf of your friends, he could blackmail me for money or embarrass me and reduce my influence."

Mahmood took a deep breath, his face contorted, and expelled his breath forcefully as if to exorcise some horrible emotion before recovering his calm. "I realize you are from Australia and do not know our customs. Your insult is forgotten and is of no consequence now. Do not worry about it."

Mahmood smiled and took a drink of tea. "When my rival kidnapped you after I agreed to deliver the ransom money, he made a grave mistake. Thus your safety became my problem. My rival has paid dearly for his interference." He settled back and regarded Hank quietly a moment. "Mister Hank, I assure you the liquid in the cup will help you. Please drink."

Hank lifted the cup to his lips with a frown and took a drink. It was bitter and slimly. He was mollified by the mention and description of Sally and decided he should drink the concoction.

"Yes, that's the way. The potion will help your stomach and aid your sleep." Mahmood pointed to the man in the green robe, who had retreated a short distance. "We will need to lance your arm. It will be quite painful, but essential if we are to save your arm and your life, God willing."

The man in the green robe knelt and lifted Hank's swollen arm turning his head away at the smell. Hank moaned but allowed the man his arm. The man produced a small knife and slit the wound. The greenish-yellow pus oozed out. The man grunted and stood, turning away in disgust. Hank gagged and steeled himself against the urge to throw up, but could not stop the impulse and spewed a small amount of liquid on the carpet. The stench from his arm was the worst smell Hank had ever encountered. He looked up afraid that he might have upset Mahmood, but Mahmood was still smiling at him.

Mahmood spoke loudly in his native tongue. The physician knelt back and accepted a basin handed to him by the boy. He washed the wound, widening the gap gently with his fingers, allowing more of the reeking pus to outflow. Hank passed out from the pain.

***

Hank awoke in a dark room. He had no idea how long he had been asleep. The light seeping under the door allowed him to see the room. He was laying on a soft rug his head on a pillow covered by several blankets. He felt a little better. His arm still throbbed relentlessly, but seemed less acute. He blew his breath out between his pursed lips as he sat up.

He remembered his dream of diving the reef with Sally and Freddy. The first enjoyable dream he had had for a long time. He lifted his bandaged arm to his face with a groan. It still smelled putrid, but the smell seemed less strong. The last thing he remembered was the man in the green robe spreading his wound and the intense debilitating pain.

The door opened and the boy came in and handed him a cup of watery gruel. The boy motioned for him to drink. He took a sip. It tasted sweet, and he smiled back at the boy, who nodded and left.

Several hours later, the man in the green robe entered the room and knelt to take up Hank's arm. The man removed the bandage and twisted his head away. He gently spread the wound and more reeking pus oozed out. Hank ughed and winced before falling back against the pillow as the waves of pain slammed against him. The man washed the gash with a stinging liquid, wound a clean bandage around Hank's arm, gave him a cup of the insipid concoction, encouraging him to drink all of the concoction, and then left. The throbbing pain from his arm sounded like the banging of a tin drum in his head as Hank reached up with his other hand to wipe away his tears.

41- LAHORE: JANUARY 26, 1970

"No cows," Sally said as they drove through the streets of Lahore, teaming with people. "I kinda liked seeing the cows in the streets in India. Made it seem friendlier. Did you see those meat kiosks with those hanging hunks of meat covered in flies? We'll have to be careful what we eat here. There's hardly any women on the streets either. Not a good sign."

"It's a strict Muslim country," Harry said. "I didn't like it when I came through. Seems the populace is kind of angry or don't like tourist. I'd advise getting across Pakistan as fast as possible."

"Well I'm beat," James said. "The fiasco at the border with the carnet was draining. I'm glad there was little hassle at the Pakistan passport control, but it still took a long time for them to inspect the van. Let's spend the night here and get an early start. Any suggestions on hotels?"

"Just keep on this road until we hit the center," Harry said. "There should be some budget hotels toward the old city."

***

They found a hotel close to the walled old city, procured three rooms and ate a light dinner. After dinner, they walked to the old walled city where the immense marble Lahore Fort, initially built by the third Mughal Emperor, Akbar, in 1556, and expanded by the other ascending Mughal Emperors, dominated the inside. They visited the outside of several mosques and lingered in front of the impressive Data Durbar Mosque with its green dome and immense marble courtyard.

"Lahore is a center of Sufism," Harry said. "Many Sufi scholars settled here. This mosque is considered the most important and largest Sufi shrine in Pakistan."

"Sufism... isn't that a mystic sect?" Bridget asked.

"Yes, the Sufi goal is extinction of the individual and a state of ecstasy with God," Harry replied. "The English couple I came with were very interested in Sufism."

"Sounds a lot like the mysticism of the Hindus and Buddhist," Bridget added.

Harry put his arm around Bridget and pulled her close. "I'm sure there are similarities, but the Sufi believe the mysticism comes directly from Mohammed, who himself was a mystic. The Koran was revealed to Mohammed by the archangel Gabriel over a period of 23 years."

"It's an interesting shrine," James said. "I'll have to look into Sufism. Mysticism has always interested me." He appraised the group. "Shall we go back to the hotel? We should probably get an early start tomorrow, so we can get across Pakistan." He was looking forward to spending the night alone with Sally. The fiasco at the Indian border was still rankling him, and he wanted to get a good night sleep. "It's over five hundred kilometers and Harry says the roads aren't that great."

***

James knocked on Harry's door as the sun was rising. "Up and at'em." Why was he using the damn army lingo? "We need to get on the road if we're going to make Peshawar today."

He thought the Pakistanis were often rude. Harry was right about the populace appearing to dislike tourists. The meat kiosks he had seen had turned his stomach. He wasn't going to eat any meat in Pakistan. He wanted to get across the country quickly as Harry had suggested. Unfortunately, he hadn't slept well. Sally had been affectionate, but he couldn't put his worry about causing trouble for Martin with the carnet fiasco out of his mind. Plus, his reoccurring nightmare had woken him in the middle of the night, and he wasn't able to get back to sleep.

"We're up," Harry's voice sounded from the door. "Meet you in the lobby in ten. I'd suggest hitting the road before the traffic gets too bad and stopping later for breakfast."

"Sounds good." James continued to Hank's room. When he knocked on the door, the door swung open and Hank stood in his underwear.

"I heard, mate," Hank said.

Monica came to the door completely nude and smiled demurely. "We'll meet you in the lobby."

James nodded and went back down the hall. Man, what a body. He didn't know who was more attractive— Monica or Bridget. There was something to be said for voluptuous women. What was he thinking? He didn't want another episode with a Swedish siren.

Sally was busy packing when he entered their room. "What happened? You look weird?" She approached James and laid her hand on his chest. "Did Hank give you some agro?"

"No, he and Monica were already up," James said. He hadn't realized that Monica's nude body had affected him so. "So were Harry and Bridget. We're good to go."

They met in the lobby, climbed aboard the van, and were off. The city traffic was just beginning. It took a good hour before they reached the outskirts of the crowded city, second largest in Pakistan.

James thought about his recurring nightmare. He just couldn't seem to get rid of it. Traveling with Sally had been an immense comfort, but why couldn't he ditch the nightmare? Was his destruction of life to haunt him forever? By right action and compassion could he ever escape his bad karma?

***

They reached Peshawar just after sunset. They had stopped in Gujarat for breakfast, and Islamabad, the new capital, outside Rawalpindi where they had an unpleasant lunch.

"It's so nice to be out of the van," Sally said as she and James relaxed on their hotel bed naked after a quick shower. "Everybody seemed to get along well considering the cramped conditions. Bridget and Harry are doing well. I wish I could say the same for Hank and Monica." She raised up. "She sure was friendly with those Germans in Islamabad. Good thing they're going the other way."

He pulled her too him and kissed her, squeezing tight before pulling away. "I thought Hank and Monica were getting on well. Why do you think there's discord?"

"Just a feeling I've got. I hope I'm wrong."

"I'm glad you agreed to sit in back occasionally to give others a chance to sit up front."

"Right on," she said and rolled on top of James. "That was a long stretch of driving. It was a good idea to let Harry drive the last leg. Hope you were able to relax."

As they lay back in each other's arms, James mused on what the future would hold. Sally would eventually have to return to Australia. Would he go with her? He would love to see Australia. Where would it all lead? He told himself to stop focusing on the future and live in the moment. And the moment was good.

There was a single knock before the door was opened. Monica entered even though James and Sally were naked on the bed. "Hope I'm not interrupting anything." She stared unflinching at the two.

Sally bounded up. "No, mate, we're finished," she said with a smirk. "What's up?"

"Dinner I hope," Monica said and moved even closer to the bed eying James's nude reclining body and smiling broadly.

Sally placed her hands on Monica's shoulders and spun her toward the door. "Okay mate, dinner it is. Give us a few minutes say fifteen and we'll meet you in restaurant downstairs." She ushered Monica out of the room.

Sally started dressing. "She has some nerve. These Swedish women are certainly unabashed. I saw the smile she gave you. I can tell you find her alluring. Just watch out, Mister. One dally with a Swedish beauty is enough." She sat on James's chest. "You hear me."

"Loud and clear." He pushed her off and rose to give her a hug. "I shall not be led to temptation." He hoped Sally was wrong about Monica and Hank, but he knew how Bridget had felt about Hank. Maybe Hank couldn't get over his infatuation with Sally. Sally was a fiery lady whose beauty and personality had certainly captivated him. And Hank grew up with her.

"Well I reckon we'll have to savor the night without any drinks or hash," Sally said as she waited by the door for James. "But we can enjoy ourselves in other ways so be prepared. No early to sleep for you, mate."

***

They had a leisurely breakfast and set off for the famous Khyber Pass. Everyone seemed in good spirits as they approached the towering arid hills of the pass from the dusty plain. The gap of the pass between the hills was formed by two streams that produced the narrow gorge. They wound up the serpentine road that rose gradually to the Fort Ali Masjid where the gorge narrowed with precipitous walls of brown rock, then further on widened into a wide valley with forts and villages. The road rose again to Fort Kotal where James pulled the van off the road.

"This is the highest point of the Khyber Pass," James said.

"Imagine all the silk road caravans that travelled through this pass," Bridget said as she was sitting in the front passenger seat. "It feels so great to experience this famous road."

"Persians, Greeks, Mughals, and of course the British all controlled this strategic pass," Harry said. "The gateway to India. Alexander the Great and his army came through in 327 BC."

Sally had been sketching the pass in the back seat as they drove and scrutinized her quick sketch as they got out to watch the traffic snaking up the pass. She added some details as the others took photographs.

"I like your sketch," Bridget said. She moved to Sally's side and placed her hand on Sally's back.

"I don't like sketching much when the van is moving," Sally said. "It makes me a little dizzy, but I couldn't pass up trying to capture this famous pass."

Back on the road they descended to a wide plain and then into another narrow gorge to the town of Towr Khan where they disembarked, presented their passports, and were allowed to enter Afghanistan. The border agents didn't even bother to peer in the van. They drove on and descended into a valley to the Lowyah Dakkah village— the end of the Khyber Pass.

James pulled the van into the lot next to the dilapidated building under the shade of the lone tree. "Damn, we should have gotten another jerry can of gas before we left Kabul. This may have been a gas station at one time, but not anymore."

"Jesus, I knew we should have stayed in Kabul," Sally said as James came to a stop. "This whole trip has gone to shit. We've had no word from Mahmood. Mahmood could be in with the kidnappers and was just fobbing us off."

Before leaving Kabul, they had filled up the van's tank and one jerry can. James had calculated that they could fill up when they reached the village of Oalat, the last supposed gas station before Kandahar, where two Germans had told them they could buy gasoline. Harry hadn't remembered the gas station, but he had taken a nap on the way out with the British couple and may have missed it. After emptying the jerry can into the tank 300 kilometers out of Kabul on the paved road the Russians and the Americans had built across Afghanistan, James had easily made it to Oalat.

"Damn," Harry said. "Those Germans either were shitting us about a gas station here or have been in Kabul too long."

"I should've listened to you, Harry," James said, "and gotten another jerry can for gas. It's about 150 kilometers to Kandahar. I think it's better to stop here rather than continuing on and running totally out of gas. I've been running on empty quite a while. At least there's some shade."

They all got out of the van except for Sally, who slumped down on the bench inside. "What else is going to go wrong?" she said with exasperation. "Out of gas in the middle of nowhere. Great."

She had argued against leaving Kabul. Traveling westward made them even farther away from Mahmood. If they needed to see him again, they would have to return to Kabul. She like everyone else had grown tired of the waiting in Kabul, but waiting in Herat would be just as tiresome.

James unloaded the camp stove and put on some water. "We'll let's make the best of our wait here—have some tea and just relax." His slack face betrayed his disappointment. "We got a late start. It will be dark soon. We'll have to stay here tonight. Tomorrow I'll hitch a ride and get the jerry can filled and buy another." He peered into to the van. "I'm sorry, Sally. I blew it. I believed those Germans about the gas station."

They had remained in Kabul three weeks after the last meeting with Mahmood. James had convinced Sally to travel onward in order to dissipate some of the despair the group was exhibiting, hoping a change of location and travel would take their mind off their worry for Hank. Sally had gone along with the idea even though she didn't like it. James had informed Mahmood of their departure in a note left at the post office.

"Maybe I should try and catch a bus back to Kabul in Kandahar to wait for Hank there and if need be go to the authorities," Sally called from the van.

"I don't think that would be a good idea," Monica said as she approached the van. "Staying by yourself in Kabul for who knows how long could be dangerous. What if they kidnapped you as well?"

"Hank and I were going to go back to Australia from India," Sally said, her face twisted in anger. "It was my idea to come overland to England. I caused this mess."

James frowned and entered the van. "Come on Sally, come outside and sit in the shade. I'm sorry I messed up. Going back to Kabul would be premature and confusing to Mahmood. Mahmood knows we're on the road to Herat. He said he would send Hank to us." He grabbed a handful of cushions and placed them outside under the tree, then went back into the van and held out his hand. "Come on Sally."

Sally clasped his hand and reluctantly clambered out of the van. "You all put so much trust in this character, Mahmood." She plopped down on a cushion to stifle her tears. "We have no confirmation that he received James's note."

When the kettle whistled, Monica poured the boiling water in the tea pot and stirred the contents. After letting the tea brew a few minutes, she poured a cup for everyone. Sally sipped her tea in silence.

James placed his arm around Sally. "We're all worried. We'll be back on the road tomorrow. I'm confident that Mahmood knows we're on the way to Herat. This little set back, although frustrating, will not make much of a difference."

"We could play cards," Bridget said.

"Yeah-yeah, let's play cards," Monica added.

Harry jumped up and pointed. "What's that?" He shaded his eyes. "There's riders coming."

A group of five blue, turbaned Afghans on horses, carrying rifles across their lap, their chests strung with cartridge belts, galloped toward them. They halted in a cloud of dust like bandits from another era. One rider slid off his horse and with his Enfield rifle dashed to the van. After perusing the contents, he spoke in his native tongue to the man with the decorated horse, who was carrying an AK-47 rifle.

The man with the AK-47 studied the group in silence before pointing at the van. "Why here?" His voice was loud and guttural.

Harry cautiously moved to the empty jerry can and held it up. "No petrol."

"Ahhh, na petrol," the headman said, his deep voice filling the air. He spoke loudly to the man inspecting the van, who rushed to his horse and vaulted astride. He and two of the other men rode off. The headman and another rider remained behind, staring at the group.

Sally was surprised by the rapid events and scared. She had no idea what the riders intended. James rose and picked up the tea pot, pointed at the pot, and then to the riders.

The headman nodded. "Bala, tea good." He pointed at Sally. "Mahmood."

Sally, slumped on her cushion, watching the cloud of dust from the departing riders, shot upright. "Mahmood, yes."

"Mahmood, great man," the headman said with a big smile.

Sally stared at the headman in disbelief. "You know Mahmood?"

The headman nodded and laughed. "Mahmood, good friend."

Sally was stupefied. How had this Afghan connected them to Mahmood? James must be right. Mahmood knows we're on the road to Herat.

James retrieved two glasses from the van and poured each a tea and added sugar. He handed the glasses to the riders, who smiled, accepted the glasses, and bowed.

The headman's horse bridle and saddle were studded with silver stars and elaborately embroidered designs with decorative tassels. The two Afghans slowly sipped their tea and continued staring. When they had finished their tea, the headman held out his glass.

"More," James said and pointed to the tea pot.

The headman shook his head. James retrieved the glasses. The group remained silent, avoiding eye contact, sipping their tea. The headman and the other Afghan would occasionally speak to each other, but mostly were silent.

Sally stood. "How did you know we knew Mahmood?" she asked.

"Yes, Mahmood important," the headman said with a big smile.

She wasn't going to get any information. The headman's understanding of English was apparently poor. Maybe he recognized her red hair, and that's why he pointed at her rather than the others. Had Mahmood told his followers to be on the lookout for a Western group with a red haired young woman? "Do you know Hank?"

"Hank," the headman repeated. "What is Hank?"

"Mahmood was going to find our friend, Hank," James said.

"Mahmood good friend," the headman said nodding with a smile.

Sally wondered where the other three had gone. Were they bringing reinforcements? Surely they didn't need more men. The mention of Mahmood had helped to ally her fears, but she was still worried about what would happen next.

After what seemed like an hour, the other three riders appeared with two jerry cans strapped to their horses. They dismounted and began pouring gasoline into the van's tank.

James exhaled a sigh of relief. He rose and bowed. "Tashakor... thank you." He retrieved his wallet and approached the headman with a wad of money.

The headman held up his hand. "Na," he said. "Koda hafez." He bowed and then spoke to his men before turning his horse and with a wave rode off. His men following.

"What a wonder," Monica said.

The group watched the riders disappear. Sally rose and grabbed James's arm. "What was that all about? How could they possibly know we were connected to Mahmood?"

"They must be allied with Mahmood," James said, placing his arm around Sally. "Mahmood may have put the word out about us traveling to Herat and your red hair to protect us."

"It was certainly scary, but how wonderful," Bridget said. "He acted like he knew about you Sally when he pointed at you and said Mahmood. This could be a good sign."

"I don't know about that." Sally said, but the talk of Mahmood had lifted her spirits. Maybe traveling westward wasn't such a bad idea. "Let's get the hell out of here before something else happens."

James pulled Sally closer. "I know it was tempting to go to your embassy for Hank. In Europe, that would have been the correct action, but here it may have caused problems. Mahmood warned us not to go to the authorities."

Sally shook her head. "I've about had it with all these crazy Afghans." she walked a few steps away from James and shouted to the air, "Where in the hell are you, Hank?"

***

"You were so calm, James," Monica said as they were relaxing in the restaurant of their Kandahar hotel. They had arrived in Kandahar a little after dark. Sally had eaten only a small amount of her food. She had no appetite. Her worry was giving her a headache and stomach pains. She knew she should be more positive.

"I was shaking in my boots until the headman pointed at Sally and said Mahmood," James said.

Monica placed her hand on James's hand. "Offering them tea was really smart."

Sally noted Monica's action and grit her teeth. Was Monica now after James? These Swedes seem to have no boundaries. She needed to snap out of it and take care before Monica usurped her place. Still Monica was right about James offering them tea. He's probably right about the Afghans riders recognizing my red hair. Maybe she should put more faith in Mahmood like everyone else.

"It was unbelievable," Bridget said. "It was like something out of the Arabian Nights. You were great too Harry."

"I was scared as well," Harry said. "The headman's comment about Mahmood was intriguing. I bet like you said, James, Mahmood had put the word out about us. He must have unbelievable influence in this country. We were lucky to find him."

"I'll go to the post office in the morning and send another update note back to Mahmood." James said. "Then we should take off for Herat. It's over five hundred kilometers. It's supposed to be an interesting city." James nodded to Harry. "Can you go to the bazaar in the morning and buy another jerry can? With both cans full and a full tank, we should be able to make it to Herat."

"Glad to," Harry said. "After, before we leave, let's all go to the mosque of the sacred cloak. It's impressive with its green marble domes. We don't have to go in. It's a couple of blocks from here. It supposedly houses the cloak of Mohammed himself. Course you can't see the cloak. It's worth seeing the outside. It won't take long."

***

With two Jerry cans full of gasoline as well as the tank, they made in to Herat with no problem although the gas gauge had been on empty for a while. Sally had been worried they'd run out of gas again and was quiet most of the drive. Upon arrival in Herat, James, smiling with jubilation, pulled into the gas station on the outskirts of town. After filling up, they drove to the center of the small town and procured two rooms at a hotel Harry was familiar with.

As soon as Sally and James entered their room, Sally slumped down on her bed and strongly expelled her breath. She was relieved to have arrived, but still extremely worried about Hank, wishing there was something she could do to aid his rescue. Just waiting for news was driving her to the pit of despair. The affair with the riders gave her hope, but also highlighted their reliance on Mahmood, who she was leery of and yet hopeful at the same time.

"What if we don't hear from Mahmood?" Sally said. "How long can we stay here waiting?" She beckoned James to her, holding her arms out. She knew James was trying his best to keep everyone engaged and hopeful of Hank's return. She would be totally lost without him. He laid down next to her and hugged her to him. She was comforted by his embrace and closed her eyes. "You were good with the Afghan riders. I'm sorry for the way I've acted." She pulled away and laid her head on his chest. "Do you really think they recognized my red hair?"

"Yeah, the head horseman singled you out. Word of your red hair and Mahmood's support must have been circulated amongst his followers. It was a good sign." He rubbed her back and kissed her cheek. "I have a feeling that we will soon hear news of Hank." He tapped her leg. "You want to go out and have a look around? Get a feeling for the town."

"No," Sally said. "I feel awful. You go and let me rest. I hope coming here hasn't been a terrible mistake."

"I'll bring you back some soup if you like."

"Yes, please. I'm sorry I'm so morose. I can't help it."

"It's understandable. I'm worried sick too."

43- BAMYAN: MARCH 24, 1970

Hank was excited to see the light from the rising sun in the window with its now open shutters. His sleep had been fitful in anticipation of being freed and reuniting with his friends. Could he actually believe what Mahmood said? He had to admit Mahmood had treated him well even though he was kept captive and isolated. He believed he would keep his arm thanks to the physician, but he wondered if it would ever be normal again. It still ached especially when he used it. He wondered how James and Sally had gotten Mahmood's help. He hoped to meet with Mahmood again and ask questions. He would be careful and try to not offend Mahmood.

How many days was it since he last met with Mahmood? He couldn't be sure, at least a week or more. The opium they gave him for the pain addled his brain, and he often fell in and out of a dazed sleep. The boy brought him stew now instead of the insipid gruel. The physician came every evening to change his bandage and inspect the wound. The usually taciturn physician actually spoke to him now. The word *khubam* was often said with a smile. He didn't know what *khubam* meant, but the physician's smile must signify his arm was progressing well. He couldn't believe he was so despondent and in such pain when the kidnappers had him that he had wanted to die. He was ashamed of his moments of weakness.

***

The next morning the boy came and escorted Hank into the big room. He indicated for him to sit. Mahmood was not present. Hank took his seat on the carpet and rested against the large pillow. Besides the predominately red carpets with black and white geometric designs and applique wall hangings, he noticed the beamed ceiling was painted in geometric designs almost mirroring the carpets. There was no doubt Mahmood was wealthy and apparently quite powerful.

Mahmood entered through a door at the back of the platform and smiled at Hank. "Salam, my friend. My physician has approved your return to your friends. My men will drive you toward Herat in the morning where your friends are waiting." He clapped his hands and Mohammed came in and served Mahmood tea. Mahmood spoke and Mohammed came down to Hank and poured him a glass of tea.

"I am heartened by your recovery, Hank. You are a remarkably strong young man. I am pleased that I was able to help you." He sipped his tea. "Go ahead drink your tea it will invigorate you."

"I'm so thankful Mister Mahmood for you rescuing me and helping me to recover. I thought for sure I would lose my arm or die."

"It was the least I could do. I am ashamed at the terrible treatment you have endured in my country."

"If you don't mind me asking," Hank said, "how did you become involved?"

"It was God's will, my friend. Your friends were directed to me by one of the hash sellers, expecting you might be in Bamyan. Why the hash seller would say this, I have no idea. It was fortuitous in any case." Mahmood took a drink of tea and gazed up at the ceiling. "Your friends were in great distress and worried about you especially the lady, Sally. She is the most beautiful young lady I have ever seen. I was most taken with her. You are fortunate to a have a friend like her. Since your friends came to me, I was honor bound to help. I asked them to be my guest for the evening while I sent my men out to search and make enquiries." He paused and spoke to Mohammed, who left the room. "Luckily my men located the hash sellers that were holding you for ransom. I agreed to act as intermediary. The hash sellers request for ransom, I thought acceptable and relayed the information to your friends. Your friends gave me the money for the ransom, but before my men could pay the ransom and retrieve you, my rival learning of my involvement had you kidnapped to get back at me. A very foolish act. He thought they could hide you away and extract money and concessions from me, but my men were able to find where you were being kept and planned an attack. They freed you and brought you here."

"Thank you so much, Mahmood. I wish there was something I could do to repay you."

"Do not worry. My reward is your recovery and your return to your friends. God has smiled on you,

Mister Hank. My defeat of my rival's forces and your rescue has undoubtedly rankled my rival to no end. You and your friends are safe while you remain in Afghanistan. My men are ubiquitous and are watching out for the safety of you and your friends while in Afghanistan. My rival is undoubtedly extremely angry and would like to get back at me anyway he can. However, his forces have been depleted, and he has gone into hiding. He will be licking his wounds and planning some kind of additional attack against me, but he is like a bee that can only cause discomfort. Still my rival may try to come after you or your friends. Please remain vigilant for yourself and your friends' safety on your journey westward. I regret I must leave and will not be here in the morning to see you off. My men will take good care of you. Go with God and keep kind thoughts in your heart for Afghanistan, despite the horrible treatment you received." Mahmood stood. "Mohammed will take you to see our marvelous standing Buddhas, wonderful sculptures and the pride of my village. The walk will do you good." Mahmood laid his hand on his heart. "It was a great pleasure to meet you and your friends. Goodbye and go with God."

"I don't think the others will want to stay here much longer," James said as he rested on Sally's bed in their room in Herat. He and the others had had breakfast, and he had brought Sally a plate of eggs, toast, and rice of which she had eaten only a small amount. "It's been two weeks. They're getting restless."

"I'm not leaving without news about Hank," Sally said loudly. "I'll take the bus back to Kabul if you want to go on." Her time in Herat had been spent mostly in her room. The waiting was driving her crazy. Every day without any word drove her into deeper despair. What could be taking so long? Nothing had changed for her with their trip to Herat except a change of scenery, which may have helped the others but did nothing for her.

"I can't let you do that."

"You don't control me." Her anger quickly boiled over like hot soup.

"I'm not trying to control you."

"The hell you're not," she shouted. "I should have never let you talk me into leaving Kabul." She felt she was even farther away from Hank wherever he was. Or course she had no idea where Hank was or even if he was still alive. "You can carry on with the others. I've seen how Monica is always eyeing you and getting close. You can go on with her if you want. Hank found her quite the woman. You should give her a try if you haven't already. I know you want to."

"I don't want to go with Monica."

"Why not? You're not fucking me." She realized her anger was misplaced, but she wished the Swedish ladies had never come along.

"Sally, I'm trying to support and take care of you. I would be glad to have sex with you. I'm not shunning you." He moved to take her into his arms, but she shoved him away

"Go on. Go to your friends and make your plans. I'll take the bus back to Kabul. Give Monica a good shake for me. I'm sure she's dying for it."

"This is a dead end conversation," he said, frowning with exasperation, and reached for her, but she slipped away.

She slumped on the bed. "Just go."

James stared at her momentarily, then left their room.

Sally frowned at the door. Jesus, how had things gotten so messed up. Where are you, Hank? God, she was going crazy and taking it out on James. She wasn't being fair to him. She needed to stop being so rude. He was doing his best. She understood why he was trying to keep the group engaged. Monica's attention toward James was contributing to her anger.

She didn't actually believe James was having sex with Monica. She didn't know why she had said it. Her anger at Monica for her attentions to James had overtaken her. It had been more than a month since James and she had had sex. She couldn't face the idea. She was punishing herself as well as James. Her actions were insidious and made little sense. She doubted that James could ignore a buxom Swede hanging on his every word for long? He came clean about Bridget. She was reasonably sure he'd remained true to her since Kathmandu, but would it last.

***

One afternoon after the weeks in Herat, James rushed into their room. "There was a note from Mahmood at the desk. Hank is safe and will be here soon. Probably in a couple of days."

Sally stared at him doubting his hopeful words. "What are you talking about?"

"Mahmood has rescued Hank. He's in Bamyan at Mahmood's compound. Mahmood is sending Hank here."

Sally stood up and rushed to James. "Oh James," she shouted. "Can it be true?"

"Yes, it's true."

"Oh, how wonderful." She started crying and kissing James profusely. "You were right James. I'm so sorry. I've been a miserable bitch." She pulled him to the bed. "Hold me. I should have never doubted you."

James laid down and tenderly took Sally in his arms. Sally cried softly, her tears rolling down her cheeks.

"I'm crying with happiness, James." She wiped her tears. "I was so sure they would kill Hank. Just wait 'til I see the Big Oaf."

"He will need our understanding," James said. "I'm sure he's been through a harrowing ordeal. We owe his life to Mahmood. What an honorable man."

"Do we need to go to Bamyan to get him?" She couldn't believe it was really true. She wanted tangible proof... no more waiting.

"No, he is coming here."

"How?"

"Mahmood didn't say." James rubbed Sally's shoulder. "He told us to stay put, and Hank would be delivered to us."

"It's so unbelievable," Sally said. If Mahmood has rescued Hank, why wasn't he already here? What was the hold up? "Oh, James, I'm shaking I'm so excited."

"Of course, it's hard to believe after all this time."

"Were you telling me the truth about Monica? Be honest. I promise I won't hold it against you."

✳✳✳

Sally shared her glee about Hank's safety with James freely. Their sexual bouts renewed her feelings for James, spurred her appetite, and she gained back some of the weight. She felt joyful and couldn't wait to see Hank. Two days after receiving Mahmood's note and after a delicious bout of love making in the morning, she accompanied James to the other room where Harry and the Swedish ladies were smoking a chillum.

"You guys look relaxed," Harry said. "Here take a hit. We've got a lot of hash to smoke before we leave for Iran. Possession for hash in Iran can be the death penalty."

James went to the window and gazed down at the street. "You guys want to walk around, take in the town again, and get some lunch. Sally hasn't been out much."

"Yeah-yeah, James," Monica said and moved from her bed to stand next to Sally. "Let's go."

***

They strolled down the dirt streets as decorated horses pulled the local cart taxis up and down kicking up clouds of dust. Afghan men and women in traditional dress shuffled along in the bright sun. Many European and American young people were about also. Herat was almost as popular as Kabul with Westerners since it was first stop from Europe where hashish was legal and plentiful. Harry led the way to the Herat Great Mosque.

Sally stopped when they entered the main gate. "What a spectacular courtyard. This is big for this small town."

"It's considered the finest mosque in Afghanistan," Harry said. "The mosque was originally laid out in 1200 AD, but was much different." Harry had learned about the Mosque on his trip out with the scholars. "Shah Ruhk, who took control of the Timur Empire after the death of Timur, moved the capital of the Empire from Samarkand to Herat in 1404, and expanded the mosque to its present day size. The Timur Empire included Persia, Turkey and parts of India. Most of the mosque was destroyed in the Anglo Afghan war that began after the Amir of Afghanistan invaded British India in May 1919. The Amir's army was quickly defeated by the superior British army. After the war, the British recognized Afghan as an independent country. The Mosque was rebuilt in 1945."

"Can we go inside?" Monica asked.

Bridget sidled up to Harry and took his arm. "I don't know about the rest of you but I'm hungry. We've seen so many mosques. Let's find something to eat."

Harry clutched Bridget's hand. "Good idea. We can always come back."

They left the courtyard and walked up the street toward the towering massive fort high on the hill.

"The Citadel supposedly sits on a foundation of a fort Alexander the Great built," Harry said, pointing at the fort. "The Citadel in its present form was also built by Shah Ruhk."

Sally was glad they came to Herat. She felt privileged to be traveling the same trail as Alexander the Great. The trip from Kabul seemed to have been a welcome change for the group despite their worry about Hank. Now everyone was jubilant about

Hank's rescue and were looking forward to being reunited.

"It's massive, but very dilapidated," Monica said as she laid her hand on James's shoulder.

Sally noticed Monica's attention. Hank needed to arrive soon. Monica on her own was turning her attention to James, but James didn't seem to be affected by her attention. She felt bad about insinuating James was having sex with Monica. She had been so nasty to James and really all of them. She was glad they had tolerated her behavior. She needed to make amends. She thought Herat was an interesting city and had enjoyed the last few days. She hoped Hank would regain his enamor of Monica, and the group could travel on happily together.

****

"This is a great little town," Sally said as she lay on their bed, catching her breath, bathed in sweat. "Imagine, all the famous people who have traveled through Herat— Alexander the Great, Genghis Khan, Tamerlane, and the Persian, Darius. Oh I'm so glad I listened to you." She grabbed James. "You were so right about Mahmood. I wish Mahmood would hurry up and send Hank to us. I can't wait to see him." She wouldn't believe Hank was really free until she could touch him. "What do you think Iran will be like?"

"According to Harry, Mashhad is interesting, but he didn't like Tehran. We need to be absolutely clean of any hash at the border."

There was a soft knock on the door. "That must be Harry," James said. "Hopefully there's word from Mahmood." He pulled on his trousers and went to the door. When he opened the door, there stood a haggard Hank. "Hank!" James exclaimed and hugged the tall Australian.

Sally burst through the door naked and hugged and kissed her friend. "Come in, Hank." She pulled him in. "You look a fright. Jesus, mate, you're so skinny." Noticing she was stark naked, she put on here shirt and pulled up her trousers. "Sit down and tell us all about it. We didn't know what to do. We found this Mahmood in Bamyan when we couldn't find you in the village where you went to buy hash. Of course you met him...."

James placed his hand on Sally's shoulder. "Easy Sally. Let Hank talk."

"I'm so glad you're safe, Hank. I don't know what I would have told my brother."

"So, Hank, go ahead tell us what happened," James said.

"Can I tell you over lunch?" Hank asked. "Coming here over the mountains, I didn't get much to eat."

"Of course," Sally said, rising and grabbing Hank's right arm. Hank's swollen left forearm was covered in a gauze bandage. "I'll take Hank down to the restaurant. Go get the others, so we can all hear Hank's story."

***

"Monica probably told you about the hash deal," Hank began as the group were sitting at the hotel café waiting for their food. "Anyway, when I went in the back room, the guy handed me various qualities of hash. I chose the best and got out the money. He wanted more for a kilo than what he had said earlier. He tried to grab the money, and I pushed him away with my other hand. My left. He went berserk, shouting at me, and pulled a knife, slashing my arm. I was about to deck him when this other man came in from another room with a rifle. That stopped me in my tracks. The guy I pushed continued yelling at me. He retrieved a rifle and ushered me outside through a back door after wrapping a rag around my wound to deter the dripping blood. He held his finger to his lips and then ran his finger over his neck. I got the message."

Hank took a drink of tea. "I was tied up and gagged in another house. I heard Harry come to the door, but I could only moan. They kept me there a few days. Then some other blokes came to the house. There was some heated conversation and they carried me out and dumped me in the back of a Land Rover. Everything was like a movie that I was watching, but not a part of. They took me up some winding dirt road for hours to another house kind of out on its own. Bouncing around in the back of the Land Rover on the terrible road was scary. I was kept at this remote house for I think more than a week." Hank smoothed his hair and took a deep breath.

"They kept me bound except when they fed me. They were gruff but not horrible. One night I heard commotion in the other room, shouting, and then gun fire." Hank paused and took another deep breath. "I braced myself and listened, wondering what was going on. Two men in black turbans burst in. One slammed me in the stomach with his rifle. They gagged me, then slammed me in the head. When I awoke, I was in a car bouncing over the road with a bag over my head." Hank stopped and closed his eyes for a few seconds before continuing. "They carried me into a house, threw me in a small room, removed the bag and gag, shoved me down, and kicked me."

Hank took a deep breath and stretched his neck. "They fed me horrible putrid food. I got the shits bad, which seemed to amuse them. They did nothing for my cut arm. The dirty rag it was wrapped in was stiff with saturated blood. My arm soon became swollen and ached terribly. Man was I scared. Afghan men would come into the room, all carrying rifles, and would shout and kick me. I didn't know what the hell was going on. I figured they would eventually kill me, but, when they didn't, I thought they were holding me for ransom. Least I hoped."

"How horrible," Sally said. "You poor dear."

When the food arrived Hank paused and ate a few bites of kebabs and drank sparingly of the tea. "I feel so hungry, but the food tastes insipid to me."

"Come on, tell us the rest," Sally said.

Hank grimaced as if the pain was still with him. He related the horrible treatment he received and his rescue by other men who drove him to Bamyan where he met Mahmood.

Hank paused and took a drink of tea, staring out across the room for several seconds. "I was scared of Mahmood and doubted that he was going to set me free despite the good treatment. When he mentioned meeting with you guys and described Sally, commenting on her red hair and green eyes, it gave me some hope. After weeks of isolation, except for visits from a boy and the physician, Mahmood told me I would be taken to you in Herat. I finally believed I might be set free. The next day two men escorted me to a Land Rover and drove off into the mountains. The road was terrible. The men sometimes had to jack up the car to get it out of pot holes. It was a beautiful journey through the mountains and valleys. When we stopped in a village, the people would crowd around the Land Rover and gawk. I was fed sparsely and we traveled until dark and then slept in the car with huge sheepskin pelts to keep us warm. The next day we arrived here in Herat. They helped me out and pointed to the hotel. 'Friends inside' they said. I just stood there staring at them. I couldn't move. They ushered me toward the door, and I finally realized I was free."

"My god, you were lucky," Sally said. "I was so worried. I don't know what I would have done without James. He believed in Mahmood when I didn't." She rubbed James back. "I wanted to go to the police and the embassy. I'm so glad you convinced me to wait, James."

Hank took a deep breath and slowly expelled the air. "I knew you would keep Sally safe, James, and figure out the best way to handle the situation." He rubbed his head and stared down at his plate. "That was my only consolation. I really thought I was gonna die."

45- HERAT: MARCH 27, 1970

Hank was thankful to rejoin his friends. Yet, the significance of what he had been through was paramount in his mind and left him somewhat bereft. He had been extremely lucky. His aggressive nature had caused his kidnapping, and he realized it was a futile way to act. It had almost cost him his life. What would have happened to him if Mahmood had not rescued him?

When Sally and James left for their room after several rounds of chillums, he was relieved. The opium Sally had given him after changing his arm dressing was kicking in along with the hashish, and he wanted to go to bed. He walked into the bathroom and brushed his teeth. The simple task seemed alien as he examined himself in the mirror. He couldn't remember ever being so skinny. His ribs stood out like the pictures he remembered of the people released from the Nazis death camps at the end of the war.

He left the bathroom and got into bed. Monica moved to his bed and gave him a kiss. "Do you want some company?"

He felt a stirring. She was a beautiful lady, but he was too tired for any company. "Thank you, Monica, but I just want to go to sleep."

"I understand. Can I get you anything?" She caressed his cheek and patted his chest.

"I'm good," he said and rolled toward the wall.

Monica rose and went into the bathroom, and Bridget joined her.

Harry walked next to Hank's bed. "I'm so glad you made it back, Hank. We were all so worried. Sleep tight my friend."

***

Hank's sleep was fitful despite the opium. When he awoke, he didn't feel refreshed. He didn't know what he wanted. His life seemed so empty. He watched Harry and Bridget asleep, entwined in the farther bed and Monica asleep in her bed with her back to him. Did he still have feelings for Bridget? No... she was an opportunist and had probably little regard for him. He suspected Monica was probably similar in her feelings toward him. Still, they had had some great times in India. She was a fun lover and would probably stick with him the rest of the journey. Everyone expected him to continue the journey, although the prospect did not seem that enticing to him anymore. Actually, nothing of his future seemed that enticing. He knew Sally really loved him like a brother and would want him to continue the journey. He had made a promise to Freddy to protect her. Instead, she had to protect him. He rolled to his side with a wince and moan.

Monica as if sensing Hank's movement, rolled to face Hank. "How are feeling, Hank?"

"Grateful to be free," Hank replied meekly, surprised by her quick awakening.

Monica walked to his bed in her underwear and tee shirt and gave him a kiss. "You appear a little better then yesterday. How's the arm?"

"It aches, but not terribly unless I move it."

"It will take quite a while to completely heal. It must have been terribly infected. I'm so glad that Mahmood had a good physician. I must confess when I met Mahmood I didn't think he would be much help. He sure proved me wrong."

"Yes, I would have been done for without his help."

"Want me to help you take a shower. I bet you'd welcome a warm shower."

"That would be nice."

She pulled him up, and they walked together into the bathroom. After disrobing, she helped Hank disrobe, then adjusted the shower. They moved together hand in hand into the spray. She washed his body, swishing the sponge in soft circles across his back while he held his head in the warm spray, occasionally moaning with satisfaction.

Hank slumped against the wall as she turned off the shower. "Thank you, Monica. That felt so good. Sorry I can't reciprocate. I just don't have any energy."

She cuddled up to him, squashing her breasts against his chest. "Don't worry about that. We'll have plenty of time for that." After toweling him dry, she escorted him back to his bed.

Harry and Bridget were sitting on their bed. "How was the shower?" Bridget asked.

"Wonderful and refreshing," Hank said.

"Is there still hot water?" Harry asked.

"Yeah-yeah," Monica said. "Go for it."

46- IRAN BORDER: MARCH 31, 1970

"Here we go," James announced as they approached the Border outpost. He was a bit apprehensive after hearing the stories Harry told of Europeans and Americans caught in Iran with drugs. He made a silent prayer that the van and everyone were completely clean of any hash or residue. They had left all their smoked chillums and pipes in Herat.

James drove through the Iranian border gate where tall men in crisp grey military uniforms and black calf-length boots stood with automatic weapons either side of the gate. The Iranian border was a stark contrast to the Afghan border they had just left where two soldiers in worn uniforms conducted the incoming and outgoing traveler formalities, their Enfield rifles resting against the office wall.

They had stayed in Herat three additional days to allow Hank to recover more. Sally changed the dressing on Hank's arm daily and gave him opium for the pain.

James was surprised when Hank suggested they go onward, since that would end the opium and hash use. Everyone was happy to get moving. He had enjoyed Herat and was glad that they had spent some time there. He understood why many of the Westerners on the hippie trail stayed a while before continuing on to Kabul. There was a friendliness that seemed genuine. He had noticed two Afghans that often seemed to be observing them while in Herat. He hadn't remembered seeing them before Hank arrived. Hank had told him that Mahmood had said that they would be safe in Afghanistan, but his rival might try something against them outside of Afghanistan to get back at him. He suspected the two men were Mahmood's men making sure they remained safe. Both bearded men were wearing black turbans and traditional Afghan clothes and kept their distance.

"This looks scary," Bridget said.

"The famed SAVAK," Harry whispered, "the Shah's police and intelligence service. Everyone needs to be on their best behavior. These guys are serious."

The men in uniform waved their guns at them and shouted for them to get out of the van and line up with their passports. The men scrutinized the passports with solemn faces and motioned for the group to sit on a bench outside the office. They proceeded to strip everything from the van and pile it in the courtyard. Periodically they would stare menacingly at the group.

After more than an hour of scrutinizing the contents of the van, they handed back their passports and told them they could go. The group hurriedly replaced all the articles— food, clothes, stove, utensils, bags, and cushions— back in the van and climbed inside.

"Okay, on we go," James said with as much enthusiasm as he could muster. He was relieved to drive onward, thankful no hash crumbs had been found.

They didn't reach Mashhad until after dark. They stopped at a restaurant that Harry had remembered when they were close to the Haram. The restaurant was crowded with young people, who were obviously enjoying their food and conversation. Harry chose an empty table.

"Good evening, I am Kohshar," a dark haired man said as he approached the table. "May I join you?"

The ladies appeared apprehensive, but Harry said, "Sure, sit down."

"I'm a student here," the young man said. "Where are you from?"

Harry made the introductions referencing the countries they were from.

"Oh, quite international," Kohshar said, opening his dark eyes wide.

"Your English is very good," Monica said.

"Thank you," Kohshar replied. "You are so kind. I am glad you have come to the most holy and best city in Iran." He paused and studied the group. "Have you seen the Haram?"

"We just arrived," James said. "Is there a good hotel near here?"

"Oh yes, not far from here is most satisfying hotel." The man had a hard time not staring at the beautiful Western ladies. "I would be very pleased to show you to the hotel. Did you arrive by bus?"

"No, we drove," James said.

"You have a car," Kohshar said and widened his smile. "Ah, very good. I will take you to a hotel with good parking for your car."

"Hey, can you get a beer around here?" Hank asked.

"Yes. Here, you can buy."

"Now you're talking," Hank said. "Beers all around."

The young man stared at Hank apparently not sure what Hank had meant.

"We'd like to buy six beers, Kohshar," Harry said slowly.

"Yes, I understand." Kohshar rose and walked to the kitchen. He arrived back with a waiter, who was a carrying a tray with six Iranian beers.

"What is good here?" James asked.

"I like the chicken and lamb combination kebabs," Kohshar said. "Fried eggplant is also very good. And of course our delicious bread, sangak."

"That sounds good," Monica said. "Can you order for us?"

"Of course. It would be my pleasure." Kohshar signaled for the waiter.

"If you haven't eaten," James said, "order something for yourself."

"Thank you. I have already eaten." Kohshar waited until the waiter departed after he had ordered for the group before leaning in. "You must be careful what you say in my country," he said softly. "SAVAK spies are everywhere." He perused the tables nearby. "I myself have been imprisoned. Turned in by someone I thought was my friend. The Shah is hated, and the SAVAK are brutal and sadistic. Trust no one." He rose and glanced behind him. "Enjoy your meal. I will meet you outside when you are finished."

***

"It's like a bigger version of the great mosque in Herat," Sally said as they stood inside the Haram courtyard in front of the massive mosque in the early morning.

"Yes, you are correct, fine lady," Kohshar said. He had met them at their hotel to show them around the Haram. "I have seen the mosque in Herat and the mosque in Kandahar with the cloak of Mohammed. We are lucky this is such a fine day to view this most holy site."

"I'm not into this much," Hank said. "I think I'll go back to the hotel."

"You feeling okay?" Sally asked. "You want me to come back with you? Do I need to change your dressing?"

"I'm just tired," Hank said. "Catch you later."

"I'll come back with you," Monica said as she grabbed his uninjured arm.

"Nah, I just want to lay down. Stay and enjoy the site."

They watched Hank shuffle away.

"He's not been sleeping well," Monica said. "He wakes up repeatedly mumbling something."

"He's had a harrowing experience," James said. He knew well how nightmares could plague one's sleep. "It will take a while for him to build up his strength and put the horrendous experience behind him. He's doing as well as can be expected."

"Is your friend ill?" Kohshar asked.

"He was," Harry said, "but he's recovering nicely."

"When did they build this complex?" Bridget asked.

"The first temple here was supposedly Zoroastrian," Kohshar said. "Do you know Zoroastrian— the ancient religion of Persia?"

"I've heard of the Zoroastrian religion," Bridget said, "but I don't know much about it."

"It was the religion of ancient Persia from 600 BC. They believed in a universal supreme god, Ahura Mazda. They believed in heaven, hell, and free will. Good and evil were in constant battle."

"Doesn't the Muslim and Christian religions have a lot in common with Zoroastrianism?" Harry asked.

"Exactly right," Kohshar said. "Persia was a great empire that lasted over a thousand years until supplanted by the Arab conquest" He smiled with a look of pride as he surveyed his audience. "Haram means forbidden in Arabic. Only the pure are allowed to see. Non-Muslims are not allowed into the shrines and mosques. This Haram is a sacred pilgrimage for Shiites. Initially a Muslim martyr was buried here, and later a mausoleum replaced the temple. In the ninth century another martyr was buried here, and a dome was built over the grave. It was expanded over the years, and mosques were added."

They wandered from courtyard to courtyard most of the morning, marveling at the blue and gold domes, incredible mosaics, and dazzling tiles decorating the outside of the structures.

"Let's go back to the hotel and get Hank for lunch," Sally said. "Go back to that nice restaurant. Will you come with us, Kohshar?"

"I would be happy to go with," Kohshar replied.

Walking back to the hotel, James saw two men watching them. For some reason he thought they looked somewhat like the Afghans, who had been watching them in Herat even though the bearded men were bare headed and dressed in worn sport jackets with western style trousers. He dismissed his thought as absurd. People stared at them wherever they went.

They walked back to the hotel and Sally went up to get Hank as the others waited in the lobby.

They walked to the restaurant on the crowded street past the stares of the men and women, many in suits as well as men in scruffy jackets and trousers. Half the women they passed had no head covering. The restaurant was again packed with young men and women, but they were able to get the last table. Kohshar excused himself and went to a table of friends.

Bridget after surveying the room smiled and said, "It's refreshing to see women here with uncovered heads like in Kabul."

"Yeah, I certainly wouldn't like to have to always cover up my hair," Sally responded.

"In your case," Bridget said with a big smile, "it would be a travesty to cover such beautiful hair."

Sally smiled back. "As it would be to cover up your hair as well."

James was thankful that Bridget and Sally were getting along so well. The return of Hank had raised the mood of everyone. The journey onward would be enjoyable again, and he was looking forward to the travels.

Kohshar joined them again at the table. "My friends were happy to hear that you enjoyed your visit to the Haram." He furtively glanced at the ladies. "Would you like for me to order for you again. Persian Fesenjun is a specialty here. It is a delicious dish of chicken, walnuts and pomegranate syrup over rice."

"That would be yummy," Sally said. "Sure, let's give it a try."

Kohshar called the waiter over and ordered. He studied the group in silence before asking, "How long are you staying in Mashhad?"

"We leave tomorrow," James said.

"You are going to Tehran?"

"Yes, and all the way across your country to Turkey," Harry added.

"This is a very long journey," Kohshar said. "I wish you much luck. I think you will not like Tehran very much. Here we are Persians. There they are Quajars...Turks. They lack refinement."

"Oh, that's good to know," James said.

"You must excuse me," Kohshar said. "I have an appointment and must leave."

"Thanks for all your help Kohshar," James said. "Will we see you later?"

"I am not sure. Perhaps I will see you here tonight."

When the chicken dish arrived it looked fabulous. The taste of the sauce was delicious and the chicken was very tender. James was happy that they had met the friendly Kohshar. Everyone enjoyed the food except Hank, who only ate a few bites and pushed around the food with his fork, looking despondent. Hank hadn't even asked for a beer. James felt bad for him.

When they finished their lunch and were sipping their tea, Hank cleared his throat. "I'm thinking of returning to Australia." He shifted in his seat, sitting erect. "I'm tired and not interested in traveling much anymore. I bet I could get a flight back to Australia from Tehran."

"What?" Sally said "Come on Hank. You're just feeling down. You'll like traveling once you recover more. It will be fun. James, talk some sense to him."

"I can understand your wish to return home," James said. "Your ordeal was frightening and brutal. Continuing on... seeing different countries could help." Traveling had helped him with his ghosts.

"My heart's not in it anymore," Hank said. "I'm sick of Muslims and their strange culture. Besides, I want a proper doctor for my arm. It still aches."

"What about me?" Sally said.

"You're with James," Hank said. "Go ahead and complete the journey."

"I don't like this one bit," Sally said.

James wondered if Sally could convince Hank to stay. Hank seemed quite adamant. Sally would be beside herself if he left. This was a development he hadn't foreseen.

***

They arrived in Tehran, a huge sprawling city, midafternoon after an overnight stop midway in a non-descript village of mud houses and peasant farmers, who were not very welcoming. They had eaten a quick dinner of chewy kebabs and crisp bread and retired to the only decrepit hotel for an early start. The woman at the hotel was very curt and unwelcoming, and the rooms were small and the beds horrible.

In Tehran they drove to a hotel in the center of town near the business district that Harry knew about. They were able to get a large room with six beds.

"This is a nice hotel," Bridget said as they arrived in their room. She sat down on her bed. "A real mattress. I saw a lot of women in business suits and uncovered hair on the street. I hope this will be a cool city."

"I wouldn't bet on it," Harry said. "I found the people here rude and often obnoxious. The woman in our party said she got groped."

"Really," Bridget said. "I sure hope that doesn't happen to us."

"I would suggest only going out in a group," Harry said.

"Let's go out for coffee and a snack," Sally suggested. "Lunch in that village was almost inedible. As Harry said, if we are in a group, we should be safe."

They went out in search of a restaurant since the hotel restaurant, nearly empty, didn't seem that inviting. They found a small attractive restaurant with modern tables and a few customers. The staff watched them enter but made no move toward them. The other customers stared at them with sour expressions as if their presence was an affront. They chose a large table. The menu, which was in Farsi, was of no help. After many minutes, a waiter came to their table and spoke in Farsi.

Harry smiled at the waiter. "Salam, see orders of bakhtiyari kebabs, bademjab, and shesh coffee, lotfan."

The waiter nodded and continued to stare at the ladies.

Hank asked for beer, but the waiter frowned and departed.

"What was his problem?" Sally said. "Probably don't get many tourists. We should have eaten at the hotel." She gently hit Harry on the arm. "Way to go on the lingo, mate. What are we getting?"

"Three orders of lamb kebabs, eggplant, and six coffees," Harry said. "It's the only thing I know how to order in Farsi. The couple I traveled with spoke a little Farsi, and I memorized the food items."

"Good on you," Sally said.

"After this, I'd like to find a travel agent," Hank announced.

"Please, Hank, won't you change your mind?" Sally asked.

"No, I need to go home," Hank said emphatically, straitening up to his full sitting height.

"Okay," Sally said. "I get the picture."

They ate their snack. The attempt to ask the waiter for the location of a travel agent was met by the shaking of his head. They headed out and walked down the busy wide street with many stylish shops.

Sally separated from the group and went to a clothing store window. "What the hell," she suddenly said and spun around on the man who had grabbed her crotch. "You asshole."

Harry grabbed for the guy, but the man fled from his grasp.

"Jesus, he squeezed so hard I bet I have a bruise," Sally said. "Fuck this. I want to go back to the hotel."

On the way back to the hotel all three women were molested and several struggles broke out between the perpetrators, James, and Harry.

"These assholes are crazy," Sally said. "What the hell is wrong with these men? Did you see them cross the damn street just to grab us— bastards."

"I've never seen anything like it," James said. "These men are crazy. Talk about frustrated idiots."

"I warned you," Harry said. "They must think we're hippie, sex freaks or something."

***

After they returned to the hotel, the Swedes took a taxi with Hank and Harry to the location of a travel agent the hotel manager had told them about. James and Sally went up to the room. James was surprised that Sally didn't want to go with the others. She seemed distraught and was fidgeting with her hair, a deep frown on her face. James decided he should let her be. He laid down on another bed and began reading, *The Heart of Darkness*, he had traded another book for with a guy in Herat.

Sally rose from her bed and came to sit next to James. She lowered her eyes with a serious expression. "I'm thinking I better go back home with Hank."

"I thought you wanted to continue on to England," James said.

"I did... I do, but I need to help Hank. He's not himself. He needs my help. My brother and family will be hurt and probably furious if I don't return with him."

James didn't know what to say. He thought of protesting, but then considered how Sally's help would be invaluable to Hank. "I understand," he replied solemnly.

He understood but was not happy. The loss of her was something he hadn't contemplated. Ever since Hank's return and Sally's rekindled romance toward him, he had felt terrific. Traveling with her the rest of the way seemed so promising.

"I'm not abandoning you," Sally said.

"You're not. Then what do you call it." He stood and realized his anger was selfish and was not helping. "Sorry... of course you should go back with Hank to help."

"It would be only temporary," she said. "We could rendezvous later. I'll join you as soon as I can."

James suspected that if she left he would never see her again. Australia was halfway around the world.

"Wouldn't your family be able to nurture Hank back to health?"

"Sure, but I need to be there to help. Hank won't want to tell the full story. He's so macho. I owe him that."

"I'm afraid I'll never see you again. I can't imagine how we would meet up."

"I'll meet you again." She said forcefully as she grabbed his shoulders. "Nothing will stop that from happening." She placed her arm around James and kissed his cheek. "You'll eventually get to England won't you? If nothing else we can meet up there."

"Yes," he said softly, trying his best to disguise his anguish.

"Well, then, what's the trouble?"

"The trouble is I want to travel with you. I'm in love with you."

"Oh, James, I love you too."

"Check out these bruises," Sally said opening her legs and displaying the bruises on her thighs after removing her trousers. "These men here are sex starved imbeciles."

"I know. It's awful." James hugged her.

Sally laid her head on his shoulders and sighed. "I'll be glad to get out of this city." She rose, dressed, and returned to the bed and pushed him back to lay in his arms.

Was she making a mistake? She didn't want to lose James. She was truly in love with him. She felt she had no choice. She owed it to her family and Hank to return with him. She had to, didn't she? Why had Hank been so stupid? If he hadn't been kidnapped, she could have had a great trip with James. She could stay. Screw Hank... the dumb idiot. Why had things gone off the tracks so? No... going back was the right thing to do, but the thought of leaving James was scary. Could she lose him?

She wouldn't let anything stop her from returning come hell or high water. How would she get the money to return though? The plane ticket to Australia would exhaust most of her funds. She'd have to get her parents to loan her the money. She'd get a job to help. How long would she need to stay to help Hank recover? He was getting better with each day. She hoped she wouldn't be there that long.

They'd probably already missed her brother's wedding. She hadn't received a letter from him since Delhi. International mail in this part of the world was so haphazard.

The door burst open and Bridget rushed into the room. "Christ, I'm not going out again," she said. "We got molested repeatedly."

"It was horrible," Monica said as she and the rest entered behind Bridget. "When Harry almost decked one of the molesters, a huge crowd of angry men formed. It was scary. We had to run away."

"I over reacted," Harry said. "The bastards made me so angry."

"I got a flight out tomorrow morning at ten thirty," Hank said. "I'll be glad to get out of this crazy city."

"I've decided to go home with you," Sally said, rising and approaching Hank.

"Really," Hank said. "What about the rest of the trip?"

"I'll join James in Europe or England," Sally said. "I need to help you. If it wasn't for me you never would have experienced such degradation."

"Hey, it was all my fault. You had nothing to do with it." He stared at Sally with a quixotic smirk. "I've enjoyed our travels together. You've been great. My stupidity is to blame." Hank lowered his head and closed his eyes. "Don't feel obligated to come back with me. I'll be all right. Stay with James."

"I've made up my mind," Sally said, raising her voice and moving closer to Hank. She pushed his head up. "I'm coming back with you and that's that," she nearly shouted.

Hank reared back and nodded, patting Sally's arm. "Okay. Freddy and the family will be pleased." He took a deep breath. "Too bad we missed the wedding."

"It's the right thing to do," Monica said. "Hank will need help traveling back."

She bet Monica was happy she was going. There'd be nothing stopping her from going after James. Would he be able to resist? Sally thought not. James didn't really seem to believe she'd return, and Monica was beautiful. Well she hoped Monica would enjoy him. When she got back to James, if Monica was still around, she'd show her how to corral a man.

"Can we take a taxi back to the travel agent to get my ticket?" Sally asked rather angrily. Lighten up she told herself.

"Of course," Hank said. "Let's go."

Sally stood up and glanced at James. "Come on, James. Come with us."

***

In the evening they ate in the hotel restaurant. They were able to get beer and toasted Hank and Sally. The food special was pretty good— a rice dish with lamb and vegetables. They went up to the room with more beers and played cards before retiring. Sally clung to James all night. She slept little, wondering if she had made the right choice.

They all came down in the morning with Hank and Sally for the taxi to the airport.

Sally hugged and kissed James. "I will find you. You need to write often and tell me where you are. I'm coming as soon as I can."

"Don't worry," James said. "I'll keep in touch. I'll wait for you."

"You better, mate."

Monica and Bridget hugged Hank and Sally, wished them a safe journey as did Harry. The taxi arrived and they were off with vigorous hand waving.

***

All during the flight, Sally was uncomfortable and worried she had made a frightening wrong decision. Men were easily manipulated by beautiful women, and Monica and Bridget had demonstrated their guile. The phrase 'out of sight out of mind' played in her thoughts. There was nothing for it. She had made her decision and needed to turn her attention to Hank and her family. Her family would be flabbergasted when they heard of Hank's ordeal. She tried to sleep on the long interminable flight but only got a few snatches of sleep.

When they came out of the airport gate in the afternoon in Sidney, her family was waiting. Hank had called them from Tehran. They rushed up and hugged the travelers.

"Cracky, Hank, you've lost a lot of weight," Sally's dad said. "What happened to your arm?"

"Yeah, I've been ill," Hank replied. "I got a cut on my arm and it got badly infected."

"I'm sorry to hear that," Sally's mom said.

"Let's get your bags and start home," Freddy suggested. "I'm so glad you came back for the wedding. I was sure you'd miss it when we got your letter from Kabul."

"When's the wedding?" Sally said. "I thought we already missed it."

"The wedding's next week," Freddy said. "Didn't you get my letter in Kabul?"

"No." Sally said. "That's fantastic." Had she somehow sensed the date? Did this contribute to her determination to return with Hank?

"I'm so glad Hank you can stand up with me. I was afraid I would have to ask Samuel to be my best man." Freddy placed his arm around Hank. "Don't worry, mate, Mom will have you fattened up in no time."

"No worries there," Sally's dad said.

The drive to Brisbane seemed short on the unclogged modern road that often was along the coast, the sun reflecting on the undulating ocean.

"I'm so happy to be home," Hank said with a barely visible hint of moisture in his eyes.

"Bet you and Sally had some great adventures," Freddy said. "We can't wait to hear all about it."

"Yeah, it was quite the trip," Sally said. "We met and traveled with some great people. Two Swedish ladies, a handsome American, and an English chap."

"Is that right, Hank?" Freddy said. "Swedish ladies... sounds fascinating."

"Did you hear that, Mom?" Sally's dad said. "Handsome American, 'ey."

"I'm sure we'll hear all about it in good time," Sally's mom said. "Get these travelers home so they can rest and have a good dinner. Roast beef and Yorkshire pudding awaits."

"Oh Mom, that sounds great. I liked a lot of the food we had on the trip. But nothing can beat your roast beef and Yorkshire pudding."

Her Mom gave Sally a kiss on the cheek. "You're such a good lass."

***

"Well Hank, tell us about these Swedish ladies," Freddy said as they were seated around the table after their homecoming dinner.

"I met Bridget in Ajanta, a cool group of caves in India north of Bombay with Buddhist paintings. She was almost as tall as me and had lovely blond hair. She joined us and went to Goa with us and then all the way to Nepal. Monica, the other Swedish lady, I met in Goa. They both came with us when we left India."

"Hank got to know them both very well, if you know what I mean," Sally said.

Freddy gave Hank a small shove. "Swedish ladies, hey mate." He nodded at Sally. "So when did you get sick?"

Hank hung his head. "I got sick in India and Nepal. Asian runs." He glanced at Sally. "The worse was when I got in trouble in Afghanistan. I was held hostage for a while and was eventually rescued."

"What?" Sam, Sally's dad, said. "Held hostage?"

Sally waited for Hank to speak. When he didn't, she said, "Hank got in a dispute and his actions were considered an insult. He was kept for over a month as a prisoner and treated horribly. He had a terrible ordeal and needs our kindness and consideration."

"Jesus, Hank," Freddy said.

"Yeah," Hank said. "If you don't mind, I don't feel like talking about it now."

"No worries," Freddy said. "We've got a lot to do before the wedding. I'm so glad you both are here."

Sally was pleased that Freddy had sensed Hank's consternation. Freddy was a sensitive person, and she loved him dearly.

***

The wedding was a grand success. Her brother's joy was obvious. His beautiful bride, Cindy, was showing a little but it did not detract from the ceremony. Cindy was a stunning, mixed-race woman, who Sally remembered fondly from school. Hank performed his best man duties, but seemed detached and morose. He hadn't expanded on his kidnaping and changed the subject whenever it came up.

Hank moped about and was often absent from home. He missed meals and seemed to shun the entire family. Freddy expressed his worries about Hank to Sally. Sally didn't know what to do to help Hank. She suggested that Hank should talk to a professional, but her suggestion was met with a scowl and his declaration that he didn't need to talk to some shrink. She didn't know how to reach him. All her efforts failed.

A week after the wedding, he moved into an apartment. Sally dropped by his apartment after her work at a local clothing store, but he made excuses for her to leave after a few minutes. A week later, he accepted a job at a cattle station near Alice Springs. She was disappointed that he left, but accepted that he needed to be by himself.

Sally spent her time when she wasn't working making water color painting of some of her sketches. The paintings fortified her memories of her travels and strengthened her determination to get back to James.

She checked the post daily, hoping for a letter from James. If she couldn't help Hank, there was no reason to hang around home. She could return to James, but where the hell was he? After four weeks a letter arrived posted from Erzurum Turkey where they were snowed in. The roads North and West through the mountains were all closed. They were waiting for the roads to open and getting bored in the small provincial town.

She was ecstatic to get the letter. She was bored herself. It would take months for her to save enough money from her job as a saleswoman at a clothing store for a plane ticket and living expenses. She asked her brother to help convince their parents to loan her money. She fantasized what James would be doing holed up in a Turkish town with Harry and the Swedish beauties. Her fantasies were not enjoyable.

James was probably already in Europe—possibly Greece. She had sent off a letter to the American Express office in Istanbul and Athens three weeks ago asking him to call. She wrote the next day and asked him again to call her at her parents. She needed to arrange a meeting place. She also sent the same letter to Frankfurt, Germany. She prayed that he would get her letters in Athens.

After another two weeks, she received a letter post marked from Istanbul. They had been there a few days and were enjoying Istanbul. Harry was going to leave the group in Thessalonica and take trains to England. He was totally out of money and was borrowing money from James. The Swedish ladies might depart in Thessalonica too. James was going to travel on to Athens.

She hoped the Swedish ladies would depart with Harry. The thought of the Swedes and James alone in Greece together was disturbing. The days seemed to stretch on interminably as she waited for his call.

48- TEHRAN: APRIL 3, 1970

Bridget was of two minds when Hank and Sally left. Sally's absence would adversely affect the journey for a time, but would allow her the opportunity to get closer to James. Not that she thought of abandoning Harry. Bridget was still infatuated with James— the proverbial one that got away. She didn't want to directly pursue James and be humiliated again or create derision in the group. They still had a long journey ahead. She just felt a special stirring whenever she was in close proximity to James— a vicarious pleasure she relished.

She felt sorry for Hank. He had had a harrowing imprisonment that no one should have had to endure. It was important that Sally went back with him. Sally would aid the return journey and his recovery. What would have happened if they hadn't found Mahmood? She remembered that Sally was the one to insist in Bamyan to continue looking for Mahmood when the rest thought of leaving. Sally had an innate intuitive sense. Putting aside her jealousy, she really did like Sally. She was beautiful and a fiery personality. She had certainly captured Mahmood's attention when they first met him. Perhaps her presence had been an inducement for Mahmood to help them. Bridget wondered how rare women with red hair and green eyes were in the world. She knew no one in Sweden with the same attributes nor had she seen anyone else on the trip with similar traits. The uniqueness of Sally's hair color and eyes must have excited Mahmood. It excited her.

She wondered how Monica felt about Sally's departure. She had seen how Monica had focused her attention on James when Sally was sick with worries about Hank. Would Monica step up her pursuit of James? Would she be jealous of Monica if Monica did? Maybe a little, but Monica's pairing with James would probably enhance the journey.

While James and Harry were packing up, Bridget whispered to Monica to join her in the bathroom. "How do you feel about Sally's departure?" Bridget asked.

"She was fun to be around. I'll miss her. She was right to accompany Hank back to Australia. He's not the same Hank. I hope she can help his recovery. He shunned me after his ordeal."

"Did that bother you that much?"

"Well yes, a little. You and I have talked about Hank as a lover. He certainly left a lot to be desired, but his heart was in the right place. I'll miss him."

"Are you going to try for James?"

"What do you mean?"

"I saw how you often paid attention to him while Sally kept to herself."

"I like him. He's a great guy. You tried and failed to take him away from Sally. He is apparently crazy about her. You think I would have any chance?"

"Yes, I do. He's alone. I'm happy with Harry and have no inclination to try for James although I would relish being with him. There's something about him that is so irresistible. He's handsome, an inquisitive intellectual, and so kind and caring. But me going after him would probably cause derision and might spoil the journey. You going after on the other hand would probably enhance the journey. I think if you play your cards right, you could snare him."

"I would like to pair up with him. It would certainly make the journey more fun."

***

Bridget quickly packed up her bag and backpack and went with the others out to the van. She could tell that James was morose, but he was trying to put a good face on it. He suggested stopping at the Golestan Palaces on the way out.

The Golestan was an impressive group of palaces that were only used for ceremonial purposes by the current Shah, who had a separate residential palace. The impressive painted walls, dazzling tiles, beautiful carpets, and stained glass windows in the group of palaces was a feast for the eyes. Most of the 17 palaces were built over the 131 years of rule of the Qajar dynasty. The Qajar family had taken control of Iran in 1794, deposing Loft Ali Khan the last Zand Shah. The site was restored to its present form in 1865.

Bridget was impressed by the gardens and palaces and would have liked to have spent more time on the tour, but could tell James and Harry were fed up with Tehran. James led the group through the palaces quickly, anxious to get on the road.

***

The road to Tabriz was relatively good, the traffic of trucks and cars constant but courteous. They made reasonable time, reaching Tabriz just after sunset. They found a pleasant hotel. Bridget was surprised by the considerate treatment they received after what they had experienced in Tehran. The people in Tabriz were decidedly different. Although stared at constantly, she was not molested or harangued. After settling in the hotel, they went to the restaurant recommended by the man at the hotel desk and were pleasantly surprised that the waiter spoke broken English, They were able to order with no difficulty. The food was tasty, and they were all happy to be out of Tehran.

"Didn't Britain and the U.S. back a coup that overthrew the democratically elected Prime Minister and put the Shah on the throne?" Bridget asked as they were enjoying their coffee.

"Yes," Harry said, looking around to make sure no one was in earshot. "Britain invaded Iran during the Second World War mainly to protect the oil fields, which a British Oil Company controlled. After the war, a progressive Iranian parliament was elected, led by the National Front leader, Mossadegh."

"Oh yeah-yeah, I remember the name," Bridget said.

"Mossadegh later became the Prime Minister," Harry said. "When Mossadegh proposed a fifty-fifty ownership arrangement for the oil, Britain rejected the proposal and in response imposed an embargo on Iranian oil. With the steep drop in the sale of oil, the Iranian economy suffered. Food and other products became scarce and expensive. Discontent in the country increased and was fostered by British agents. In 1953, after Mossadegh's growing loss of support in the Parliament over the suffering economy, Mossadegh dissolved Parliament." Harry paused as he gathered his breath and bathed in the smile from Bridget. "This gave Britain and the CIA the excuse they needed to support a military coup. The military took control of the government and imprisoned Mossadegh. The Shah, who had fled the country during the coup, was invited back and became the supreme power."

"Yeah-yeah, Harry," Bridget said. "Good synopsis. Do you think most Britons know this history?"

"I doubt it. I didn't know it until the couple I rode out with explained it to me."

***

In the morning they all toured the covered Tabriz bazaar maze with its many carpet, spice, and hat

421

shops. James took the group into a carpet shop. They inspected many different carpets, and drank endless cups of tea. Bridget was in awe of the many different beautiful carpets and purchased a stunning blue, black red, and white small carpet. Monica purchased a small carpet as well. Then they continued around the bazaar.

As they were leaving the bazaar, James stopped outside. "Did you see the two men in the bazaar looking at us?"

"What two men?" Harry asked. "Everyone in the bazaar was watching us."

"There were two men outside the carpet shop that watched us leave. I thought they kinda looked like the men in Mashhad."

"What men in Mashhad?" Harry asked.

"Two men outside the Haram, who were lingering at the entrance when we left. I thought they looked like the guys we saw in Herat."

"The men in Herat were wearing typical Afghan dress, had turbans, and beards. I didn't see anyone that looked like Afghans here? I thought you felt the men in Herat were Mahmood's men checking on us."

Bridget vaguely remembered the men in Herat James mentioned, but she thought the men in the bazaar were just typical Iranians watching Westerners. Maybe he was so distressed by Sally's departure that he was seeing things. Perhaps Mahmood had sent men to watch over them in Herat, but the same men in different dress watching them in Mashhad and then here in Tabriz was a stretch of the imagination.

"Yeah, I'm probably being unreasonable," James said, squinting. "Hank is gone. Mahmood's men wouldn't still be following us for protection."

Monica edged up next to James. "We're so used to looking over our shoulder. It's understandable. It will take some time to put Hank's kidnapping behind us."

Bridget was glad Monica was subtly ingratiating herself more with James. He definitely needed the distraction, but Monica needed to take it slow and not appear too obvious as not to chase him away. He was quite morose and understandably fragile. She was one to talk. She hadn't been that subtle with James. Maybe if she hadn't moved so fast in Benares and Kathmandu, she would have had more success. Of course circumstances were much different. Monica's pursuit would be much easier now that Sally was gone.

***

After they left in the morning for Turkey, Harry warned James that the people in the Turkish Border town, Gurbulak, were unpleasant and belligerent when he came through. He suggested James not stop in town until they reached the petrol station.

After clearing Turkish customs with no problem and no search of the van, they drove into Gurbulak to the central square where a large group of men were gathered, many spilling into the street. All the men were wearing flat type wool caps. As James slowed and honked to wait for the men to get out of the way, several men began pounding on the van, their faces contorted in gruesome stares. One of the men opened the van backdoor, but Monica pulled it shut and locked it. Another man climbed atop of the luggage rack and was trying to undue the jerry cans.

"Step on it," Harry shouted.

"Jesus, what's up with these people?"

"Just keep going."

The man on the roof sprang off as James sped away from the square, honking continuously through the crowd of angry men. He pulled into the petrol station on the outskirts of the village. Many of the angry men followed them. The station owner came out with a shot gun and shouted at the men. Most of the men dispersed, but a small group stayed in the street.

Bridget was stunned by the town's behavior. She couldn't imagine what had happened to these people. James and Harry got out and asked the station owner to fill the tank. Bridget and Monica remained in the van with the curtains closed and watched the people in the street through the gap.

A young boy came out of the station and walked up to James and Harry. "Hello, how are you," the boy said with a giant smile.

The station owner stopped pumping petrol and approached the boy with a frown. He shouted at the boy in guttural Turkish. The boy cowered, but remained staring. The owner moved to the boy and slapped him, splitting the boy's lip. The boy screamed, grabbing his mouth as the blood dripped through his fingers. He fled back into the station, crying, where a portly woman dressed in black hugged the boy and shouted at the owner.

James looked to Harry, who shrugged, then paid the owner in Turkish lira that he had exchanged in Tabriz. The owner nodded to them and said something in Turkish. James nodded back, thanked the man, and hopped back into the van. As they drove from the station, the men in the street banged on the van, shouting something. James accelerated as fast as he could through the crowd.

Several kids ran down the road after them, one carrying a shotgun. James, watching the kids in his side mirror, hunched his shoulders. "Everybody down, they've got a gun."

Bridget was relieved when they rounded a curve and the group was no longer in sight. "God, what happened to that town?" Bridget asked.

"No idea, but it was way worse than when I came through," Harry said. "Maybe there was some incident with tourists or something."

"Did you see the owner backhand his kid and split his lip for just talking to us?" James exclaimed. "I hope the other towns in Turkey we go through are not like this."

"I don't think they'll be," Harry said. "For some reason the Gurbulak people are incensed idiots. I didn't have much trouble in the rest of Turkey on the way out."

They proceeded across Eastern Turkey through the various scattered villages without further incident. There was little traffic on the paved road except for massive trucks loaded to the hilt. James often had to pull off the road to let them pass when they hogged the entire road. The Turkish truck drivers in their decorated trucks seemed to think that the road belonged to them.

In the afternoon they passed the snowcapped twin volcanic peaks of Mount Ararat rising up from the plain in the northern distance— the supposed resting place of Noah's ark. Bridget was thrilled to see Mount Arat even though she gave no credence to the biblical story of the ark. She thought it was an allegorical children's tale to scare people into following the precepts of Judaism. Possibly a retelling of the flood story from Mesopotamia.

49- ERZURUM: APRIL 4, 1970

They drove into the town of Erzurum at sunset. The town was majestic surrounded by high snowcapped peaks. There were several mosques in town and a citadel high up on a hill. The unusual Medrese School, a Muslim seminary, with its tall minarets and peaked cone roof was the largest building in town.

The short stocky men of the town watched them as they climbed out from the van in front of the hotel Harry was familiar with, but to their relief did not accost them.

"Every man has the same flat cap," Bridget said as they walked into the hotel.

"Yeah, they are very popular in this region of Turkey," Harry said. "We call them cabbie hats in England. Ataturk in 1925 outlawed the fez hat, which had been mandated in the Ottoman Empire instead of turbans. These guys must have decided on the cabbie hat instead."

"So much for variety," Bridget said.

They went into the hotel and obtained a room with four beds. They were glad to bed down, drained by the journey, the hassle in the border town, and the repeated bail-outs to the side of the road.

James laid down in his bed and cupped his arms behind his head exhaling deeply, glad to be out of the van. He thought about the mayhem in the border town, wondering what had happened to make the town so unwelcoming. Bridget laid down with Harry. He was glad Harry and Bridget were getting along so well even though he felt a little jealous.

"It feels so good to be in a town that seems civilized compared to that border town," Monica announced as she slumped down on her bed. "My god that place was scary. I need a shower to wash away the irk I feel from traveling through that town." She reluctantly pushed herself up and tottered to the bathroom. When she came out from the shower, she was naked with a towel wrapped around her head. She passed closely by James, giving a big smile.

As James watched Monica cross the room, he felt a stirring of desire, compounded by her enticing smile and curvaceous body. He expected she was feeling lonely without Hank like he felt without Sally. He had trouble getting to sleep as the image of Monica continued to corrupt his thoughts as well as worry about the resurgence of his nightmare. Sally had provided such a comfort that was sadly missing now. He awoke in the night, sweating despite the cold of their room, the vivid nightmare gripping his mind like the claws of a tiger. He could not fall back asleep and watched the group, soothed to a small extent by their untroubled sleep. In the morning, he was first up and quietly plodded to the bathroom for a hot shower. He felt refreshed somewhat after the shower and went to sit on his bed to watch the rest of the group wake up slowly. He couldn't keep his eyes off the Swedish ladies as they rose, stretching their perfect forms in the morning light suffusing the room. They spoke to each other in their sing song Swedish cadence, then dashed together into the bathroom for their wake-up shower. They were a delight to watch, and he was thankful he was in pleasant company— fortunate not to be alone.

After everyone had showered, they left the hotel in good spirits and were shocked to find the ground covered with more than a foot of snow. "Damn, this a lot of snow," Harry said. "Look at the mountains. They're completely covered."

"Is this a problem?" Bridget asked.

"I don't know," Harry said. "We'll ask at the restaurant."

They hurried the several blocks to the restaurant and filed inside. "Lot of snow," Harry said to the proprietor, who spoke English, and remembered Harry.

"Yes, it is unusual for this time of year," the proprietor said. "I'm afraid that all the roads west and north have been closed. Much snow in the mountains."

"We can't leave for Trabzon?" James asked.

"No, it is forbidden," the proprietor said. "You will have to wait for the roads to reopen."

"When will that be?"

"It is unknown," the proprietor said. "Please sit. Would you all like Turkish coffee?"

They nodded. "Yes, please."

"At least this town is nothing like that crazy border town," Monica said. "People seem to be friendly. The hotel is comfortable. A couple of days here won't be so bad." She trailed her hand across James's back as she followed Harry and Bridget to a table. James watched her retreating form. He could still feel the brush of her hand.

"Good coffee," Bridget said. "Nice that the owner speaks English." She leaned into Harry. "Good restaurant choice."

They ordered eggs with sausage and dug in as soon as their plates arrived. The food was hot and enjoyable. They ordered another coffee and savored the congenial atmosphere of the restaurant. They were the only Westerners. The patrons in the café after their initial stares thankfully ignored the group.

When they finished eating, the owner came to clear the table and asked them about their journey. When Harry told him about their troubles in Gurbulak, the proprietor said he had heard similar stories from other travelers, but did not know why the village was so angry and belligerent.

"The proprietor is nice and it's great that he speaks English," Bridget said after the man departed and rubbed Harry's shoulder. "This town is so much different than that border town. Those guys were animals."

Monica leaned toward James and placed her hand on his arm. "Are you sad, James?" She rubbed his arm gently and placed her other hand on his back. "Don't worry things will work out. We probably won't be here too long." She stared unflinchingly at James, then smiled before taking a sip of her coffee. "I know you're missing Sally. She was such a bright star. Do you really think she'll be coming back to join you in Europe?"

"I don't know," James replied glumly. "Hard to say how she'll feel once she's back with her family." He looked away briefly to mitigate the intensity of Monica's gaze. "Hank's recovery will take a while. A flight from Australia to Europe will cost a lot. She'll need to get a loan from her parents to be able to meet me in Europe or England. That could be a problem if her parents aren't too receptive."

"Hank was a shadow of his old self when he showed up in Herat," Monica said. "He lost all interest in me. I tried to reignite some passion, make him feel better, but he wasn't having it."

"Yeah, I thought as much," James said. "It was good you tried."

Monica laid a hand on James's cheek and widened her eyes. "You are such an understanding man." She withdrew her hand. "Sally said you had a terrible time in Vietnam. It's such a crazy war. What happened there?"

"I'd rather not talk about it now."

"Okay. If you need a sympathetic ear, I'm here."

***

Each day when they arrived at the restaurant, they hoped to hear the roads were open, but were repeatedly disappointed. They spent a lot of time playing cards or lingering in the warm restaurant.

James accepted Monica's increased overt attention toward him with good nature, and although often embarrassed by her attention, he felt good that Monica was concerned about him.

One night when it was colder than usual, James felt a warm body against his back. He thought he was dreaming of Sally. When he realized it wasn't a dream, he twisted around.

"I was cold," Monica said. "It's much toastier in here with you." She kissed him and pressed her ample breasts against him. Her hand went to his crotch. "We could really warm each other up."

"This isn't a good idea," James said.

"Oh James," Monica replied, squeezing even tighter against him "Why deny yourself. Sally's gone and I'm here. You may never see her again. Just relax and enjoy." She kissed him again. He savored her soft lips as the phrase 'you may never see her again' repeated in his mind like a broken record.

She pulled down his underwear, and James did not resist. She rolled onto her back, pulling James on top, and grasped and pulled his hips into hers. The spark of lust stung James, dispelling any other thoughts, and he entered Monica with frantic energy. He pumped vigorously, rocking the bed noisily as Monica cried out in orgasm.

Bridget laughed. "Hey, we're trying to sleep over here."

***

After another week in which he and Monica slept together nightly, an ease settled over the group now that they were paired. James accepted that Sally's return was unlikely and decided to make the best of his pairing with Monica. She was a nurse back in Sweden and was not shy. She didn't have the enthusiasm for art and culture that Bridget had, but she was quick-witted and had a sunny disposition. The group made their walks to the restaurant each morning, hoping that they would be told the roads would open, but accepted the news of the continuing road closure with measured acceptance.

Near the end of the second week, they were informed at lunch they could go north in the morning to Trabzon if they had chains. James purchased chains and a short stocky man with wrists the size of heavy lumber agreed to install them for a small fee. As James stood by the man installing the chains, he noticed two men come out of a tea shop, who momentarily stared at him. He hadn't noticed them in town before. They were bundled in thick wool coats, were clean shaven, and wore the pervasive flat caps. James watched the men with curiosity, thinking they were similar to the men he wondered about in Iran. He knew that anyone following him into Turkey made little sense. He needed to stop worrying anyone was following them. It was an absurd notion.

The next morning they set off. The road climbed steadily up and they had to go slow, following the caravan of trucks that had accumulated in Erzurum. The icy road was treacherous, and he spun out several times, but was able to stop before going over the side of the road into the deep chasm. It was a nail biting, slow journey.

They reached Trabzon in the evening. The Black Sea, illuminated by the swollen moon, stretched out in front of them to the horizon. They quickly obtained a room with two double beds in a small hotel and fell into bed exhausted. James was glad that Monica sensed his exhaustion and didn't press for sex.

***

The next morning, they drove along the road full of traffic that ran near the shore of the Black Sea. The going was slow from town to town after their late start. They stopped at Samsun, a shipping hub and modern city in the late afternoon. They got two hotel rooms.

James, having regained his energy, went after Monica as if he were competing in a marathon contest. Their antics dispelled any lingering guilt he felt for betraying Sally.

They left early the next morning to beat the traffic. The highway soon left the banks of the Black Sea and went inland. The traffic was much lighter and they made good time reaching the outskirts of Istanbul in the late afternoon. They drove through the swarming city to the Bosporus, parked, and got out.

Hank was pleased they made it back for Freddy's wedding, but didn't enjoy the ceremony that much. The joy of everyone just seemed to make him more depressed. He shunned Sally's interest in his wellbeing and moved out of the home he had so loved. It was too painful to be there. Just seeing Sally reminded him of his ordeal and his stupidity. He went on a date with his previous girlfriend Vivian. Vivian was eager for a relationship, but Hank found little enjoyment being with her.

The grip of morose remembrances from his kidnapping haunted his waking and sleeping thoughts. He could have easily died in Afghanistan. He wanted to push his ordeal in Afghanistan out of his mind, but his efforts were futile. He started running in the early morning even though it made his arm ache. The pain reinforced his feelings of failure.

He knew he should be eating more, but most food tasted insipid to him. He seldom cooked for himself and often ate out or consumed frozen dinners. He had frequent bouts of diarrhea, which served to despoil his appetite. When Sally came to see him at his apartment, bringing food, her presence reminded him of his ordeal and made him more morose. Plus, her talk about wanting to reunite with James in Europe and moaning about her parents reluctance to loan her the money, made him angry. James, Sally, and Harry had saved him by finding Mahmood, and he owed them a debt of gratitude, but he hated her talk of James. He just wanted everyone to leave him alone.

He left Brisbane and got a job at a cattle station near Alice Springs— way away from Sally and her family. He kept to himself and worked hard. He welcomed the isolation and the work especially with the horses. His nights in the bunk house were an agony, fraught with horrible nightmares. He often awoke in a sweat and went out to the stables to be with the horses. Just laying hands on them calmed him. They accepted him as he was— a damaged individual.

He admired the station owner, Richard Andrews, a no nonsense rugged man, who occasionally stopped to talk to him, complementing him on his work and expertise with the horses. The other hands were friendly enough, but he kept to himself and made no close friends. When the crew went in town to the pub, he stayed at the station. Beer, which he had consumed with glee before his ordeal tasted bitter, and the intoxication that he had so relished seemed debilitating. He felt best riding the range alone, searching for strays and working the cattle. He gained back some weight, but still often felt nauseous when he ate.

One afternoon Richard came out to greet Hank after a long day as Hank was unsaddling his horse. "You got a call this afternoon, from your brother, Freddy Compton," Richard said as he patted Hank's beige stallion. "He asked that you call home."

"Oh... well... thank you."

"I didn't know you had a half-brother."

"I grew up with him, and consider him a brother, but he's not my blood brother."

"I see. Why don't you come up to the house after you clean up and have dinner with me," Richard said. "After dinner you can call Freddy. He seemed very anxious to talk to you."

"Has something happened?"

"No. He said there was no emergency. He was worried about you, since you hadn't written or called."

***

Hank knocked at the big house with trepidation. He wasn't relishing a dinner with Richard nor a call to Freddy.

"Come on in," Richard said as he opened the thick pine door.

"Thanks for inviting me," Hank said, placed his hat on one of the pegs near the door, and followed Richard past the rustic living room into the dining room with its long pine table.

"I had some of the boys cut out a nice steer," Richard said as he indicated a chair near the head of the table for Hank. "We've got fresh T-bones."

"Sounds inviting." Hank took his seat. He glanced around the sparse dining room. On the sideboard were a host of photographs. The chandelier over the table was made from an old wagon wheel, and the mostly bare plaster walls were painted a cream color.

"I couldn't help but notice when you first came here you were quite skinny. You've gained some weight, but you're still quite light for your height."

"Yeah, I was quite sick for a while."

"That's a nasty scar you have on your arm."

"Got cut with a knife. It was a terrible wound that got badly infected. My arm is not yet fully recovered, but it's so much better than it was."

"You couldn't tell that by me. You don't let it interfere with your work. You're one of the best workers I've ever had." He paused and took a drink of his beer. "I've been meaning to invite you up here. You've really impressed me, Hank, and I want to offer you the job of foreman. My last foreman left soon after you came, and I've been assuming his duties. My daughter will be coming back from college soon, and I want to be able to spend more time with her." He paused and exhaled. "Plus I'm getting too old to try to ramrod you young men. You can think it over if you like."

"Gosh, Mr. Andrews, I don't know what to say other than I'd love to be your foreman."

"I'm so glad, Hank." Richard raised his glass and held it out toward Hank. Hank raised his glass, and Richard clinked it with his. "Cheers."

"Cheers," Hank replied and took a drink of beer. He knew he should happy with the major promotion, but felt joyless and didn't know why he had accepted right off the bat. It would mean more money, but he didn't care about the money. Would he be able to handle the increased responsibility? Before his trip and ordeal he would have been stoked at a chance for a foreman job.

The elderly Aborigine cook shuffled in with the dishes of food on a big tray and set the plates of T-bone steak, roast potatoes, and mixed vegetables on the table. Richard grabbed the platter of steaks and laid one on his plate and handed the platter to Hank. Then proceeded with the other dishes.

"So tell me about Freddy," Richard said.

Hank glanced out the window and took a deep breath. "Freddy was my best friend when we were kids. We went everywhere together. My parents died in an auto accident when I was ten, and Freddy's family took me in and raised me as their own. I don't know what I would have done if they hadn't."

"I'm sorry for you loss, Hank. Losing your parents at such a young age must have been devastating." Richard cut a big chunk of steak and placed it in his mouth and chewed vigorously. "I must tell you there's nothing like fresh steak. Almost melts in your mouth."

Hank cut a piece of steak and chewed vigorously. "Yes, Mr. Andrews this is so tender and delicious."

"Call me Richard." Richard took another bite of steak and a fork full of roast potatoes. "Why haven't you contacted Freddy since you've been here? Did you have a falling out?"

"No, I was concentrating on the work and trying to get my arm back in shape."

***

Hank assumed his foreman duties with nervousness. He knew the work well enough, but wasn't sure how best to proceed. He slowly discarded his shell and engaged the workers more. He soon figured out who were the good workers and who were the slackers. He surprised himself. The workers seemed to accept his authority. He gave the good workers more autonomy and supervised the slackers closely. The two Aborigine wranglers were good workers, but kept to themselves. It was obvious most of the other workers didn't like the Aborigines. One was an artist and Hank liked his work. When Hank asked to buy a painting, the man gave him the painting, saying it pleased him that Hank liked his work, and he wanted to honor Hank. The gift had almost brought tears to Hank's eyes.

After several weeks as foreman, Richard's daughter, Amelia arrived. Hank could tell Richard was delighted. Amelia was a beautiful blond with a luscious face and lithe body. She reminded him of Bridget, but was not nearly as tall. He made a point of avoiding her. Yet, when she wasn't looking, he couldn't keep his eyes off her. He didn't know how to deal with his infatuation with the young woman. He didn't need any entanglement or humiliation.

Amelia went out riding the first few weeks of her appearance often accompanied by her father. As the weeks passed, her rides with her father diminished, and she was often by herself. Hank would ride out in the same vicinity, but was careful to keep out of sight, watching her sweep across the dry landscape.

One late afternoon when Amelia returned from her ride as the sun was beginning to set, Hank was feeding the other horses. He heard her arrive and stayed in the barn, hoping to avoid her.

Amelia tied her horse up to the hitching post and walked into the barn. "Hey up, Hank, will you help me rub down Lightening? I stayed out longer then I should have. I don't want to make Dad wait for dinner."

"Sure," Hank said, and walked out with her. "I can see you've put Lightning through her paces. I can rub her down if you like and put her up, if you want to get going."

"Why thank you, Hank," Amelia replied. "But I can help. Shouldn't take too long." She unbuckled the saddle strap, and Hank grasped the saddle and slung it on the corral fence. "My Dad said you've done wonders with the workers. He really likes you."

"Thank you. Your Dad is such a great guy." Up close her face was even more beautiful with her welcoming smile and eyes like tunnels of blue.

"So where are you from?" she asked, moving even closer.

"I grew up in Brisbane."

"What brought you out here?"

"I've worked on cattle stations before. I like the work and being in the outback."

"I've seen you riding about. You are a natural horseman. We should go riding together."

"That's quite a skyline," Bridget said. "What's that huge mosque on the hill?"

"Hagia Sophia," Harry said. "That section of Istanbul over the Bosporus is considered the beginning of Europe although it's very much Turkish, and I wouldn't categorize it as European. Of course Constantinople was the seat of the Greek Empire for many years. Hagia Sophia as you probably already know was originally a Christian church."

They hopped back in the van and crossed over the bridge into the supposed European section. They chose a hotel near a police station not far from the Blue Mosque. James at Harry's suggestion went inside the police station and offered the policeman at the station counter a cash incentive to park his vehicle on the street at the side of the station, hoping that the location and incentive would keep the van safe from vandalism. Istanbul was notorious for vehicle break-ins. They left many of their purchases in the van, but took their rugs and a few other purchases in with them to decorate their rooms. James had his camera equipment locked in the hotel safe.

***

"It was originally the greatest Greek Orthodox church in Christendom," Harry said as they stood in front of the Hagia Sophia in the early morning. "Now it's a museum." They continued into the massive building.

Bridget stopped and gazed up at the ceiling. "The dome is immense and those half domes on either side are dazzling. What an unusual and unbelievable sight."

"After the Turkish conquest of Constantinople in 1453 it was turned into a mosque and the minarets were added," Harry said. "My English traveling companions gave me a history lesson when we were here. It was considered the most accomplished architectural achievement of its age. When it was built in 537 AD, it was the largest building in the world."

They mounted the steps to the second floor gallery and strolled around the gallery admiring the fine mosaics.

"The Turks plastered over the mosaics when it became a mosque," Harry said and strolled to the balustrade to look out at the vast expanse of the interior. "I'm overwhelmed by the beauty and size of this building whenever I come here."

"I'm surprised the mosaics weren't destroyed," Bridget said. "I'm glad they weren't. They're so beautiful."

After several hours, they left Hagia Sophia and sauntered arm in arm across the inviting park with its multicolored spring flowers to the Blue Mosque.

"Sultan Ahmet built this mosque to compete with the Hagia Sophia," Harry said.

Bridget glanced back at Hagia Sophia before turning to the mosque. "It's not nearly as big. I like the cascading domes from large to small. Nice touch."

"I've not seen another mosque with six minarets," Monica said. "Most have only four."

Harry laughed. "According to legend, the Sultan wanted gold minarets and the architect thought he said six instead of gold. The two words are similar in Turkish. The mosque was completed in 1616."

"I heard them calling to prayer last night from the minaret," Bridget said. "So they pray five times a day. That takes a lot of dedication."

"Yeah, intense dedication," James replied. "All the religions have their dogma. Sometimes I think dogma gets in the way of religious belief."

"Yeah-yeah," Bridget said. "Religious dogma can be stifling." She never ceased to be in awe of James. She disliked religion in general although she had found Greek mythology, Hinduism, and Buddhism fascinating. Her family never attended church. Religious observation in Sweden had diminished over the years since the Second World War, which she thought was good. Religion was responsible for enumerable wars and human suffering throughout the ages and had fostered misogyny. She detested the male only priests and preachers. Celibacy among catholic priests was unnatural and any mention of nuns incensed her.

They went inside the mosque. Its domes, pervasive blue tiles, and stained glass windows were stunning. They continued through the mosque to the stark courtyard before leaving.

"The Blue Mosque is an incredibly beautiful mosque, but I liked Hagia Sophia better," Bridget said as she grasped Harry's arm.

***

After a late lazy morning as Bridget and Harry relaxed in their hotel room, Bridget, announcing her hunger, dragged Harry out and roused James and Monica. They all went to an early lunch. After a delicious lunch of iskender kebabs and rice with assorted vegetables, they walked to the Topkapi Palace with its massive, twelve foot, high walls.

"I didn't have time to come here on my first stop in Istanbul," Harry said. "So, I'll leave the tour to you, James."

James referred to the tourist pamphlet as they stood outside in the warm sun. A plethora of bulky clouds had assembled in the sky, periodically blocking out the sun as the clouds swam across the sky. "This Palace was the center of the Ottoman Empire from the fifteenth to the nineteenth century," James said as he started for the entrance. "The Ottoman Empire encompassed southeastern Europe, western Asia, and northern Africa. It was known for its art and military control. The First World War saw the defeat of the Ottomans and the dissolution of their vast empire."

They strolled through the Imperial gate to the park and then to the Archaeological Museum. The museum had innumerable Classical and Hellenic artifacts.

They continued on into the second courtyard through the crenellated Gate of Greeting with its twin towers topped by cone roofs.

"Another park," Monica said. "Isn't the Harem in here?"

"Yes, to the left," James said.

They entered the famed sultan's harem building through the Tower of Justice, the tallest structure in the palace. The first area was the eunuchs section, decorated with seventeenth century tiles. They proceeded to the courtyard of the concubines, which was surrounded by baths, fountains, and private apartments.

"This place is giving me the creeps," Bridget said. "It's like a comfortable prison. Talk about misogyny. Let's get out of here." All through the tour of the harem, she felt a chill and creeping sensation up her back. She thought the misogyny inherent in the Muslim religion medieval.

"Just think what Henry the Eighth had to go through to marry another woman while the sultans had their pick of hundreds of women," Harry said

"I suppose you think the sultans had it made," Bridget said and punched Harry. "Hundreds of ladies to choose from."

"Well it must have been a lavish life style."

"It must have been awful to be a concubine," Monica said.

Bridget was well aware that men had been subjugating women since time immemorial. She wondered sometimes if deep down she actually disliked and disdained men. Even in Sweden men mostly held the reins of power. Compared to other countries in Europe, Sweden and the other Scandinavian countries had been at the forefront of incorporating women into the power structure. Still there was a long way to go before women were equally represented. Misogyny still ruled the day.

"The concubines were all slaves— mostly Christian women from the Caucasus," James said. "Muslim women could not be enslaved."

"Oh, how sick," Bridget said and quickly exited the harem.

They walked across the gardens of the courtyard to the Treasury building. The Treasury contained gold and jewel encrusted armor of the sultans, decorated Korans, jewel encrusted daggers and utensils, the famed Spoon Maker's diamond, the seventh largest in the world at eighty-six carats, and untold other jewels all in bullet proof cases.

"I remember this diamond from the movie,' Topkapi'," Bridget said. "I'm glad we were able to see it."

James pointed at another door way "In here are the Islamic paintings."

"Let's skip the paintings," Monica said, grabbing James from behind and nuzzling his neck.

"I'm going to go through quickly," Bridget said. "I'll meet you in the courtyard."

"Come on let's all go," James said.

Monica and Harry agreed, and they proceeded quickly through the rooms of many paintings—portraits of the various sultans and ceremonial painting with amazing detail. They exited into the fourth courtyard with its gardens and large pool, and out to the terrace overlooking the Sea of Marmara.

***

The next morning they entered the Istanbul Grand Bazaar, a covered warren of shops selling all manner of goods— the largest covered bazaar in the world. Sounds of Turkish music wafted from the many shops and gave a carnival air to the bazaar.

They had eaten a quick breakfast in their favorite restaurant where the previous evening they had been offered a hashish joint. Bridget was surprised by the offer since two policeman were in the restaurant. James had quickly declined the joint. Bridget was glad, thinking it was a possible set up for entrapment, but wasn't sure since the policemen were very friendly and had sent glasses of raki, an anise liquor, to their table. It was obvious that the policeman were captivated by her and Monica. In any case taking risks in Turkey was foolish and stupid.

"I want to get some leather skirts and pants," Monica said as they strolled through the area of the rug merchants."

"Let's check out some carpets first," James said.

"What's with you and carpets?" Harry asked.

"I've always liked oriental carpets. I'd like to see what they have and the prices."

They entered a large carpet shop "Welcome, my friends," the owner said. "I'm happy you are interested in carpets. I have the best carpet shop in all of Turkey. We have fine Turkish carpets and kilims as well as carpets from around the world." He bade them all sit and had tea brought in for them. He then proceeded to unroll carpets and kilims one after the other. The parade of carpets was impressive.

Bridget thought about purchasing one of the amazing large flowered carpets and have it shipped to Sweden for her apartment, but her funds were getting low, and they all were helping Harry, who was nearly out of money. The price for the carpet was tantalizing, but in the end she decided against the purchase.

James seemed interested in a few carpets as well but did not purchase any. After many cups of tea and the viewing of numerous carpets, they left much to the dismay of the merchant.

Monica and Bridget ordered leather trousers and skirts at one of the leather shops, and James ordered suede trousers and waist coat. Harry selected a leather vest. Their made to order items would be ready the following day.

After wandering around the bazaar for hours amazed by the gamut of goods offered, they walked back to their hotel, each couple to their room.

***

When Bridget awoke to the call of the muezzin, she studied the twilight streaming through the window and gave Harry a shake. "Shall we get James and Monica and go to dinner."

Harry opened his eyes and smiled. "Lovely idea. I feel refreshed, energized, and we worked up quite an appetite." He placed a hand on Bridget's thigh. His smile encompassing his entire face.

Bridget was enjoying her pairing with Harry. He was a considerate lover, but he didn't stir her passion to the extent that her brief dalliance with James had. Istanbul was interesting and she was grateful she had come overland, despite the despondency the kidnapping of Hank in Afghanistan had caused. She wondered how she'd feel leaving James behind in Thessalonica and taking the train with Harry and Monica to Paris and on to Sweden. Maybe she should continue on with Harry to England for a while. See where he lived and tour around England with him. Although maybe that wasn't such a good idea. Monica wouldn't want to come and wouldn't like traveling back to Sweden from Paris on her own. Since Harry was basically out of money and would need to get a job in England— James had been loaning him money and Bridget had often paid for his share of the meals— she didn't think she would want to hang around his hometown or wherever he found work. Probably better to end it in Paris and continue on with Monica to Sweden.

Bridget couldn't help being jealous of Monica's relationship with James. She hadn't gotten over her failure to completely capture him in Kathmandu. She doubted that Sally would be returning, but it was obvious James hadn't given up all hope of her return. She and Monica had invited him to come to Sweden after he finished visiting Greece, Europe, and England. He seemed receptive to the idea. She would enjoy seeing him in Sweden and showing him around. She might even be able to renew a relationship. She still remembered the gratification she had tasted briefly in Kathmandu. They would be a good couple together.

She had had a lovely day visiting the bazaar. The variety of items for sale was impressive and the pervasive Turkish music and alluring smells almost made her swoon. Returning to Europe seemed pedestrian after the riches of the East, and she was feeling a little disheartened about leaving in the morning and soon ending her association with James. She would miss being around James probably more so than missing Harry. What was it about James than defied explanation?

In the evening the four went out to dinner to their favorite restaurant where the Turkish music played was more traditional. She liked the traditional music better than the popular music that one heard almost everywhere. The traditional music was less jarring and flowed together harmoniously.

As Bridget was discussing the wondrous merchandise, she had seen in the bazaar, Monica announced out of the blue, "I'm going to continue on with James to Athens."

Bridget stared at Monica a few seconds trying to understand where this left her. "I thought you were coming on the train with me."

"I was, but I asked James if he would mind if I came with him to Athens. I want to see Athens and the Acropolis." She leaned into James and gave him a smile. "He was all for it." She turned to Bridget. "Would you like to come along too?"

"I've never been to Athens," Bridget exclaimed. Visiting Athens undoubtedly would be more interesting than a train journey with Harry and then having to continue to Sweden alone. Plus she would savor more time with James. She turned to Harry and placed her hand on his arm. "Would you be disappointed if I didn't come on the train with you?"

"Of course I would, but I understand if you want to see Athens. I've been and it is an amazing city. You should go. If I could afford it, I would come too."

"I could loan you the money."

"You all have helped me out so much already. I can't in good conscience accept more of your kindness. You'll need your money to get back to Sweden. No, I'll take the train. If you don't come visit me in England, I'm definitely coming to Sweden. Hopefully in the fall."

"Oh Harry, that would be wonderful," Bridget said. "I don't know what to do," Bridget looked from

Monica to Harry. "I feel bad about abandoning you." She pulled Harry's hand to her chest. "We've had so much fun together."

"Hey, I'm a big lad. Not to worry. Go with James and Monica. I insist."

Bridget leaned over and gave Harry a kiss. "Thank you."

***

In the morning they went to the bazaar, collected their leather goods, and returned to the hotel to pack up and check out. When they got to the van, the passenger window was broken out, and most of their souvenirs were gone. The inside of the van was strewn with utensils and food.

"Fuck, can you believe it," James said. "They broke in right next to the police station. My bribe to the police was useless."

"Turks are brazen," Harry said.

James rubbed his head. "We should have taken everything inside the hotel."

"Our Afghan coats and all the saris and shirts," Bridget said. "Damn. Lucky we took our rugs inside." She was unhappy about the loss of all her souvenirs, but had never put much stock in material things. She favored experiences over artifacts.

"There's nothing for it," James said. "Let's clean up and take off."

They tidied the van and started off, winding their way out of the city through the congested traffic.

They saw two men jump on a truck ahead of them full of watermelons. The men threw four melons to the small truck behind them before jumping off.

"Did you see that," James said. "Broad daylight— unbelievable."

*****

They reached Edirne near the Greek border in the afternoon and drove past the three spectacular mosques in the center of the town. "The Selimiye Mosque has the tallest minarets in Turkey and a cupola higher than Hagia Sophia," Harry said. 'You want to stop and go inside?"

"I'm anxious to get to Greece," Bridget said. "I've had enough of mosques."

"Greece it is, then," James announced.

52- GREEK BORDER: APRIL 26, 1970

"I see you have come from India overland," the Greek official said and studied James, Harry, Bridget and Monica in turn with a slight squint, lingering his gaze on the women.

They had whisked through the Turkey side of the border with no problems, but had been stopped on the Greek side and ushered into an office.

"Yes, that's right," James replied.

"We know that you are smuggling hashish," the official said with a smile that changed to a frown.

"No we're not," James said, staring back, trying to keep his face neutral. The frequent suspicions and harassments at borders were tolling on him, making him angry.

"It will go easier on you if you confess and tell us where it is hidden," the official said. "If we have to tear your van apart and find the hashish, you will all go to jail for a long time." He peered intensely at the group. "Our prisons are not a place you would enjoy."

"Go ahead and search," James said. "We're clean."

The official stood. "I will give you some time to discuss this among yourselves." He left the room.

"What's with this— we know shit," Monica said.

Harry leaned forward. "They might try this approach on all the people they think are hippies," he said softly.

"Nothing to do, but sit and wait," James said. "They can tear the van apart, like the others, to no avail." He suspected that they were being monitored.

After twenty minutes, the official walked back into the room. "Yes, now tell me where the hashish is hidden."

"We don't have any hashish," James almost shouted. He took a deep breath and cautioned himself to keep calm.

"I urge you to reconsider and tell us where the hashish is hidden."

"Hey, we've been thoroughly searched at most border crossings," James said in a much calmer voice. "Go ahead and search."

The official watched each in turn for several minutes without speaking. "That will not be necessary. Here are your passports. You are free to go."

James and the group walked slowly to the van and drove off. "That was weird," Monica said. "I'm surprised they didn't search the van."

"Probably too lazy," Harry said.

"Thank god for that," James added. "Destination Thessalonica. It's good to be in Europe. I've never been."

***

James drove until early evening, stopped near Alexanderpolis for the night, and the four slept in the van. The next morning they ordered a breakfast of yogurt, cheese, and bread at a restaurant near the sea. The fresh sea air was inviting and the weather was warm as the brilliant sun reflected off the blue sea. They drove on and arrived in Thessalonica in the afternoon. James followed the signs to the train station.

They all accompanied Harry into the train station. After purchasing his ticket, Harry turned to the three. "I'll never forget the great time we had together." He hugged James. "It's been a fantastic journey my friend. What adventures we had. It's hard to believe all the great things we've seen and experienced— amazing memories to last a lifetime. I'll see you in England. Have a great trip." He moved to Monica and hugged her. "I'm glad we met. It was a joy to travel with you. Take care of James." He grabbed Bridget and kissed and hugged for a long time. "I'm going to miss you. You have to come and visit. You'll like England. Don't worry, we'll see each other again. If you don't come to England, I'm definitely coming to Sweden. Enjoy Greece. Off with you. I don't want to start crying."

They watched him walk away his pack slung over one shoulder. "I'm going to miss him," Bridget said. "He was such a great guy. I'm a little sad I didn't go with him."

Monica slipped her arm around Bridget. "Don't worry, as he said you'll see each other again." She clapped her hands together. "Athens here we come."

They piled into the van and drove off. They were all silent for a time before Bridget started enumerating the fabulous things they had seen together. After dark, they pulled off alongside the road and bedded down "I'm missing Harry already," Bridget said as she lay on the other side of Monica. "When I get back to Sweden, I'll try to get my dad to loan me the money and go visit Harry before I start school again."

"Why didn't you go with him?" James asked.

"I wanted to see Athens and the Acropolis," Bridget said. "When Monica said she had decided to come with you, I couldn't pass up the opportunity. I've always wanted to see Athens. I've studied Greek mythology and have been fascinated by classical art." She smiled and gave her head a shake. "I'm sure I'll see Harry again. Besides you're great company, James."

Two interesting ladies. He felt a very lucky chap. "I'm glad you came along."

***

They reached the outskirts of Athens in the late morning and threaded their way through the city to the Plaka area below the Acropolis high on the hill. They got a room with three beds and went to lunch.

"I loved the feta cheese in the salad and these baklava are to die for," Bridget said as they were sitting at an outdoor café finishing their desert and coffee. "Shall we go up to the Acropolis this afternoon or tomorrow morning?"

"I'm rather tired," Monica said. "I could do with a nap. Besides, it's hot already. Let's go early in the morning."

Back at the hotel they laid down. The ladies fell asleep, but James was wide awake, still buzzing from the drive. Eventually he fell asleep. When he awoke, the ladies were whispering among themselves.

"What's up?" James asked.

"We want to go out shopping," Monica said. "You want to come?"

"Sure," James replied. "I feel better after the nap."

They walked among the tourist shops in the Plaka area. They stopped in a restaurant after perusing several shops and ordered beers. "Check out the menu," Monica said. "This may be a good place for dinner. She grasped James arm. "I liked the restaurant we had lunch in, but this place looks classier." She snuggled her head on James shoulder while Bridget stared at them her eyes wide and lips parted.

The Greek and European men, who passed on the cobblestone street, all gawked at the Swedish beauties. James became apprehensive when a handsome Greek young man approached their table.

"Hello," the young man called. "Where are you from?" He was of medium height and lanky with a curly, dark head of hair and a charming smile.

"We're from Sweden," Bridget said laying a hand on Monica's shoulder. She put her other hand on James's shoulder. "James is an American."

"Fine countries... may I join you?" the man asked.

"Sure," Bridget said and pulled out a chair.

James had been set to ward off the man. He wondered what Bridget intended.

"I am Vasili," the man said before shaking hands with the three as they declared their name. "How long have you been in Athens?" he asked as he stared at the ladies in turn, then concentrated his gaze on Bridget.

"We arrived today," Bridget answered.

"You must come to the bouzouki tonight," Vasili said. "You will see the real Greece."

"Where is it?" Bridget asked.

"I will show you," Vasili said. "It is a little hard to find. Please, when you finish your drinks, we shall go. It is not far. I can meet you there tonight if you like."

"Oh, that would great," Bridget said. "Would you like a drink?"

"You are very kind," Vasili replied. He motioned for the waiter. "One ouzo and three more beers. Let it be my treat."

***

"This place is great," Bridget said as they entered the small bar. "Do you see Vasili?"

461

The ladies were wearing summer dresses and had applied make up. James felt majestic in their company as they each hooked their arms in his.

"Here he comes," Monica said.

"Good evening, my friends," Vasili said. "I have reserved a table for you."

"Do you work here?" James asked.

"No, the owners are friends of mine," Vasili replied. He led them to a table near the dancefloor in front of the stage. The band, two bouzouki players and a woman singer with a tambourine, were just setting up."

The place was crowded with young and old. Most of the crowd appeared to be Greek with a few scattered tourists.

"They are renowned musicians, the best bouzouki players in all of Athens," Vasili said. "What would you like to drink?"

"I want to try ouzo," Bridget said.

"Me too," Monica added.

When the glasses of ouzo arrived each took a sip. "This tastes the same as the Turkish raki," Bridget said.

Vasili frowned. "Raki and ouzo are very similar, but ouzo is far superior."

James thought they tasted exactly the same, but knew the Turks and Greeks had been enemies for centuries and accepted Vasili's assertion without comment.

When the band started playing, the melodic sounds of the twin bouzoukis enthralled the crowd. Then the woman began to sing a haunting melody as she swayed with the music, tapping the tambourine on her ample hips. Several Greek men jumped up and began to dance.

"We Greeks love to dance," Vasili said and joined the dancers, often eyeing Bridget as he glided and skipped to the music.

"Isn't he handsome," Bridget said. "I love the dancing."

Vasili returned to the table when the song finished. "Before the Junta, the Regime of the Colonels," he said with distaste, "patrons would break dishes to show their appreciation of the music, but it is against the law now." He smiled and stared at Bridget. "In the islands, you can still see it."

***

"Thank you, Vasili, for showing us a wonderful evening," Bridget said as they stood outside their hotel. She placed her hand on his shoulder and gave him a kiss on the cheek. She was quite inebriated.

"May I see you tomorrow?" Vasili asked.

"Perhaps tomorrow night, Vasili," Bridget said. "We'll come to the bouzouki club."

"Thanks for a great evening," James said. "The music was excellent."

They entered their hotel and waved goodbye to the disappointed Vasili.

"He wanted to come up," James said.

"I know," Bridget replied. "I'm nearly drunk and involvement with him is the last thing I need."

53- ATHENS: APRIL 28, 1970

Bridget was elated that she was in Athens. Although she missed Harry and was a feeling a little guilty that she hadn't traveled on the train with him. The prospect of visiting the Acropolis and seeing the ancient art of Greece overshadowed any guilt she felt. Her interest in James burgeoned with their closeness. He was such a magnet. She wouldn't try to take him away from Monica, knowing it would devastate their friendship. Maybe she could breach the subject of sharing with Monica. She and Monica had never participated in such an arrangement in Sweden, but she had confessed to her the threesome she had had with Lisa last year. Maybe with some subtle persuasion Monica would be willing to share James.

While James was taking his nap, she saw her chance to talk to Monica. She roused Monica and, putting her finger to her lips, indicated with a toss of her head for Monica to join her in the bathroom. Monica looked up with a confused expression. "Come on," Bridget whispered. She helped Monica up and escorted her into the bathroom.

"What going on?" Monica whispered as soon as Bridget softly closed the bathroom door.

"I wanted to talk to you in private," Bridget whispered. "I told you about Lisa and our threesome with her boyfriend last year."

"Yes, I remember."

"Well, I don't want to offend you, but I was wondering if you would be receptive if I joined you and James in bed."

Monica face stretched in surprise, followed by a confused look. "I thought you had given up on James and were devoted to Harry."

"I like Harry. Traveling with him was fun, and I plan on visiting him if I can't induce him to come to Sweden. I don't know what it is, but James really turns me on."

"Jesus, Bridget." Monica shook her head. "I don't know." She paused and just stared at Bridget.

"Are you in love with James?" Bridget asked. Maybe she had been mistaken about Monica's feelings for James.

"I like him. He's a great guy, but I wouldn't say I'm in love."

"Well, what would it hurt then?"

"Do you think he'd go for it?"

"I think he might. I was able to seduce him fairly easy in Benares and Kathmandu before Sally caught on." She placed her hand on Monica's shoulder. "Hey, if he rejects the idea, it would be no biggie. He's not going to kick you out of bed. If he kicks me out, I won't be devastated." Actually she would be disappointed, but it was well worth the risk.

***

After the delightful night at the bouzouki bar and the intense pursuit by the handsome Greek, Vasili, Bridget's passion was on high. She had considered inviting Vasili up to the room, but decided intimacy with Vasili wasn't a good idea. Besides, since they all had a fair share of ouzo, she believed tonight would be an excellent opportunity for her plan.

After saying good night to Vasili, the three climbed the stairs to their room. Bridget nudged Monica and smiled. Monica smiled back. They continued into their room and disrobed for bed. Bridget and Monica went into the bathroom together.

"You're still good with this?" Bridget whispered.

"Yeah, the more I've thought about it the more excited I've become. Let's give it a try."

They completed their absolutions and came out of the bathroom laughing. James rose from his bed and started for the bathroom. "That was a great night. The music was wonderful. You ladies are sure in good spirit. I'm so glad you both came with me to Athens."

"Yes, it was a wonderful night," Monica said, trailing her hand across his back as he passed by her to enter the bathroom. Bridget grabbed Monica's hands and they exchanged big smiles.

After James came out of the bathroom, he climbed into bed. "That ouzo sure goes to your head."

Monica turned the light out and joined James in bed. She moved over him to the side near the wall, then Bridget slipped into the bed on the other side. The lights outside seeped through the window to softly illuminate the room enough that Bridget could see the naked muscular form of James's body, spiking her desire.

"What's up?" James said as he moved closer to Monica to give Bridget more room.

"You... that's what's up," Monica said. "Tonight we are putting you through your paces."

"Just relax and enjoy," Bridget said. "I've been waiting for this."

***

They went down for breakfast in the early morning despite having spent a good part of the night in their sexual gyrations. After breakfast, they began their long walk up to the Acropolis. The morning was already heating up, and Bridget was excited at the prospect of being on top of the Acropolis. She had thoroughly enjoyed their romp and was looking forward to another night of entwinement.

"Man, it's hot," Bridget said as she stopped to rest. She raised her hair off the back of her neck and glanced at Monica.

Monica laughed, adjusted her tank top and wiped her forehead with her handkerchief. "I think we maybe overdid it last night. I'm tired already."

James laughed. "Come on we can do this." When they reached Propylaea, the covered temple like entrance to the Acropolis, he stopped and took several deep breaths. "We made it."

"The ancient Acropolis of the greatest Greek city state," Bridget said moving into the Propylaea. "It's dedicated to Athena, goddess of wisdom, courage, justice, mathematics, strength, and the arts." She laid her hand on James's shoulder "She was worshiped as the warrior goddess and considered the epitome of beautiful. When I studied Greek Mythology, I found it fascinating. Athena remained a virgin and only fought for just reasons. The opposite of her brother, Ares, who loved the savagery of war."

Bridget noticed her talk of war had disturbed James. She wondered if he would ever get over his experiences in Viet Nam. War was such a destructive force. The US involvement in Viet Nam was criminal. Anticommunist and anti-Russian propaganda was spouted in Sweden by the conservatives, but thankfully they were a minority. Sweden hadn't allied with the Americans in the stupid war. Demonstrations against the war had taken place in Sweden. Even government ministers took part in the demonstrations. It seemed Americans were easily manipulated by the anticommunist propaganda. She knew James carried considerable pain about his experience in the War, and she so much wanted to soothe his mind and of course his body.

They walked on to the Erecthion with the famous porch and marble columns of maidens. "It's so amazing to see these maidens close up," Bridget said. "I've marveled at photographs of them."

After contemplating the exquisite maidens for many minutes, Bridget hooked arms with James and Monica and spurred them on to the Parthenon where they gazed up at the massive columns.

"The Parthenon was completed in 432 BC," Bridget said. "These columns taper in size as they rise and actually lean inward slightly."

"I can't believe I'm standing at the birthplace of democracy," Monica said. She walked to the side of the Acropolis. "You can see all the way to the sea from here." She grabbed James around the waist. "I'm so happy."

Bridget thought about the immense power that the Acropolis extolled. She imagined the hilltop full of citizens in their togas, discussing the events of their empire. The tryst last night had enlivened everyone. She was so glad she had chosen to come with James and Monica. She would be reluctant to leave James, but she and Monica were getting low on funds, and although she knew James would be willing to loan them money, she didn't want to diminish his traveling money, hoping he could still come to Sweden. Although James believed that Sally might return, she had her doubts. She hoped that if and when James came to Sweden after he finished his excursion of mainland Europe and England, she could seduce him thoroughly to herself despite what it might do to her relationship with Monica. She would delight in having him all to herself.

"Let's go down to the amphitheater," Bridget said, grasping James's hand. "It's gigantic."

"It must have been quite a sight in its heyday," James said.

"It's the theater of Dionysus." Bridget pulled James down the steps. "Dionysus was the god of theater, wine making, fertility, and ecstasy," Bridget said, emphasizing 'ecstasy' and winking at James. "A most popular god." She laughed and shoved James. "What say you, James?"

"Undoubtedly."

***

The next morning they took a taxi through the busy streets to the National Archaeological Museum in the center of Athens after a quick breakfast near their hotel.

"This place is huge," Monica said. "This is going to take a while to see."

They had spent the night in a much larger room with two double beds. The rollicking encompassed both beds and was an unforgettable night. James had not made it to American Express, and they had skipped the bouzouki night club.

They proceeded inside to the prehistoric collection with artifacts from a thousand BC to the seventh millennium. Bridget scurried to a display case where many people were gathered. "Agamemnon's gold death mask," she announced with enthusiasm and pulled James closer. "It's from Mycenae." She ignored the people next to her and pulled Monica to her other side. "It's so much more impressive than the pictures I've seen."

"Where was Mycenae?" Monica asked.

"It's in the Peloponnese about fifty miles from Athens," Bridget said. "The Mycenaean period was from 1600 to 1100 hundred BC."

They continued on into the sculpture section. Bridget stopped in the classical period section in front of the life size, bronze statue of a man with his arms outstretched. "So life like."

James mimicked the pose. Monica shoved him and laughed while Bridget read the plaque at the base of the statue.

"It's from 460 BC," Bridget said. "Their casting expertise was incredible. This statue rivals even modern day sculpture."

They continued on into the Hellenistic period, and the Roman period. They hurried through the metalwork section to vases and minor art.

"I studied some of these vases in school," Bridget said. "This is amazing, to actually see them."

They continued on through the museum until early afternoon and caught a taxi back to the Plaka.

***

"I'm tired," Monica said as they were sitting at a restaurant in the Plaka after their late lunch. "The museum was awesome, but we must have walked miles seeing it all. Are you guys still up for the bouzouki place again tonight? I bet Vasili was disappointed last night that we didn't come. I'm not complaining. I thoroughly enjoyed our frolic."

"I'm good with whatever you ladies decide," James said. "The music was great last time."

"What's the plan for tomorrow?" Bridget asked.

"There are more temples in Athens we could go to, or we could drive out of town to the Poseidon Temple, which is on the coast."

"Oh, that sounds inviting," Monica said. "I'd love to see the coast. How far is it?"

"About seventy kilometers," James said.

"I like that idea," Bridget said. "Tonight I'm up for going back to the bouzouki place. The music was fantastic." She pushed her lips out. "But I don't want to stay long." She stared at Monica and raised her eyebrows. Monica nodded back. "Monica and I have been talking. We know you want to go to Crete to see Knossos. We thought of coming with you, but we think we better head back to Sweden. We want to stop in Rome on the way back. I've been but Monica hasn't."

"I'm not much for boats," Monica said. "I get sea sick. Plus our funds are getting low." She placed her hand on James's shoulder. "We can't ask you to pay for us." She raised her wine glass. "James you have been so wonderful. This has been a trip of a lifetime. We owe you so much. We plan to leave the day after tomorrow."

"Oh, James, I'm so glad to hear your voice," Sally said when he called from American Express after retrieving her letter. "Where are you?"

"I'm in Athens," James replied.

"Your letter from Istanbul arrived a few days ago. How do you like Athens?"

"It's great. We went to the Acropolis, the National Museum, and the Temple of Poseidon. The weather has been nice. Hot, but a welcome change from the snow in Turkey."

"Whose we?"

"Monica and Bridget."

"I thought they were going to leave in Thessalonica with Harry."

"They wanted to see Athens."

"Are they with you now?"

James could hear the anger in Sally's voice. "No, they left yesterday."

There was prolonged silence. "I'm not going to ask what you three got up to." Another extended pause. "I want to fly and meet you. My family is getting on my nerves. Hank doesn't want my help and has gone to a cattle station. I'm going crazy here. I want to be with you."

"That would be wonderful." Was she really coming back to him?

"Are you just saying that? You seem to be enjoying yourself without me. Do you really want me to come to you?"

"Of course I want you to come back to me. I'm missing you terribly. I'm trying to make the best of my travels, learning about ancient Greece. Viewing amazing temples and artifacts. It's more enjoyable to travel with friends."

"Friends... I bet." Sally paused. "I'm working on my brother to help me get my parents to lend me the money for the plane ticket and traveling money. They seem receptive, but haven't volunteered the money yet. I'm hoping with Freddy's help they'll agree soon. My Dad is reluctant to sell some of his stock to get enough funds because the market is down. The waiting is driving me crazy. Where could we meet? I'm dying to see you."

"I'm going to Crete tonight. I want to see Knossos and other parts of the island. I'll call you when I get back to Athens. Then maybe you'll know when you'll have the money, and we can set a date and location to meet. As you know, I need to go to Frankfurt to redeem my plane ticket. Meeting in Frankfurt could be a plan. I can't wait to see you again."

"Call me as soon as you get back to Athens... as soon as you get back, you hear."

"I will, I promise. Traveling together again will be great."

"Yes, James, for sure. Okay then... bye."

He didn't really know how he felt about Sally in light of her departure and his relations with the Swedish ladies. He had enjoyed the Swedes company and those steamy nights. He still held a grudge for Sally leaving him although he understood why she had to go back with Hank. He was surprised that Hank shunned her and went to a cattle station. He would have thought Hank would have welcomed Sally and Freddy's company. He even thought Hank would try wooing Sally again. Hank's ordeal must have really changed him. He could commiserate with the guy. His own ordeal in Vietnam had certainly changed him and was still wreaking havoc with his psyche.

Could he welcome Sally back with the same enthusiasm he felt for her before she left? He wanted to, but was not sure. He thought of the Swedes and what fun they could have if he visited them in Sweden. What if Sally's parents wouldn't loan her the money for her return? He'd be disappointed wouldn't he? Sally was much different than the Swedes. She was effervescent and made him laugh. He felt she had actually loved him while he thought the Swedes were just interested in experiences and pleasure. Sally and he had been good together until Hank's abduction. She had really made him feel special and pushed his haunting memories to the background. Forget the thoughts. He'd find out soon enough if Sally was ever coming.

***

The sea was fairly calm as James sailed out of Piraeus for Crete. He was sad to be all alone. It would be so much more enjoyable if Sally was here with him. How would she react when she found out about his relations with the Swedes? It would come out. He wouldn't lie to her anymore. He strolled around the ship looking at the gamut of passengers, mostly Greek but also a good number of European tourists. None looked familiar.

The next morning the ferry arrived in Crete at Heraklion. As they sailed into the harbor, he could see the square like Koules fortress at the headland to the bay. The bright morning sun in a deep blue sky void of clouds reflected off the brown stones of the fort and the brilliant blue water of the bay.

When he disembarked, he felt a little woozy from the voyage. At one point in the night, he was nauseous and had to go up on deck to get some fresh air. He got a taxi at the port into town. After getting settled in the hotel near the main square, he decided to go exploring.

He strolled down the street toward the museum, feeling excited about learning more about the Minoan civilization. Inside the interior of the modern two story building, he ambled around the many artifacts. He marveled at the thin wall vases produced around 1900 to 1700 BC. When he came to the bare-breasted goddess statuettes holding a snake in each hand, he was spell bound. He had seen pictures of the statues in books, but seeing them up close was magical. The ancient artistry was impressive.

He recalled the beautiful pottery from the Indus valley that was contemporary with the Minoan. The artistry of ancient civilizations was an enlightening window into their culture. He took pleasure from seeing the artifacts up close. He proceeded upstairs to view the exceptional frescos. He especially liked the famous bull leapers. He tried to imagine the athletic skill the dangerous bull leaping required. Did the legend in the Iliad of the Minotaur and the Labyrinth derive from the bull leaping or was there an actual labyrinth at Knossos? After several hours, he left the museum, enthused about going to the ruins of Knossos.

***

The taxi ride to Knossos was short in the warm sun. He entered the palace ruins that stood on a hill next to the Kairatos River where he met two young Englishmen, who had just entered the site. He toured the complex with them. They had come back to Heraklion from a place called Matala on the southwest coast where many young travelers were hanging out in caves.

Knossos was inhabited from about 6,000 BC to 1375 BC. The first actual palace was built around 1900 BC. James tried to envision the site in its heyday. The serpentine layout of the corridors reminded him of the Minotaur and the Labyrinth legend. Seeing the unfortified layout of the city he understood how the Mycenaeans were able to conquer the palace in 1450 BC.

The throne room was the highlight of the complex with its water management and closed sewer systems. He thought about the terrible sewage systems or lack of in India. The Minoans were quite advanced for the time period. When he and the English chaps finished their extensive excursion around the ruins, they shared a taxi back to town.

The Englishmen retrieved their packs from their hotel and joined James for dinner. They were catching the night ferry to Athens. All three lingered over their coffee until it was time for them to go to the ferry. Their continued talk of Matala aroused his interest in Matala even more. Sounded like a cool place. He decided to go have a look and perhaps stay a while. Then when he got back to Athens, Sally would hopefully have a better idea when if ever she would have the money to rejoin him.

***

James started hitchhiking toward Matala after breakfast, his visit to Knossos still occupying his thoughts. The ancient civilizations, the beginning of humans living together in complex societies, he found fascinating. He got a ride with a truck driver, who took him to the end of the pavement and turned off. It was several hours before he scored another ride with three German men, Hans, Fred, and Karl in a Volkswagen bus, who were also going to Matala. The dusty dirt road was in poor condition with numerous ruts and the going was slow. Just before sunset, they arrived at the end of the road on the horseshoe bay.

"This must be the place," Hans said. "I'm thirsty after eating all that dust. I heard there was a great taverna here? A beer is calling my name." His laugh was infectious.

James and the three Germans strolled onto the beach to the beat of the drums of a group pounding in accompaniment to the descent of the sun. James pointed to a building on the far end of the beach. "That must be the taverna down at the end."

The small bay with the caves in the cliff to the north and another cliff to the south was beautiful in the golden sheen of the sinking sun.

They walked down the beach and up the steps of the open air taverna, the Mermaid Café, as Led Zeppelin's *Dazed and Confused* was playing from the outdoor speakers. Several of the tables on the raised concrete slab were occupied by young men and women in bathing suits. A large tree grew out of a hole in the concrete, offering some shade. The bar, store, and kitchen was a one room affair, white-washed with a blue band around the bottom of the outside wall.

Hans ordered beers all around. "I'm going to like it here," he said as he hoisted his beer. They watched the sun slowly descend and disappear into the iridescent colors reflecting on the expanse of the bay to shouts, cheers, and crescendo drums. The play of rainbow colors was spectacular.

James thought of the great times he had in Goa. He wondered how Monica and Bridget were getting on. They'd probably be enjoying Rome on their way back to Sweden. What a change back in Sweden would be for them. He missed them. When he got back to Athens, he hoped Sally would know when she'd have money for her return, and they could arrange a meeting place. He was feeling rather lonely.

The Swedish beauties had assuaged his distress and disappointment after Sally's departure. If Sally managed to return, he hoped he could recover his devotion.

"Hey cats, you wanna score," a bushy headed and bearded young man with a New York accent said as he drifted by the table.

"Yeah," James said.

The man pulled out the vacant chair. "I'm Juice. You want hash or grass?"

"Both." They agreed on a price and the sale was made. "What's the story on the caves?" James asked.

"You looking for a cave?"

"Yeah," James replied. He wasn't sure what that entailed... but why not.

"A cat I know just moved down to a better cave. If you want, I'll show you where his old cave is."

James finished his beer and walked with Juice halfway down the beach. The group, drumming and cheering, had started to break up. Some were moving toward the caves and others toward the café.

Juice pointed toward the cliff. "See that cave on the left near the top. That's the one Henry just moved out of. It's not much of a cave. Dirt sleeping platform and floor. Better than sleeping on the beach though."

James thanked Juice and walked back to the Germans at the café. "What are you guys going to do tonight?" James asked and took a swig of the new beer Hans had gotten for him.

"We'll stay here and eventually sleep in our van. We paid plenty to get it here."

"I'll get my pack from the van and stash it in the cave."

"Cool man, come back. We'll keep your seat. I bet this place is going to get crowded."

***

James slept in the small cave the first night and each day quizzed the cave inhabitants to learn of better caves being vacated that he could move into. People were always coming and going. His reoccurring dream plagued him most nights. He made friends with many of the cave dwellers and enjoyed the camaraderie.

He and the Germans, who had given him the ride, were often together smoking chillums at the cafe. He had saved a few unused chillums and was glad to share them with the Germans. After a week of many moves, he scored a beautiful cave on the first level from which he could dive out into the sea. He bought a little kerosene stove from one of the departing people and sometimes cooked his own simple meals from produce he could buy at the café.

The cave— actually a catacomb—had an ancient painting on the back wall of a maiden with a lamp. The walls were rock hewn and the sleeping alcove where a cadaver would have resided had a foam mattress. Most nights he would go down to the café or to jam sessions in the big cave, which could hold about fifty people, where nightly gathering of music were held.

One evening while James was sitting in the big cave, a lady with long brown hair in a ponytail moved through the group and chose a vacant space next to him at the back of the cave. Two guitar players were playing and singing the Dylan song, *Like a Rolling Stone*, accompanied by many drummers on plastic jugs and metal pans.

"Hi, I'm Betty," she said and held out her hand.

He shook her soft hand. "I'm James."

"How long have you been here?"

"Almost a week."

"I arrived yesterday," Betty said. "Are you touring Europe?"

"Sort of," James said. "I came from India overland. Came to Crete to see Knossos. Heard about the caves and the scene here and decided to check it out."

"India?" She had brown eyes with a hint of yellow around the outside of the iris. In the lamp light her eyes seemed to glow. "That must have been an amazing trip."

"It was incredible. Sometimes, I can't believe it really happened."

"I'm a psychologist from L.A. on vacation with my girlfriend. We heard about Matala in Athens and decided to come and have a look."

"Cool." He studied her face with those luminescent eyes and small up turned nose. She had quite a few lines around her eyes and an entrenched tan. He gaged she was quite a few years older than him. He was surprised that the notoriety of Matala had reached Athens.

"Are you in a cave?" Betty asked.

"Yes, I have a great cave on the first level."

"We're staying with two other women in a cave on the second level. It's kind of tight for the four of us. We met the ladies at the café, and they graciously offered to put us up. Wish I had a better sleeping mat. The rock floor gets hard after a while."

She concentrated on the admirable music and was silent for several songs until the guitarists took a break to toke on the communal pipe.

"The food at the café is surprisingly good for such a small place," Betty said. "I didn't see you there."

"No, I had some fish stew left that I ate for dinner."

"You cook in your cave?"

"Sometimes," he replied. "Of course the food at the café is much better."

After a short break the music continued. Before it ended, James excused himself and left. He had gone on a long swim during the day and was tired.

The next morning after a quick dip, he went to the café for breakfast. As he ascended the stairs, Betty waved at him and asked him to join them. The four ladies were eating omelets and having Nescafé coffees with milk. They introduced themselves. Beside Betty there was Maggie, Joann, and Carol.

"You've been swimming already," Betty said, placing a hand on his wet hair that was now down to his shoulders.

"Yes, I like to dive out of my cave in the morning. It's a brisk wake up."

"That sounds inviting," Betty said. "Would you show us your cave later?"

After breakfast all of the ladies accompanied James across the beach to his cave and crowded in the small cave.

"This is wonderful," Betty said. The other ladies agreed, remarking on the mural on the back wall. The three ladies excused themselves and left while Betty remained. "That's a cool little stove."

"Would you like a Nescafé," James asked.

"That would be great. Thank you."

Betty, sitting on the foam bed, watched James make two cups of Nescafe. "Sugar and milk?"

"Yes please."

James closed the translucent plastic cover to the entrance for privacy and joined her on the bed.

"This is such a cool cave," she said as she swung her legs in and out and sipped her coffee. How did you manage to snag it?"

"I changed from cave to better cave as I learned people were leaving. Eventually this cave came open when a New Yorker, we called Juice, was leaving. I met him my first day here. He was my supplier for hash."

"Juice?" Betty said. "How'd he get that name?"

"He was always drinking juice. Never beer, wine, or coffee. Only juice. He was the main dealer here. Crazy guy. Called everyone cat."

"Sounds like a character. I'm sorry I missed him." She studied the painting on the back wall. "How old is that painting."

"I don't know for sure," he said. "Someone told me they were made by the Romans in the first century AD."

It's amazing. The colors are still quite vibrant for something that old. Does it bother you that this was a catacomb— someone's grave."

"Not really, but I've had some strange dreams in here." In fact it did bother him, but he had gotten used to the eerie feeling and his frequent reoccurring nightmares.

"When I first arrived and learned the caves were catacombs, I was a bit leery of staying in a cave," she said. "But since there is either the beach or the caves, I opted for the cave." She finished her coffee and handed the cup to James. "That was nice. Thank you. Well, I think I'll go for swim. Joann says that they go over the cliff to a secluded area on the rocks to swim. Do you know it?"

"Yeah, people go there for nude sunbathing. Often Greek men come to the beach to ogle the ladies. Many of the cave dwellers go over the rocks for privacy."

"Will you be coming?"

"Yes. I'll meet you there later." He watched her leave, thinking this was a welcome development. She was pretty and had a tight curvaceous body. He was missing the Swedes.

***

As James was sitting at the Mermaid café with Betty and her friends after nearly a week with Betty, he noticed a tour bus coming up the road. He watched as a group of Greeks, mostly men with a few families, disembarked. Elias, the café owner, came out to watch the tour group.

"What's up, Elias?" James asked.

"I had heard that they were going to run tours here," Elias said. "They're going to clean me out. I will need to go to Heraklion for more supplies."

James studied the tour group, most of whom were walking toward the beach gawking at the few so called hippies lounging on the sand. Some of the ladies lying on the beach were topless, which seemed to be a big attraction to the men. The ladies soon donned their tops. A few Greek families spread out their beach blankets and stripped down to their swim suits. Others were coming to the café.

"We better settle up and go to the rocks," James said. "This is not good."

"It's a freak show," Betty said. "Let's go."

***

The group spent most of the days on the rocks to avoid the Greek tourists. The arrival of tour buses increased to an everyday occurrence. After a few days of the tours, several Greek men, watching the trail of people over the rocks, followed them across the rocks to watch the naked hippies. When they arrived, most of the young people jumped into the water.

The Germans left the day after the scene at the rocks. The next day, Betty and Maggie left. The last days with Betty had been difficult as she often seemed irritable. Why, he never found out.

James knew he should go but lingered. He was curious how the scene would adapt to the tours. He became friends with an American, George, and two attractive French women, Monique and Antoinette. Monique was with George, but she flirted openly with James while Antoinette ignored him, but he often caught her staring at him.

A few days after Betty's departure, the Greek military showed up in combat dress and forced all the people to leave the caves. James along with George and another American, Cary, and the two French women left together in the back of a produce truck. James told them he had a van in Athens and would be driving to Germany if they wanted a ride and were willing to share expenses.

***

When James arrived in Athens after a night on the ferry from Crete, he and the two Americans and two French ladies took a taxi to the hotel near where his van was parked, and he and the Swedes had stayed. The two Americans and French women continued on to the youth hostel. After checking in and inspecting his van, James telephoned Sally from the lobby phone booth.

"Hello, can I speak to Sally?" James asked

"Is this James?"

"Yes."

"Sally flew to Athens to meet you. I'm Sally's brother, Freddy. Where are you calling from?"

"Athens."

"Why are you calling from Athens? Why aren't you and Sally together? What's going on?"

"I just arrived in Athens from Crete. I didn't know Sally was coming here. Where is she staying? When did she arrive?"

"She arrived last week. She called a few days ago. She's worried that you've already left for Germany? Have you a pen? I'll give you her address in Athens. I hope she hasn't left for England. She said if you didn't show she would leave her uncle's address in London at American Express, and you could meet up there."

James grabbed a pen and wrote down the address. "Don't worry Freddy. I'll find her."

"I hope so. Get her to call home as soon as you find her. I'm worried."

"I will Freddy. Bye."

He asked the hotel receptionist the location of the address, which was only a few streets away. With a deep breath, he headed off. He noticed the two men in the Greek fishing hats eating at a café across from his hotel, who looked up as he walked away. He liked the look of the Greek fishing hats and thought about buying one for himself. His Hong Kong straw hat was nearly in tatters and wouldn't last much longer. As he neared Sally's hotel his apprehension crept up his spine like a slow moving tarantula. If Sally arrived last week, she wouldn't be happy about his absence.

When the weeks passed after Sally spoke to James in Athens, and she did not hear from James again, she got worried. Was he blowing her off? She needed to be with him. She wasn't going to lose him if she could help it. She realized after they had hung up that she had been less than polite. Her anger over his time with Monica and Bridget had gotten the better of her. Had she scared James?

If she had the money, she would fly to Athens and connect somehow with James when he came back from Crete. Would he have already returned? No he would have called. She needed her parents to commit so she could make plans. Fuck the damn market.

As she fretted, she became more insistent with her brother and parents about the money. Finally her Dad relented, sold some stock, and loaned her money. At last she could make plans, but why hadn't James called? Damn, she wanted so much to get going. If she flew to Athens, she could surprise James. She could call home when she arrived and give Freddy her hotel address so that James would find out where she was when he called. It would give her time to see the attractions in Athens.

Yes, that was what she would do. Heck with this bloody waiting at home. Hank was gone. She needed to get back to James to work her magic and dissipate his memories of the Swedes.

She flew to Athens from Sydney the next week and got a hotel in the Plaka area. The first week she kept herself busy, visiting the Acropolis, National Museum, and other temples, making her sketches and waiting. By the second week her anger fumed like a simmering fire.

Near the middle of the second week, she was morose and angry. Coming without talking to James first had been a mistake. She called home, but James had not called. What was she going to do? She'd stay in Athens at least a few more days. If James didn't show, she'd continued on to England to her uncle. She'd already sent her uncle's address in a letter for James care of American Express to Frankfurt and London. If he had already left for Germany, he'd surely check American Express for any mail, wouldn't he?

Her plans had fallen apart. She was stupid for coming without first talking to James. Her impulsive wish to be reunited as soon as possible had been a mistake. She wiped away her tears and laid back on her bed.

There was a knock on her door. The maid had already been. She rose and went apprehensively to the door. She cracked the door, keeping the chain engaged, and peered out. There stood James. She dragged the chain out and slung the door open to burst into his arms.

"Where in the hell have you been?" She exclaimed, pulling him into her room.

"I was in Crete in the caves at Matala," he said. "I would have come earlier if I'd known you were here. Why didn't you say you were coming to Athens in our last phone call?"

"Because I hadn't decided then," she said and pushed him down on the bed. "What's this caves in Matala?" She got on top of him, straddling him. "Why did you stay so long?" She grabbed his face between both hands. "Is there another woman?"

"You know... the place was full of travelers. It was cool. The weather was great, smoke was plentiful, and some great musicians passed through. It was fun until the military kicked us out."

"You mean you'd still be there. You left me hanging. I was so worried that I'd missed you." She stood up. She bet he had a girlfriend there ... the two timing shit-head.

"I didn't know you were coming here." He stood and embraced her.

She pushed him away. "They don't have telephones on Crete?"

"Not in Matala. The nearest town with an international phone would have been Heraklion. I never left Matala once I got there."

"Who was she?"

"Who was who?"

"You trying to tell me you spent weeks with a bunch of travelers without some dally with a woman?"

"I didn't know if I'd ever see you again. I stayed in Matala because there was a cool community and it was a fun, beautiful place."

"Right. I bet you were screwing your brains out while I was stewing in Brisbane." She shoved him away. "Did you bring you girlfriend with you?"

"I don't have another girlfriend. You're my girlfriend. I did come to Athens with some people from Matala that I agreed to drive to Germany."

"So you did bring your girlfriend. You two timing asshole."

"The women are not my girlfriends. They're just travelers I met in Matala. They wanted to go to Germany and agreed to share expenses." He again attempted to embrace her, but she pushed him away.

"Where are these travelers?"

"I told them I would meet them at a restaurant this afternoon. They are staying at a hostel. I wanted a comfortable hotel where I left my van."

"You better be telling the truth."

"I am, I swear."

"Oh James," Sally pulled him to her. "I've missed you so much."

***

"Hi guys," James said as he and Sally approached the group at the restaurant. "I want you to meet my traveling companion, Sally Compton. She'll be coming with us. We plan to leave tomorrow."

494

"Hi, mates," Sally said. She and James joined them at the table.

"Monique and Antoinette are from France," James said, "and George and Cary are Americans. We all met in Matala."

"Right on," Sally said.

James observed the group silently a few seconds. "Sally and I traveled together in India and overland to Tehran. She had to go back to Australia with her friend Hank, who was injured. She came to Athens to hook back up. I'm so glad we are reunited." He pushed his arm around Sally and pulled her to him.

Sally didn't think the group were particularly friendly. Monique smiled. George and Cary stared. She stared back. Go ahead blokes have a good gander. Sally and James sat down.

Sally thought Monique was somewhat friendly as Monique extended her hand. Cary acted like Sally's arrival was an affront with a sour scowl. James had told her that he was a Vietnam vet, who saw a lot of jungle fighting. Wars and their horrendous devastation. Antoinette seemed to be withholding judgment. She didn't know about George. He seemed detached and the look he gave her made her skin crawl. James said he and Monique were together. Well good luck Monique.

Antoinette took out a cigarette and lit up, blowing smoke to the side. "It's going to be crowded with six." She fixed her dark eyes on James.

"Well if any of you want to find alternative transportation— feel free," James said.

All right, James. Let sour puss have it. If any decided to bail that would be so much the better.

"I'm sure we'll manage fine," Monique said.

"Good," James said. "Have you ordered yet?"

"No chéri," Monique said. "We were waiting for you."

***

They left Athens in the morning and drove toward Yugoslavia through the Greek mountains, sleeping in the van late in the evening. They crossed the border in Yugoslavia without much of a hassle other than a prolonged search of the van. While the van was being searched, James saw a gray sedan cross the border with two men, who seemed to stare at him while they waited for their passports to be approved and stamped. The first night in Yugoslavia, they pulled off the road in what they thought was a deserted spot in the mountains, but soon were accosted by two young girls in worn colorful dresses, who asked for money. Sally gave them a dinar each, and the kids scampered away.

Sally thought the group were tolerating each other congenially despite the cramped conditions and the standoff manner of Cary and Antoinette. She was surprised that George and Monique got on as well as they did. Monique was pretty but perhaps a little overweight. George was not ugly nor handsome, but he had a crude personality. She would have dumped George like a hot potato if she were Monique. It was obvious that Antoinette didn't like George and could barely tolerate Cary. Sally didn't think Antoinette was happy that Sally had joined James. She bet Antoinette had thought of seducing James on the trip until she arrived. Antoinette was pretty in her dark Roma-like appearance with a definite alluring body. James had sworn he hadn't had a liaison with either of the French ladies, and she believed him. He had confessed his pairing with Monica across Turkey and both Swedes in Athens as well as the short affair with the American in Matala after her prolonged grilling. She had been hurt that he couldn't stay true to her, but glad she had come back when she did. James seemed to attract women like ants to honey.

As James was getting the stove out to fix something to eat, a dark haired man with a deep red scarf around his neck and a trilby hat approached. He smiled and made the sign of eating. James offered him some bread they had bought. The man shook his head, waved his hand, and motioned for them to follow him repeating 'food'.

James turned to the group. "Shall we go with him and check it out?"

"I'm not going with him," Cary said. "It may be a trick."

"Okay," James replied. "I'll go."

"Leave your keys to the van," Cary said.

"I don't think that's necessary," James replied with a frown and started off after the man.

"I'll come too," Sally said and caught up to James.

"The nerve of that asshole, Cary," Sally whispered.

"He's a trip. I knew guys like him in Nam, who hated their experiences there. I try to cut him some slack, but he can definitely get on your nerves."

They walked with the man through the forest and soon arrived at a camp in a clearing with a roaring fire. Colorful wooden caravans were circled around the fire where ten adults were sitting while a group of children, including the two who had come to the van, were roaming about. Steaming pots were suspended over the flames. The group rose and studied the two. The man went to the fire, retrieved a ladle, and held up the stew in the ladle.

"Good food," the man said. "Come... bring friends."

"Thank you," James said. He leaned close to Sally. "I think they're Roma," he whispered. "We need to accept their hospitality. We don't want to offend them. Go back and get the others."

James stood when he saw all the group coming. The Roma gave up their stools and stumps and filled plates for them with the steaming stew.

The food was good, and they were offered seconds along with a clear alcoholic liquor that burned the back of Sally's throat. James declined seconds, but Cary, George, Monique, and Antoinette accepted. After they ate and had consumed numerous glasses of the liquor, the Roma retrieved instruments from their caravans— violins, accordions, drums, and guitars. The lively music began, and the rest of the Roma started dancing in a circle. They pulled James and his group up and got everyone dancing. The dancing and drinking continued late into the night.

They thanked their hosts and staggered back to the van. Cary bedded down in the front seat and George, Monique, Antoinette, James, and Sally bedded down in the back. It was a tight squeeze.

"That was some strong drink, mates," Sally said as she scooted into her sleeping bag.

"I'll have a hangover for sure," Monique said as she wrapped the blankets around her and George.

Antoinette waited for the rest to settle before she scrunched down in her sleeping bag. "This is close, but should keep us warm. It's getting cold." She wedged herself between Sally and Monique "Bonne nuit."

After James fell asleep, Sally slipped into his sleeping bag. "I'm cold," she said. "Do you mind?"

James obviously surprised wrapped his arms around Sally. "It's fine, nice and cozy."

She rotated around and grabbed his arm and pulled it across her chest. "Sweet dreams, James." She pushed her panty clad buttock tight against him. She enjoyed the warmth of him against her and the stiffness her proximity elicited. She wished they were alone. Their steamy night in Athens was so welcome and fulfilling. She was glad that the liquor made it easy to fall asleep.

In the morning Sally rotated to face James. She kissed him and slammed her hips against his. "We need a bigger bag and more room." She laughed, squirmed out of the bag, pulled on her jeans, and left the van. Antoinette had made a show of moving to accommodate Sally's movement. George and Monique were wrapped tight in their blankets still sound asleep.

Antoinette sat up in her sleeping bag and frowned. "It was really cold last night. I could hardly sleep." She scouted closer to James and scrunched down in her sleeping bag.

James pushed himself out of his sleeping bag, causing Antoinette to huff and squirm away. He dressed outside, and he and Sally walked toward the Roma camp to thank them again. They were all gone. Only the dirt covered fire pit remained.

"That was a fantastic night," Sally said. "The music was wonderful." She hugged him. "Aren't you glad I came?"

"Of course. I'm sorry there's so many of us. If I had known you were in Athens, I wouldn't have agreed to take the others to Germany. I would have loved to travel just the two of us."

"Oh, I'm so happy to be with you again. Forget the others." She hugged him tight "I was going crazy at my parents. When I first got to Athens, I was a little mad when you didn't arrive back. After a week, I was afraid you left without checking your mail. The second week, I was livid. I was afraid I'd have to travel to England by myself."

"I'm sorry I stayed so long in Matala."

"You should be." She gave him a shove. "No worries. It's all good now."

Sally's face suddenly became still, her eyes wide as a man stepped out of the forest. He was not one of the people from last night. She looked at James whose face was stretched in disbelief. She turned to look where James was gazing and saw the other man.

"What's going on?" Sally said.

James turned to look at the other man behind him. "Oh no," he whispered. He recognized the men as the men in the gray sedan at the border.

The men approached them slowly their pistols held out in front.

"Jesus, stay still," James whispered.

"Do not try to run," one of the men said in his foreign accent. "We do not want to shoot."

James grabbed Sally tighter. The man, who spoke, slammed his pistol on the back of James's head, and James fell to the ground clutching his head. The two men grabbed Sally and dragged her into the forest as she screamed at the top of her lungs.

56–YUGOSLAVIA: JUNE 1, 1970

James, his vision distorted, saw Sally dragged into the forest, her screams echoing long after in his mind. He forced himself up. What should he do? Should he run after them or go get Cary and George to help? His quandary was solved when all the group ran into the clearing.

"What's going on?" Cary asked, holding a pistol. "We heard Sally's screams."

James shook his head to try to clear his vision. "Two men took Sally," James said. "They each had a gun. They were the men I saw in a gray car that entered Yugoslavia when our van was being searched. I heard one say that they were going to be rich as they dragged Sally away." He shook his head again and looked at Cary's pistol. "Where did you get the gun?"

"I had it hidden in a secret compartment in my pack. Who were these men?"

"I don't know. They might be men that followed me from Afghanistan."

"Why would men follow you from Afghanistan and be here in Yugoslavia to kidnap Sally?" Antoinette asked with a frown of disbelief.

"What are you talking about?" Cary said. "Are you delirious? This makes no sense."

"No... maybe not," James replied. "Never mind I'll explain later. We need to go after them."

"Monique and Antoinette, go back to the van and lock yourself in," Cary commanded. "Come on James and George. We'll follow the men. Stay behind me and be ready to take cover."

The three started off into the forest, Cary in the lead, and James and George following him. James was amazed at the alacrity of Cary as he moved forward without making hardly any sound following the apparent path of the men. Cary must have been a consummate jungle fighter. Suddenly, after 15 minutes, Cary held up his hand and ducked down. George and James took cover also.

Cary held his finger to his lips and motioned for them to stay put as he slipped forward. He reappeared after a few minutes and went to James. "They're tying her up," he whispered. "She appears to be unconscious. They have a car on a dirt road that is a dead end. I'll go forward and circle around. You need to approach the road silently and when I fire, you start shouting. George, you spread out from James and shout when I fire also."

"What are you going to do?" James asked as he took hold of Cary's arm.

"Kill them. What else is there to do? They both have guns."

"Wait. We can't just kill them. There's got to be another way.

"Yeah," George piped up. "It would be murder."

"It's self-defense," Cary said.

"No... let's think this through," James said, trying to think of an alternate action.

"They're not kidnapping her for fun," Cary said. "They mean her harm."

"What if we follow them and look for a chance to free her?" James didn't want any more killings on his conscience.

"How we gonna do that? We're back on another road. Are you going to run after their car?" Cary shook his head. "Get real, man. We have no other choice. We kill them and bury the bodies."

"No," James said squeezing Cary's arm tighter. "The dead end road they're on has to meet up with the main road. Let's go to the next town, which if I remember correctly from the map, they will have to go through. Then we follow and wait for an opportunity to overcome them and free Sally."

"You're crazy," Cary said with disgust. "She's your girlfriend. If you want to risk her life this way, it's no skin off my nose. They know your van and will know we are following them."

"Please, let's try my plan," James pleaded. "Let me go see for myself."

James snuck up to the forest edge and watched the men place the unconscious Sally bound and gagged into the back seat of the car. He memorized the license plate of the gray sedan and returned to George and Cary.

"Okay, let's go back and speed to the next town to await their arrival."

"This is stupid," Cary said. "We have the element of surprise here. You're risking her life, you fool. They could go the opposite way back to Greece."

"No, they have to go to the next town to go either north or south. Please, let's go." He grabbed Cary. "Please, I beg you, help me?"

"Okay, as long as I'm not putting my life on the line," Cary replied. "I didn't slug my way through death and destruction in Nam to die in Yugoslavia for some hair-brained plan."

"I'm in," George said.

"Back to the van then."

The three ran back to the van, and James sped away.

"What's going on," Monique said. "Where's Sally?'

"The kidnappers have her. They've tied her up. She appears to be unconscious. They have to go through the next town. We'll speed there and try for an opportunity to rescue her."

"Why didn't you try to stop them?" Monique said. "Why did you let them take her?"

"They both had guns," James said. "We had no chance to overpower them."

"He's an idiot," Cary said with a scorn of disgust. "I could have killed them both and freed her, but Mister Namby-Pamby didn't want to kill them."

"Couldn't you have gotten the drop on them and forced them to surrender?" Monique asked.

"It would not have been a winning strategy," Cary said. "I wouldn't have risked it. Two guns against one. You've been watching too many Westerns."

"I'm glad you didn't kill them," George said." I want no part in murder."

"Hold on," James said. "The decision was made. Let's not beat it to death. We need to concentrate on how we are going to get Sally back."

"Let's go to the police," Monique said.

"By the time we explain what happened to the police these guys will be long gone with Sally," Cary said. "What I want to know is why in the hell these two guys went to all this trouble to kidnap Sally in Yugoslavia."

"If I'm right, it is a long story. The short version is we ran into some trouble in Afghanistan and apparently got in the middle of a feud between two Afghan warlords. These men or others, I believe, may have been following Sally and me since we left Afghanistan, and they've been following me since Sally's departure in Tehran. They could have easily kidnapped me after Sally left, but they must have wanted Sally and somehow knew she planned to return to me in Europe." He remembered the attention Mahmood paid Sally and the headman of the riders singling her out. "The whole scenario is unbelievable... it's too crazy. I don't know." James frowned. "I can try to explain it later. What we need now is to come up with a plan."

"That's up to you, James," Cary said. "Mine would have worked. I have no idea how were going to get her back now."

***

When they arrived in the town at top speed, James quickly pulled the van behind a gas station that was at the intersection of the two roads believing that the kidnappers would have to be on one of the roads. He had formulated a plan that might work if the kidnappers stopped. If not they would have to follow. He prayed that they would stop. "You ladies stay in the van," James said. "George and Cary let's get out, spread out, and hide. If I'm right, they will be driving into town. I doubt they would have raced here like we did with a kidnapped woman."

"Then what?" Cary asked.

"I don't know," James replied. "If they stop maybe we can overpower them somehow. Let's split up and hide. Since you have the gun, Cary, go behind the gas station. That might be the most likely stop. I'll go across the street from the station, and George you go across the other street."

Carry shook his head. "All right, I'll give it a try."

After a short time, sure enough the grey sedan came up the other road. The car pulled into the gas station. James looked up and thanked providence. He waited anxiously as the man not driving got out of the car while the other man stayed behind the wheel. The man, who exited, entered the outside door of the station bathroom. This was their chance. James sprinted across the road and went to the open driver's window. As soon as he arrived and reached for the surprised man, the man pointed his pistol at James. The man didn't see Cary sneaking up on the other side.

Cary pushed his pistol in the open window on the other side of the vehicle. "Hands up, asshole," Cary shouted. The man started to turn and James grabbed his gun hand.

"Drop it or I'll shoot," Cary said.

The man dropped the gun. James opened the door and retrieved the gun. He slammed the gun on the back of the man's head and shoved him down on the seat. Cary was already moving toward the gas station bathroom. James pulled the unconscious Sally from the backseat, lifted her onto his shoulder, and ran to his van. He deposited her in the back with the other ladies and sprinted back to the front of the gas station. Cary had his gun pushed against the side of the other man, who had come out of the bathroom. Surprisingly, the attendant in the gas station was watching the scene nonchalantly as if the activities he had just witnessed were nothing to get excited about.

Cary pushed the man toward the car. "You are making a big mistake," the man said. "You will pay with your lives."

Cary ground the pistol harder into the man's side. "Shut the fuck up, asshole, or you'll be the one paying with your life."

James opened the back door and Cary slammed the man on the head with his pistol and shoved him inside.

"What now, James?" Cary said. "You are one lucky bastard. Someone is smiling on you."

"Let's get out of town quickly. You drive their car out of town. Then I'll join you and we'll tie them up."

"Okay, let's hit it," Cary said. "I don't want to tarry here. The gas station attendant saw the whole thing. He'll probably call the cops. Take the back road behind the station to get out of town so the attendant doesn't see your van. Hopefully he didn't pay attention to it when you drove into town."

"Okay."

James sprinted to the van followed by George. He started the engine and turned to the back. "How is she?"

"She's unresponsive, but breathing," Monique said.

"It's like she's been drugged," Antoinette added

James drove off and met Cary driving the car on the main road. Cary stopped on the shoulder a ways out of town and got out. James pulled behind and got out with lengths of rope George had cut and some rags.

Cary grabbed the lengths of rope and rags James handed him. "You tie up the guy in the front seat. I'll do the guy in the back. Tie up their hands behind them and bind their feet. Stuff the rags to gag them and tie around their heads so they can't spit the rags out."

"Okay, after we tie them up, you drive the car to some secluded spot in the forest while I follow and then we can ditch it," James said. "Then we should head as fast as possible to Austria."

"I still think we should kill them."

"No, please... let's just do what I suggest."

"All right," Cary replied, shaking his head.

Once the tying and gagging was complete, Cary jumped back in the men's car and drove off. James followed. A few kilometers further on Cary pulled onto a forest road and after about two kilometers drove the car into a gully in the forest. He rummaged in the men's pockets, then jumped out, ran to the van, and slipped into the front seat as George climbed into the back. James drove off, staying at the speed limit.

"I've got their passports and guns," Cary said. "You were right. They're Afghans. Man, Sally must have made one hell of an impression in Afghanistan to cause men to follow you all this way to wait for her return. This is the craziest story I've ever heard. Jesus, we were lucky that those assholes stopped. What the fuck happened in Afghanistan?"

"I'll tell you later. I sure hope those men aren't found for days."

When James drove onto a bridge across a roaring river, Cary told James to stop. He got out and threw the Afghan passports tied to the three pistols into the river and climbed back in. "Let's go. I hope your luck holds out, James. I imagine the gas station attendant has called the police. God, I hope we make it to Austria before the police find us. Otherwise we could be fucked."

"While you two were knocking out and placing the Afghans in the car, I watched the attendant," George said. "He made no move to use the telephone. He didn't even seem surprised or interested in what you guys were doing."

Sally regained semi-consciousness many hours after her rescue late in the evening. She was groggy and still fell in and out of sleep most of the night, often mumbling incoherently. James driving the speed limit did not stop except to get gasoline and things to buy to eat in the van. Early the second day, they reached the Austrian Border, having driven along the coast most of the way.

Sally was still feeling a little groggy and disoriented from her drugging and kidnapping, but was glad to have reached the border without incident. She roused herself to be able to present herself for expected scrutiny— put the horrors the kidnappers may have intended for her out of her mind. The incident was too unbelievable and made little sense to her. Were the kidnappers intending to take her back to Afghanistan? It was too crazy for words.

On the way, James had explained why he thought the two men kidnapped Sally, telling the group about the abduction of Hank in Afghanistan by the hash sellers, the finding of Mahmood, Hank's abduction from the hash sellers by a rival warlord of Mahmood's, Mahmood's rescue of Hank, Hank's return in Herat, and their journey to Tehran where Hank and Sally flew back to Australia. He reasoned that the rival warlord of Mahmood must have sent the two men to kidnap Sally. Mahmood had been particularly taken with Sally, but how his rival knew about that could have only come from an informer inside Mahmood's men. He detailed his occasional sighting of two men in Herat, Tehran and Turkey, who he thought might be the same men or similar men following him, but had pretty much discounted the sightings at the time, thinking he was being paranoid. The men had kept their distance and changed their appearance to blend in with the population.

Sally was terrified that the men would still try following them. She hoped the kidnappers had been stuck in the ditched car for days if not longer. They would probably know they had driven north to the Austrian border. Made more sense that going back to Greece or hiding out in Yugoslavia. They needed to get through the border and back on the road as soon as possible.

When they reached the Austrian border, the Austrian border guard peered into the van as James stopped at the barricade. He raised the barricade and ordered James to pull the van to the side of the border crossing. The guard ordered everyone out, gathered their passports, and then escorted them to an office where he herded them into a small room.

After what seemed a long time as they were sitting in the small room in silence, exhausted by the kidnapping ordeal and long drive, a male and female guard came into the room and announced they all would be searched individually. Sally looked at James in disbelief. She wanted to scream. They needed to get on the road. How could James have possibly smuggled drugs across all the countries he had visited. It was stupid to search and keep them.

The respective female or male guard took them one by one out to a smaller room and strip-searched them. Sally was enraged, but submitted to the search without comment. She realized that they could deny her entry, which would be disastrous. They needed to get as far away from Yugoslavia as quickly as possible. When her strip search was completed, including a demeaning anal cavity search, she was escorted back to the communal room where she saw out the window the guards taking everything out of the van and even removing the paneling. The male and female guards remained in the room without speaking.

After what seemed like more than an hour, the apparent leader of the guards stomped in the room. "We smell that you have been smoking hashish," he said in his thick German accent. "You must tell us where it is hidden. We will find it."

"I bought the van in India as you can see from the sales agreement and carnet," James said. "I had no control over what the people did in the van before I bought it."

"You lie," the guard said and spoke in German to the other guards in the room, who laughed. "The smell of hashish is fresh. Tell us."

Sally stood up. "We're not lying."

James snatched Sally's hand and pulled her back to her seat. "Easy," he whispered. "Relax."

You relax she said silently in her mind. These assholes have no right to treat us like this. We're in Europe. She realized she needed to calm herself. They needed to get back on the road, and causing a disturbance would be stupid.

Two of the guards left the room while the spokesman remained, glaring at the group. "You will go to jail for a long time when we find the hashish. It will go easier on you if you confess the hiding place."

"We have no hash or any other drugs or illegal contraband," James said. "We are traveling to Germany and do not want any trouble. Go ahead and search. We're clean."

After a few minutes, the leader came back and handed them their stamped passports, telling them they were free to go. They went out to the van and were surprised that everything had been neatly put back.

"Jesus, those fucking fascists," Cary said as they drove off. "Fucking dicks. Man, that was the most thorough search, I've ever encountered. I'm sure glad I threw my pistol away with those of the Afghans. If they had found my weapon, we would've been screwed."

"Asshole Germans," Antoinette said. "I hope they liked my asshole. They at least put everything back in the van."

"They were Austrian," Monique said.

"Hitler had big support in Austria," Antoinette replied. 'They're the same as Germans."

Sally didn't dislike Germans. She had met many nice ones. Of course she knew the French never forgave Germany for the Second World War. The Austrian border had been the worse border so far with the strip search and haughty attitude. Iran had been scary because of the dictatorship and death penalty for drug smuggling, but they were in no hurry then. She felt a great sense of relief as they drove off into the mountains. The reality of what happened in Yugoslavia was paramount in her mind, but seemed like a dream. She had been incredibly lucky. The hours wasted at the border she hoped wouldn't prove detrimental. The kidnappers wouldn't know the route they took after the border. Maybe they would give up. Oh god, let them give up. She rubbed her arm where they had injected her with the debilitating drug.

"The guards had a good sense of smell," Monique said, obviously trying to lighten the mood. No one laughed.

"The mountains are beautiful," George added, following Monique's lead. "I'd sure like to go skiing here."

Sally was glad of the comments. She needed to stop focusing on her ordeal and worrying that the kidnappers were hot on their trail.

"You want us to let you out," Monique said.

"Wrong time of year. No, I'm coming to France with you, Babe," George said. "You're not trying to get rid of me are you?"

"We are all free spirits, *mon chéri*," Monique said and hugged George. "But of course I want you to come with me to Paris."

They drove on across Austria only stopping for gas and food to eat in the van.

***

Going through the German border outside Salzburg was fairly easy. The border agents did not search the van or the group. They reached Munich early in the evening. James dropped Cary, George, Monique, and Antoinette at the train station, and they said their goodbyes.

"Alone at last," Sally said. "Let's find a park and relax. I'm exhausted with the nonstop traveling and border crossings… not to mention I'm still scared to death of what could have happened to me. You saved me, James."

James drove to the English Park in Munich and parked. They both got into the back and lied down.

"It's ironic that the big park in Munich is called the English Park. It's a lovely park." She exhaled audibly. "What a trip. I'm so glad to be stationary. How did you guys overcome those two men? Monique told me Cary had a gun. What really happened?"

"After you were abducted in the clearing where the Roma had camped, Cary, George, and I followed. We found them on a dead end forest road tying you up. Cary wanted to kill the two, but I stopped him. I didn't want their death on my conscience or yours."

"Jesus, James. You think he would have killed them in cold blood?"

"Yes, I think he would have. In Matala he told me he had collected the ears of the Viet Cong he had personally killed. I doubt a few more killings would have bothered him in the least."

He described how luckily the men stopped at the gas station in the nearest town where he and the group were hiding, awaiting the hoped for arrival of the kidnappers, and how they overpowered the men, rescued Sally, drove the car out of town, tied up the men, and ditched the car in a forest with the men inside.

"Do you really think those men were sent by Mahmood's rival? Why didn't they kidnap you? How could they have known I was meeting you in Athens? Why didn't they snatch me in Athens when I was there by myself?"

"I can't answer your questions. I don't know the answers. I imagine they were following me, believing that you would return to me. You said you would in Tehran. Perhaps they overheard this or someone else told them. They could have checked at our hotel. You were quite vocal about your plan to return to me in Europe. Maybe they didn't know you were in Athens until I returned and met you. Why they waited for you when they could have easily taken me in Turkey or Greece, I don't know. Maybe because you're a beautiful woman, and Mahmood was quite taken with you. Mahmood's rival may have thought that kidnapping you would be a great way to get back at Mahmood. When they took you, I couldn't stop thinking about the horrible things they might do to you."

"God, James, what if they hadn't stopped in the town and drove through. What would you have done?"

"Followed and hoped for another opportunity to rescue you."

"Did you see these men following you the whole way after I left in Tehran? Did you see them in Matala?"

"I definitely didn't see them in Matala. They would have stood out like a sore thumb. I saw them or others in Herat, Tehran, Erzurum, and Istanbul. I was never sure if they were the same men or if I was imagining men were following me. I didn't notice them in Athens." He realized he had been so absorbed by the Swedes that he hadn't noticed much. "I definitely didn't see any men who could be following me in Crete.

"Could they still be after me?"

"Yes, I would think so, but I don't know how they could have followed our trail. We didn't stop until now. In Austria we could have taken many different routes."

"God, James what shall we do?"

I don't know." He grabbed his head with both hands. "I don't know... I don't know." He shook his head back and forth.

58- ALICE SPRINGS: JUNE 3, 1970

Amelia and Hank's late afternoon rides, became a daily experience. Hank was invited to the house for dinners and became almost like one of the family. One evening at Amelia's invitation, he snuck into her room through the window. He allowed Amelia to control the action, remembering Sally's rebukes in India and his disastrous liaison with Bridget. He thought it was the most enjoyable sex he had ever experienced. The gymnastics in her room became a common occurrence, and he reached heights of infatuation.

Hank gradually revealed to Amelia his loss of parents, his childhood with Freddy and Sally, his misplaced fascination with Sally, and his journey to Hong Kong, Bangkok, India, Pakistan, Afghanistan, and Iran. She told him about the death of her mother, who died of cancer when she was fifteen, and her dad's depression for years. He glossed over his kidnapping in Afghanistan, but Amelia wouldn't let it drop and drew out the hideous details of his abduction and imprisonment. On his time off, they went everywhere together. Amelia convinced Hank to invite Freddy to visit the station. She wanted so much to meet Freddy, his foster brother, and Freddy's wife.

When Freddy arrived with his new wife, Sonya, Amelia welcomed them with open arms. Sonya's pregnancy was apparent and her dark face was full of happiness. Sonya declined the daily rides that the three took and spent the time talking to Robert, Amelia's Dad, who obviously enjoyed Sonya's company. Hank thanked Amelia for insisting that Hank invite his foster brother and wife to visit. Restoring the bond with Freddy helped Hank deal with his isolation and imbedded embarrassment over his kidnapping.

Freddy told them about Sally's flight to Athens and her reunion with James. He related Sally's plan to drive across Europe, eventually heading for London to visit their uncle, Jeb. He expressed his disappointment that he and Sonya couldn't travel to see them.

Hank wasn't sure how he felt about Sally's reunion with James. He told himself he should be happy that Sally got her wish. Was he still mad about James's and Bridget's betrayal?

After Freddy and his wife left, Amelia stopped on one of their afternoon rides under a lone tree and dismounted. "I'm so glad Freddy and Sonya were able to visit," she said. "I think seeing Freddy and Sonya has been good for you. It has opened you up more. You seem more relaxed."

"Yes, I enjoyed seeing Freddy and Sonya. I'm glad you suggested it. I was a gloomy recluse at their wedding. Something I regretted. When I left Brisbane, I was ashamed of my kidnapping. I'm glad you made me talk about it. Seeing and being with Freddy was a release of sorts. Something I can't explain and don't really fully understand."

Amelia embraced him. "Your ordeal will haunt you to some extent for a long time. You are making wonderful progress."

"Thank you. You have been so wise and adept."

"You know… I think seeing Sally and James would help you a great deal. I think you have unfinished issues with them as well."

Hank studied her face, digesting her statement. "That may be, but they're going to London and will probably be in England a long time. I don't know when if ever they will come to Australia."

"What do you think about going to London to visit them?"

"That's not possible. I've got your Dad's station to run."

"I've always wanted to visit England." She tilted her head and smiled. "I bet I could get my Dad to agree. He can run the station while we're gone."

"That wouldn't be fair to your Dad. I'm enjoying being here. I love the work. I did my traveling."

Amelia let the conversation drop. Over the next few days, Amelia brought up the benefits of going to London. She got her father's approval for the trip. After continued discussion with Amelia and Robert, Hank dropped his adamant opposition to the trip. He began to consider the possibility, but still had a nagging apprehension. Coming face to face with James and Sally would bring his abduction and his weakness to the forefront. Eventually, Amelia's enthusiasm won out.

He called Jeb to apprise him of their idea of a trip to London and to find out when Sally might arrive. Jeb was overjoyed of the idea of Hank and Amelia visiting and insisted that they stay with him. He even offered to pay for their flight, but Hank said the flight would be no problem.

Jeb didn't know exactly when James and Sally would arrive. He had received a call from Athens and knew they were going to drive through Yugoslavia, Austria, and Germany to Frankfort, then on to Paris, and possibly other places before making their way to London. He suggested they come as soon as possible, so they'd be there as a surprise when Sally arrived.

As they approached the outskirts of Paris, the traffic became thick but rather orderly. The Parisian drivers were aggressive and favored their horns, but nothing like the haphazard traffic in India. They drove to the center and found themselves in the large multilane traffic circle around the immense Arc de Triumph. They had driven straight through only stopping for two nights in Frankfurt, sleeping in the van so James could get his refund for his plane ticket.

"There's so many roads off the circle," James said. "I've no idea which one to take."

"Can we park and walk along the Seine?" Sally asked

"Sure if I can find my way," he said with dismay as he continued around the circle.

"In this guide book, the river is south of the Arch. Head toward the Eiffel Tower."

James drove around the grand circle several more times before he was able to exit toward the Eiffel Tower in the distance. They reached the river and drove down the side. He turned off on a side street and found a parking space a few blocks from the river. Sally was glad to be out of the traffic. They walked to the river hand in hand.

She was still a little fearful that somehow the kidnappers had been able to follow them. It seemed impossible that they could have. She had studied every face she saw since Yugoslavia and was positive she had never seen the two kidnappers. Their faces were burned indelibly into her memory. Maybe they should slow down and try to find some enjoyment—see the wonderful attractions of Paris and try to put her abduction behind them.

"Oh James this is so romantic," Sally said when they reached the river. She grabbed his hand and dragged him down the stairs. Spying a docking point for the river cruise boats up ahead, Sally erupted, "Let's take a cruise on the Seine. My treat."

***

As they sailed down the Seine River, Sally snuggled next to James enjoying the quiet respite. She felt more secure in Paris. The kidnappers should have no idea where they were or where they were going. They had slept in the van— no hotel records. Surly the kidnappers had given up and returned to Afghanistan. She would continue to study faces, but was determined to push her fear to the background and enjoy the famous city.

She wondered how Hank was fairing. She hoped he was making progress on putting his Afghanistan ordeal behind him. She knew it would take her some time to put her abduction behind her although it was not nearly as horrific as Hank's. It could have been. She remembered how fortunate and happy she felt when she had joined James in India. Rejoining him in Athens had elicited even greater joy and raised

525

her expectations to new heights. Things had changed so abruptly in Yugoslavia.

She was lucky that Cary and George were with them in Yugoslavia. James would not have been able to overpower the kidnappers without their help. If the kidnappers had been successful what would have happened? They apparently didn't want to kill her. They possibly wanted to take her back to Afghanistan and use her to extract ransom from Mahmood or turn her into a sex slave as retribution against Mahmood. The whole scenario was unbelievably crazy.

She worried about the future. Would James stay with her? She sure wanted him to. Could they overcome the horrors of their ordeals? Why didn't James talk more about their future together? She suspected his experience in Nam and the ordeals in Afghanistan and Yugoslavia had damaged him so much he couldn't believe in future happiness. It was as if he was running away from himself. Just like Hank ran away from his horrendous kidnapping. She was determined not to run away from her ordeal. She had been reluctant to confront James about their future together even though it consumed her thoughts. She reasoned that this needed to end.

She raised her head and gazed intensely at James. "I know we can never forget what happened in Afghanistan and Yugoslavia. Maybe we need to do something for joy. I doubt the kidnappers have followed us here. We need some fun. Let's get a hotel after the cruise and spend some time in Paris."

***

They found a quaint hotel with a double bed in the Latin Quarter. After stowing their packs and a refreshing shower together, they strolled outside in the warm summer sunshine and settled at a sidewalk café for a coffee and croissant.

"It's lovely here," Sally said, basking in the hot sun as she watched the flow of pedestrians along the sidewalk, feeling refreshed from their shower together that helped to wash away the nearly nonstop escape from Yugoslavia. "Shall we finish our coffee and test out the bed," she asked with a sweltering smirk. "After all, we are in the City of Love." She gave him a shove and laughed. "Then we can go to the Eiffel Tower. Tomorrow I want to go to the Louvre."

"I see. So you've got it all planned out?"

"You bet. I'll be the maestro. You just sit back and enjoy it." The banter enlivened her. She needed to laugh and enjoy the life that had been given back to her.

***

"It's great up here on top of the Eiffel Tower," Sally said as she gazed out across the skyline and hugged James. "I'm so glad to be here. Paris is such a beautiful city."

"Yes, I'm so glad I could experience it with you."

"Let's go back to the hotel freshen up and have dinner."

Back at the hotel Sally changed to a dress. They walked a few blocks from their hotel in the warm evening and chose an attractive restaurant that didn't seem to expensive. They ordered a bottle of Beaujolais and both had onion soup to start. James ordered the Sole Meniere and Sally had Cod Provencal. For dessert they had mocha pots de crème and crème brulee with cognac.

"What a delicious meal," Sally said. "I'm stuffed. Let's walk for a while. It's such a lovely night." They strolled toward the river arm and arm.

She had been right to rejoin James in Athens despite the incident in Yugoslavia. She had missed out on Turkey— not to mention being able to fend off Monica. At least James owned up to his relationship with Monica. The Swedish ladies were intrepid. She had forgiven James. Well mostly. She would never forget his betrayal with Bridget. Monica was understandable. She knew James doubted that she would ever return to him. In light of the disaster in Yugoslavia, his dalliances were of no real importance. She had remained true, but had not been tempted. Was she that much different? She had used Hank to her own ends and had been drawn to James at first for selfish reasons.

At the river they watched the brightly lit tour boats and gazed across the river at Norte Dame, bright and resplendent in the flood lights. "Oh, James, we are so lucky to have found each other. That I would fall in love with a Yank is beyond my wildest dreams."

***

"The Louvre is immense," Sally said as they stood outside in the morning. She opened the guide book. "In the sixteenth century it was the royal palace. Louis the Fourteenth moved the royal palace to Versailles and decreed that the Louvre become a museum." She grabbed his hand and started for the entrance. "Let's go to the paintings first. I want to see the Impressionists and the Mona Lisa."

When she stood in the group in front of the Mona Lisa, she had to wait for the crowd to thin so she could get close "Do you think this is the most famous iconic painting in the world?" she asked, leaning into James. She liked how Da Vinci had captured the women's enigmatic smile. She wondered if she could paint something as accomplished as this.

"I'd say so," James replied.

"You know it's beautiful, but it doesn't really strike me emotionally. I liked most of the Impressionist paintings better."

"Da Vinci painted this in 1519. Long before the Impressionists. Her mysterious smile is world famous."

Sally loved art and felt blessed she could see one of the most famous museums in the world. Art was such an important part of history and culture. She recalled the ancient art of Thailand, India, Afghanistan, Iran and Greece she had seen. Artists throughout the ages produced phenomenal art. What an amazing and valuable aspect of the human experience. She didn't know that much about art history before her journey and had learned a vast extent about art around the world. In the past she had liked the doing more than the studies, but had come to realize that understanding the history of art would make her a better artist.

Bridget studied art history while she studied the skills to make art. She was glad that she had met Bridget despite Bridget's attempt to take James away from her. She would pursue her art with renewed vigor when she was settled— whenever that might be. Despite the trauma of her journey, the excursion had been so rewarding. Most importantly she had found a wonderful soulmate to share her experiences. She was truly a very lucky person and had much to be grateful for.

They took a break and had a light lunch at the museum. They resumed their tour whipping through the Egyptian, Near Eastern, Greek, Etruscan, Roman, and Islamic Antiquities.

***

Sally opened the guide book as they stood inside Norte Dame in the early morning. "This was begun in 1163. There were two churches here before, and, back to Roman times, there was a temple to Jupiter." She gazed upward. "The ceiling is 115 feet high."

They had entered Norte Dame after standing outside studying the pinnacle Rocco steeple, flying buttresses, and myriad fascinating gargoyles.

"The rose windows still contain the original glass," Sally said. "The arched flying buttresses on the outside were needed to hold up these towering walls. Quite an engineering marvel."

After they left the cathedral, they wandered over to the Holy Chapel, which paled compared to Norte Dame. "Louis the Ninth had this built to house the supposed crown of thorns and a piece of the cross," Sally said with quixotic smile. She doubted their authenticity. She didn't know if she believed Jesus was an actual person. She had learned about so many religions on the trip, all of whom claimed to be the true religion, except perhaps for Buddhism, which really didn't claim to be a religion.

***

"We've seen the Arc de Triomphe, the Louvre, Norte Dame, Holy Chapel, Jardin de Tuileries, Rodin Museum, and cruised down the Seine," Sally said as they lounged on their hotel bed. "I'm so happy we stopped and had fun. This is such a beautiful city. I'm so glad I was able to see it, but I'm anxious to get to London. Are you ready to move on?"

"Yes, let's leave in the morning. I haven't seen anyone watching or following us. I think we're safe."

"I agree," she said. "You know you still call out in your sleep." She paused and scooted closer. "I know something horrible happened to you in Vietnam. You need to tell me."

"You're right." He took a deep breath and watched her face for a few seconds. "When I received my draft induction notice, I was devastated. I was adamantly against the Vietnam War, but accepted induction into the Army, believing I didn't have any other acceptable choices. I had thought about going to Canada, and had even driven to the border, but eventually decided leaving the US was a cop out. Once in the Army, I tried to somehow avoid going to Vietnam. No such luck. Upon arrival in Vietnam, I was dejected and angry. I hated being in Vietnam and hoped to complete my tour without killing anyone. Totally naïve."

He paused and looked away as if he had to reach deep to recall his experience. "At the artillery base I was sent to, I fired into the forest on many occasion when the base was attacked, but I fired high not wanting to kill anyone. Of course the artillery bombardments we launched undoubtedly killed innumerable people, but I couldn't do anything about that. I hated myself for being a part of the killing. I kept my head down, and followed orders, determined to wait out the terrifying ordeal. But the night I killed a Viet Cong face to face was something I couldn't ignore or forget."

He stared for a time at Sally as the tears welled before shaking his head to staunch the flow. "I interrupted him while on guard duty. He was trying to blow up the ammunition building." He paused again before continuing, his voice cracking. "I got the drop on him and tried to get him to become my prisoner, but he went for his rifle. I reacted and shot him twice in the chest. As he fell, I rushed to him, held my hand on the wound to staunch the blood, and yelled for help, but he died before the medic arrived. Not that the medic could have done much. I must have hit an artery because the blood just kept spurting. It was horrible. His face, staring up at me as his life slipped away, has haunted my sleep and waking life. He just stared at me as if he needed to fix my face in his memory."

"Oh, James, how horrible. It was self-defense. The Viet Cong chose his path. What if the ammunition building had exploded? Wouldn't people at the base have died?"

"Yes, I know." His face was in agony. "Compared to the guys in jungle combat, who killed people regularly, my regret is small. Even so, why should my life be worth more than that Viet Cong.? I've tried to rationalize my actions, forgive myself, but I can't. He was fighting to drive out the American invaders. I was fighting to selfishly remain alive while my country destroyed the people of Vietnam for no good reason. I didn't have the courage to go to prison for my convictions. Stop communism... what a load of crap. That face as his life drained away is an image I know I'll never forget."

Sally grabbed and hugged him tightly. "I'm glad you told me. Now I understand why you feel so guilty. You have nothing to be ashamed of."

"I most certainly do," he said loudly, separating far enough to peer into her eyes. "I know I will have to live with my regrets and take each day as it comes. I'm so glad we were able to rescue you in Yugoslavia without killing anyone. If we hadn't rescued you, I don't know if I could have carried on in life. I love you so much."

She kissed him, allowing his declaration of love to wash over her like the soothing water of the first slip into a warm bath. She grasped him to her and laid back with him in her arms. "Go to sleep, My Love." She pushed his head against her chest and caressed his hair. No wonder he was hiding from his memories.

They fell asleep in each other's arms. Sally's sleep was fitful. Upon waking, she remembered her ghastly dream of standing next to James as the Viet Cong man died. She couldn't imagine the actual horror of watching someone you shot die staring up at you as the person's life leaked away. James's confession would help him put the experience behind him. Well, not behind him, but offer a path toward coping with the debilitating memory. His sharing could lead to more sharing. They needed to talk about their future together.

***

In the morning Sally slipped out of their Paris bed quietly, making sure to not wake James, and dressed. She went downstairs to the hotel lobby and phoned her uncle, Jeb, in London, explaining that they were expecting to arrive in London today.

"Julie has your room ready and we're looking forward to meeting your friend, James," Jeb exclaimed. He told her how to get to London and to his house in Chelsea from Dover. Sally wrote down the directions.

"I'm so excited to see you and Julie," Sally said. "I can't wait."

"We are looking forward to your visit. It's been ten years since we've seen you. We want to hear all about your travels. There's a surprise waiting here also."

"Surprise?" Sally replied. "What kind of surprise?"

"You'll see. Someone I'm sure you'll be happy to see."

"Jeb, who are you talking about. I don't know anyone in England except you and Julie. Don't pull this on me. Come on, tell me who is it."

"You'll find out when you get here. A friend from down under."

"What? Jeb, who are you talking about. Don't do this to me."

"It's Hank. That's all I'm going to say, so don't ask any more."

"Why would Hank be there? You're pulling my leg."

"No, he's here. The sooner you arrive the sooner you'll find out why. Goodbye."

"I can't believe it," Sally said to the air in the phone booth as she replaced the phone. "He hung up on me."

She left the booth, shaking her head, raced upstairs, and roused James. "Come on, we need to get going. When I phoned my uncle to say we were coming, he told me Hank was there.”

“What?” James rubbed his eyes as he rolled over. “Why?”

“He said we’d find out when we got there.” She pulled his blanket off. “My uncle is quite the joker. He knows that my not knowing why Hank’s there will drive me crazy. I haven’t seen Jeb for ten years, and he pulls this on me. Come on. Let’s hit the road.”

60- BRUGES: JUNE 10, 1970

In Belgium they stopped for lunch in the quaint city of Bruges with its canals, cobblestone streets, and cookie cutter houses, then went on to Ostend where they caught the ferry to Dover. Sally with her Commonwealth passport went quickly through passport control, but James was told to wait. Sally saw him sitting on a bench next to a man, who looked like he was from India or Pakistan. After James was escorted away, it was nearly an hour before he appeared and walked out of passport control. They went together to the van and drove to customs where agents only made a cursory inspection of the van.

"We don't seem to do very well at borders," Sally said as they left the immigration area and looked for road signs to London.

"Apparently not," James replied.

"What took so long at passport control?"

"They kept me waiting in a room on my own for some time. I imagine they were watching me to see if I became nervous or something. Then two men in suits came in. They asked me a bunch of questions: why I wanted to visit the UK, what my plans were, and how did I plan to return to the US. I gave them the standard tourist answers, enumerating some of the attractions I wanted to see. They wanted to know what I did on my travels, and why I had been traveling for so long a time. I told them I traveled to the various countries I visited to broaden my knowledge of the world before I planned to resume my career as an engineer. I explained that I had saved enough money from my work and time in the Army to allow me to travel extensively. It was obvious they didn't like my looks. I showed them the traveler's checks I got from the refund on the rest of my plane ticket, which proved I had enough money for my visit to Great Britain. I told them when I finished my visit, I would buy a plane ticket back to the US. They wanted to know about you. I said that you were a friend, and we were visiting the UK together. I didn't mention your uncle not wanting to cloud the water. Since I had enough money and gave them acceptable answers, they let me in."

"I was worried that they might refuse you entry. I didn't know what I would do then. Jesus, we've been hassled at almost every damn border."

"This one wasn't that bad. You whisked right through, and they didn't unload everything from the van." He glanced over at her and laughed. "Hey, we made it. London here we come. I hope we get to your uncle's before dark. You sure you know the way?"

"I wrote down the directions. We'll see. We can always stop at a call box and phone if we go astray."

They made it to Chelsea with only a few wrong turns and stops to ask directions. Her uncle's house was a large three-story brick row house with ornate windows in a block of similar houses. They had to drive around awhile before they found a parking space on a side street.

"Let's not tell them what happened in Yugoslavia," Sally said. It will only make Hank more despondent, and freak out my uncle."

"Okay. Yes, it will be our secret."

They walked quickly to Jeb's house— Sally nearly dragging James with her. She banged the door knocker and waited in obvious anticipation.

Hank opened the door and stared in wonder a few seconds before rushing outside. "Hey up, mates. You made it. So good to see you again."

"Hank," Sally exclaimed and dove toward him, hugging him tightly. "I'm so glad you're here" She held him at arm's length. "You look great."

"You're a sight for sore eyes yourself," Hank said. "Where's your bags?"

"We left them in the car," Sally replied.

Her uncle came up behind Hank and pushed past to hug Sally. "The red-haired beauty from down under. So happy you're here. It's been too many years. You're all grown up. You are so beautiful. Come on, come inside, and have a cup of tea."

"Uncle Jeb, this is my friend and traveling companion, James."

Jeb grabbed James's hand and shook it vigorously while he pulled him inside. "Welcome... welcome. We were just going to have our tea. Your timing is impeccable. Course you can always have something a little stronger with your tea. I've some special reserve single malt scotch that is excellent." He pushed Sally and James ahead of him. "My god, world travelers. What stories you can tell. Hank has been describing some of your antics. He's been on pins and needles awaiting your arrival. When you called from Paris, I thought he was going to jump out of his skin, he was so happy."

They were ushered into the living room where Hank's new girlfriend and her aunt were sitting opposite each other on Victorian style pink couches. Plant stands with fresh cut flowers and potted plants were numerous around the room, and pink velvet drapes adorned the windows. A silver tea service with plates of scones and finger sandwiches were sitting on the low mahogany table between the couches and chairs. Her aunt Julie and Hank's girlfriend stood up.

"You're finally here," Julie said, advancing toward Sally. "I love your hair longer. I'd forgotten what a sumptuous color it is." She hugged Sally. "Just in time for tea."

"This is my friend, James," Sally said. "My aunt, Julie."

James shook hands with Julie. The blond shapely woman was beautiful in her tight fitting gold dress, her hair in an elaborate bun, her brown eyes heavy with makeup. James was surprised how much younger she was than Jeb.

"This is my girlfriend, Amelia," Hank said.

Sally slipped up to Amelia and gave her a hug. "Are you from Brisbane?"

"No, I'm from Alice Springs." Amelia was dressed in a green silk shirtdress and her blond hair was cut short. Her blue eyes sparkled warmth in her tan oval face.

"How'd you two meet?" Sally asked.

"Sit down and let's enjoy our tea," Julie said.

Hank crossed to Amelia. James and Sally took their seat on the matching vacant couch.

Jeb went to the mahogany sideboard and poured a glass of scotch. "Who's having scotch with their tea?"

"James and I will give it a try," Sally said. "Hey, James?"

"By all means," James said.

Amelia wanted scotch, but Hank and Julie declined.

"I know Hank," Jeb said as he saw Hank's raised head and stretched face. "I'll get you a beer."

They settled down to their tea, sandwiches, and drinks.

"So Hank how'd you two meet and what brought you to London?" Sally asked.

"You remember, I left Brisbane and went to work on a cattle station near Alice Springs. Amelia's dad is the owner. When Amelia came back from college, I was mesmerized by her." He placed his hand on Amelia's arm. She smiled broadly and blushed slightly.

"And?"

"When Freddy visited and told me of your letter from Athens and your plan to visit your uncle, Amelia suggested we fly to London to meet you.

Amelia like me has never been to England. I was reluctant at first. After her Dad supported the idea, I gradually became open to the visit. Amelia's Dad is such a great guy. I never really properly thanked James and you for saving my life, and of course I wanted to introduce you to Amelia."

"We didn't save your life," James said.

"Without you finding Mahmood and getting his help, I would have been a goner."

"Well, I'm so glad we were able to help," James said. Actually he remembered that Sally was the one who adamantly insisted in Bamyan that they find Mahmood when he had thought of giving up.

"You're looking good, mate," Sally said. "You gained back your weight. I'm so glad you're here. Seems you found a lovely friend. So, Amelia, you grew up on a cattle station in the outback. How was that?"

"I loved it," Amelia said. "Riding horses on the land. It was idyllic. I went to Victoria College in Melbourne and was homesick most of my time there. I was so glad to get back home after graduation. I love being out in the outback. When I saw Hank, Dad's new foreman, I was curious about him. I thought he was handsome. He was very shy, kept to himself, and seemed detached somehow."

"How was Paris?" Julie asked.

James saw that Sally was obviously perturbed by the interruption, but forced a smile at Julie. "What a beautiful city," Sally said. "We had such a good time."

"I've always loved going to Paris," Julie said. "We haven't been in a few years. Jeb works so hard. We did go to the States last year— New York and Miami. Bustling cities. Very interesting. Where are you from, James?"

"Alton, Illinois. It's across the Mississippi River from St. Louis."

They continued their conversation. Sally related the amazing sites she saw in Athens and their travels through Yugoslavia, Austria, and Germany, leaving out any mention of her abduction.

After several hours, Julie suggested she show them to their room. Sally and James followed Julie to the second floor bedroom with its view of the extensively landscaped back garden.

"I assume you want to share a room," Julie said. "There is another bedroom if you want separate rooms."

"This will be great," Sally replied. She walked around the room surveying the contents: oak floors, immense oriental carpet, red velvet drapes, which matched the red in the carpet, and the large four poster mahogany bed with a white bedspread sprinkled with red rose designs. She peeked into the bathroom with its claw foot bath and separate tiled shower. "You've done a fabulous decorating job. I see your deft hand all over the house. It's beautiful. Thank you so much for putting us up."

"Of course— nothing is too good for Jeb's favorite niece," Julie said with a hint of sarcasm. "If there is anything you need, don't hesitate to ask. Dinner will be at eight." She left, closing the door.

James waited to make sure Julie was out of ear shot. "Is there some deal between you and Julie?"

"She's an uptight socialite," Sally said and began stripping off her clothes. "I'm crazy about my uncle, but I've never really liked Julie. His first wife was much nicer and a genuine good person. Julie enticed uncle Jeb away from her. She's beautiful, but I'm not sure she even likes Jeb... but she sure likes his money. I'm dying for a shower. Will you be a darling and bring the luggage. I need to change my clothes. Get Hank to help you." She disappeared into the bathroom naked. "If you hurry you can join me in the shower."

They had made it to the end of their journey. They had not seen anyone following them since Yugoslavia, and he truly believed they would never see the kidnappers again. This phase of his life's journey was over. He would need to figure out what he would do next. He still had money in the bank in the US and could travel more for a short time. He would have to get a job eventually. He wanted to stay with the spirited Sally. She was the woman for him. Would they stay in England or would they go to Australia? Would she want to go to the US with him? Should they get married? So many questions to answer.

He marveled how Sally had put her kidnapping behind her. She was an amazing woman, and he was lucky that she had come back to him. The future was ahead and only time would tell if they would be able to bind together despite the uncertainty and traumas they both held.

545

ABOUT THE AUTHOR

Donald Houser is a writer of three previous self-published novels, *Cloud Of Death* (2020), *Death In The Peru Rainforest* (2019) and *Escape From The P*residio (2015). He is a retired engineer, who is interested in the peoples of the world. He enjoys reading informative and captivating books, traveling and learning about other cultures, and hiking in the wonders of nature. He is a long time resident of Santa Fe, New Mexico.